FREAKS AND GREEKS

TIMOTHY BOWDEN

Tar & Feather Publishing

SYDNEY

Timothy Bowden/Tar & Feather Publishing.
www.tarandfeather.com.au
tarandfeathergroup@gmail.com

Cover design by Nick Hamilton
www.thehammo.com

Book Layout ©2015 BookDesignTemplates.com

Freaks and Greeks. Timothy Bowden. -- 1st edition.
ISBN 978-1-68411-243-2

For Sandy,

I told you...

THRACE
Apollonia
Hellespont
Chersonesus
Lemnos
PERSIAN EMPIRE
Sardis
Ephesus
Miletus
Delphi
Athens
Marathon
Naxos
Sparta
ANCIENT GREECE

PROLOGUE

....

O*nce...*

This mouth had tasted wine, and laughed, and kissed the lips of a woman with hot desire.

These hands had grown sure and calloused, working stone and wood.

These feet had walked to market, to temple, to home. The paths of men.

But now...

The mouth is torn. Lips ripped away. Teeth broken and gapped. Maw black and red with crusted gore.

Hands are curled and blackened claws. Fingertip skin tattered and peeled.

Feet limp onwards, unstopping, stalking a different path. The path of hell on earth.

....

The sun stood high and blazed down on the figure crossing the dry grasslands beneath. The thing was heading nowhere in particular: it was merely answering a deep, base urge to find that which it craved. Sometimes it had walked in company and sometimes, like now, alone. It made little difference to the creature.

And sometimes it encountered what it endlessly sought: food - red and glorious – and it bit and tore and gorged to quell the unquenchable fire that sat in its belly. That unstoppable cold ache.

It had three parents, this monster. The first two had brought it into the world, with warmth and love. The third took it out and bequeathed to it instead this mindless, endless quest.

It did not – could not – remember where it came from now, the village far to the south. It could not remember the fateful trip into the steaming jungle that had led to its current existence. That chance encounter with a walking, rotting nightmare so outside his lived experience that it froze the man in his tracks, made him easy prey.

That thing. The thing that had turned the man from a 'him' to an 'it' had, in turn, been begat by another walking dead horror, and so the lineage continued. It had begun somewhere, deep in the jungle, some terrible confluence of a man, an infected animal bite, some oozing mud used to soothe the wound, a bacteria, a tiny seed of death awakened from its slumber. An infection. And so it began. Pure chance.

Or perhaps fate.

Now, when the net flicked up in front of it, it recognised that there was movement, and it turned its head side to side, dull eyes searching for prey. But it didn't spot the hunters lying concealed in the grass around it, and it didn't resist as the net raced forward and over it, the tough cords bearing it off balance and down. Only when the men ran out and revealed themselves, to swiftly bind its hands and feet, did it react, straining and rearing, seeking to take their warm flesh between its teeth. When the hood came down over its head, cinched tight beneath its working jaws, it felt no discomfort or panic. It could smell the sweat of the men who now strapped it to a pole, and hear their curses and shouts, and so it kept struggling to reach them, as the skin rubbed away at its wrists and ankles, exposing white flashes of bone beneath grey-black skin.

It didn't stop. Day and night, as long as it sensed their presence, it sought to reach them. Its efforts were in vain, for not enough thought lit its mind to try to actually undo the knots, or trick its captors. At times, the men who bore it laughed at its antics. At other times they grew weary of it, the smell and the horror, and sometimes hit and kicked it, till they were lashed into order by the sharp tongue of their leader. On they bore their burden.

Northward.

....

PANDORA'S BOX

The Captain of the Gate Guard was not best pleased to be disturbed at his gambling. Not while the dice were running hot, the wine jug full and fairly free of sediment and the oil lamps not even guttering. That it was the newest recruit who had come to fetch him from the tavern- wide-eyed and with his larynx spasming like he was one of the Royal Crocodiles swallowing a miscreant- pleased the Captain even less. He could not remember the recruit's name, and it didn't matter. Some stupid ape from some one-camel town out in the boondocks. Correction: zero-camel town. Undoubtedly the stupid bastards would have eaten it, if they had one. Or shagged it to death.

As they neared the main gateway that opened to the south, the Captain's rhythmic booting of the recruit's ass was interrupted by the sound of raised angry voices. Hurrying forward he found his squad holding up a hide-covered wagon, his lieutenant in a heated exchange with a man in the passenger seat. Apart from him, the Captain quickly noted three others, all cloaked and shifty-looking. He relaxed. His squad of ten men, encircling the wagon with spears lowered, was more than a match if anything kicked off.

"Report!" the Captain barked, stomping up beside his lieutenant.

"Sir, this lot seek entry. Despite the hour, and despite not having a pass."

"I told you already..." hissed the passenger in a high, accented voice.

What was that, wondered the Captain briefly; maybe Numidian? Hard to make out features in the wavering light of the torches mounted high in the sconces by the gate.

"And I told you to shut it!" said the lieutenant, thrusting a finger at the man.

"All right. Let's all calm down." The Captain was busy calculating what kind of bribe they could extort from the wagoneer versus the likelihood of the wine shop having any of that latest drop still available if he tarried here too long; the one the barkeep kept hidden behind the counter, for 'quality'. As if any toffs were likely down this end of the city.

"Captain," said the passenger. "Listen, please. My cargo, it is very precious. We are expected, we must get to..."

Whatever the passenger was going to say was interrupted by a low groan coming from beneath the hides.

"What was that?"

"That? Nothing. Nothing at all."

There was another moan, and the taut hide trembled.

"Nothing?" asked the Captain.

The passenger bit his lip. "Nothing that need concern you."

"Now that," said the Captain, "really does concern me." His eyes ranged over his men before fixing on the recruit who had summoned him. "You."

The man gulped. "Sir, my name is..."

"I don't care. Just check under that cover. And you," swinging back to point at the passenger, "don't move. Or any of your boys. If you don't want to be skewered, that is."

The recruit walked around to the end of the wagon, and examined the lashings.

The passenger and his men exchanged worried looks. "I really think..."

"Don't. Just shut up. Get on with it, man."

The Captain didn't fail to notice how the wagon crew- while obeying his order not to move- seemed to lean away from the wagon. The recruit undid the first rope, lifted a flap and peered inside.

"Sir, it's some sort of cage. There's someone in there!"

"Ah!" gloated the Captain. "Illegal slave-trading, is it? Or kidnapping? Big fines, either way!"

"You don't understand!" hissed the passenger.

There was a sudden shout of alarm from the rear of the wagon. The Captain jumped back, sweeping his curved sword from its sheath.

"What?!"

The recruit was pressed up tight against the back of the wagon, eyes bulging horribly. "S...Sir! Something's got my arm! It's..." And then he threw his head back and screamed.

"What in the name of Osiris is going on?" The Captain pricked the passenger under the chin with the point of his scimitar. "Release my man!"

The passenger shook his head. "Too late," he mumbled. "Too late now..."

With a high pitched shriek the recruit managed to get his feet against the wagon and pulled backwards with all his might. With a terrible wrenching sound something gave way and he fell back into the dirt. Several soldiers ran forward to help, but winced in horror as a fountain of blood sprayed from the recruit's arm. His hand was gone at the wrist.

"Kneel!" bellowed the Captain, and the passenger, holding his hands above him, awkwardly climbed down from the wagon and knelt in the dirt. "All of you!"

The rest of the wagon crew followed the example of their leader and dropped to their knees, covered by the soldiers. The recruit lay rocking and keening on his back, while two men tried to wind a cloth around his ragged stump.

The Captain swung his sword, and the passenger blanched, but the blade bit instead into the rope holding the hide covers down, slicing it cleanly though. The passenger fainted, falling to the ground, and with a grunt of disgust the Captain stalked around the wagon, cutting rope after rope, before pulling the hide covers free with a savage jerk.

An iron cage was revealed, someone – or something – squatting inside, its hands to its mouth as it chewed and gnawed on...

"Gods above and below! Kill it!"

Soldiers crabbed forward, aiming their spears at the gaps between the bars. The occupant displayed no fear or even notice. A foul stench wafted from it.

"Hold!"

The gateway was flooded with sudden light as a procession of torchbearers emerged swiftly from the city, the light glinting on their bald pates. The speaker strode forward, long robes billowing.

"Hold, Captain!"

"High Priest," said the Captain, grinding his teeth. "You have no jurisdiction here. This is city security, it's army business."

The High Priest smiled coldly, no part of it reaching his kohl-rimmed eyes.

"Do not presume to come between the Son of Ra and his business, Captain. Behold!" He thrust his hand high, revealing a golden scarab clutched in his fist. The soldiers instantly dropped to one knee. Slowly, the Captain followed, bowing his head.

"As Pharaoh wills," he muttered. "So we obey."

The High Priest nodded. "As it should be. Now, we shall take the wagon." He hesitated briefly. "And that man there." He pointed at the wounded soldier lying holding his arm.

The Captain hesitated. "You will take good care of him?"

"We will do what is necessary."

The Captain did not like the glittering look in the priest's eyes one little bit, but meddling in their affairs for the sake of one stupid trooper really didn't seem worth it. He waved his men aside, and they watched dumbly as the wagon creaked into the city, the wounded soldier carried in after, his eyes wide with shock and fear.

"I'm sure he'll be fine," the Captain muttered. But he didn't even convince himself, let alone any of his men.

....

And so the creature came into the hands of the priests. For a while it was left alone somewhere dark and quiet, and it was still. It didn't think, didn't dream. It just was.

But finally when the quiet steps of the priests returned it could almost be described as coming to life; as it registered their presence and moaned with terrible hunger. Its movements were more sluggish now – it had been a long time since it had last eaten – and it was easier to control. It was carried down narrow passageways, through doorways, up staircases, and finally into a vast room, lit by the flickering golden light of many lamps and torches.

It was set down on its own feet, but held tightly, so that when it staggered it did not fall. And then the hood was lifted swiftly away.

The lights blazed in its eyes, though they didn't blink. The pupils struggled to react within the dry orbs. It heard the gasps from people about it, but didn't register the emotion behind the sound. It tried to move towards the closest knot of courtiers, but was held in place by the strong hands of the priests controlling chains wrapped about it. It opened its mouth and a loud moan of frustration rattled its shrunken throat.

"So," said a voice drifting down from a high golden throne at the end of the chamber. "This is it, is it?"

"Yes, oh Pharaoh, God King, Son of Ra," said the High Priest. He bowed low, his high headdress almost brushing the floor.

The divine royal nose sniffed.

"Is that...it...I can smell?"

The High Priest caught the attention of one of his underlings with a subtle move of his head. The acolyte swung his pot of glowing myrhh more energetically. Scented smoke drifted across the floor. Some nearby courtiers coughed.

"It isn't quite as I imagined."

The thing that Pharaoh, ruler of Egypt, was staring at stood within a ring of priests, chains attached to its neck, waist, wrists and ankles. It was naked, its body blackened and withered – dessicated, like meat left too long by the fire.

"The gods work in mysterious ways," intoned the High Priest.

"Undoubtedly," said the Pharaoh, dipping his head. "But even so... It doesn't look particularly blessed. Does it?"

The High Priest did not respond.

Pharaoh sucked on his bottom lip.

"Where on earth did you find it?"

"It has been delivered unto you from many miles away, sire. From across the burning wastes beyond the Nile, from deep in the steaming jungles, it brings to you the Gift of the Gods."

Pharaoh stared, drumming his fingers on his throne.

"You would think," he said finally, "that the gods would choose a more appealing vessel to hold the Gift. But still, who are we to judge? And so, how exactly will the sharing of this gift happen?"

"Through the Kiss of the Gods."

"The Kiss of the Gods?"

"Yes, Oh Pharaoh."

"I have to kiss it?"

"Err... Not quite. I believe it has to bite you."

Pharaoh rubbed a finger across his brow, trying to smooth it out. He could feel it furrowing, and he worried about wrinkles.

"Did you say bite me?"

"Yes, Oh Pharaoh."

"Not on your life."

"The gods work in mys-"

"Yes. Yes, I know. Still." Pharaoh coughed. It really did smell. "I'm going to need a little more proof, I think."

"Certainly, Son of Ra. Observe."

The High Priest snapped his fingers, and a muscular priest stepped forward from the shadows, armed with a short spear. The Royal Guard stirred uneasily.

With a swift, practised move, the priest brought the spear down in position, ran forward and thrust it into the creature's back. The chains clanked as the thing was pushed forward by the blow, then with a faint cracking sound the silver point of the spear appeared in its sternum, breaking completely through.

The creature hardly reacted. It glanced down, and tried to raise one arm slowly, as if to touch the spear head, before the chains impeded the gesture. With a crunch, the priest retracted the spear, again causing the being to stagger slightly, before it resumed its silent stance.

"You see, Oh Pharoah? Completely unharmed."

Pharaoh's eyes glittered. "Where does it have to bite me?"

The High Priest smiled, though it never reached his eyes. "Wherever Pharaoh desires."

....

The news leaking from the throne room promised a golden age for Egypt, a time when their god king would commence his unceasing reign of a thousand years. The people spoke of it with wonder. Successions were always risky times, when the chance of wars between competing royal relatives was high, so this promised a period of peace and stability to be marvelled at. But then a little after that came further worrying gossip, actually, it seemed the Son of Ra was gravely ill, wracked by a vicious fever. Courtiers and slaves alike held their breath.

An hour past midnight, news came that the Pharaoh had died. A great lamentation arose from the courtiers and officials gathered in the Great Hall. Garments were torn. Kohl streamed in black rivers from red-rimmed eyes.

An hour after that came a correction: it turned out Pharaoh wasn't so dead after all. He was alive.

Stunned silence met this proclamation, followed by great cries of joy. Truly, he was the blessed Son of Ra! A knot of the most senior courtiers, the High Priest shoving into the lead, ran for the Pharaoh's private chambers. Forgetting decorum, they threw the doors open to behold the miracle themselves.

The sight of the god-king squatting on a mound of blood-ied, dismembered corpses that had until recently been his four body servants- busily chewing on a piece of purple intestine- tarnished the moment somewhat.

"Y-y-your majesty?" stammered the High Priest.

But Pharaoh would not answer, his mouth stuffed as it was with what appeared to be the liver of his favourite Numidian body slave. He did, however, become seemingly aware of their presence, and turned his red and weeping eyes upon them. He sprang forward, and there was a desperate battle at the door to get out; and if that meant leaving some other unfortunate to a private counsel with the Son of Ra, then so be it. The High Priest managed to thrust himself clear, applying some judicious and vicious elbow jabs as he did so – after all, one didn't get to the chief priesthood by being especially nice. The heavy doors were finally swung shut -to the despairing shrieks of a lower chancellor trapped inside- and barred.

Over the following days, various doctors were dispatched into the royal chambers to attempt a cure, often at the point of a spear, as it soon became obvious that whoever went in wasn't coming out, and the screams that echoed from the chamber sug-gested a fairly unpleasant trip to the realm of the gods.

Worse, it appeared that the Pharaoh now had company.

Such was the glut of offerings available, it appeared that even an appetite as insatiable as the Pharaoh's had now become was unable to completely devour every part of every servant, doctor and courtier trapped in the room. Those left more or less intact, minus a few missing choice cuts, had apparently followed suit and risen from the dead.

It was alarming to discover that the Gift of the Gods could be so... arbitrary. It seemed to threaten the whole basis of society, and as such really needed to be hushed up. This was certainly the opinion of the High Priest.

A most learned Greek physician was discovered to be visiting a nearby city, researching Egyptian medical practises. The courtiers sent for him, not even balking at the princely sum of money the physician charged for making a house call. He thus became the first Greek to set eyes on the Hadesmen.

"Hmmmm..." he said, while peering through a narrow gap in the door to the Pharaoh's bedchamber, held in place by half a dozen of the biggest, burliest men from the Royal Guard. Even they grunted, feet struggling for purchase on the polished marble floor, as the creatures on the other side thrust and pounded to get free.

"Well, doctor?" asked the Upper Vizier. "Have you seen the like?"

"Can you cure him?" asked the Chamberlain.

"Ah," said the doctor. "Just him?"

"Well, yes. He is the only one that matters. All others in the room are... expendable."

"Highly expendable," added the High Priest.

The physician grimaced.

"Yes. Quite. Look, it's just that I thought I caught sight of one of your top doctors in there. Fellow I came to consult with, in fact. Moving about, but missing enough pieces now that I think he would find himself a fascinating case study."

"Of course we consulted our own top healers," said the Vizier, bridling. "Nothing but the best for the Pharaoh."

"Right. Anyway, I don't much want to end up like that, so the rest are going to have to go. And I'll need a net."

A platoon of armoured axemen was summoned to the Royal Bedchamber. The captain in charge sucked at his cheeks as he considered his orders.

"So basically, we are to go in, chop everyone in there into pieces..."

"Very small pieces!"

"Right, very small pieces – except for the Pharaoh?"

"Correct."

"All the while in full armour, helmets and all?"

"Yes, yes, that's right. What's the problem? It's what you do, isn't it?"

"Well, it's just that in that environment, with restricted visibility, heat of combat and all that, it can be a bit hard to tell who is who..."

"You don't know what the Pharaoh looks like? Your sovereign and holy ruler? Is that what you are saying? Haven't you seen him in hieroglyphs?"

"Well, sure. But you mean to tell me that's what he really looks like?"

"Of course!" shouted the official in charge of the Royal scribes.

"It's the whole flat art thing," said the Captain. "Real heads are round, and aren't always side on... And everybody knows you lot always make 'em look better than they really do."

"Listen, soldier boy, our artists are bloody top notch! We don't need some meathead with no sense of art coming in here and criticizing..."

"What do you suggest?" interrupted the Upper Vizier.

The Captain considered.

"One of you lot comes in with us, and points him out."

The Upper Vizier and Chamberlain exchanged a look.

"I believe the High Priest would perform admirably in that role."

"What??"

"Oh calm down. You know you're in the shit anyway. Might as well do something before the whole inundation falls."

The troop lined up before the door, the quivering High Priest behind the Captain, his sweaty hands locked on the buckles of the soldier's scale armour.

"Ready, boys? Remember, chop fast, and anyone who goes down is unfortunately also for the grind. So don't go down. Or if you do, do us all a favour and try to take your helmet off so the rest of us can get a good go at you. Ok, go go go!"

The door was flung open, and the line of men thrust into the room. The doors were swiftly shut behind them, and barred. The sounds of the combat within easily carried through.

"Right, form up! Shit! Get that one!..."

"Where's the Pharaoh?"

"There! There!"

"That one?"

"No! That one! Don't kill that one!"

And through all the shouting came the meaty whacking sound of blade on flesh and bone, or the higher chink as expensive marble floors were chipped and gouged. Then finally it was over but for the screech of one remaining creature, the one that had been the Pharaoh, now pinned beneath cursing, sweating soldiers. The rest of the room was a stinking charnel house of pieces of flesh and splintered bone, rotten as if they had lain there for days already, worse in sight and smell then any battleground.

"Right," said the Greek. "Net?"

He took the proffered bundle and entered the room, closing the door on the anxious noble faces behind him. There was a jostling for position as ears were stuck to the heavy door, and hisses for everyone to be quiet came from everyone else. Except for the High Priest, who slumped against the opposite wall, and slowly slid down, leaving a smear of cold sweat down the plaster.

"Now then, your majesty," the rest heard the Greek doctor say. "What seems to be the trouble?"

When he emerged some time later, the courtiers took him through to the council chamber to report.

"I don't know what you have done here," said the doctor gravely. "But it is a terrible thing."

"Now see here, you impudent pirate!" spat the Chancellor, but the Vizier restrained him with a gentle hand on the arm.

"You do not have a man in there anymore," continued the doctor. "You somehow have an animated body, which by all rights ought to be dead."

"He is immortal," whispered the High Priest. "It is glorious..."

"It is disgusting. And I bet he would tell you the same, if he could still speak."

"He doesn't need to speak!" snapped the Vizier. "Only rule!"

"Yes?" said the doctor, narrowing his eyes.

"What else did you find out?" asked the Chancellor.

"He – or rather, 'it' – has an insatiable appetite. But only for raw meat. Especially human, it seems... Maybe to balance one of the humours, which in this state is very much out of alignment. Or maybe the withholding of such a diet will create balance. I will know more once I can do further study..."

"So it isn't so disgusting you don't want to research it?" asked the Chamberlain dryly, but the doctor was staring into the distance, absently plucking at his beard.

The doctor and Egyptian officials found that by binding the Pharaoh tightly in linen bandages, they were able to somewhat contain his murderous ability. His strength was still great, but with his hands wrapped so that his ragged nails and protruding tips of finger bones couldn't scratch and grab hold or rend, and with his face completely covered, so tightly he could barely work his jaw, he was – more or less – safe to let loose within the palace.

And so the Son of Ra staggered about, bouncing off walls and sending eunuchs and slaves shrieking down hallways before him. The Greek doctor noted with interest that even in death the creature still relied upon sight and sound and smell to locate food. Bandaged as he was, it was much harder for him to sense living humans, unless he was very close. He did not seem able to reason that it was the linen wrappings making things difficult, and seek to remove them.

A sub-human level of understanding, thought the doctor. With basic urges to destroy and eat not driven by hunger, or at least not by the usual living version of hunger, where food would serve to fuel the workings of the humours within the body. Maybe a hitherto undiscovered humour? A dark humour? But present all along, or caused by the bite of the creature the painted officials had grudgingly told him about?

The Greek doctor, having moved in to the palace complex, had planned to continue his study of the Pharaoh, and then return to Greece to get his research published. He almost rubbed his hands with glee thinking how he would be able to choose whatever city he wished to set up his own teaching school in, pride of place in one of the nicest public stoas in the agora, out of the sun in summer and protected from the rain in winter. All the rich young lads clamouring to come and learn from him...

So the coup caught him, and the rest of the courtiers, completely by surprise.

While the Pharaoh's interest in immortality had been well-known in royal circles, his successor's disinterest in it was less understood. The First Royal Prince, who was the Pharaoh's oldest nephew, was less of a fan of the idea that his uncle would reign forever, while he would grow old and die awaiting his place in Ra's holy light. He had been away suppressing some Libyan tribes when news reached him of events back in Memphis. He was a warrior, with a warrior's simple solutions to complex problems, and several companies of extremely loyal troops at his disposal.

The first the Greek doctor knew of the change was when he strode into the royal council hall and went skidding across the floor, fighting to keep his balance. He looked down at the red smear he had made across the marble, and back at the large pool of blood he had walked through.

"Greetings, good doctor."

There, on the throne, sat the First Royal Prince, the double crown of Upper and Lower Egypt upon his head, the royal flail in his hand. He was flanked by soldiers, and a small arc of stunned courtiers stood before him. Another arc of courtiers, the Vizier and Chamberlain among them, lay sprawled upon the floor, quite dead.

"Ah."

"I regret to inform you that your services are no longer required, doctor. Feel free to pack up and leave. Within the hour."

"My duty is to my patient – your uncle."

"Very noble. But you Greeks have a way with words, don't you? And in this case 'patient' is in fact a bit wide of the mark. Strictly speaking, he has to be alive to be a patient, doesn't he? In this case, the feather-light soul has long left the body."

"Your uncle can see, and hear, and smell. He walks, and sometimes makes sounds like speech. Are these not signifiers of life?"

The new Pharaoh frowned. "But he feels no pain –and yearns for human flesh. That is not human!"

"It is different, granted. But not without precedent. Certain head injuries I have seen can reduce a man's capacity to feel some sensations. And cannibalism has been practised by many cultures for religious reasons..."

"Are you going to try to tell me that my uncle simply banged his head and has converted to some new cult?"

"No... There is something at work here that I do not fully understand. If you would permit me to continue working with him..."

"I'm afraid that won't be possible, doctor. Even if I was at all interested, which I am not. My uncle will not be here much longer. Frankly, and I am sure you can understand this, it hardly helps the new regime to have the old one banging into door-ways and trying to eat the envoys."

"You can't kill him."

"Your notes tell us that when enough damage is done, tech-nically you can."

"That would be regicide. And murder. Besides which, you must see his worth to the scientific community..."

"You are hardly in a position to tell me what I can and can-not do!"

"I beg you..."

"Enough! The sun is moving, doctor, and the royal croco-diles are hungry."

The doctor could see there was nothing more that he could do, and rapidly took his leave. Packing his belongings, and head-ing for the river to catch a dhow to the coast and a ship back to Greece, he felt as if his chance to make a name for himself had slipped forever from his grasp. No school of medicine named after him now.

Little did the doctor know, but his words had planted a seed of doubt in the new Pharaoh's mind. He had enough fear of the gods to wonder what would happen if he had his uncle chopped into bits with axes, thus ensuring he would not be able to be whole in the afterlife. After all, his uncle had enjoyed a long and peaceful reign – that suggested he had some godly favour. No, it wasn't worth risking it. The trouble with coming to power by force was it sometimes gave others the same idea. Especially if they could accuse him of being out of favour with the gods: one long drought or some pestilence early in his reign would be all they needed. The old Pharaoh had to go, but it had to be clean.

And so late one night, far out in the desert, a small pro-cession entered a ravine. By the light of torches, a tomb dug into the rock face was unblocked and six swearing soldiers man-handled a struggling bundle inside. There was further muffled swearing from deep inside, then all six bolted out. As the last cleared the entry, workers levered huge stone blocks back into place. The stones had been dressed well, and slid neatly into the space, one by one, leaving the barest of gaps. And if it sounded like some angry hissing came through these gaps from within as they worked, to a man they ignored it and worked as fast as they could. The reward they had been promised for this job beckoned, and thirsty work and money meant beer aplenty when they got back to the city. Finally, a small avalanche of natural rock was allowed to fall over the face of the tomb, disguising it. Tools were collected, and soldiers and workers trudged back towards the lights of the city.

Halfway back, the swishing sounds of chariot wheels and drumming hoof beats carried to them easily in the still night air. Surprised, but pleased to find they warranted such an escort, they stood together and waited until the chariot troop came trotting towards them. The leader of the burial party held up a hand in greeting, and the gesture was returned by the chariot troop leader, except his hand cut down abruptly, almost as if he was ordering an...

"Attack!"

The first arrows started to fall, and as the troop passed down one side then up the other of the burial party, the archers easily picked off their incredulous targets. They were masters at standing balanced on the balls of their feet as the chariots swung on their rope suspension, and the moonlight provided more than enough light. When no more men were standing, the troop commander signalled a stop, and the drivers tied off their reigns and jumped down with sickle knives to ensure there were no survivors. The commander was well pleased – the entire unit would be celebrating for a week after this action, thanks to the gift paid into their troop fund.

He was less pleased two days later, when the entire troop, nursing crippling hangovers and several diseases, were shipped off to fight Libyan brigands on the furthest extreme of the kingdom.

A period of mourning began with the announcement of the death of the old Pharaoh – due to natural causes - followed closely by a longer period of thanksgiving on the accession of the new Son of Ra.

The tomb lay forgotten.

Months passed. The new Pharaoh ruled from Memphis, and the ancient land went on as it had for time immemorial. Grain grew fat, fed by the waters of the Nile. Merchant ships plied their way between Egypt and Phoenicia, Carthage and beyond.

And still the tomb slept.

Until one dark evening, when the moon was nothing but the faintest of slivers, spilling a mere cupful of light onto the desert floor. A deeper patch of darkness wound its way along the ra-vine, stopping at the scene of an old rockslide.

"You are sure this is it?" hissed one shadow to another.

The mass broke apart, and revealed itself to be half a dozen men: one short and fat, one tall and thin, along with four burly labourers from the docks.

"Well, Tesh? Is it?"

The thin man cast about, squinting at thick dark lines drawn on a piece of parchment in his hand. There was just enough light to get the general idea of the terrain features it depicted.

"Yes, Bes. This is it. Tools!"

The dockworkers pulled lever bars and mattocks from sacks on their backs.

"And you can trust your source?"

"Oh yes!"

Bes grunted at that. He and Tesh both came from a long line of tomb robbers, a much misunderstood profession which called upon a wide-ranging skill set: intelligence gathering, geography, mathematics, physics, diplomacy, and of course espionage and blackmail, to name a few. If Bes was sure, it was good enough for him. Not that he trusted Bes completely, of course – nor, he supposed, did Bes fully trust him. His thoughts turned to the small dagger concealed in the back of his belt, and wondered where his partner was keeping his own 'argument of last resort'.

The party set to, with no extra lighting, and making every attempt to reduce noise; the sound of iron on stone could carry far in the desert at night, and one never knew who was skulking around: patrols, nomads, shepherds, even other grave robbers. Getting caught could mean death – and the horrible thought of priceless treasures passing through unsavoury and plebeian hands.

You had to know the market, both Tesh and Bes liked to state to each other. It wasn't enough to just set up a booth in some marketplace and flog gold leaf covered canopic jars to slaves doing the household shopping. You had to know where to sell, how high to go, how to explain away your possession of holy jewelled scarabs to suspicious officials. You also needed a strong back.

All hands were needed to lift the first of the square blocks from the tomb doorway. Sharpened levers had to be thrust into the gaps, and the stone gradually walked clear, until they could, grunting, let it topple to the sand. There was no need to make the hole too large – just enough for them to squeeze through. It was important to keep an eye on where everyone was, and who was inside – it didn't do to have your hired muscle strolling in and pocketing any gems or other small moveables they could see.

"I'll go first," said Bes.

Tesh nodded, quietly fingering the blade at his back. He watched his partner disappear headfirst into the inky blackness of the tomb interior. The four dockworkers stepped back, and he rolled his eyes. Superstitious clots. No doubt this tomb, like the rest, had warnings of dire consequences for any who dared disturb the occupant's earthly remains written around the doorway, meant to frighten off such as he.

Tesh stuck his head and arms through the hole, and thrust. Damnation, the hole was just a little too high off the ground for him, he was on tiptoe and couldn't quite get the traction necessary to push himself in. He could call to the men, but they were outside, and that would mean having to yell quite loudly. Just then two dry hands wrapped around his wrists, and he let out a short mewl of fear.

"Oh, be quiet. It's me."

"I knew that."

"Are you stuck?"

"No... Yes. A little."

Bes hauled on his arms, and he slithered into the dry, cool interior, banging his knees on the hard floor.

"What did you say?" asked Bes.

"I didn't say anything."

There was a brief flash of sparks, and then the wan light from a single taper. They allowed themselves this much light and no more to search tombs.

"To business," said Bes, and the taper moved away, sending flickering yellow shadows chasing each other across the rock walls and ceiling. "Inventory..."

Tesh rubbed his knees and stood, following cautiously. Tombs were often filled with bric-a-brac, piled in with no idea of layout, and it was easy to trip or stub your toe.

"Let's see," said Bes up ahead. "Hmmm. Bit dismal. Couple of chests worth looking at... Some hangings..."

"A chair over here."

"Good, see if it's a set. Another chest."

"Yes – another chair here."

"..."

"Just some rags here – wait, what did you say?"

"Chair?"

"No..."

"..."

"There, that."

"That wasn't me."

"Not you?"

"No."

"Oh."

"Shit..."

The dockworkers outside were nervous already. It was only the promise of making a month's wages in one night that had lured them out here in the first place. At the sound of the first screams, however, they were uncertain – maybe they should lend a hand? But the sight of Tesh, blood-spattered and thrusting desperately out of the hole only to be dragged back in by something, followed by horrible tearing sounds, and a high pitched scream abruptly cut off, was enough. They ran for the entry of the ravine, and didn't look back.

Of course, they left the tomb open.

....

For the new Pharaoh - somewhat more corpulent and less warrior-like now after months of high living - news of the sighting of a monstrous, bandaged, unstoppable nightmare came as a great disappointment. He was sure it was his uncle, somehow released from his tomb and still bent on eating more of his old subjects.

This was not good. The royal family was extensive, and while there had been no doubt that he was the next in line for the throne, there were always those not happy with the position the gods had given them, looking for their moment to ascend. It simply wouldn't do to give any ambitious upstart the chance to parade the old Pharaoh around, and claim to be acting under his wishes. The court was full of adders, frankly.

He summoned the new High Priest for a private meeting.

"Your lot started this, dragging that creature out of the southern desert," said Pharaoh. "So your lot can finish this."

The High Priest clicked his teeth, thinking. "Leave it to me, your highness."

The creature was tracked down, and teams of men – elephant hunters by trade – were dispatched with all their equipment to capture it. Soon enough, late one night, another caged wagon, securely covered in hides, was quietly let into the city – all the proper passes, and trusted men on the gates - with no fuss. It was conveyed by back roads to the main temple building, and once the nervous horses were unhitched, was pulled inside by bands of priests.

Pharaoh's orders had been exact, there was to be no extermination via pulverisation. The priests were charged with finding a way to end the creature's existence without doing more damage to the body than they had to. There was to be nothing done that could lead to charges against the Pharaoh of leaving his uncle disabled in the afterlife. Just in case.

The creature was strapped to a heavy marble table, and the remaining bandages cut away. The body revealed was withered and desiccated by the dry heat of the desert. And yet, without pause, the creature struggled to get free, and followed the movements of the priests with hungry, dead eyes.

The High Priest took personal charge. A sharp blade was placed in his hand, and with barely a tremor he sliced along the creature's side. Other priests took hold of the wound, and pulled it wide, choking on the stench of old decay that wafted from inside.

"It makes no sound?" muttered the High Priest, and thrust his hand into the cavity. He cut, and tugged free rotting internal organs, dropping them into waiting canopic jars. The only organ that seemed whole was the stomach, which was bloated and full as a new wine skin. The priest sucked his lower lip, deciding there was no need to open it. The whole mess was glopped into a waiting jar.

Still the beast lived, staring at the High Priest fixedly, snarling and gnashing its teeth. The priest stared back into its black, blank eyes in return, thinking. So, where did its weakness lie? It showed no fear of anything. Senseless...

"Pass me a cranial hook, and hold its head still."

He took the proffered wire hook, and, leaning in, thrust the end up one of the monster's nostrils. This certainly got its attention. It thrashed and roared, almost bucking clear of the half dozen men almost lying across it.

"Hold it!" yelled the High Priest, grunting as he thrust the wire higher, then twisted and pulled. As if a torch was blown out, the creature suddenly went still, and at the same time the priest pulled the wire clear, a glob of blackened brain matter attached to the end.

"Here is the answer," said the priest, holding the wire with its awful addition aloft.

"We will need a bigger hook than that," said the vizier from the doorway. "We have had reports. He was not the only one. It is spreading. Fast."

"Shit," said the High Priest of Egypt.

....

TWO

ICARUS ASCENDING

"You're wanted," said the man at the door. "They want to see you."

Miltiades sighed. There was no need to ask who 'they' were. The only question was why him, and why now? He really hadn't thought he would be on their agenda any more. Hadn't he done his bit, shown he was willing? But the thing with tyrants, he thought wryly, was that they didn't need a reason, nor did they have to explain themselves to anyone.

"Say," said the messenger. "Wasn't your dad-"

Miltiades slammed the door in his face.

"Fucking Eupatrid bastard!" snarled the lackey as he stamped away - loudly enough for Miltiades to hear.

If only the former, "fucking" part, was true - at least true more often. But apart from the odd flute girl at a party, Miltiades couldn't see that changing any time soon, either. As for the middle accusation- Hades, was there a correct term for the middle item of three? Former, latter, and...something? Had he forgotten everything he had once learned, sitting with the other boys on the stoa steps, listening to their teacher, Photios? His shoulders twitched involuntarily, as if expecting the swish of the pedagogue's rod, even now. Anyway, his status was what it was. Class was class. And as for the latter accusation - well, a pity it wasn't true, in some ways. The lack of responsibility, of expectation-sounded quite pleasant.

Anyway, no point dreaming about how things may have been. Miltiades took his cloak from the peg by the door, ran his fingers through his hair, and stepped out into the street. Wouldn't do to keep them waiting. He walked down the narrow avenue, heading for the agora. It was a good street to live on - it had a proper covered drain, so you could walk without fear of where you were treading. And his neighbours were discreet and quiet, keeping their outer doors closed and the inner world of their homes sealed off. They were all lucky - lucky they hadn't lived in homes at the base of the Acropolis, where the new marketplace now stood. Those poor buggers couldn't believe it when they had been told by their new ruler that they were going to have to make way for progress.

"Progress? Why??" they had yelped.

"For the good of the people," was the smug response.

And the thing was, the sanctimonious bastard was right. His ambitious plans had indeed greatly benefitted Athens - benefitted them all, really, though he doubted you would get many of his fellows in the Eupatrid class to agree. You could see their point - after years and years of sharing the rule amongst themselves, along comes Pisistratus, this populist upstart, who installs himself as tyrant, and bang goes a lot of their privileges. And political control.

You had to hand it to old Pisistratus, the man who would not take "no" for an answer. Not content to stick to the old system and share the rule with others of the Eupatrid class, he had wanted it all for himself. It took him three goes to get it. The first time, he had roughed himself up, wounded his own donkey, and then dragged himself and the poor beast into the assembly, declaring he had been set upon by political enemies who were displeased with his championing of the common folk. The other Eupatrids rolled their eyes at the obvious con, but the common folk liked the sound of being championed- since it hadn't happened before- and asked Pisistratus what he wanted.

Bodyguards, he answered. Lots of really big bodyguards. Burly men with clubs. In case his enemies tried to do away with him again.

And so the people voted to give him what he wanted, while the Eupatrids hurried home to hide under their beds, suspecting they were about to get a flogging. Instead, Pisistratus promptly marched his new little force up onto the Acropolis and declared himself sole ruler. His reign lasted as long as it took the upper classes to don their armour and storm the ramp to throw him out.

Undaunted, he tried again. This time, while touring the countryside, he came upon a peasant girl of great height. Seeing a possibility, he dressed her in armour, complete with full helmet on her head, and rode with her in his chariot into Athens, with heralds preparing the way, declaring Athena herself had come down from Olympus, such was her desire for Pisistratus to rule.

And the people, the poor simple people, stood and gaped with slack jaws – Athena herself! - and promptly handed over control of the city to this showman. If Athena herself wanted Pisistratus to rule, what else could they do? His rule lasted a little longer this time, since he safeguarded himself by marrying the daughter of one of the other powerhouse families. But shortly after, the poor girl fled home to papa, crying that all he wanted to do was practise acts of debauchery upon her sweet, rich flesh, and again the power of the wealthy came together and threw him out.

The final time he went for simple and direct: he simply hired an army of mercenaries, and took the place at the point of the sword. Those who openly opposed him died or were banished. Those he suspected had their precious sons or daughters taken as hostages and farmed out to friendly city-states, as insurance for ongoing support. And so the rule of the Pisistratids began.

And while old Pisistratus, the man himself, was dead and gone, his two sons now ruled in his stead. And wanted to see Miltiades.

What in Hades for?

He'd played along, hadn't rocked the boat. Even did a year as archon, though every decision had to go through the Pisistratids, to make sure it "suited the people".

He ignored the stallholders in the marketplace who shouted at him to peruse their wares. Stepped around the line of gossiping women lined up with their amphorae at the new public fountainhouse. Nodded in the direction of the temple. Up ahead, smack in the middle of the agora, at the base of the rocky outcrop of the acropolis, was a huge mansion – the home of the Pisistratids. Where else would you build a house, if you wanted to convey the not-so-subtle message that you were now at the heart of everything that happened in Athens? No good being perched up on the Acropolis itself, tucked out of the way in the temple precinct. Not to mention the inconvenience of having to continually hike up that ramp. No good either building out on the assembly ground, where the citizens eligible to vote met to perform their sacred duty, while the poorer masses could only stand on the edges, watching. Again, too removed. No, best to be here, in the true bustling heart of the city – the agora, the marketplace.

"Hey!" a man shouted at him. The man held up three fingers, and grinned and pumped his other fist in the air. "Yeah! Three times! Three times!" He held pretend reins, and lashed at pretend horses, whooping all the while.

Others were stopping and looking first at the man, then at him. Miltiades smiled tightly and strode quickly towards the door of the house. Two Scythians leaned against the wall, their ridiculous pointed hats like a pair of dicks, as far as he was concerned. He didn't actually say that, of course, thanks to their much less ridiculous bows and quivers full of arrows. The

Pisistratids' pet police force. Foreign mercenaries, really. Just what every good tyrant needed. Or pair of tyrants.

The Scythians squinted at him, but made no move to bar his way or waylay him, so he pushed open the door and entered the cool darkness of the interior. The oversized andron on the right was where the brothers conducted their business, as if their household business was one and the same with the business of the city-state. Oh, the arrogance of it. Like their father building this mansion right on top of where the original council chamber had stood.

Inside the andron, there were a pair of simple wooden chairs down one end – well, they could hardly use thrones, could they? No kings in Athens, after all. Hippias sat in one, erect, his mean little beard on the end of his jutting chin, while his brother, Hipparchus slouched in the other.

A gaggle of councillors stood along the walls, trying to convince themselves that they were still actively engaged in the government of the city-state. Ha.

Miltiades pushed into the middle. "Gentlemen."

Hippias studied him, while Hipparchus glanced up once and then went back to chewing on his fingernails.

"So," said Hippias. "The horseman cometh. Son of the superstar."

There was a pang of pain in Miltiades' gut, but he bore down on it and forced himself to breathe slowly and evenly.

"You wanted to see me?"

Hippias smiled, and blinked rapidly. Hipparchus yawned.

"Indeed," said Hippias. "Weren't busy, were you?"

Miltiades stayed silent, waiting.

"Though it has been some time, we - my brother and I - wished to express our regret at the passing of your noble father."

"Murder," said Miltiades, before he could stop himself.

"What was that?"

"You mean the murder of my father." He should shut up. Why poke the snake? But some part of him just couldn't seem to help it.

Hippias frowned. "Yes. I know how he died. That is, we all heard how he died. And we want you to know, that you have our full support, if you ever find out who was responsible and seek to bring him to trial. Isn't that right, Hipparchus?"

"Sure," said Hipparchus. "Murder. Trial."

"Must have been awful," said Hippias. "Stabbed to death in some rank alley, lying bleeding to death in the sewerage. A long way from the Olympics, I suppose. Still, fly too high and there are always bound to be jealousies. Aren't there?"

Miltiades put his hands behind his back, and stabbed his thumbnail into the palm of his hand.

"Oh, that's right!" said Hipparchus, sitting upright. "That was your father! The chariot guy. Three times victorious with the same team of horses, right? Only equalled once before. Man, you are famous. Or rather, your dad is famous. Was famous."

"What about you?" asked Hippias. "Any aspirations in that field? Going to seek Olympic glory?"

"Chariot racing isn't really my thing," said Miltiades.

"Any aspirations in any other fields, then?" asked Hippias quietly. His eyes were suddenly much harder. Even Hipparchus stilled, and waited.

"No," said Miltiades eventually. "I served a year as archon. As you know. That is sufficient public life for me. I have no desire for acclaim. Of any kind."

Hippias nodded, and looked around the room. "Here is wisdom. Well spoken, sir. That being the case, you won't mind being away from Athens for a while. You see, we have a little job for you."

Some Time Earlier

He was a crewman on a merchant ship, plying its way between Egypt and the Phoenician city-states on the Sinai coast.

They had stopped at a small town to reprovision and caulk a leak, and Smitagees, in search of a woman, had slipped away by himself. The town seemed too small and sun-scorched to host a proper brothel, but questions in the market place directed him to the outskirts, and a small, dim building pretending to be an inn. He bargained with a dim-eyed crone in the main room and was thrust down a hallway and through a greasy curtain into a windowless back room. There was a bolted door, and a small pallet upon which sat a glum looking woman of indeterminate age.

Ah well, thought Smitagees. Any port in a storm.

He had approached the woman and was pulling at his clothing when a low growl surprised him, emanating from behind the door. He paused. The listless female did not respond at all. Had he imagined it? But no, the growl came again. Not a beast, or certainly not a beast that he recognised. This was beginning to smell bad in more ways than one. Fearing a trap – some snarling dog perhaps, to be set upon him when he was at his most vulnerable, all his coin taken – he pulled his knife from his belt and strode over to the door. He pulled the bolt – not stopping to think why it was bolted from this side – but a cry from the girl, suddenly more animated, caused him to turn.

Don't, she cried in alarm. We trapped it in there last night!

Trapped what, he asked. Some poor dupe?

It came out of the desert! she cried, but that made no real sense to him.

At that moment, something behind the door charged, and it was only by the grace of his strong sea legs that he was able to keep his balance and shove back against whoever or whatever was trying to get out. Human hands, the flesh green and peeling from the yellow-white bones beneath, reached through the gap, and a nightmarish head tried to follow. He punched it hard in the mouth, once, twice, until it staggered back into the dark. Seizing his chance, he slammed the door and threw the bolt home. The monster beat against it, but the door at least was soundly made and held.

The female sagged back upon the pallet, giving him a wan smile. Smitagees looked at her for a moment, but was unsurprised to find that encountering ferocious, rotting monsters did nothing for his desires. His prick was as shrivelled as if he had been bathing in ice water. He thrust back past the curtain and down the hall, pausing only long enough to hold down the crone and extract his money. He strode off back towards his ship, her curses ringing in his ear. His knuckles stung – he saw that there was a tear in the skin, blood welling. He stuck it in his mouth and sucked.

Over the next two days, he was dismayed to see that the wound appeared infected. Despite sluicing it with seawater frequently, the cuts deepened into angry weeping holes, the skin across the rest of his hand feeling hot and tight, the veins dark and throbbing. He wrapped a rag around it and went about his duties.

A day later, the headache struck – a mere annoyance, at first, until it became so intense he could barely see, and that afternoon he found himself crashing to the deck from the rigging. His shipmates threw him into a hammock below decks – there was no doctor on board, he would have to wait until the next landfall.

But later that day, Smitagees died.

A death on board ship was not uncommon, but still no favourable omen. The captain ordered that the body be wrapped and buried overboard as swiftly as possible. As the men went about their duties, they were surprised to hear a commotion from below deck where the burial party had gone to wrap and weight the corpse. They were even more surprised when Smitagees reappeared, in hot pursuit of the sailors fleeing before him.

A crazed melee ensued, until finally with bill hooks, oars and fishing nets, the horrified crew were able to despatch him overboard. The entire company lined the railing to watch as he sank beneath the swell, chilled by the last glimpses of his dead black eyes. Like a shark's, they muttered to one another, only worse.

By this time, the ship had been carried in close to shore, and the captain hurriedly set the men to the task of trimming sail to carry them safely back out to deeper waters. A cry from the lookout brought him back to the railing – a black shape was bobbing in the water, just near land. As he watched, it resolved itself into Smitagees' head, then torso... The dead man was staggering somewhat drunkenly to shore.

"Shit," said the Phoenician captain.

There were villages in the hinterland. For a moment the captain considered beaching the ship, sending out runners with warnings – or of even trying to catch and re-kill his old crewman. But where was the profit in that? No, either the gods had a reason for keeping Smitagees moving, in which case it had nothing to do with him, or whatever it was that had caused it was sure to wear off sooner or later. The dead couldn't keep going forever. Time, tide and profits, on the other hand, waited on no man.

He gave the order to set sail.

....

Miltiades was walking. His usual instinct would have been to go home, polish off the amphora from last night – but instead the urge hit to get moving, try to make sense of what he had heard. He slipped out of the new agora as quickly as possible, heading across the site of the old market place and around the base of the acropolis. He didn't feel like trudging up the steep slope to the temples and public buildings at the top. Far too likely to run into fellow Eupatrids up there. Instead his course took him around the inside of the city wall, amid the noise and smell of the poorer households.

This did not mean he found himself any more comfortable here, amid the simple folk. No, he did not have the gift of the common touch. Pisistratus used to tour the countryside, pressing flesh and dispensing justice, building a following among the poor farmers and labourers. He had the knack of making everyone feel they were part of something, something more than just their own little lives. As trade grew, the potters could swell their chests at the knowledge that it was their amphorae that carried Athenian oil across the Aegean. And the farmers who grew the olive trees could see the wealth of the city grow and feel a catch in their throat that it was their solid work helping build this new polis.

But nor did Miltiades feel any more real kinship with his fellow Eupatrids. He was realistic enough to know that it was just luck that he was born into the wealthy Philaid clan. It had taken no special skill on his part, except for emerging alive and bawling from between his mother's legs. The accident of birth didn't stop others of his class conducting themselves as if they personally had slain the minotaur or been handpicked by Zeus himself.

Where did he fit? Where did he belong? If not with the people, if not with the upper class, then where? Not with the merchant class either, surely. All that fussing over an abacus and trying to screw your supplier's price down to the minimum while bloating your own - no, that wasn't for him either.

The sound of hammers caught his attention. He glanced up, squinting his eyes against the flare of sunlight on unpainted white marble. He had come upon the Temple of Olympian Zeus, the biggest temple in the whole city, currently under construction under the orders of the men without title or position, Hippias and Hipparchus. He had to admit that it was beautiful. The height of the columns was truly breathtaking.

"What an eyesore," said a languid voice behind him. "Ostentatious, or what?"

He turned. Damnation. Company, and Eupatrid company at that. "Oh, hello Cleisthenes. Didn't know you were back. Always hard keep up with whether your family is currently exiled or not."

The other man smiled thinly. "Oh yes," he said, coming to stand beside Miltiades. "The brothers kindly overturned the last banishment and invited the Alcmaeonid clan to return to Athens. So here I am. Though what exactly I'm doing here I don't know. What are you doing here?"

"Just out walking."

"Just out walking. Still, what else is a Eupatrid to do, when there is tyranny in town? Can't exactly get on with the usual business of wheeling and dealing and politicking. No, hang on a minute: you let them make you archon, didn't you?"

"I stood for archon. I was elected. Besides, I seem to recall you serving the year after."

"Yes," said Cleisthenes with a smile. "Although I did it... ironically. But my point stands – things have changed. Though maybe things have to change even more." His face was suddenly serious.

"You mean, to go back to the way they were?"

Cleisthenes shook his head. "No, not necessarily. Though you are right that that is what most Eupatrids desire." He kicked at a chunk of marble. "The Pisistratids have started something here, something we should maybe see through, if we could but learn to put aside base self-interest, which they cannot... Look, I'm having a symposium next week, a few sympathetic souls. Why not come? See where the wine and talk may take us? Then have a flute girl play your flute?"

Miltiades looked up at the workmen chipping away on the upper reaches of the temple. He didn't think he could stand the height, personally. "I can't. There's something I need to do."

"Life can't be all horses and racing, Miltiades," said Cleisthenes. "Sometimes you have to pick a side and stand your ground."

"I'm not..." Miltiades stopped. It was pointless arguing. "Look, politics just isn't my thing."

"And you call yourself a Eupatrid!" laughed Cleisthenes. "It's what we do! Correction, it was what we did. Scheming, plotting, competing to see who could fund the biggest public building." He gestured towards the Temple of Zeus. "Until the Pisistratids became the only show in town."

Miltiades stood silent.

"Well, what's this thing you have to do, that is so important?"

"I have to take a trip," said Miltiades.

"You have to take a trip," Hippias had said.

"Oh?" Miltiades had replied guardedly.

"Yes. It's about your uncle, he who is also named Miltiades. Heard from him lately?"

Memories rushed through him at the mention of his uncle – the ready smile, the easy manner. He was quieter than his brash, louder brother, Miltiades' own father. Miltiades had always felt understanding when his uncle had looked at him, when he would clap him on the shoulder and ask him what he was reading. They had spent less time together than he might have liked – his father seemed to harbour a vague dislike for his brother, so did not extend an invitation to visit very often. How many times had Miltiades wished that it was his namesake he called father instead?

"What about him?"

"You recall, no doubt, that your father sent him to the Chersonnese, on the Hellespont, to establish a colony?"

Of course Miltiades did. Pisistratus won a lot of praise for that shrewd move. There was one thing the people of Athens feared more than any other: more than Thebans, or barbarians, or disease, or even the Spartans. They feared hunger. It was no secret that as the population grew, the capacity of the thin soil of Attica to feed everyone was sorely tested. And so, when Pisistratus announced he was sending brave Uncle Miltiades and a bunch of land-hungry colonists far away to establish a city-state on the entry to the Black Sea, there was much rejoicing. For that narrow waterway led to gold – the dusky gold of endless fields of wheat. With a military and trading presence right at the head of the straits, Athens was guaranteed a steady supply. Miltiades' father rejoiced for another reason – he and his brother had fallen out a year or two earlier, meaning Miltiades had not seen him for some time before the expedition, and was now even less likely to see him again.

"The ships have stopped coming. And there hasn't been word from him in months."

"Send a messenger."

"We did. He hasn't come back, either."

Miltiades sucked his teeth. "And you want me to...?"

"We want you to take a ship and go see what is going on. If your uncle still rules there, remind him of his duty to Athens. If something has happened to him... well, we want you to take over. Set up a base. Get some crops planted and trade for more. Get the grain flowing again."

"Gentlemen," said Miltiades. "I'm not sure that I'm your man. I don't think I'm the adventurer-entrepreneur type..."

"Gods!" groaned Hipparchus. "Not this, not that. What kind of man are you then?"

"I quite like reading," said Miltiades calmly. Hipparchus guffawed.

"It doesn't matter," said Hippias, with a glance at this brother. "You're going. We'll give you a ship and a captain, and some funds. You advertise for settlers. We will make a proclamation at the next Assembly to that effect. Cheer up, Miltiades. A chance to feed the city? You'll be a hero."

....

Some Time Earlier

Astyages, King of the Medes, was far from happy. For one thing, his war chariot did not have any seating, and both the horses out front and the driver beside him were sweating and stinking in the midday heat. On top of that, there was the whole issue of dealing with this uprising by the lousy Persians, whom he had previously thought of as loyal vassals. So here he was, in the centre of his royal army, waiting to inflict annihilation on the ingrates, instead of being back in his nice cool palace enjoying the charms of his concubines.

He glanced left and right, surveying the ranks of his forces: rows of spearmen at the front, ranks of archers behind them, and large bodies of horsemen on the two flanks. He frowned as he made out the figure of Harpagus, one of his kinsmen, given command of the cavalry this day. Harpagus was sitting stock still on his horse, staring straight ahead across the plain. If he could feel the eyes of his king upon him, he made no sign. What was that old saying? Keep your enemies close, but keep your kinsmen closer still, for they shall surely try to screw you if given the opportunity?

Astyages sighed. It was all such a bother. Who would want to be a king, really?

The current trouble, if he thought about it, had all started years ago. With that cursed dream.

Astyages had been troubled by recurring and disturbing nightmares about his daughter, and summoned the Magi to interpret them for him. It was more embarrasing than he had imagined, describing to the old greybeards the nature of the visions. He couldn't help but wonder if they were secretly laughing at him. But still...when he had finished explaining, the learned men sucked their teeth and clicked their tongues, sadly shaking their heads of curled and perfumed locks.

"What?" demanded Astyages.

"It's not good, sire," replied one of the Magi. "It means any son your daughter produces is bound to overthrow you."

The wise men left, eager to return to their quarters and discuss what a pervert their king was – imagine the old boy having dreams like that?

The interpretation did not please the Median king. He had recently wed his daughter to a Persian nobleman. At that time the Persians were mere subjects of the Medes, and the move was a political one to keep them in line – it was an alliance of increasing importance due to confused reports of hordes of strange raiders appearing in the lands to the south.

This daughter had just given birth to a child, a boy named Cyrus.

Asytages confided in one of his nobles, this very kinsman, Harpagus. The child has to go, he said. Quietly. And permanently. Very, very permanently. Harpagus had licked his lips, but he knew better than to question Astyages. A favour was an order in the noble houses of the Medes. And yet, later, as he stole away from the royal precinct with the gurgling baby hidden beneath his cloak, he was uneasy. He had confided his orders to his wife.

"But can you imagine what happens when Astyages dies and his daughter takes over?" he asked his wife. "The fact that her child disappeared won't have escaped her. She's going to want to track down who did it. And then..." He shuddered at the thought.

"Well, you are not going to harm a hair on that child's head," his wife declared, and that was that. Harpagus winced: now he really was in a bind, stuck as he was between the two people on earth with the most power to make his life hell.

There had to be a way out.

And there was. It presented itself in the form of a herdsman who lived on his property. A herdsman who wouldn't mind adopting a baby to raise as his own son...

Astyages shook his head as he glowered across at his supposedly loyal subject. What a fool. Thought he'd got away with it. But fate moves in mysterious ways, and the king discovered his little ploy. It had all come out when some of the other nobles had complained that some upstart of a kid, some herdsman's son, was beating up all their noble-born sons until they declared him their king in some wargame they were playing. It just wasn't right, complained the nobles, they were quality, after all. Get rid of the little brat. Bring him before me, commanded Astyages. He hated some of these nobles's kids – such snotty, whining brats. He just had to meet the young fellow who had given them their comeuppance. And of course, once the cocksure little bugger was standing before him, it was obvious in his looks and bearing that this was no mere herdsman's boy. It hadn't taken much – just a slight bit of torture – to get the whole story: the herdsman reported that Harpagus had given him the boy to hide away and raise as his own.

On the plus side, because the kid, Cyrus, had already been named king by the other boys, the Magi were of the opinion that had satisfied the fate foretold in the dream – he had become king through violence - and he wouldn't be king in any other way. On the minus side, Harpagus had disobeyed an order from his king, and had acted on an indepenedent thought. A very dangerous precedent.

Astyages had responded – he had invited Harpagus to dinner...

"You appear greatly amused, my lord. Can you share the joke?" Harpagus had asked. Even with a feast in full swing, from his position at the king's side, the noble couldn't miss the smirk on Astyages' face.

"I'll tell you in a minute," said Astyages. "Good?" he asked, as Harpagus took a big bite of the meat on his silver salver.

"Delicious. Young and succulent."

Astyages blew wine out his nose, and collapsed for some minutes, only recovering after his bodyguard pounded him on the back.

"Sorry, sorry," he said, wiping his eyes and giggling still. "Oh, this is rich."

"Ah... It is certainly pleasing to see my lord in such high spirits..."

"Yes, well," said Astyages coyly, playing with his wine cup. "I've received some good news. About my grandson."

Harpagus stopped chewing for a moment, and swallowed carefully. "Indeed?"

"Yes. Turns out he's actually still alive. No, sit down, Harpagus."

"My lord... I don't know what to say... This is happy news..."

"Isn't it? There is, however, the little matter of you not obeying my instructions. I really can't let that slide. So, don't take it personally, but I had your own son kidnapped and...ah...served up to you."

"...what?"

"Your meal. That was your kid."

"We had lamb, not goat..."

"No, we had lamb. You had your boy. Not a kid, your kid."

"It can't be... You wouldn't..."

"Oh, it is, and I did. I'll prove it."

Astyages clapped his hands, and a slave brought in a platter covered by a lid. With trembling fingers, Harpagus lifted it, glanced at what lay beneath, and fell back against his chair, the blood drained from his face.

"So the moral is, always obey me, right?"

Harpagus nodded. He had aged noticeably. "If you will excuse me, my lord..." He rose on unsteady feet and tottered toward the door.

"Don't forget your leftovers!" cried Astyages.

Harpagus accepted the dish from the slave, and took what remained of his son for burial. And from that moment on, worked tirelessly to bring down the Median king. The agent he chose was Cyrus, the now reclaimed grandson of Astyages.

"Irony," the hunched and grizzled noble could be heard to mutter as he absently paced his villa. "Irony."

When Cyrus had grown up to be one of the bravest and most popular men in Persia, Harpagus acted. He sent a secret message urging Cyrus to rebel, and assuring him of the support of many Median nobles tired of Astyages' arrogance and harsh rule. This was music to Cyrus' ears. He saw himself as a Persian, like his father, and bitterly resented his people's subservient position to the Medes. He acted swiftly, sending out messages ordering all able bodied Persian men to meet on a particular date, at a particular place.

It hadn't taken much talk from Cyrus to convince the Persian host that things were out of whack – that it should be they who were ruling the Medes, not the other way around. They would rise up and take their proper place in the world, as masters, not servants. The crowd loved it. There was a great celebration, with much wine consumed and little care taken to set an effective, sober watch. So that night as they lay sleeping, none noticed the shambling handful of figures appearing out of the darkness to the south until it was too late...

Reports reached Astyages of the Persians' rather haphazard advance into his kingdom. He gathered his kinsmen and nobles to him, and directed them to raise their troops.

"It is time to teach this little boy his place," he told them.

He completely missed the knowing smirk Harpagus bestowed on several of the more powerful noblemen.

And so now the Mede army was drawn up on a plain not far from the capital. Astyages positioned himself in the middle, and had no doubt they would deliver a decisive blow to this rebellion. For some time nothing happened. The men stood or sat in position. Servants brought him snacks of sweet meats and wine infused with honey. And then a dust storm appeared on the horizon, heralding what must be the approach of the Persian force. Astyages waggled his fingers, and watching trumpeteers blew their signal. The Medes got to their feet, wiping off their hands and took firm grip of bow and shield and spear.

Astyages waited, impatiently, for the Persians to draw into sight. When they did, he was a little surprised. There seemed to be no order in their ranks at all – just a mass of swarming men. And these seemed somewhat drunk, or fevered, going by their odd, shambling movement. No cavalry, either.

Astyages smiled toothily. This would be, he thought, a piece of honeycake.

Stirrings on both his wings caught his attention, and he was displeased to see huge chunks of his cavalry riding forward. He hadn't given any order to attack, what was going on? Who was in charge around here? But then he spotted a rider at the front of the troop on the right. Harpagus...

Harpagus grimly led the Mede cavalry towards the Persians at the canter. When he judged they were close enough, he signalled the ranks behind him to slow, stop. And turn about. They now faced the Median forces – who were now somewhat exposed on the flanks.

Bastard! Astyages gripped his sword hilt so tightly his hand was shaking. Sneaking, turncoat little bastard! Now the Persians had plenty of cavalry, and he had hardly any! Traitor! Treachery!

Harpagus stared at the distant figure of Astyages with satisfaction. Oh yes, this was sweet. Once the Persian infantry swept by, he would lead the horsemen forward in a looping charge. He glanced back – come on, Cyrus, get your boys moving...

He was surprised to see the Persians splitting into two groups, one pack coming up behind his troopers, another heading for the cavalry stationed on the far side. What tactic was this?

Astyages watched as the Persians seemingly attacked and overwhelmed the cavalry on the flanks. A double double cross? Now? Wouldn't Cyrus have wanted to use them in the battle, and then get rid of them? That's how he would have done it. But sure enough, rider after rider was being hauled down and covered in swarming figures. And not just the men – some of the horses, too, seemed to be pulled down. A few dozen realised fast enough what was happening and spurred their horses back towards the Median army. Astyages let them get within a few score paces before signalling his archers to shoot them down. Never trust a traitor. Especially, as it turned out, if they were related by blood.

The chaos before him gradually cleared, and the Persian force was surging forward again. The Median archers let fly, but still the attackers came on, those in the front fairly bristling with arrows. The distance between the lines shrank and shrank, and now finally some of the crazed Persians were dropping, feathered shafts protruding from eye sockets or mouths, but the rest moved forward, arms outstretched, mouths gaping. And now the Medes could see what confronted them, see the already present wounds, the spoiled flesh, the exposed bone. They could hear the tortured groans. They could smell the corruption. And the lines began to dissolve as men's nerve broke, and they ran.

The king's bodyguard drew in tight about him, forming an island in a sea of putrid flesh as the monstrous Persian force flowed around, many continuing in pursuit of those who had fled, but others turning to grab at the armoured spearmen about Astyages. The terrible creatures were without pain or fear, continuing to press forward even after swords had hacked their arms from their bodies, thrusting their gaping maws and clacking teeth toward the Medes.

And more figures were joining them – bodies lying strewn about the field were stirring, rising.

Astyages recognized one loitering at the back of the pack – it may have been missing half its face, and seemingly all its bowels, but there was no mistaking the man who had betrayed him.

"Harpagus, you stupid bastard! With all your scheming you could have made yourself king, but look at you! I always thought you were gutless!"

And it was with this last desperate laugh in his throat that the lines collapsed and the dead surged over them all.

....

On top of a nearby mountain, a man leaned upon his long, notched sword, watching. "A blessing," he murmured.

"My lord Cyrus," said one of the score or so men standing in an arc behind him, "A blessing? Surely these things are the work of darkness, not the light."

Cyrus did not turn. He rubbed one of his forearms – bound in leather strips that were scored and furrowed – across his brow, leaving streaks of clean skin showing through the grime of travel and battle. "And yet, see," he said finally. "These things have carried the Medes before them. The kingdom is there for the taking."

"These things used to be our own forces," said another. "My own brothers walk down there amongst them..." He broke off, throwing his cloak over his head.

"It is true that it is hard. Hard to take, and even harder to understand," Cyrus turned and looked at them each in turn. "Our way is hard. The way of the light. For surely, I say these things are the work of Ahura Mazda, god of light. They shall be like a fire, burning away the power of the wicked like Astyages. We shall rise, we shall rule."

"Those of us who don't get eaten," muttered someone at the back.

The others glanced at their leader uncertainly, but he smiled, his teeth white against the dirt and sunburn of his face. He threw his head back and laughed, and walked among them, clapping them on the shoulders.

"Yes! Those who are not eaten. But you are not seeing them as clearly as I. I tell you, the cities shall be safe. These creatures know no siege craft. They will flow on, like a tide of fire, and we will ride before it and after it, guiding the people to safety, and leading the tide onward. We will let it do its work, and go on, to the north."

"Where will it end? Where will this tide end up?"

Cyrus shrugged. "Who knows? It won't be our problem. Cheer up, all of you! You are witnessing the birth of the Persian Empire. All births are painful. But we shall rule for a thousand years. For us, the light! And for those who oppose us, a sea of darkness..."

....

THREE

THE 12 LABOURS
OF HERACLES

Miltiades hesitated. He realised that he had been about to knock, but this was his house, damn it, and he could go where he liked. It was just that the door leading from the main section of the house into the women's quarters was not one he used much himself. With no wife, the rooms had previously stood empty, used as storage. But that had all changed with the death of his father.

"You'll be a hero," Hippias had said. Fat chance of that, if he couldn't face his own mother.

Don't overthink it, he said to himself, and pushed on through. It was darker in this section of the house. The nicer rooms with better light were toward the front. These rooms were attached to the kitchen, and smelled smoky. One of the slaves directed him toward his mother's bedroom, which surprised him. Wasn't she even getting up to oversee the work of the slaves?

Her room didn't smell of smoke – instead it was filled with a cloying mixture of incense and perfumed balm. It filled him with revulsion.

"Mother," he said, and the white shape sprawled on the bed turned towards him.

"Miltiades? My son? What is it? What's wrong?"

He could hear her voice tighten with anxiety. He rarely came here, so she was surprised.

"Mother, listen. I am going away for a while. I have to sail to the Chersonnese within the week. To visit Uncle Miltiades."

"Go away?" she said. "Go away? But who will look after me?"

"Well...the slaves. Just like always. I'm not taking everyone. Just Zander."

"Don't leave me. I don't want you to leave me. What if your father's killers come back?"

He didn't feel like offering any words of comfort – this path was too well travelled already. He couldn't tell her that following these orders was probably the best insurance against further trouble. Just go along. If he confided in her, he feared what she would do, what she would say. She would stir the pot, but it would be him, as head of the clan, who would pay the price.

"Listen, I have been given a great honour. To sail to the Hellespont and safeguard the food supply for all of Athens." He laughed a little. "I may be the hero of the hour."

"You?" she said, and the flatness of her tone reminded him of why he loathed her as he did.

"You should get up," he said. "You should dress, and direct the slaves. You should do something. Weave, something."

"I should do something?" she said quietly, and he knew she was thinking of past days, of his father parading in his glorious chariot, the people cheering, the envy of her neighbours. Her glory days. But Miltiades also recalled the stench of shit as he was called to identify the stiff body lying in the filth. He did not wish to end that way.

"I will write," he said, and there was a moment of weakening when he could have leaned forward and kissed her, but she made no move to proffer her cheek so instead he turned to walk out.

"No doubt you will," she said, to his stiff retreating back. "That's pretty much all you do."

The sound of the smashing wine cup brought Zander running. He stopped when he reached the doorway of the andron and took in Miltiades' hard white face.

"Oh dear, oh dear. What has the gorgon done this time, Perseus?"

Miltiades let out a bitter bark of laughter at the use of their boyhood jest. He looked up at his main slave, the head of his household staff, who had been his companion since childhood. Zeus, but he had some grey hairs on the sides of his head now. He unconsciously ran a hand through his own hair, though Zander was a few years older than him, as close as they could work out. The slave's memories of his early years were hazy. Still, they were boys no more.

"Alas, she has not turned me to stone. For then I would not have broken this wine cup."

Zander looked down at the broken shards. "Oh. One of your nicest ones, too. The one with the pornographic scene at the bottom. Now what am I to amuse myself with when I clean in here?"

"When you clean in here? When do you clean in here? You mean when you order the slave girl to clean in here while you watch her bum wiggle."

Zander shrugged. "Such is the prerogative of the limited power you grant me."

"One day, it is off to the silver mines for you."

Zander now smiled at the use of their other longstanding jest. "Well, I have always wanted to travel."

"Ah," said Miltiades, suddenly growing serious. "Funny you should mention that. How do you feel about sea voyages?"

....

The sun was already higher than he would have liked when Miltiades walked out of the gate in the southern city walls and headed down towards the port of Phaleron. The Assembly had gone on longer than he'd expected, what with Hippias having to go through some elaborate charade of consulting the priests on what the oracles portended for the expedition. He had left Zander to set up with a small table in the agora, to take down the names of citizens interested in trying their luck in the north. Miltiades had no doubts that there would be enough takers – second sons, failed merchants, non-citizen metics sick of the snobbery of the Athenians. Oh yes, there would be enough willing to face an uncertain future for the promise of some nice fat farmland.

"Oh, cousin?"

He turned, working to hide the frown that threatened to darken his face. A slightly older man with a balding pate was walking hard to catch up.

"Nicomedes."

"Cousin Miltiades! I... hold a moment..." The other man mopped his red face with his cloak. "Really must get to the gym more often... Let me congratulate you on your appointment. An honour, rivalling that of your uncle and even, dare I say, your poor-"

"Best walk with me, Nicomedes. I must get down to the docks."

"The docks?" Nicomedes squinted at the collection of buildings marking Athens' main port, a couple of miles across the plain. "Oh, I don't think so. Nasty, smelly places. Quite lower class."

"Well, thank you and good day then," Miltiades nodded and turned to go.

"Hold up! I won't keep you." Despite these words, Nicomedes had taken hold of his tunic sleeve. Miltiades looked at the older man's fingers with growing annoyance. "It's my boy. My son, Callias. You do remember him?"

Miltiades nodded noncommittally. He did have some vague picture of a young stripling at some clan feast or other.

"He's currently serving his time as a cadet on the border. I am wondering if you would consider taking him with you? You will be needing assistants, will you not? Junior officers?"

"I don't know how long we will be gone. And it might be dangerous – we don't know what has happened up there."

Nicomedes waved his hand. "Oh, I'm sure he will be safe with you. And a little danger never hurt anyone. Between you and me, I'm hoping to separate him from a friend of his." Nicomedes glanced about and leaned in, though they were quite alone. "They are getting a little too close."

"Nothing wrong with that."

Nicomedes pursed his lips. "Not in certain situations, no. If the other fellow was older, and an upright cititzen, and Callias was gaining from the alliance, it would be perfectly acceptable. For a time. Why, I myself was protégé to old Sophon and I certainly learned a thing or two there. Apart from the times when he was trying to bugger me – but that was only when he was drunk. And I never let him, of course. I'm not like that. Just let him wiggle it between my thighs, like any normal lad. Ha! But there is something... a little vicious about this. No, it must be stopped. The boy needs some toughening up."

Miltiades stared out at the sunlight glinting on the distant water. Family obligations were a heavy weight he had really been hoping to escape. Still, he remembered his own year serving in the cramped forts that dotted Athens' northern border, on the lookout for raids by the Thebans. He'd been miserable.

"I'll take him. Go tell Zander to add his name to the list. He's in the agora."

He strode off with Nicomedes' unctuous thanks following him.

Down on the waterfront, he picked his way through the bustle. There were fat bodied merchant ships – with fat bodied merchants standing around them arguing. Sleek war triremes pulled up onto land, while wiry oarsmen strutted about carrying their oar and the little cushions they used for their blistered backsides. Funny how the ships and the men associated with them came to match. Which raised the question – what would his appointed ship look like? Something a little nondescript, nothing that stood out, he surmised wryly. But hopefully up to the task.

He scanned the row of little wine shops along the docks and picked out the one he was after, down the far end. He had to negotiate around donkeys and men, both laden with trade goods coming into Athens, and sweating dockworkers loading uniform amphorae of olive oil heading out. And everywhere the sunlight glinted on the silver owls of Athens as coins passed backwards and forwards. The wine shop was not much more than a shack, with a couple of trestle tables set up out the front. There were three hard looking men sitting at one, with jugs of water, wine and a mixing bowl set between them. He could feel them eyeing him up and down as he approached – the gait of a land dweller, the cloak and tunic of someone with money.

"Phillipus?" he asked.

The men stared at him.

"Well then, if none of you gentlemen are Phillipus, can you tell me where I might find him?"

"Why would you want to find him?" grunted one.

"Not that it is any of your business, but I have work for him."

"You have work for Phillipus? If you have work, best come to us instead, if it is a ship you are after."

"A ship captained by somebody sane," chipped in one of the others. The third spat on the ground.

Miltiades worked to stop his mouth twisting in disgust. "I'm afraid choice of captain was lifted out of my hands by the brothers. This commision is at the behest of the Pisistratids."

The three exchanged a look. The Pisistratids were no champions of the men of the coast. Their own champion, Isocrates, had seemed likely to take power, with the promise of favour to those traders and merchants and business men who formed his backers. But that all came to naught when Pisistratus the

Elder marched into Athens at the head of his mercenary army and took power for himself. So, no, they were not fans of the Pisistratids around here – but they had to respect them.

"He's inside," The first speaker gestured at the thin material serving as a door. "But be warned; don't mention Egypt, whatever you do." And they snickered unpleasantly at some private joke.

"Thank you. I will take your advice on board."

Miltiades pushed through the greasy curtain and into the gloom of the interior room. It seemed even darker at first after the glare of the outside light, but as he stepped cautiously forward he could make out a counter at the back, and a scattering of benches and tables. A man sat slumped in the far corner. He stepped up to the counter and pressed a coin onto the damp wood, and the old woman standing there quietly place two jugs, a mixing bowl and drinking cup before him. It seemed one didn't have to stipulate what wine one wanted here. It was the house special or nothing. Light flared, and he was aware of the three drinkers from outside following him in and taking seats at a corner table, opposite to where the solitary man sat.

Miltiades nodded his thanks to the crone, and mixed himself a cup of watered wine. He figured the wine was probably marginally safer than the water here, so chose to make it fairly strong. The aroma was one of vinegar. He carried it over to the man's table and sat across from him.

"Captain Phillipus?"

"Fuck off," grunted the man. There were sniggers from the table behind him.

"So what's the story with Egypt?" Miltiades asked. The laughter cut off behind him.

A sense of breath being held.

The man reared up spluttering, revealing wine-reddened eyes. He held up a shaking finger. "You... You just fuck off... Fucking Egypt?... You... Fuck!"

"Tell me, do you kiss your mother with that mouth?"

The man's eyes narrowed. "No," he said. "But maybe I kiss yours."

"Inadvisable," said Miltiades. "Firstly, you'd have trouble getting your arms around her. Secondly, you'd have to catch her between mouthfuls."

The man let out a bark of laughter. The tension eased. "I actually do like a woman with a healthy appetite. And something to hold onto."

"Well, I'll be sure to introduce you when we get back."

"When we get back? Where are we going?"

Miltiades looked into the captain's eyes, and somewhere beneath the watery surface he felt like there was something else, some iron. "The Pisistratids have named you as the trirarch to take me to the Chersonnese."

"The Chersonnese? What's there?"

"My uncle, hopefully. A colony, at any rate. Or there will be."

Phillipus rubbed his whiskered chin. "I don't much care for your employers."

"Enough to turn down their silver?"

"Well... Perhaps not enough for that, no. Tell me more."

"We are to embark within the week. Myself, and a number of settlers to be determined. Either to reinforce the existing colony or establish a new one. Apparently, we will be hailed as heroes of Athens, when we return with baskets full of golden grain."

"Hmmm," Phillipus looked down at the table, swirling his fingers through spilt wine. "I'd want a hundred proper oarsmen for the journey back. You could make up the rest with colonists, if they are prepared to row."

"How long to get to the Chersonnese?"

The captain sucked his lips. "If we don't just hug the coast, and instead cut across to some of the islands like Lemnos, I'd say four or five days. Depending."

"How long to ready your ship?"

"Not long. I take good care of my trireme. It's here in dry dock."

Better than the care you take with yourself, Miltiades felt like saying.

"Good. I'll be sending my slave Zander to liaise with you." Miltiades stood.

"Wait," said the captain. "Why me?"

"I was hoping you would know the answer to that."

Phillipus slowly shook his head.

"Could it have something to do with Egypt?" asked Miltiades softly.

He could see Phillipus' face harden. "Do not mention that place to me again."

Miltiades grunted. The captain's hand shot out and locked onto his wrist. It was a rough, strong grip – the grip of a sailor.

"I mean it."

"Very well," Miltiades slowly pulled his hand clear. "I'd leave you a coin for wine, but maybe you had better start sobering up."

"I'll take your damn coin. I don't have to be sober to sail."

And that was it, thought Miltiades as he pushed back out into the light. You are probably completely expendable. Which means so am I.

....

He came fully awake. He blinked in the darkness and stifled a curse. It had taken him a long time to get to sleep, the blanket twining about his restless legs like a python. His mind had been full of lists – names, supplies, all the odds and ends and minutiae that seemed to have to go into this venture. It wasn't like that in the stories – Jason, Odysseus... everybody in the stories just got in a boat and went. Not that things weren't coming together. After his first meeting with Phillipus, he had walked back to the agora, to Zander. He found his slave set up outside one of the stoas, with a pair of men waiting before the table.

"Citizens," Miltiades nodded at the men. By the look of their attire, none were particularly well off. "How are we going, Zander?"

"Good, good. With these gentlemen here, we will have near forty by the end of the day."

"Really? That many already?"

"A good chance for a new beginning, sir," said one of the men waiting.

"You're prepared to move so far away? From Athens?"

The man shrugged. "A man's polis is where his land is. If you give me land there, then that shall be my home."

"You're a farmer, then?"

"Not we two, no," said the man, reddening. "Stone masons, actually."

"Stone masons? Why would you want to leave? There is plenty of building work for you here, surely."

"Well, sir, it is just that Hermolaos and I aren't the very best of masons, you might say. And the Pisistratids only want the best, so we don't get much of a look in. And since no one else is really building…"

"Agathon doesn't tell it right," broke in the other. "We do good, solid work. But we aren't into all that fancy stuff the Pisistratids want."

"Well, welcome. I dare say we shall need stonemasons as well as farmers. Especially those who can do good, solid work. I don't think we'll have much call for fancy pediments. Not for a while, anyway."

But now something was wrong. No dream had roused him. What, then? He lay still, opening his senses. Something felt different – some change of pressure in the house. Quietly he swung his legs over the side of his bed and sat up, listening. He could hear nothing. Perhaps it was just one of the slaves going to the privvy. Or perhaps it was something else.

It seemed unlikely that he would be able to sleep without going and checking. He could call to Zander, or one of the other slaves sleeping not far away, but that would disturb his mother, who would demand to know why her sleep was being interrupted, which would only disturb him further... And besides, there was something about the silent darkness that stifled his voice in his throat. As if calling out might bring some horrible creature to his door. Apollo's balls, was he a child again?

He lifted his cloak from its peg and hung it about his shoulders: the night air was chill. For a moment he wished he had a weapon of some kind nearby, but his arms were locked away in a closet deep in the house. At best he had a couple of thick scrolls. Maybe a stylus.

He stepped out into the corridor, and slowly drifted towards the inner courtyard. And there, dark against the lighter shade of the wall, he saw the cause of his waking. The door to the street stood open.

This door was always locked at night. Always. He slowly scanned the courtyard, ears straining. Something moved. He spun. A figure moved towards him.

He felt a stab of disappointment amongst the fear. So this was how it was to end? Murdered in his home, in the dark, alone. His father flashed into his mind, and he could almost have laughed that they should share this, share this end. At least he wasn't in some foul alley.

And yet, another part of his mind cried out: but why? I haven't done anything.

I haven't done anything.

I want to do something before I die.

The figure halted before him, covered in an immense black cloak, cowled.

"*Hear me,*" said the man.

"Just get it over with," said Miltiades. "No wait! Tell me at least who sent you. The Pisistratids? The Alcmaeonids? Who?"

The man chuckled. Not a very pleasant sound.

"*Those who sent me are beyond your ken.*"

Miltiades had been carefully scanning the darkness about him. He had assumed there were more accomplices, hiding, but instead it seemed as if this intruder was alone. In which case, one shout would rouse the household slaves.

Maybe tonight was not his time to die.

As if guessing his thoughts, the man thrust a hand towards him, and Miltiades reeled back – but it held no weapon. Instead the man pointed at him with a long white finger. He suddenly felt hot and cold, all at once.

"*Hark!*" cried the dark intruder.

"*Man of inaction, now must action take*
Not for self, but for the people's sake.
Thrice betrayer, thrice betrayed
With living flesh is debt repaid.
To live to see the setting sun,
tortoise must rise up and run."

The man stepped closer, and within the shadows of the hood, Miltiades could just make out his bearded features.

It appeared to be an older version of himself, pale and care-worn.

"What the hell?" said Miltiades, and then the courtyard swam and he fainted to the floor.

....

"And you're sure it wasn't a dream?" asked Zander, as he slid the door's oiled locking bolt backwards and forwards. "You did finish all that cheese last night."

"I told you. I'm sure." Miltiades sat shivering on a bench, a blanket about his shoulders and a cup of wine in his hand. The household slaves had found him still unconscious on the ground just before dawn, the door firmly locked. "And it's my bloody cheese. I can finish it off if I want to."

"Well, it's just that I sometimes have trouble telling if a dream is real or not, that's all."

"Dangerous for a slave to dream too much," Miltiades said, and instantly regretted it.

Zander didn't comment. Miltiades glanced at his face, but that told him nothing.

"That leaves us with a crazed burglar who doesn't take anything, spouts poetry then locks the door behind him, or..."

"Or?"

Zander shrugged. "Or a visitation from the gods."

"Oh, come on."

"I'm just outlining your choices," Zander threw his hands up. "You are free to choose."

Before Miltiades could reply, there was a knock on the door that made them both jump. The messenger was, at least, entirely human. Another summons from the Pisistratids.

When Miltiades was shown into the andron of the Pisistratid mansion, it was far emptier than the last time he had been there. There was only Hipparchus, who was standing at a window, gazing out into the agora and absent-mindedly plucking at his lower lip.

"Exquisite," he said softly. "He is just exquisite. What a waste."

Miltiades coughed. Hipparchus turned to him and looked him up and down, face blank.

"Oh, goody. The librarian." He sauntered over to his chair and draped himself across it, feet dangling.

"I'm hardly a librarian..."

"Do you own books? Yes? Then you're a librarian."

"Ah... Where is Hippias?"

"Not here. Obviously."

"He sent for me."

"No, I sent for you. I am equal to him, you know. Joint ruler."

Miltiades bit back a comment about how neither of the brothers actually held any magistracy or other title. They may like to maintain the outward trappings of the old government, still allowing yearly election of the three archons, but it was still a tyranny they led. "Of course," he said. "Then what can I do for you? The expedition is coming together-"

"You should be careful who you are seen hanging out with," Hipparchus interrupted, swivelling to sit upright in the chair.

Miltiades blinked. "What? Who...?"

"Why did you hold a meeting with that Alcmaeonid dog, Cleisthenes?"

"I didn't hold any... Oh, I ran into him at the... Wait, are you having me followed?"

Hipparchus smirked.

"I don't believe it. I'm doing what you want, I'm getting this stupid little expedition together..."

"That's right. You are doing what we want. And you will keep doing what we want, if you know what is good for you. It would be nice to think that not all Eupatrids are as patently untrustworthy as the Alcmaeonids. Just you remember, Miltiades, that our father didn't rule for as long as he did without always being a lap ahead of your sort. And we will be here just as long and beyond. If you had a kid, we'd have taken them hostage by now, but since you don't... Well, we will just have to keep our eyes on you, won't we? No matter where you go."

"You have a spy in my party? Is that what you are saying?"

That smug smile again. Miltiades just wanted to smash it off his face.

"No more meetings with untrustworthy elements, Miltiades, that's all I wanted to say. Run along now. And take that look off your face. Go cry to Hippias, if that will stop you bleating. You're boring me. He's up on the acropolis in his vault. Actually, you'll like it up there. Plenty of paper and dust."

Once outside, Miltiades decided he did want to confront Hippias, who was a little easier to deal with. His temper had cooled a little by the time he walked the Panathenaic Way up the ramp, up to the top of the Acropolis. As usual, there were a number of beggars standing by the Temple of Athena. He had no coins on his person, and felt uncomfortable, planning to keep his gaze fixed firmly ahead – but one of the figures caught his eye.

"Master Photios!"

He was older than when Miltiades had sat on the stoa steps, listening to him, with Zander sitting several steps below, ostensibly there just to carry Miltiades' slate and scrolls but taking part in the lessons, too. But then, with his bushy white beard and eyebrows, he had always seemed old to the young school boys.

"Master Photios, what are you doing here?"

It pierced Miltiades' heart to see how the old man moved to hide his begging bowl behind his back, and drew himself up straight and tall, adjusting his tattered old cloak about his bony shoulders.

"All citizens have the right to consult with the gods from time to time, young...uh..."

"Master, it is me. Miltiades."

"I know that! There is nothing wrong with my memory. It is just that... it takes a little longer for the memory to find form in speech."

Miltiades took in the gauntness of the older man's cheeks. The deep lines.

"Master," he said gently. "Why aren't you teaching?"

To his horror, Photios' bottom lip started to tremble. "Listen, Master," he said hastily. "I have business inside – but please, go down to the Agora and find Zander. You remember Zander? I need your help with something."

"You are a little old to be taking lessons, Miltiades. Unless... Have you a son?" The older man's eyes lit up.

"I do not. But it isn't your teaching I need you for. I need your brains for other things. I need an administrator. Find Zander, he'll explain."

The old man glanced at the other beggars standing nearby. He looked back at Miltiades and tried to speak, but his voice caught in his throat. Miltiades reached out and squeezed his skinny bicep, and the old man nodded, then turned and walked slowly for gateway.

There was work going on within the Temple. The Pisistratids had ordered extravagant marble statues to be added to the pediments, and workmen and artisans were busy chipping away. The statue of Athena herself, made of simple wood, seemed rather forelorn to Miltiades as he made his way past it to the rear of the building. Here he found what he was looking for, a handful of Skythians lounging about outside a door leading to an inner chamber. They watched him with that same air of arrogant, dismissive suspicion as he ducked through the low opening and into the lamplit interior.

Inside, he hesitated. The interior room was full of shelves, and most of these were packed with scrolls. He gazed about in wonder, at the smoky light from a dozen oil lamps flickering across the yellow rolls of paper. All that knowledge. This was, to him, a true temple.

"What do you want?" asked Hippias, barely glancing up from where he stood bent over an unfurled scroll on a small desk.

"What is this place? Is this your own library?"

Hippias squinted at him. "None of your damn business. And put your tongue back in your mouth. You aren't getting your greedy paws on any of these. At the risk of repeating myself: what do you want?"

"This expedition," said Miltiades carefully. "Is this just an elaborate scheme to do away with me?"

"Do away with you? Why ever would I want to do away with you?"

"If you have some cause to distrust me, and wish me dead..."

"Dead? Oh come, Miltiades! Don't be so dramatic!"

"A man broke into my house last night. I thought sent by you."

"To do what? Murder you in your sleep? I can assure you, Miltiades, if I sent someone to do that, you wouldn't be walking around now. My Skythians can be quiet as mice when they need to be. So, this man in your house. He attacked you?"

"No. He... Actually he spouted some poetry at me, then disappeared." He chose to leave out the detail of his own fainting spell. And the fact that the man had looked so much like him.

"Poetry?" Hippias chuckled. "Some out of work actor, hoping you'd fund a play?"

"It sounded like some kind of warning..."

"Not from one of the comedies, then?"

"It sounded personal. Meant for me."

Hippias stood upright and fixed Miltiades with an intense look. "Tell me of this poetic warning, then."

Miltiades repeated what he could remember. It was halting, out of order, and sounded stupid to his own ears as he said it. Hippias scoffed.

"That does not sound like much of a prophecy to me."

"That's probably due to my retelling..."

"Listen, Miltiades. I have a personal interest in prophecies. That is what you see before you. On these scrolls are written the words of the gods themselves, as relayed through the best oracles across Greece. So I know what I am talking about."

Miltiades gazed at the hundreds of rolls in wonder. "So many? But why?"

Hippias narrowed his eyes. "Forewarning."

"Your brother is having me followed. Did you know that?"

"So? I'm actually pleased he is taking an interest. Usually more preoccupied with where he can stick his cock. And since you are hardly his type, I'll assume his motives are political."

"I don't need to be watched."

"Oh, but you do, Miltiades. All you Eupatrids do. I know you aren't planning any sabotage or revolution, but...well, politics is in your rather expensive blood. Now stop grinding your teeth. Your little expedition represents a large investment. And it isn't going too far to say that the happiness and stability of this city-state rests on your success. I want to see big fat trading ships pulling in to Phalerum loaded with grain. And you can stamp your smiling face on every sack, if you like, and I'll make sure the people pour libations in your honour every tenth day, for saving them from hunger."

"And on the other days they pour in your honour, for having the idea to send me..."

Hippias smile broadly. "Of course. So long as we understand each other. Now, if you will excuse me..."

Miltiades turned to go, then turned back. "These prophecies, do any speak of my uncle? Or this voyage?"

Hippias stared at him. "No. No, there is complete silence from the gods on that score. So apart from the mysterious words of your visitor, I guess that means you are free to write your own destiny."

···

Miltiades found Zander and his old teacher in the agora. The slave rolled his eyes as Miltiades approached.

"Master Photios has been correcting the spelling on my lists..."

"If it is worth doing," said Photios crankily, "then it may as well be done correctly."

"How are our numbers?"

"You have sixty names here."

"Right. Listen, Zander, I want you to send some messengers to all of them who are of hoplite class. I want them all on the assembly ground tomorrow with their full panoply."

Zander arched his eyebrows. "Are we expecting much trouble on this trip?"

"I don't know, but things are taking on a flavour I don't much like."

"Very well. I'll hire some messenger boys. What about you? Get all your gear out too?"

"Yes, me too."

Zander scratched his head. "I'll have to remember where I put it. Weren't we using your cuirass as a fruit platter?"

"Ha ha. Just get on with it, will you?"

He watched Zander walk off. When he turned back, Photios was staring at him.

"I do recall you, you know, Miltiades. You were always a quiet lad. Never any bother."

"Is that a compliment or a criticism?"

"Neither," said Photios, looking at him curiosly. "Everything depends upon context. In this case, it was simply an observation."

The next day Miltiades, Zander and a couple of other household slaves left early to lug his weapons and armour down to the assembly ground. He was pleased to find Photios already there, and about a dozen men standing about while others were arriving even as he watched.

There was a cough behind him. "Cousin Miltiades?"

Two young men came up to him, both clad expensively in the newest style of armour, made of stiff layered linen and leather. They each held a full Corinthian-style helmet under one arm, and sported bright bronze greaves. Slaves carried their large round shields and spears. Miltiades looked enviously at their armour as Zander lifted his heavy old bronze breastplate into position and started strapping him into it.

"You are Callias?" he asked the one who had spoken, who looked vaguely familiar to him. The young man nodded. He had the air of an over-excited puppy, hoping for a pat on the head but half expecting a smack. Miltiades looked to the other youth standing beside him, and took an instant dislike to him. There was something far too smug about his manner.

"Thank you for this opportunity, cousin. Fort duty was becoming very tedious... For both of us."

"And you are?" Miltiades asked the other young man.

"Teron," he said. "Of the Alcmaeonid clan."

"Well, Teron, I'm sorry you have wasted your time this morning... Hades!" Miltiades kicked at Zander, who squatted at his feet, a grieve prized open between his two hands. "You are pulling half the hairs on my leg out!"

"Well, do more exercise," grumbled Zander "Your calf is fatter than the last time you wore these, and I doubt its muscle."

Teron smirked. Miltiades felt like punching him in the mouth – it was just that sort of face.

"As I was saying. Callias, I have agreed to take you with me as a junior office. But Teron, there is no place for you."

"Now there's a shame," said Teron. "I could see myself fitting right in here."

"Cousin," said Callias. "It was my idea he come this morning. I felt sure you would allow him to accompany me... us."

"Has your father spoken to you about this journey, and about his wishes?"

Callias flushed. "He is an idiot. He doesn't understand. Teron and I... He is my best friend, my brother. My Achilles. He..." Callias looked to his friend. Miltiades was embarrassed to see tears glinting in his kinsman's eyes. He was poised to admonish Callias for speaking like that about his father, but the lad was already overly emotional, and besides... Who was he to give such advice?

"Yes, well. He is free to stay and watch, but he cannot accompany us. That is final." Miltiades wanted to end the matter as quickly as possible. He was aware of a growing audience standing nearby, watching, and did not want a family member to disgrace himself. He turned to face them, to give Callias time to compose himself.

"Greetings, men," There were about fifty gathered before him in a loose crescent. He could see that maybe half had the full panoply of breastplate, helmet and shield. The rest all had spears and shields, but no proper chest protection beyond a thick jerkin and maybe a leather cap or basic open helmet. "Thank you for coming. You have all signed on to my expedition, to either reinforce my uncle's polis in the Chersonnese or establish a new colony. Since we will be living together, I thought it a good idea to get together today, and start forging some bonds."

One man, with a large build and sporting a long red beard, laughed. "And a very pretty phalanx we make, too!"

"Let's form up," said Miltiades. "We will make a line twenty five long and two deep. Best armour in the front, from the right, those lacking are behind."

Miltiades took his helmet from Zander and sat it high on the top of his head, rather than pull it down over his face, so he could see and hear. He took up his large round shield, taking the weight on his left shoulder by hooking the rim over it, and grasped his spear.

"Come with me," he said to Callias and walked towards the right hand end of the line, the traditional place for the commander. The large red head man stood there. His panoply was all bronze, and he too had a full helmet, but one of the more expensive kind with hinged cheek flaps that could be lifted up allowing the wearer to hear, then snapped back into place for battle.

"Nice panoply, citizen," said Miltiades.

The man shook his head. "Thank you, but I'm no citizen. I'm a metic. Name is Metramandes."

Which meant he was a Greek, but not born in Athens.

"Tell me, why does a non-citizen want to be part of this expedition? Especially one as wealthy as you, if your armour is anything to go by."

The big man shrugged. "Wealth I have, it is true. But there is something valuable I do not have – Athenian citizenship."

"That is not in my power to offer."

"I know that. But it may be that as a citizen of a colony state, I have a better chance of earning full citizenship here."

"You love Athens that much?"

The big man laughed. "It is a very nice city. But, truthfully, it is the financial and legal benefits that come with citizenship that I would truly love. You will take the lead position, I take it?"

"As commander, of course."

The right hand position was always the place of honour, and the most dangerous. Whereas every other man had his neighbours' shield to partially cover him, the man on the end was exposed. Miltiades had no great confidence in his fighting skill, but one could hardly expect men to do what you said if you relegated this position to someone else. At least he had more room to work his spear and sword, without anyone crowding him in.

"Then next in line should stand your young friend there, with the fancy cuirass."

Miltiades shook his head. "No, I want him behind me, not in the front line."

"Custom has it that the men with the best panoply place themselves where danger is greatest."

"Men, yes, but not boys."

"I am ready to take my place, cousin!"

"You should be ready to take orders, if you think you are coming on this trip. Behind me. Form up!"

Metramandes shrugged. The men moved in, interlocking shields, those in the second row pressing theirs into the backs of those in front.

"Right, spears up!"

With a clattering and cursing the two rows brought their long heavy spears up into position, held above their right shoulders. At six feet long, the points of the second row extended past the right ear of the man in front, making a double wall of spearheads for any enemy to contend with. And the interwoven shields made a solid mass that was very hard to break through. Miltiades drilled them for an hour, having the row move forward, halt, and practise both the overhand and underhand spear position. He also had them break apart, and at a whistle move as quickly as possible to take up their same position, facing whichever direction he dictated. By the end, they were all dripping sweat and breathing hard. Several had cuts from mishandled spears, and tempers were fraying. He decided it was time to stop, before the exercise went from team building to civil war.

Zander jogged over to him, a small jug of water in hand. Miltiades took it, and was embarrassed at how his hand shook with fatigue as he gulped it. He should really have been exercising more regularly.

"Not too disastrous," murmured Zander. "As long as you aren't expecting a war."

Miltiades watched the rest peel off their armour, and thrust their shields back into their covers. "They will do. We will buy up some javelins for the rest, for those who are below hoplite class. They will serve as skirmishers."

"So...we are expecting a war?"

"I'm not expecting anything. Which is to say, I'm expecting everything. That's wise, don't you think?"

Zander nodded glumly. "Though true wisdom might lie in finding a way out of this mission."

"And miss our chance to be in our own epic? Come, where's your sense of adventure?"

"Wherever you order it to be, I suppose..."

The night before they sailed, Miltiades sat writing instructions for the manager of their family estates. A knock at the door of the andron disturbed him.

"Come."

"The mistress wishes you to give this to your uncle, sir," said a sallow faced slave at the door, "When you see him." He held a sealed piece of parchment in one thin hand.

Miltiades squinted at him. "Who in Hades are you?"

"Oh, I'm new, sir. Purchased by the mistress this morning, sir-"

Miltiades snatched the letter from the man's fingers and shoved him aside, tearing it open as he strode towards the women's quarters.

"Mother!" he shouted, sending a slave girl scurrying away in fear as he reached her room. He barged in. "What in blazes is this?"

She sat on her couch, blinking at him, a tray of crumbs resting on her bosom, honey glistening on her lips and chin. "What?"

"In the name of the gods, wipe your mouth."

Rather than use her napkin, she stuck her tongue out and rolled it around her lips, removing the glinting honey. The sight revolted him.

"Why are you writing to Uncle Miltiades? What is the meaning of this?"

"What is wrong?"

"This. You have written to ask him to return to Athens, to the family lands. Why?"

"I only thought that since you are going there, then he could come back here. Then I could live with him."

"What? I am head of the family."

"Yes, but if he came back, and you stayed there, he could be in charge."

"You want to live with him? Why?"

"Well," she said, picking at the fatter crumbs on her bosom. "His household would be more lively, more fun for me."

"He's probably dead," said Miltiades acidly. And there it was, the admission to himself in the same moment – his uncle, his strong, bold uncle, with the deep creases at the corner of his eyes when he laughed, probably lay dead, slain by barbarians in that far flung backwater. The same one he sailed to on the morrow.

His mother stared at him. "How can you say that? How dare you say that?"

"So you are stuck with me, and my boring ways, for a while longer, mother. Unless you intend to remarry."

"It should have been..." she muttered.

"What did you say?"

"First your father. Then your uncle. It isn't fair. Not while you..." She trailed off.

"Finish that sentence. I dare you."

She sniffed, shook her head. Miltiades stiffened like a statue. "Goodbye, mother."

He spun about and strode from the room, shredding the parchment as he went, trying to make the words disappear.

"Wait!" she cried after him. "Don't go! Don't leave me!"

But he ignored her tears, and returned to his desk where he sat staring sightlessly at his letter, hands shaking.

FOUR

••

ODYSSEY

The day of departure seemed blessed by the gods – the sun was warm, and the Bay of Salamis was smooth and glassy. There was no great fanfare, just a small crowd of family members farewelling the colonists. Neither Hippias nor Hipparchus made an appearance, but Miltiades caught sight of one of their tame councillors skulking at the back, watching.

The trireme sat tied to the dock, stained black by a recent coat of pitch. Wooden boards covered over the outrigger for the top level of rowers, and on this deck was a pile of gear running the length of the ship, covered and lashed down tight. The ship's mast lay tied down alongside, ready to be raised and set in place should the wind be right.

Miltiades poured a libation of wine to the gods and handed over to Phillipus. The captain seemed in a foul mood, but sober as far as he could tell.

"Right," said Phillipus. "Colonists, you lot are going to be the fart-sniffers, down the bottom of the ship. And don't bloody groan at me. It will be all hands to stations till we've had a good shake out, then we will proceed at half on, half off. If you haven't already bought yourself a sheepskin cushion, I suggest you go do that now. Otherwise your arse is going to be sorer than the new boy at the brothel by the time we get where we're going."

The professional rowers laughed. They were easily identifiable, sun burned, lean and muscled, each carrying his own oar and cushion. Phillipus turned to Miltiades.

"Everyone takes a turn at the oars. Except maybe him." He pointed at Photios, who bristled.

"I can do my share like everyone else!"

Phillipus shrugged. "Have it your way, then. Let's load!"

The colonists boarded first, awkwardly climbing down into the lowest of the three tiers of rowing benches. Their positions were not much above the waterline, their oarholes covered by a leather patch. There was much clattering and cursing as they ran their oars out into the water. By contrast, the experienced oarsmen taking their positions in the middle and top tiers climbed nimbly into position, and were settled before the colonists had all set themselves. A couple of sailors stayed on the deck, ready to untie the lines. One had a flute thrust through his belt – it would be his job to play and help the rowers maintain their rhythm. A grizzled old sea dog manned the steering oar aft.

"What is that smell?" asked Callias.

"That's the pitch," replied Phillipus. "Keeps the sea worms out of the timber. Or else, you better hope it does."

"Why? What do sea worms do?"

"They burrow into the wood. They can grow up to a foot in length. And you'll never know they are in there until the ship falls to pieces around you."

"Hades..." murmured Callias, looking down at the deck.

Phillipus laughed and clapped him on the shoulder. "Welcome to the exciting life of the sailor, boy!"

The ropes were cast off, and the slender ship turned and moved out into the Phaleron harbour, toward the straits and then the Aegean sea.

Miltiades turned and watched the city of his birth slowly slide from view, the last thing to disappear the cluster of temples atop the Acropolis. When that too had faded from his sight, he wondered what that might mean – that the gods no longer watched over him, or that he was free of their judgement? He turned to say something to Zander, then remembered that he was down below, at the oars. He turned back to the shore, feeling ill at ease. He was used to having the quiet of his study or garden to retreat to if he felt like being alone, or Zander to talk to if he felt like company. He resolved to take a turn at the oars as well, to at least give him something to do.

He noted how denuded of trees the land around Athens was becoming; not just in those flat places where farm land stood, but also on the slopes of the rough hills. All that timber was going into the ever-expanding Athenian fleet, which was needed for the ever-increasing Athenian demand for trade goods. It caused a worry to settle in his heart, strangely – an odd fear that to so alter the landscape, they were doing something wrong... a wrong that surely could not escape punishment.

He shook himself. Amazing how taking a man from what he was used to reduced him to superstition.

A movement from the supplies caught his attention. A tarpaulin was moving. He stared, wondering what on earth it could be. A rat? But then a hand thrust out from under it, followed by a sweating lithe body.

"Hades, it was hot under there!" exclaimed the figure.

"Teron!" shouted Callias, clambering up onto the deck with a laugh. The two young men embraced.

"You had better," growled Miltiades, "have a damned good explanation for this."

Callias let go of Teron and stood between him and Miltiades, thrusting out his jaw. "It was my idea, cousin."

Teron smiled sweetly over his friend's shoulder. Miltiades shook his head.

"I should throw you overboard and make you swim back to Athens."

Neither Teron nor Callias could resist the urge to look across at the distant shore of Attica sliding by. It wasn't very far, but if you weren't a confident swimmer...

"You, Teron. Can you follow orders?"

"I always listen to my betters."

"That's not what I asked. I asked if you can follow orders. Because if you are to come with us – for now – you must do whatever I, or Phillipus, or Photios, or anyone else I put over you, tells you. Can you do that?"

The boy looked him boldly in the eye. "Oh, I can do all sorts of things."

Miltiades turned his back, pretending to study the horizon. He wasn't sure how to handle the stowaway. Turning back would waste a lot of time, and he couldn't risk the life of a member of the Alcmaeonid clan by actually making him swim for it. Drowning one of the sons of the richest family in Athens was not a good idea. No, it looked like Teron was coming to the Chersonnese, but that didn't mean he had to stay there. Miltiades resolved to send him straight back with Phillipus.

"Arrogant little whelp," said Photios, appearing at his side. "Needs a good caning."

"I'd be worried he'd enjoy it."

Photios laughed. "You know, I don't recall needing to cane you much."

"No, I was ever the good student. I liked learning. Still do."

"Is that what this enterprise is about?" asked the teacher, turning to look at him.

"Maybe," said Miltiades.

"Learning about ourselves, what we are capable of, is truly the most interesting study," mused Photios. "Though the lessons are not always pleasant."

Miltiades looked at his old teacher fondly. He was looking better. Employing him to handle accounts and logistics had been a good idea, and he congratulated himself for it. The old man's eyes looked clearer, sharper, and some decent food had added a few pounds to his skinny frame.

The going was slow. The flute player kept the pace deliberately slow while the colonists found their rhythm, but there was still a raggedness to their strokes compared to the cleaner thrusts of the two upper decks. The experienced oarsmen laughed and yelled insults down into the ship every time two oars clattered together, jarring the hands of the men who wielded them. But stroke by stroke, they drew closer to Laurium, where they would turn to the east and round the point, and commence travelling up the Euboean channel.

Once around the point and heading north, the wind was still not with them enough to warrant raising the mast and sail, but the tide was, so Phillipus released half the oarsman at a time. Those that wished could clamber up onto the deck and sit with their feet dangling over the side, letting the sun and wind and spray clean away their sweat. The colonists appeared with dazed expressions and red aching palms.

Miltiades found Zander standing and staring at the coastline slowly passing by. The slave didn't seem to notice his presence.

"What are you thinking about?" Miltiades asked.

Without turning his head, Zander answered "I was just think-ing that Acarnania must be over there. Over those mountains."

"Acarnania?" Miltiades asked, puzzled, but then remem-bered: "Ah, of course. You were born there, weren't you?"

Zander nodded.

"Do you...miss it?"

Zander snorted. "Hard to miss what you have never known. I was taken as a wee lad. Can't remember my home at all. Or family. But I can remember the man who took me captive. At least, I seem to be able to. A giant, from the point of view of a child. I remember him picking me up and throwing me over his shoulder. That was the start of my new life, as a slave."

Miltiades stayed silent, feeling strangely awkward. These topics didn't tend to come up in his usual life in the city.

"Still," continued Zander, "it must be fairly normal for any man to wish to one day return to where he came from, to stand in that place. To feel that here he belongs."

"Maybe one day," said Miltiades, unsure what else to say. He had the urge to pat Zander on the shoulder, but worried it might seem patronising.

"Maybe."

They beached the trireme well before dark, on a flat section of the Attic coast. There was a bay here, with a shallow shingle beach. Phillipus had them all at the oars, pulling hard, then shouted to lift clear as the ship ran up onto the beach. The sailors threw a half dozen round logs onto the shore, then leapt overboard with lines of rope. Stiffly the oarsmen climbed from the depths of the warship and clambered over, some of the colonists falling onto their backsides in the low surf, their legs muscles protesting at the movement. All hands took hold of the ropes, while the sailors positioned the rollers under the bow. On a signal from the captain, they heaved, and the ship rolled forward out of the water, seawater dripping from its oaken sides. The anchors were dropped and tied off, to hold it steady.

Firewood was collected, and soon several bonfires were burning as the sky turned violet overhead. A stream of visitors arrived – local farmers who had spotted the fires, and now came down from the low hills with baskets full of bread, cheese and olive oil to sell. There was a brisk trade – buying here meant saving their rations, which seemed wise, given they didn't know exactly how things would be further on.

Miltiades sought out the captain. "So, where are we?"

"This? Bay of Marathon. Good spot to land – except for the marsh at the northern end. Have to watch out for that."

"You know the area well?"

"Well enough."

Miltiades gratefully took a cup of wine from Zander.

"Can't promise anything," said his slave. "Might be a bit rough."

Miltiades sipped, and coughed. "It is. Hope you didn't pay too much for it."

"Found out something interesting. This is Pisistratid country. This is where the clan hails from."

"How bloody convenient," said Miltiades darkly. It seemed he was not yet free from tyrants. But then, when would he be? Somebody here in the company was most likely a spy – but who? It was Phillipus who brought them here, but he seemed too obvious, given he was the brothers' selection for trirarch. "Who told you that?"

"The big red-haired metic. Metramandes."

The wealthy man who was seemingly prepared to risk it all for the slim chance of citizenship? But then again, what a tempting reward that might make.

Thrice betrayed...

Ridiculous. He shouldn't let his mind get carried away. He was not about to start believing that the Olympians found it necessary to employ shadowy figures to warn the leader of a minor expedition about lurking traitors.

Phillipus wandered back, a sloshing jug in one hand and a cup in the other.

"How can you drink that muck?" asked Miltiades.

"My capacity to discriminate has long since been burned away by the fine wares on sale in Phaleron. So, I salute you, tyrant." He drained his cup.

"Don't call me that."

"No? What is it to be then? Archon? I mean, let's assume the worse and say your uncle and the rest are gone -"

"How nice, thank you."

Phillipus bowed. "-so you and your little band set up a new colony. What, are you going to hold elections for archon? There's more here than you who would like to lead." The captain looked meaningfully towards a nearby fire where the broad shape of Metramandes could be made out.

"This is my command," said Miltiades.

"Of course," said the captain. "I'm all for strong leadership. There's only one captain at sea. That's how it should be

– especially when you are heading into a storm. Same holds true on land, as far as I'm concerned. Don't get so caught up on words, Miltiades, that's my advice."

Miltiades nodded, but did not feel comforted. Words could be extremely powerful, in his experience.

....

Some Time Earlier

"Oh Great Ahura-Mazda!" cried the Magi priest. "Look upon thy subjects!"

It was still dark, but Darius supposed that shouldn't matter to a god. Besides, it was into their hearts he was supposed to be looking, not simply at their carefully curled beards and magnificent robes. The seven nobles sat on their horses, facing the east, where the sun was yet to appear.

"We await thy sign!" the Magi continued, "that we may know who has thy blessing!"

He was getting quite into it, which was good. But then, since the seven nobles had just freshly returned from murdering another Magi, he probably felt a good performance was warranted. And he was right.

What were things coming to, wondered Darius, when even priests became uppity and thought they might proclaim themselves king?

"First came your great servant Cyrus, glorious first king of the Persians!" cried the priest. "Then came Cambyses! Now, oh god, we ask who thou wouldst wish to rule thy people next."

It had bloody well better be me, thought Darius. He glanced sideways at the men beside him. He could hear old Megabyzus quietly straining next to him – as if he was sitting in the privy unable to void himself. Darius guessed that the old bugger was trying to squeeze his horse with his flabby thighs, trying to force a noise out of it. Idiot. As if that was going to do it. He resisted the urge to look around to check on his own insurance policy.

It had been one of his loyal followers, Datis, who had suggested it. He had approached Darius shortly after the assassination, when the blood was still wet on their hands, with an offer to help him fulfil his destiny.

"And what do you expect in return?" Darius had asked.

Datis had smiled. "Just that you remember this day," he said. "And remember me."

It was cold in the predawn light. It would have been far more comfortable enacting this charade mid-morning, but appearances were important, especially at such a time of turmoil. The old king was dead, and in his place up popped a man pretending to be his brother. It wasn't true, of course; he was an imposter. But the awkward fact was that most of the empire had no idea that Cambyses had already seen fit to have his actual brother killed. Darius knew it was true, because he had been the one, as the King's Lance, to do the offing. So they could hardly call out the imposter publicly without revealing some rather sordid details. Instead, the group of like-minded nobles had banded together to assassinate him, just like the real brother. It had proved surprisingly easy – being from the Magi class, rather than a Persian or Median noble family, he had taken fewer precautions than he ought. He hadn't realised how easily a few bribes and a few threats opened doors. Including doors to where one lay sleeping unprotected, but for a few naked concubines.

But who was to rule? And how to sell it to the people, especially those from the increasing number of regions falling under Persian control, who were itching for any sign of weakness or division, in which case a rebellion would be on? Quarrelling between the assassins could lead to a break up of the fledgling empire, which no one wanted. Someone - Darius could not even remember who, now: they had all been drunk – proposed this dumb show. That they sit astride their horses at dawn, and the first horse to neigh as the sun rose would be recognised as king by the others. It had seemed a damn good idea at the time, and they had all sworn to abide by it – while at the same time sending their grooms to find their most skittish, nervous mounts.

As the first glow of dawn appeared beyond the distant hills, the tension rose sharply. In the growing light, Darius looked at his groom, standing by the horse's head. He seemed shorter than usual, and appeared to have one arm stuffed up inside his tunic. Darius frowned.

"Hey-" he began.

The man turned and he could see the gleam of teeth. At the same moment the man pulled his arm free, and stuck his fingers beneath the horse's nostrils. Darius felt a thrill run through his mount's back. Its ears flicked, and it stamped a foot. Darius held his breath. He saw Megabyzus turn to look at him.

Golden light poured over the horizon – and Darius' horse let out an almighty whinny.

"A sign!" cried the Magi.

"Shit!" snarled Megabyzus.

Darius dropped his head, and let Ahura-Mazda's light bless and anoint him. He squinted at his groom, and finally recognised Datis, grinning at him triumphantly.

"How did you manage that?" he asked later, after the other nobles had pledged their loyalty to him, and he had a moment to sit back and relax with one or two most trusted adherents.

"Had my fingers up a mare's cunny for ten minutes before I came and gave your boy a whiff."

Darius laughed. "Truly, the work of God!"

"I myself have found Him many a time myself, when between a woman's thighs. At least, I have called out to him. Incidentally, you may wish to let your mount mate, or he may be a little bad tempered."

Darius laughed again.

"Who is this?" asked Datis.

Darius looked up. A sombre looking man stood in the room, holding a casket. The others came to their feet, hands straying to the hilts of their swords. An assassination attempt, already? How bloody typical.

"King of Kings," spoke the man, his voice strangely accented. "From the Magi I have come, to reveal this unto you."

Darius squinted, thinking. He had killed a Magus to take power, and the priestly class appeared to be cowed – but who was to say they hadn't planned some horrible, supernatural revenge?

"Mardonius," he said, to one of his cousins. "Have a look."

Mardonius shot him a look, but stepped forward. The Magi stepped back.

"It is the responsibility of the King of Kings to open, look and learn."

His black eyes were blank, but Darius felt a challenge. He gestured at the man to come forward, and the Magus strode to where he sat and set the casket on his knees.

"Behold," he said, and lifted the lid.

"Holy mother fucking fuck!" shouted the King of Kings, knocking his chair over backwards. The Magus neatly caught the casket before it could spill its contents. "What the hell is that?"

"Thy doom. Unless you are eternally vigilant. This is the flame that burned away the sinners, and allowed the Persians to come to power. First came Cyrus, who followed the flame across the land, until it vanished into the great north. Then Cambyses, who stemmed the flow in the ancient land of Egypt, lest it blaze again. Now, Darius. The flame has passed on, but may return and burn the lands again. Fear it, oh king."

Darius nodded. "So the stories are true. I had thought them legends. So be it." He thought quickly. "I hereby decree a series of roads to be built across my empire, with riders and horses stationed a day's ride along them. If there is any sign of these things returning, I must know at once."

The Magus nodded. "This is wise." He turned to go.

"No," said Darius. "Leave that."

The priest glanced at the casket. "There is great danger here…"

"There is great danger here, too," he said, patting his sword. "Put it down, and go."

The priest narrowed his eyes, and looked at the men standing about him. Slowly he bent and placed the casket on the floor, then bowed slightly, and strode from the room.

"What is in it?" asked Mardonius.

"I'll show you," said Darius, and he strode to the casket, opened it, and lifted something high. The others gasped, for he held in his hand a severed human head, but though there was no body, the eyes rolled wildly, and the leather-like tongue flickered from between savage white teeth.

"What the hell is it?" cried Datis, holding his nose.

"A weapon," said Darius.

On the second day, once the ship was launched back into the channel, they made better progress. The oarsmen were finding their rhythm, and towards midday the wind came up behind them and Phillipus ordered the mast raised and the great rectangular sail was set free, catching the breeze with a crack. Callias laughed aloud as spray hissed up from the bow, while Photios -still to find his sea legs- stumbled and cursed until he went sprawling, tunic riding up and revealing his skinny white legs. The oars were shipped, though the rowers had to take turns at their stations, as there was not enough room on deck for everyone at once.

Miltiades made his way to the stern, where Phillipus stood with the helmsman. "Slight change of plans," he said. "I want you to drop me ashore here and wait for me."

"That wasn't part of the plan. Wait for you how long exactly?"

"Just a day. It isn't that much. We could just as easily hit a storm and be delayed more than that anyway."

"But where are you going?"

"Delphi."

He'd made a decision. It was information he needed, not imagination. And the best place to get that was at the great Oracle at Delphi.

"Callias and Zander will come with me," he told his officers. "We'll hire horses at Opus."

"What about me?" asked Teron. "I want to come, too."

Miltiades shook his head. "Sorry. I'm not wasting coin on hiring unnecessary horses. We don't know what kind of expenses we might encounter ahead."

"I can hire my own horse," replied Teron. "So there will be no harm in me coming along, will there?"

"Where are we going, anyway?" asked Callias.

"To talk to a god."

It was late afternoon by the time they trotted in to the temple complex at Delphi. The great Temple of Apollo dominated the area, but there were a series of smaller shrines, storehouses and vault-like treasuries. They were not the only ones arriving – a steady stream of visitors walked up the stairs into the temple, to consult with the oracle. When they had beached the ship near the small city-state of Opus, Miltiades had been pleased at first to find that the chief magistrate did indeed have horses he was willing to hire – but only three. Grumbling, Teron had disappeared while Miltiades counted out coins and they saddled up. This was the part of his plan he was not looking forward to. He disliked horses and was no natural rider. He was still struggling to mount when Teron reappeared a little later grinning broadly astride an excellent stallion. Miltiades fought down the urge to ask him where he had managed to find such a mount, since the young pup was obviously bursting to tell him. His mood only worsened when, on the journey inland to Delphi, Teron kept volunteering to scout ahead, since he had the best horse.

Miltiades had aching buttocks by the time they reached Delphi. Here he had some revenge, for he ordered Teron to wait and mind the mounts – after all, his was the most expensive.

They sought out a goat to purchase just outside the temple precinct and paid the outrageous price asked. Callias was given the job of leading the bleating creature along behind them.

"Know thyself," said the young man, reading the words carved into the pediment of the Temple. "That's strange. I know who I am – I'm Callias. I don't get it."

"Ask Photios when we get back," said Miltiades.

"Don't," said Zander with a groan. "At least, not in my hearing. I can't bear it. I have no urge to go back to school."

Know thyself. What good did that do, Miltiades wondered. He did know himself. He knew that in a city of vibrant colours, where the glare of fresh white marble competed with the rich tones of painted buildings and dyed robes – red, yellow, blue and green – a sea of colour made possible as trade grew and merchants gained access to ever more pigments and dyes... He knew that in that swirl of colour, he existed as a small piece of grey. Like a single piece of shale. What else could he be? In the face of his father's boisterous volume, and his mother's simpering and preening, he had chosen to fade into the background. And then, once he was a man, and the Pisistratids had come to power, he had chosen to maintain that colouring, avoid notice, and in that way avoid the knife in the guts and his own deep red ichor spilling into the mire. True, he had agreed to serve as chief magistrate for that one year, but his time in that position was not marked by anything memorable and he had only done it to avoid further attention. Indeed, refusal would have elicited more suspicion. Even agreeing to this current venture was basically easier than refusing. You had to go along to get along. And maybe that was the point of the message painstakingly carved into the marble: don't get ideas of about being more than you are. Don't get ideas above your station.

They made their way into the main hall of the temple, where the statue of Apollo looked out unblinkingly over the supplicants. Behind the statue was a set of heavy metal-bound doors, guarded by a row of priests – beyond these awaited the Pythia, the priestess who spoke in riddles containing messages from the gods. She sat above a smoking fissure in the rock that led directly to the centre of the world.

"What are you going to ask her?" whispered Callias.

"Ask her? Nothing," said Miltiades, accepting a piece of parchment and a charcoal stick from a slave. "It's the priests I'm asking."

Callias frowned. "I don't understand."

"Callias, you may find this shocking, but I do not believe the Pythia to be the mouthpiece of the gods. The priests here, however, maintain ties with all the other major temples across Greece, and in Asia, too. As well as being disgustingly wealthy, they are probably the best source of information in all of Greece. And don't look shocked – you aren't about to be struck down by the gods for impiety."

He scribbled on the paper, and folded it neatly in two.

"So...so what are you asking the priests?"

"If they have heard anything of my uncle, and the colony on the Chersonnese. The lack of news isn't sitting right with me. If there had been some kind of attack on them, by the Thracians or whoever, surely news would have come out. Now come on. We'll give this to the priests, who will pretend to take it in to the Pythia, then they'll come out and hopefully tell us what they know."

They handed over their goat, and some coins, and a middle aged priest took their paper and slipped through the heavy doors. As they closed, the rest of the priests resumed their line across in front of them. Miltiades thought they looked fairly bored.

"And now we wait for the theatre to be conducted-"

A shriek rent the air, so loud it seemed impossible it could have come from a human mouth. Callias looked fearfully towards the statue, even though it was obvious the sound came from behind the heavy doors. The priests had all spun around, looking at each other in consternation. The scream came again, louder, and then the doors rang dully as something ran into them – hard – from the other side.

"Uh, I think the temple is closing for the day," called a grey haired priest. "If everyone would kindly-"

The doors wrenched open, and everyone took a pace back. A woman stood there, the very vision of a Fury. Her clothing rent, hair wild, and her terrible eyes bulging white and black. A priest tried to take hold of her from behind, to lead her back into the interior of the chamber, but she spun, lashing out, and he fell back with a cry, his face scoured by her uncut nails. The others formed a loose circle, trying to usher her back with soothing voices. The Pythia ignored them, staring about the room – then her eyes locked onto Miltiades. She pointed at him, and grunted, spit spraying from her mouth. She ran at them, bare feet slapping the floor.

"What in Hades?" Miltiades shoved Callias behind him.

"Go, go!" cried Zander. "She's crazy!"

The priests dove on her, bringing her to the ground. She heaved against them, clawing towards Miltiades, who stood stunned. The rest of the visitors had fled but for his small band.

"Wait," said Miltiades, and walked forward.

"No!" cried Zander and Callias together.

Miltiades squatted near the woman's head. The tendons in her neck stood out like rope. The grey haired priest laid a hand on his arm.

"Sir, please..." The Priests, of course, did not wish any injuries. Bad for business.

Miltiades stared into the woman's face. Her eyes were locked on his, her mouth was working. She looked at him desperately, tears trickling down her sweat slicked cheeks. It was like she was trying to talk past a mouthful of stone.

"What is it?" he asked her.

Her eyes rolled back into her skull, the effect terrifying, and she sagged. A stream of drool ran from her mouth onto the marble floor. The priests started to drag her back towards the doors. But then she stiffened again, and her eyes snapped back. She spat a mouthful of blood, filled her lungs, and screamed a single intelligible word:

"RUN!"

They ran. Back at the horses, they untied the halters with fumbling, trembling fingers, while Teron kept asking "What? What?" Despite the assurances they had given to the archon of Opus, they whipped their horses hard and left the area at the gallop.

But panic does not hold a man forever in its clutches, and after a while Miltiades signalled for them to slow down, and walk their blowing horses.

"What was that?" asked Callias, his face pale despite the exertion.

"Can we just not talk about it?" asked Zander.

"Cousin, she was looking right at you... She was trying to talk to you."

"That's talking about it," groaned Zander.

"Shut up, slave," hissed Teron.

"Look," said Miltiades, holding up a hand. "The poor girl had obviously been breathing in too many fumes and lost her mind. We just happened to be the first people she saw when she came through the door. Let it go. We didn't get the information we came for, so we'll just let it go. I don't see any need to tell anyone back at the ship. Especially Phillipus – he doesn't need much excuse to get drunk anyway." There was grudging agreement.

But the image of the poor girl's face played on Miltiades' mind. She had seemed to recognise him. Which, disturbingly, meant the message was for him... But run where?

Or from what?

They were forced to camp overnight, sitting huddled and quiet about a fire and chewing down stale bread. They set off again next morning as soon as it was light enough to see, and were glad when Opus came into view. With the horses returned, and a lighter wallet attached to his belt but still no clear idea of what to expect at the Hellespont, Miltiades ordered them to put to sea. From here they rounded the northern tip of Euboea, and finally the painted eyes of the ship gazed out across the open Aegean sea.

"So," said Callias, swallowing. "No land now till – when?"

"Depends," said Phillipus. "We'll make for the island of Lemnos. But it depends what old Poseidon has in store for us."

"Wouldn't it be safer to keep to the coast then? I mean, we'll still get there that way, won't we?"

"That would take a long time," said Miltiades.

"Are we in a rush?"

Miltiades felt for him – he, too, felt uneasy at the thought of being so far from land. He fancied there would be more than a few in the company feeling the same, but Phillipus laughed. "Don't you worry, boy. I'll get you there safe and sound. Now, get yourself below. Time to row."

The winds were not in their favour, and the first leg out into open water was laborious as the men bent their backs and pulled. But by midday, the breeze shifted, and again the mast was raised and the sleek ship hissed through the blue water.

It was growing dark when the rocky hills of Lemnos finally appeared on the horizon, and the men's hearts lifted, for it was not natural to be out on the water when darkness fell. Rather than beach the ship, they tied up at a simple dock in the small harbour where the polis sat, a fairly solid place with stout walls encircling it. Their arrival had been marked, and as they disembarked a town slave approached Phillipus bidding him appear before the town council.

"I'll go," said Miltiades. "Photios and Zander will come with me."

"Not me?" asked Callias.

"Not this time." It was actually Teron he wanted to avoid, and it was just easier to guarantee that by leaving Callias out of it.

The three followed the slave up the main thoroughfare to a marble hall in the centre of the town agora. Inside, a dozen men in expensive robes sat on benches.

"So," said one as soon as the doors closed behind them. "What business does an Athenian warship have this far north?"

"Private business," replied Miltiades. There was an unhappy shift amongst the oligarchs. "Which is to say, my individual business. I am simply leasing this ship to transport my men and I to the Hellespont."

"To what purpose?" croaked an ancient on the right.

"You are bound for the Chersonnese," added a third, "Are you not?"

Miltiades dipped his head in acknowledgement. "No doubt you know of our daughter colony, established there by Miltiades of Athens."

"We do," said the first man. Since he was sitting in the centre, Miltiades assumed he must be the leading magistrate.

"All you Athenians know how to do is stir up trouble," quavered the old man. "Yours is a hungry city, and in your hunger you disturb the status quo."

"So there has been some kind of trouble?" Miltiades asked, looking at each of the men in turn. "A disturbance? Something has happened to the colony?"

He caught the looks that the oligarchs shot at each other, but the chief magistrate held up his hand.

"We do not know anything. We have had no communication with that polis for some time."

"Then what was the last communication you did have with them?"

This question was met with silence.

"An arrogant request," hissed the old man. "That they should dare ask for our help, after-"

"Silence!"

The old man grumbled, but held his tongue. The magistrate turned his attention back to the Athenians. There was a shifty look to his eyes. Miltiades felt chilled. Something had indeed happened to his uncle.

"You may remain overnight, but must be gone within an hour of first light. We want no dealings with Athenian pirates or adventurers. Your presence is unwelcome. As was theirs."

The doors opened behind them. Miltiades turned to leave, then turned back to the oligarchs.

"By the gods, if you abandoned my uncle in his time of need, then know this: the next time I touch these shores I will be coming in force, and show you just how hungry Athens can be." And he marched from the room, flanked by Photios and Zander, while the councillors exclaimed behind him in outrage.

Miltiades fumed as they strode back towards the docks. A tavern caught his eye, and he swerved towards it.

"I need a drink."

Photios raised his eyebrows at Zander, who shrugged and followed inside.

There were oil lamps inside on every table, and a scattering of drinkers. It was smoky, but a pleasant enough place. Miltiades chose an empty table and signalled for wine. He downed his first cup without tasting it, then sat twisting the cup in his hands.

"What is going on?" he asked, without looking up. "What am I leading us into?"

"The gods know," said Photios in between sips. "Which is to say, men do not. Or at least I doubt those men do."

"Then we are all in good company," said Zander gloomily. He poured Miltiades some more, in an effort to stop the nervous twisting of his hands, which was unsettling him.

"Hey!"

The shout came from the open door. A gang of six young men had come in, their flushed faces revealing the wine they had already consumed. Their clothes and hair styles suggested this kind of cheap bar was not their usual establishment.

"Shit," murmured Miltiades. "Now what? They've sent the boys to give us a beating?"

"Two each," said Zander. "Gods damn it. This is going to be ugly."

"What?" squawked Photios.

"Get ready to run..."

But then they saw it wasn't them the young men were looking at, but a lone drinker the next table over.

"Hey you! Trembler!" shouted their leader.

The men pushed forward, and as they neared the lone man he raised his head to look at them. Despite their threatening manner, there did not appear to be any fear in his face. He was a gaunt looking fellow, with deep creases around his eyes. The leader of the gang, the one who had been doing all the shouting, slammed a coin down on the table.

"Let's play, Trembler!"

The thin man stared at the coin. He picked up his cup and drained it. "I don't want to." He made to stand. The leader looked at his men, and two thrust him back down into his seat.

"And I say, you do! Well? What's it to be?"

The Trembler stared at the table, then shrugged. The men laughed, and the leader sat down across from him, rubbing his hands.

"Good to see you aren't too afraid! Come on then, you old soak! Let's do it!"

One of his fellows came over to the Athenians' table, and took their oil lamp with a laugh. He turned and sat it down next to the identical one on the Trembler's table. The gang leader slapped his hands down on the table.

"This is more like it! Bets! Bets!"

A number of the other patrons in the bar had drifted over, and some did indeed hold coins up to bet.

"What in Hades is going on?" murmured Zander.

The leader held his hand out high above the yellow flame dancing in the little clay oil lamp.

"Come on, come on you useless sap! Let's go! Let's see what you have got!"

The Trembler sighed, and raised a hand to match the other man's, still gazing down at the table. One of the other men took hold of both their wrists, squatting till he was on eye level with both, making sure they were level. "Go!" he cried.

Smirking, the leader dropped his hand a quarter of the way to flame. The Trembler matched him. Grinning around at his fellows, the younger man dropped his again. Again the other matched him. The oily smoke was now curling around their hands. The young man glanced at the Trembler, licked his lips, and moved his hand a fraction lower. He grunted as the heat of the flame started to make its presence felt. The Trembler hesitated for a moment, and then his eyes snapped up to look at the other younger man. They were not a drunk's eyes, nor an old man's. There was something in them now that to Miltiades looked brutal. The Trembler lowered his hand – then dropped it further still. It was only a few inches now above the flame. Some of those watching gasped. Gritting his teeth, the young-er man moved his hand down to match. He held his on the same level, writhing in his chair, then beating his feet on the ground, then suddenly snatched his hand away with a curse. The Trembler held his eye, then slowly lowered his hand down until he cupped the lamp, and the flame went out.

"Fuck!" spat the leader, holding his hand. "You fucking dirty freak! Why don't you fuck off back to where you came from?" He staggered to his feet, and lurched towards the door, his minions following, shooting evil glances back at the Trembler.

"Wow," said Zander.

"It must be a trick," said Miltiades. "He must have known they were coming, and has something painted on his palm."

"Why don't you go ask him?" said Photios.

Zander put a hand on Miltiades' arm. "Don't. Leave him. He's mad."

"Hey," the bartender called out. "You better drink up and go."

The Trembler nodded, and stood, gathering his stained grey cloak about himself. He was tall and thin, with hunched, rounded shoulders. With his eyes down, he walked out the door.

Miltiades caught the gleam of silver on the table he had been sitting at. The coin still lay where the younger man had left it.

"Come on," he said, rising to his feet and leaning over to scoop up the coin.

Outside, they looked about until they spotted the tall man striding down the street towards the docks. They hurried after him.

"Hey!" said Miltiades, drawing alongside. "Stop. You forgot this." He held out his fist. The Trembler stopped and opened his own hand. Miltiades caught hold of it and turned it to catch the light of torches burning at the front of another wineshop.

"Mind if we see your trick? Hades..."

In the centre of the man's hand was a bright red burn, weeping liquid.

"Do you not feel pain?"

The Trembler also looked at his hand, and flexed it several times. "Of course I feel pain."

"But..." said Zander, "then how did you do that?"

"What do you mean?" said the Trembler. "I just did it, that's all."

"A better question," said Photios, "would thus be why do it?"

The thin man slowly grinned. "Ah. A better question indeed."

"And the answer?" asked Miltiades.

The man cocked his head to one side. "Hmmm... Hubris?"

"There's the cocksucker!"

The shout came from further back up the street. There came the slapping of sandals, and the six men from the wineshop came running, the leader with a bandage wrapped hastily around one hand. They were quickly surrounded.

"You are going to pay for that, motherfucker," snarled the leader. "You other pricks, get out of the way. We're going to kill this Spartan dog."

"Spartan?" asked Miltiades.

"I'm going home. Someone is waiting for me." The tall man went to walk on.

"Get him!"

It almost seemed to happen slowly, yet Miltiades could hardly track what occurred. The two youths closest to the Trembler grabbed at his arms. He let them take hold, then suddenly bent his knees and dropped his weight, jerking them towards him, and as they stumbled forwards he leaned in and headbutted one square in the face, then turned and swiped an elbow across the other's jaw. But by then the other four were on him, two of them bearing him to the ground with a heavy thud. The remaining two – the leader, and one other – moved around the writhing mass, kicking hard.

"Cowards!" cried Zander. "Six on one!"

"Come on!" said Miltiades.

With a roar, Zander dived on the back of one, dragging him down. Miltiades took hold of the leader's tunic, and swung him around till he tripped and fell. There was a shriek behind him. He spun to see one of the others crawling free from the Trembler, cradling an arm with an obviously dislocated elbow. The other was now lying under the Spartan, desperately trying to shield his face from the short sharp blows the Trembler was inflicting.

"Look out!" cried Zander.

Miltiades turned, hands out ready. The leader was up, but there was a knife in his fist. Miltiades felt the blood drain from his face. This was getting too serious. He stood taller, holding his palms up.

"That's enough. You don't want to do that..."

"Fuck you!" The leader sprang forward, and Miltiades went flying as the Spartan appeared, jerking him to the side. The youth stabbed at the Trembler's midsection, but the latter turned, allowing the blade to slide past, then grabbed the leader's wrist. His other arm snaked across the young man's throat, and he spun, overbalancing him. As he slipped to his knees, the Spartan twisted his hand and the knife fell free. The Spartan scooped it up, and held the point to the leader's throat, where a nerve twitched.

"I have your coin, and I have your knife," said the Spartan. "Shall I have your life?"

"Please..." whispered the youth, his bottom lip starting to wobble. The rest of his gang limped around behind him, cradling their injuries and keeping a respectful distance.

"Let him go," said one. "You know who his father is."

"I don't care," said the Spartan. "I told you I am going home. Someone will be worried." The point of the blade bit into the white neck.

"Friend," said Miltiades. "Come on, let him go. He isn't worth it."

The Spartan stared for a moment longer, then relaxed. He gestured at the youth to go, and the young man scrambled back to his friends. They turned and ran, hissing curses as they went.

The Spartan walked off. Miltiades looked at the others and trotted after him.

"You're a long way from home, Spartan."

"Home?" asked the Spartan.

Miltiades waited, but the man said nothing more. "You can't stay here now. They will be after you for sure after that humiliation."

The Spartan nodded. "I know."

Miltiades glanced at Photios and Zander. "If you like, you can come with us. We have a ship. An Athenian ship. We're heading for the Chersonnese. We can give you passage."

"There is not just me."

"Your companion is welcome to come too."

The Spartan walked in silence for a full minute.

"Very well. I will gather my belongings and join you."

Miltiades and the others trotted on back to the ship. Somewhere behind them in the city, a horn sounded.

"Oh shit," said Zander. "Who is his father?"

They broke into a sprint, even old Photios.

"Phillipus!" bellowed Miltiades. "Untie! Launch the ship!"

"What in Hades have you done?" asked the captain grimly.

The horn sounded again, and then a third time. Phillipus pointed at his flute player, and the man nodded and started blowing the same high pitch pattern over and over. Oarsmen and colonists came running – thankfully none had travelled far from the first available wineshops right by the dock. Angry yells could be heard coming from the direction of the agora.

"We are going to need more time," said the captain. "Or they burn the ship at their leisure as we try to get some speed up."

Miltiades nodded. "We may have to fight, bloody their noses a bit."

"You," said Phillipus, jabbing his finger into Miltiades' chest. "You fight. I'm getting my oarsmen aboard. I'm not starting a war between Athens and these pig-fuckers."

"Just get your bloody tub moving then. Colonists! Colonists! Form up! Shields and spears!"

The knot of colonists on the dock stared back at him, glancing at the oarsmen lining up to slip down into the rowing benches. Finally Metramandes stirred into action, jumping across onto the trireme's deck and tearing at the covered cargo.

"Come on!" he shouted.

It broke the spell. More men jumped over, passing spears and heavy round shields back up to the others on the shore.

"They're coming..." warned Zander.

Miltiades turned. Torchlight was flickering from further up the road, and the slap of many feet carried through a drone of angry voices that sounded like a hornet's nest. Callias appeared by his side, hoplon and spear in one hand, Miltiades' sword in the other. Miltiades took it and drew it from the scabbard. He scratched a long line in front of the ship in the dirt.

"Here! Form phalanx here."

And the colonists remembered. Few had their own shield, but they moved to their positions, and formed a double line, covering most of the length of the ship.

"Here comes that Spartan," said Zander, pointing. "But that's odd, he's alone."

From the other direction the tall, thin man came jogging, a pack on his pack and a bundle under one arm. He wore one of the short stabbing swords the Spartan's favoured on a belt over his shoulder.

Miltiades raised a hand in greeting, and the Trembler joined them. "I thought you said you were bringing someone."

"I did," said the Spartan.

Miltiades frowned, but at that moment a storm of noise broke over them and an angry mob poured around the corner and filled half the dockyard. Some held torches, others held weapons or simple clubs. Miltiades could see a couple of hunting bows.

"Lock shields!" he cried, and with a shout the colonists brought their bronze-covered hoplons into position, each overlapping that of the man to the left. The short, sharp movement brought the mob up short. Miltiades took his position at the end of the line on the right, wishing Callias had brought him his shield and not just his sword. His young cousin was waiting, biting his lip. Teron was not in position behind Metramandes, who stood frowning at the yelling mob before them.

"Where is your bloody friend?"

"Putting on his armour!"

"There isn't time for that!"

Miltiades turned to face the Lemnians. They were yelling curses, psyching themselves up to close the distance. The colonists were mostly silent, grim in the face of the numbers before them. A few Lemnians ran forward, flinging rocks which rattled off the Athenian's shields. If one of us goes down and the line breaks, thought Miltiades, that is going to be the end. They will go for us like a pack of wolves. Beside him, the Spartan pulled his sword from its sheath, steadily watching the shouting mob.

"Hold!"

The mob slowly calmed, and grudgingly opened a channel in the middle. A figure clad in full panoply strode through it, flanked by several other hoplites. It was the chief archon from their disastrous meeting.

And his open-face helmet confirmed what a prick he was, thought Miltiades, since generally the more money a man had, the more covered up he was, especially his face. Only poorer hoplites or show offs determined to be noticed would sport a helmet leaving the face fully exposed.

The archon stopped between the two lines. Miltiades risked a glance back at the trireme – all the oarsmen were below the deck, and the ropes were cast off. Phillipus and the crewmen stood ready to pole them away from the dock, but it would take several pulls and too many minutes to get them far enough away to avoid a torch.

"You! Athenian pirates!" bellowed the archon. His voice carried easily in the night air. Must have been taking lessons in public speaking, thought Miltiades. "How dare you offer such insult to the polis of Lemnos!"

"No insult was intended," Miltiades called back. "If you recall, we merely sought information. After that, yes, there was an incident. We simply intervened in an unfair dispute."

"Dispute? You attempted to murder my son! We demand you hand over the Spartan dog, and all others involved. Which apparently includes you, Miltiades."

"We do not hand Athenian citizens over to other states. If you have a dispute with us, we welcome you to bring a charge in an Athenian court."

"Oh, and I am sure we would get a fair hearing there!"

"Fairer than whatever prison you have on this dungheap of an island."

The archon frowned. "Careful, Athenian. You are not far off dying here tonight."

Miltiades paused. He mustn't let his temper carry him away. He was aware of the watchful silence of the rows of colonists to his left, Phillipus standing silent on the deck behind them – and the steady flow of reinforcements entering the square, more and more of them dressed in their armour.

"Surely there is another way to resolve this."

"Why, yes," said the archon. "There most certainly is. Pay a fine of a thousand drachma. And then we will allow you to leave."

"He must be joking," Metramandes muttered beside him.

Miltiades did some quick calculations. It would bankrupt the mission before they had begun. They would arrive at his uncle's colony as paupers. He licked his lips.

"Actually," he heard himself say. "I was thinking individual combat. You and me."

The archon's mouth dropped. He heard Metramandes grunt beside him, and Callias mutter "Yes!" behind. He couldn't see Zander, but he could imagine the look on his face nonetheless.

"I... I, uh, may be able to find a champion," said the archon, looking behind him. Many men were suddenly unable to meet his eye.

"No,' said Miltiades. He pointed with his sword. "Just you and me. We end this now." He noticed the blade was shaking slightly. He lowered his arm before anyone else could notice. He glanced at the rows of Lemnians – they were curious, and a little calmer. The chance to watch a personal challenge match rather than risk dying themselves was attractive, as Miltiades had gambled.

"It may be," said the archon, "that I was overhasty in setting the fine. Just as you are, perhaps, being overhasty now. Perhaps a more realistic amount would be... five hundred?"

Miltiades fought down the urge to answer. Wait, he told himself, just wait. Let silence speak, and let this man fill in the spaces.

"All right, how about two fifty? That seems fair."

"No! More!" cried a voice from the crowd. "Make 'em pay more!"

"Just kill them all!" yelled some hothead.

He had to act quickly, before the mob could become too agitated and confident.

"Done!" shouted Miltiades. The archon's face twitched in relief. He heard Metramandes curse beside him, imagined a snicker coming from Teron. "Zander! Bring the chest! The rest of you, get aboard!"

He couldn't allow his spine to relax until the money was paid, and the colonists were all aboard. But finally the ship pulled slowly away from the dock. As the distance grew, he stared back at the mob on the dock. He didn't know if he was angrier at them or himself. There had been some strange looks from his men. What did they want? He had extricated them from a delicate situation, all in one piece. Wasn't that good enough?

....

FIVE

TROY

"Who in Hades is that," asked Phillipus, "and what has he brought onto my ship?"

It had been a hard night. It was too dangerous to try to find somewhere else on the island to beach the ship, away from the city. Instead they spent the night at the oars, rowing just enough to slowly move northeast without encountering land until it was daylight. When the sun finally did start to rise, it was to reveal a sky covered over with low grey clouds.

The captain was pointing at the Spartan, who sat cross legged towards the bow, his bundle held in his lap. The bundle was moving. Something poked its head clear, and two long ears rose like spears.

"Is it," asked Callias, "is it a rabbit?"

Phillipus blinked, and marched forward. Miltiades, Photios and Zander followed. Before the captain could speak, Miltiades coughed. "Uh, friend Spartan? This is the trirarch, Phillipus. I'm Miltiades, of Athens. We didn't get a chance to exchange names before..."

"It is!" cried Callias. "It is a rabbit!"

The small creature had crawled from the Spartan's lap, and sat back on its haunches, sniffing at the air. It took a few hopping steps along the deck, leaving half a dozen small brown pellets in its wake.

"It's shitting," said Phillipus. "The bloody thing is shitting all over my deck."

He took a step towards it. In an instant, the Spartan was fluidly on his feet, and in between. He kept his gaze averted, over the captain's shoulder, but in his stillness was the threat of violence. Like a black cloud on the horizon, on an otherwise sunny day.

"Rabbit is not to be touched."

The captain's face screwed into a frown.

"Phillipus," said Miltiades. "Please."

Phillipus spat over the side, and stalked back towards the stern, grumbling. The Spartan relaxed and squatted by his pack, rummaging inside. He pulled out a handful of hay, and waved it about. The rabbit sniffed the air, and came hopping back. It rested one paw on the man's bony hand, and chewed at the hay, small jaws working with surprising speed.

"When you said you had to get someone, I thought you meant a woman. Or a young man." Miltiades knelt beside the Spartan. "I was at least expecting a someone, not a something."

"This is someone."

"It's lunch," scoffed Zander, behind them. Miltiades shot him a look.

"May I touch him?"

"Her," said the Spartan.

Miltiades slowly reached out and ruffled the small animal's head. She stopped chewing, and half closed her eyes. "She is very soft. What is her name?"

"She has not revealed that to me. And so I must simply call her Rabbit."

"He's mad," Zander muttered. Miltiades winced, but the Spartan either didn't notice or didn't care.

"And you? What is your name?"

There was a pause. "You can call me Tresantes."

"Tresantes? That is not a name I have heard before."

"It is a name I chose for myself. In the language of Sparta, in the Doric tongue, it means 'trembler'."

"Ah. That is what they were calling you, back on Lemnos. Why 'trembler'?"

"Because it is what the Spartans call me. I am a coward."

"You? Then you're the bravest bloody coward I've ever met. I've never seen anyone fight like that."

Tresantes shrugged.

"But your people think you are a coward?"

"Not my people. I don't have a people anymore. I lost my citizenship."

"They kicked you out? You are an exile?"

"No. I chose to go. I was free to stay – but none would speak to me, none would share fire with me. I must make way for everyone. I could not come to the assembly. I could not marry. None would befriend me. That is not life. Instead I chose to leave."

Miltiades nodded. "Understandable. To lose all that... I would leave, too. Well, there are many on board who are hoping to make a new life for themselves on this expedition. Maybe you can stay with us, do the same. There are no citizens or non-citizens where we are going."

"I will come with you," said the Spartan after a long pause. "As long as Rabbit likes it."

By early afternoon, a smudge of land appeared on the horizon, and the trireme aimed for the straits of the Hellespont, sticking close to the rocky cliffs of the northern shore. To the south lay the coast of Asia, and although Greek cities were dotted along it in the region known as Ionia, there was a deep fear of the Persians, whose kingdom extended from these lands down to the deserts beyond Egypt and Arabia.

For a time, the shore to their left rose steep and formidable just beyond a narrow rocky beach. Then the two coastlines drew ever closer together, until they passed through a narrow choke point, where a triangular peninsula thrust out from the Asian shore towards them. Further along, the channel widened again, and a broad sweeping bay opened up to their left, the land flatter beyond, and here they found both a landing site and destruction. A simple wooden jetty ran out into the water, but to one side a small galley lay sunk and awash in the swell. Inland sat the charred ruins of a small town. Phillipus manoeuvred the ship close to the end of the dock, and had the anchors dropped. The water was fairly shallow here, and the ropes did not have far to run before they stopped, and then went taut as the ship pulled against them. Those not at the oars stood and looked at the ruins.

"So here lies the colony of your uncle," said Photios.

"Now we know why no messages were coming back," said Mitiades. He felt a deep ache in his chest. He rubbed his hand across it.

"But where is everyone?" asked Callias.

"Maybe they are all dead?" suggested Teron. "Or else they have fled?"

"But no one holds the town. If they had retreated, why not come back? And if they had all been killed, who killed them? Where are they?"

"What do you want to do?" asked Phillipus.

"Land, of course," said Miltiades. "We are here to find my uncle. And re-establish this colony."

Before they docked, Miltiades ordered all the settlers up onto deck, and to arm themselves in their full panoply. This caused some consternation, as equipping themselves on a narrow crowded deck, in a slight swell, was frightening. The prospect of falling over the side in full armour didn't bear thinking about. But finally they were ready, and Phillipus brought them carefully alongside the empty side of the jetty, handling the tiller himself.

There was a definite tingle in Miltiades' legs as he tensed and jumped across onto the creaking platform. Callias, Zander and the rest were close behind. Once up on the shore, they formed up in their double lines, while Phillipus backed the trireme out into deeper water. Apart from the shifting of the men, the clank of spear shaft against shield rim, and the gentle slap of the trireme's oars, there was no sound. No voices, no cattle lowing, no birds. Every hut was a pile of ash and charred timber. The few stone buildings in the centre of town appeared gutted, their roofs burned and collapsed, soot streaking the stone above the few narrow windows.

Satisfied that they were alone, Miltiades gave orders for half the men to divest themselves of their heavy armour and shields, to scout the destroyed town and the homesteads dotted further out, while half stood ready. He detailed Callias and Teron, and two of the youngest colonists called Larmenes and Crotus, to explore further up the peninsula. He waved Phillipus in and asked him to use his oarsmen to unload their supplies. Leaving Metramandes in charge of the remaining phalanx, he took Zander and Photios into the empty ruined agora. The Spartan he left plucking grass, his rabbit wrapped in his cloak in the crook of one arm. For some reason, the Spartan's lack of concern for their surroundings gave him some comfort. Declared coward or not, they were still the most militaristic polis in all of Greece, and if he didn't feel at risk from ambush, even given the destruction about them, then that could only be good news. Unless of course he was totally mad...

They paused at the doorway of what may have been a council chamber. It was dark and empty inside.

"What's that?" said Photios. He bent stiffly and rooted in a pile of debris, and extracted what appeared to be a grey stick. He blew ash from it.

"What is it?" asked Miltiades.

Photios frowned, and rubbed it with the end of his tunic. "It appears to be a bone. Human, I would say." He rubbed a finger along it, and then brought it right up to his eye. "It's rough. Strange marks on it. Little indentations. Teeth marks?"

"Wolves?" asked Zander, glancing about.

"Possibly. But..."

"Ho! Cousin Miltiades!" Callias appeared on a distant rise to the north, waving. "Come and see this!"

Photios opted to stay put, leaving Miltiades and Zander to trot through the ruins and up the gentle slope. By the time they got to the top, both men were breathing hard. Miltiades made a silent vow to get some training in as soon as he had a chance. This was ridiculous.

"Look at this!" Callias stepped back, sweeping his arm.

Beyond the hill, the peninsula narrowed to maybe three miles across before broadening again. Water was visible in both directions. But it wasn't the view that Callias was pointing at. Someone had built a wall spanning the entire neck. The centre mile or more seemed the best built. Three figures stood on that section, waving. Their presence gave it scale – it looked to stand around seven or eight feet high, and was obviously wide enough for them to stand on comfortably. The rest of the wall looked less carefully laid – there were gaps between unshaped stones. At one point, down to their left about a mile distant, it seemed to have been blown inward, with a gaping hole that ten men could march through abreast, stone spread around it.

"Impressive, huh?"

"The natives here must be decidedly unfriendly," said Zander. "That's some fortification. And that is some breach."

"Are you sure it's a breach?" asked Callias. "I thought it was because they didn't leave space for a gate."

"You're right," said Miltiades. "They don't seem to have left space for one. That section looks like it was knocked in, with a ram or something."

Zander rubbed his hand through his whiskers. "This is really getting strange. Who builds a wall without a gate?"

"Now who's that?" said Callias, pointing.

Inland, on a high distant slope, sat several horsemen.

"Shit," said Zander. "The unfriendly natives?"

There came a yell from the three men on the wall. They were waving wildly.

"Yes, thank you, we can see them."

"No," said Miltiades. "They are pointing the other way."

As they watched, two of the men disappeared over the edge of the wall while the last stood watching. At the same time, the horsemen started picking their way down the slope, disappearing behind a fold of the wooded hill.

"What in Hades is going on? Shall I call up the men?"

"Wait, wait. Let's get down there." Miltiades stirred his weary legs into action and started jogging down towards the wall, Zander and Callias in his wake. As they got closer, he could see that the base of the wall was well-dressed stone – whoever had started building had meant it to be strong and to last. But once the first couple of layers had been set, the work deteriorated, as if the builders suddenly found they had less time than they thought.

"Teron!" Miltiades called to the youth on the wall. "Can you see the riders?"

"What riders?"

"Then what were you pointing at?"

There was a shout from the other side of the wall, and Teron turned and squatted. He leaned forward, and hauled a bundle up from the other side. Larmenes and Crotus appeared, shoving it from underneath. Teron coughed and turned his head, losing his hold and the thing landed on the top of the wall. The other two shoved him aside and eased it over, and now it was apparent that it was a person, for thin limbs could be seen thrashing weakly.

"Zeus, she stinks!" spat Teron.

Crotus and Larmenes set the woman on her feet as the others arrived. She was old, and haggard - or at least so it appeared - and she was clad in long ragged robes so that only her wrinkled hands and face were visible. She stared at them with clouded, rheumy eyes and hissed, her dry lips pulling back and revealing empty gums. They coughed and stepped back. She staggered forward, arms held out, towards Zander, who recoiled in horror.

"What is wrong with her?"

Crotus took her arm and pulled her stumbling back. "Sick. Or mad. Or both. We spotted her limping around on the other side. Thought we should bring her in for questioning."

"Can she even speak?" asked Callias.

The old woman turned towards him and stepped forward, mouth open, and again Crotus tugged her back.

"Steady, the young gent doesn't want a kiss. Well, we couldn't leave her just wandering around out there. How would you like it if she was your mum?"

"Now, that could be interesting..." murmured Zander.

At that moment, the drumming of hoofbeats carried to them.

"You two get her back to camp. Have Photios take a look at her, get some food into her. You're right, she might know something about what happened here. The rest of you, with me."

He took hold of the top of the wall and hauled himself up.

"Hang on, hang on!" cried Zander. "What if they have javelins?"

But he was already lying across the top, and didn't want to lose face by sliding back down. He raised himself up onto his feet, squinting at the trio of riders trotting towards them at a leisurely pace. He could see that they did have javelins – at least two each. But they didn't look particularly hostile.

"Ha! Look at this!" laughed Crotus. He was holding a hand up, and the crone was sucking greedily on his finger. He took a few steps, and she stumbled after him. "Like leading a calf!"

"That's disgusting," said Callias.

"At least he isn't using his cock," said Larmenes.

Crotus laughed in delight. "Don't give me ideas. Actually, it feels kind of nice. I banged that finger climbing over. Took the nail off. Come on, mum, back to camp. Ow! Gentle, please! Less gnawing with the gums, thank you."

He walked backwards, leading the hobbling woman after him, while Larmenes brought up the rear.

Miltiades shook his head and turned back to the riders.

They were wearing the same kind of pointed hats that the Skythians wore, but were lighter of skin. Each wore a patterned cloak and had a small shield slung over his back. Their horses were big – as big as well-bred Greek horses from states like Thessaly. Miltiades lifted a hand in greeting, as Zander, Callias and Teron climbed onto the wall beside him. The trio reined in, and studied the Greeks on the wall. One of them spoke a few words, but Miltiades shook his head.

"Do you speak Greek?"

"Some little bit," answered one.

"Good. Who are you?"

"Who are you?" returned the horseman pointedly.

"Before I answer, I want to know if I am speaking to friends or enemies. Did your people attack this place?"

The riders glanced along at the hole in the wall. "No."

"Then who did?"

The cavalrymen conferred. One gesticulated emphatically at the speaker, pointing back the way they had come. The speaker shrugged.

"You come to our bria, talk to king."

"Not a chance," said Zander. "You are not going anywhere with these barbarians."

"Tell me who your king is?"

"Is King Olorus. King of Dolonci. King of all this land." The rider purposefully let his gaze run across the wall. "Now, who are you?"

Ah, thought Miltiades. Thracians, not Skythians. Still considered barbaric by true Greeks, but maybe not quite as strange.

"I am Miltiades of Athens."

All three reacted to the name.

"No!" said the rider. "You not him."

"You know him? You know another by that name? That is my uncle. We share the same name. You know where he is?"

The rider frowned. "You talk to king."

"How far?"

"Oh no, no, no, no," said Zander.

"Some far. You ride with us. This many." The man held up three fingers, and pointed to the three horses.

"Right," said Miltiades, turning to the others. "Zander is coming with me. Callias, you go back and tell Photios what is going on, and get Phillipus to get the ship unloaded but not to leave until we get back. Teron, you come with us."

"What, me?" asked Teron.

"Yes. I might need you." He didn't speak the thought out loud, but Miltiades wondered whether they would be required to leave a hostage with the Thracian king, in which case the young Alcmaeonid seemed the most expendable from his point of view. "Come on. And cheer up, Zander. We're going to find out where my uncle is."

Or at least, what happened to him and the men with him.

They each climbed up behind a rider, locking their legs around the broad flanks of the horses, and holding on to the cloaks of the men in front. The cavalrymen turned about, kicked their mounts and trotted back towards the slopes rising to the north.

The landscape seemed wild and rugged to Miltiades' eye. He was used to seeing the order and precision of olive groves, pasture, vegetable plots and grain fields. The rock and scrub, and stands of trees, made this land seem older, and leant it a malevolent air. The horsemen clucked at their horses, and picked their way down barely discernible paths, until the thin blue smoke from cooking fires could be seen curling into the sky from a valley ahead hidden between folds of steep sloping hillsides.

They rode into a town of rough timber huts grouped around a large central wooden hall. There were no stone buildings anywhere, and the only defence was a simple palisade manned by stern bearded sentries with long thrusting spears.

"This is where your king lives?" asked Miltiades.

"Sometimes," grunted his rider. "He travel. Sometimes this bria, other times other bria."

That made more sense. Even a barbarian king would surely have a more splendid home if it was his permanent address. A group of warriors lounged near the doorway of the hall, and a couple came forward to take the bridles as the men dismounted. Zander rubbed his buttocks and groaned.

"That was worse than rowing that stupid boat."

Teron smirked. "I don't suppose a slave normally has much call for horsemanship."

"Shut up, Teron," said Miltiades. The young man scowled, but held his tongue.

The doors were swung open, and they stepped into the interior. Inside, it was better appointed than the Greeks expected. The floors were well-planed boards, and the walls were hung with brightly woven tapestries.

"King Olorus," said their guide, ushering them forward.

The king was a large middle-aged man with a knotted red beard streaked with grey. He sat on a simple wooden throne at the end of the hall, with a few elders seated on benches to the sides. There was a fire in the middle of the room, sending smoke up through a hole in the middle of the high ceiling. Hangings screened several doorways at the back of the chamber.

"Greetings, King Olorus," said Miltiades. Zeus, I hope he speaks some Greek.

The king nodded. "Why you come here?"

Accented, and incorrect, but good enough, thought Miltiades. "King, we have come from the polis of Athens to seek my uncle, called Miltiades, who had established a colony here on the Chersonnese."

"On Dolonci land," said the king.

"Ah... Athens, of course, wishes good relations with those who are neighbours. We do not look for conflict. We..." Miltiades faltered to a halt. This playing at diplomat suddenly seemed ridiculous. Who was he, to be trying to negotiate with these people? He had no experience in this kind of thing. He felt like a fake, an imposter, and could easily have mumbled an apology and walked out were it not for one burning question that now found its way to his lips. "King Olorus, please, do you know what happened to my uncle? Was there...trouble between you?"

The king was silent, staring at them thoughtfully. At that moment, one of the curtains twitched and a girl pushed through – no, not a girl. A young woman. She was tall, and her face was tattooed with lines and other shapes – Miltiades saw it was the same design occurring on the cloaks the men wore. How different she looked to the pale, wan daughters of Eupatrids that he was used to. The sort of girls who spent their entire lives indoors, engaged in nothing more taxing than weaving and gossip. She looked them over, her gaze lingering on Miltiades, then drifted over to the king, bending down to kiss him on the cheek. He closed his eyes and cupped her face for a moment, then she knelt and sat by his throne, leaning against his legs and watching.

"My daughter, Hegesipyle."

Miltiades bowed. The young woman's mouth twisted in a grin.

"I did not kill your uncle, Athenian," said the king.

"Who then? Their village was attacked and destroyed. And there is the wall. Why did they build that?"

"I think," the king said slowly, "I think you would not believe me if I told you."

"What do you mean?"

"You Athenians... You like the facts, yes? Moon follows sun, winter follows summer. Tide out, tide in. Fact, fact, fact, yes?"

"I'm not sure I follow..."

"Sometimes, Athenian, one thing not follow another. This I could tell you, but you not believe."

"Try me."

Before the king could answer, there was a shout from outside and a sweat-soaked man ran in. He spoke rapidly in the Thracian tongue, and the king frowned, firing back several questions. Then he smiled grimly, leaning back in his throne.

"Good, this is good. Now you see. See is better than talk." He stood, and shouted. His warriors ran in. The king pointed at two. "Bolinthos, Embades." They grinned. The others cursed. Olorus smiled at Miltiades, and held his arms out to the sides. The two warriors took long strips of leather and began binding the king's arms with them.

"King Olorus, what is going on? What will we see?"

"That sometimes one thing not follow another." The king looked down and spoke to his daughter, Hegesipyle. She rose to her feet and disappeared through one of the curtains. "You ride with us, Athenian, and I will show you."

Hegesipyle returned, carrying what appeared to Miltiades to be the biggest sword he had ever seen. The blade was as long as a man's leg, with a slight curve to it, and the hilt was half as long again. Olorus took it from her, wrapping his two meaty fists around the hilt.

"That's quite the sword," said Miltiades.

"Rhomphaia," said the king. "Come."

Outside, horses had been saddled and were held ready. Three for the Athenians, three for the king and his two warriors. The man who had brought the message was there, too, but apparently on a fresh horse, since it looked dry while he was saturated.

"Master," said Zander, and his use of that term told Miltiades how nervous he was, "what are we doing?"

"We are learning. Don't worry, we'll be all right. There can't be much danger if the king is taking so few men."

"I feel I should point out he is bringing his bloody great meat cleaver, too – oh good, now everybody is armed to the teeth. That isn't comforting."

The warriors Bolinthos and Embades jogged up, one with a pair of javelins, the other with a boar spear – a stout shaft fitted to a broad bronze head, with a cross bar just behind it to stop any beast thrusting forward along the shaft to get to the wielder. The scout was armed with a long lance. The king mounted, pulling himself up onto the horse easily despite his years. Miltiades watched Teron likewise swing himself skilfully across his mount's back, and approached his own. He had been on horseback more times in the past week than the previous three years. He was not a great horseman, never had been. In truth, he found the creature's size unnerving. Could never understand how easy his father was with them – as easy with horses as he was with people. Except for his own son, of course. Gritting his teeth, he placed his hands on the blanket covering the beast's back, and launched himself up. He had to kick to swing himself up and get his leg over, and there was no grace about it, but he was pleased he hadn't fallen off. When he looked around, Zander, too had managed to mount, though he was looking a little white. Miltiades hoped his own colour was not betraying him.

Hegesipyle ran out, holding an older style bronze helmet in her hands. She held it up to Olorus, who waved her off. She spoke angrily, and whacked him on the knee with the helmet. He raised a hand as if to strike her, and she raised the helmet again, but he ruffled her hair instead. Angrily she stepped back out of range and adjusted her locks. She caught Miltiades watching her and he looked away, feeling suddenly embarrassed.

"Come," said the king, and he set his heels into his horse's flank and trotted for the gate. Miltiades concentrated on squeezing his mount's sides with his knees to hold himself in place, and wrapped his hands in the leather harness. His sword bounced awkwardly against his ribs as he jogged along after the others.

They followed the scout north, higher into the forested hills. The pace was fairly fast, and Miltiades tried to take note of the path they took as they wound their way into a valley. Very quickly they left any signs of habitation behind – there were soon no tilled fields or small flocks of sheep or goats. They started trotting downhill, the trees opening up before them to reveal a river. Miltiades wondered if they were going to try to ford it, and wasn't looking forward to the prospect going by the apparent depth and speed of the current. But thankfully the scout turned to the right and led them along the bank.

Miltiades started to worry about how long they were going to be gone. What was happening back at the encampment? Hopefully all the stores were unloaded, and the men were working on building shelters for the night, and maybe a couple were out hunting. Their stocks of provisions would not last long. They would have to get by on what they could catch while they got the fields cleared and planted. They would also need to visit the independent city-states that lay around the Black Sea – that was where the grain stood, far more than they could ever hope to supply themselves.

He shook himself. He realised he hadn't been paying attention at all to his surroundings for the last few minutes, surely a dangerous habit when in unfamiliar territory with men he didn't know. There was much he had to change about himself, to do differently, if he was going to make a success of this. His uncle would have known what to do. Arriving at that site, no building, no farms, he would have set to with a will, to claim order from the wild. And one of the first things he had seen fit to do, was to put however many men it took to build that bloody wall...

But whatever had happened, had happened anyway...

With a start, he realised the others had stopped. He glanced about. There was a sharp bend in the river here, and the woodland pressed down close to the bank. His horse shivered. And then he saw what the others were looking at. Three figures stood in the peninsula formed by the river's curve, seemingly staring across to the other shore. Miltiades couldn't tell what they were looking at, but supposed they were working out how to cross.

The king snapped an order, and the scout kicked his horse and cantered forward. The sound of the horses' hooves obviously carried to the men, for they turned – and to Miltiades' great surprise, all started hurrying forward towards the rider.

The scout lowered his lance.

"But," said Miltiades, turning to the king. "They don't appear to be armed. Who are they?"

Olorus grunted. "Watch."

One man was a little ahead of the others. He appeared to be reaching for the scout as he rode up – beseeching him? But the scout did not stop or slow – the point of his lance caught the man in the midriff, and pierced right through him. The momentum carried him stumbling backwards, as the shaft slid through him after the point. With a final thrust the scout buried the point in the ground and let go, riding clear, leaving the man caught on the lance like an insect on a thorn.

Miltiades felt his gorge rise.

The other two figures did not pause to try to help their injured companion, but separated, one following after the scout while the other came on, having noticed the cluster of horsemen. What did they hope to do? Why did they not run? Olorus spoke again, and Bolinthos and Embades rode forward. Bolinthos, javelins in hand, rode after the one, while Embades swung from the saddle and waited, boar spear held in both hands. The final man came at them in a shambling run.

"Is he insane?" asked Zander.

"Clearly he should surrender," said Teron.

Miltiades frowned. Something was not right. Something about the way the man moved.

Embades casually lowered his spear, muscles bunched. The other man made no attempt to avoid the point or defend himself, just came on, and as he reached the Thracian, the warrior thrust forward, catching him under the chin. The Thracian shouted and pushed forward, overbalancing the man and sending him sprawling. The warrior stood over him, grunting, working the shaft and twisting it, embedding the spear head inside the man's skull. Sickeningly, Miltiades heard the scraping sound of the point and sides grinding on bone.

Meanwhile Bolinthos had ridden up behind the other man, and launched a javelin. It caught him in the shoulder, spinning him around. The Thracian threw again, and the second missile glanced off the side of his head. The man staggered backwards and fell into the river, the current catching him and whisking him downstream.

Olorus cursed and shouted. Embades swiftly withdrew his spear and swung back up onto his mount. Together, he and Bolinthos rode off downstream in pursuit.

"What is the problem?" asked Zander. "If he doesn't drown he'll bleed to death."

Olorus looked at the three Greeks, then called the scout over to hold his horse. "Come," he said, brandishing his rhomphaia. The scout grinned at them as he dismounted and took their reins as well.

"Gods, that one is still alive!" Teron pointed at the man struck through by the scout's lance. He was still struggling. He couldn't get his feet properly under himself, and was obviously too weak to catch hold of the shaft. Miltiades couldn't imagine what pain he must be feeling. He led the others after the king.

And then the smell hit him.

Not the smell of blood and shit, the usual stench of the battlefield at the end of the action, but the insidious cloying reek of decomposition. The foul miasma that was left when one side or another were slow with their clean up of the field and burial of their dead.

They came first to the figure of the man speared by Embades, and gawped. For they saw that there was something terribly wrong – the great gaping wound in the throat was there, like a second mouth, but there were other injuries, too. Chunks of flesh were missing from the arms and torso. A blackened loop of bowel was visible through one such tear, the ripped tunic stiff with brown dried blood. Some blood was oozing from the spear wound, but it was very dark and sluggish, not the burst of bright red such an injury should cause. And the stench had them gagging.

"I don't understand," said Zander. "He was alive, and now he looks long dead..."

"Is he sick? Diseased?" asked Teron, drawing away and holding a fold of his cloak over his mouth.

"Come," said Olorus grimly.

He led them towards the other man, still struggling on the lance. They faltered as they drew near.

"Gods of Olympus," murmured Miltiades.

They saw that this man was much the same as the first, his flesh rotten and sagging. Half the skin on his face and head was missing, revealing bone darkened by crawling flies. Yet the man glared at them with shrunken, milky eyes, and snapped his teeth at them. He strained, reaching for them, and managed to heave himself a little further along the lance shaft.

"This is not possible. How is this possible?"

Olorus stepped forward, gripping his rhomphaia with two hands. "You see? Sometimes one thing does not follow another as it should. Death follows life, but then life follows death again."

"That isn't life..."

"No?" Olorus placed the tip of his blade beneath the thing's chin. "You see? It wishes to eat us. It wishes to eat us because it sees us, hears us, maybe smells us. It lives."

"I meant, not a natural life. Not a life worth living. To be like that..."

The king nodded. "True, any man would not wish to be such a thing. And so we end it."

He drew the sword back and swung, and the blade hacked through the thing's neck, sending the head bouncing along the ground. At once all the motion in the body ceased, and it sagged, hanging on the lance.

"Gods, look at the head!" groaned Zander, and Miltiades saw that the thing was still staring at them, the mouth opening and closing like a landed fish. He walked towards it.

"Beware," said Olorus. He moved forward, placed one boot on the head to hold it steady, and thrust his blade through the eye socket into the brain cavity. The mouth sagged open, the tongue protruding obscenely.

The king thrust his rhomphaia into the ground to clean it, then walked back towards where the scout held their horses. The Greeks were quiet, each lost in his own thoughts. The scout held the king's mount steady with one hand while Olorus strapped his weapon across it and then took hold of its mane.

Something broke from the cover of the trees, coming straight for them. A terrible strangled groan came from its torn, black lips. The horse reared, a hoof striking the scout and sending him staggering and falling backwards. The king fell too, heavily. The horse spun and bolted, immediately followed by the other mounts. The scout sat up groggily – and threw an arm up, crying out as the thing was upon him, grabbing hold of him and bending its skull-like head. There was a piercing cry, and the Thracian thrashed sideways, holding his face, blood spurting between his fingers. The monster straightened, jaws working, chin reddened by gore. Its eyes rested on the king, on his knees, breathing hard.

It had all happened so fast, Miltiades felt fixed in place, mouth open in shock. But now he felt energy returning to his limbs. His hand found the hilt of his sword – a short, chopping macheira blade, designed for use in the press of the phalanx when the spears were all shattered and the lines were pressed tight together. He really wished he had a longer sword.

"Come on!" he cried to the others, saw Zander drop to his knees, shaking his head, saw the spurt of liquid shit running down Teron's shaking leg. So he turned and ran at the horror alone. It was intent on the king, who still knelt, shaking his head groggily. Miltiades yelled, and it looked up at him. He swung his sword at it, and struck it on the upper arm. The blade bit deep, cracking through bone, and he jerked it to pull it free. The creature's arm came clear, too – but already it reached for him with the other, the finger tips nothing but sharp bone, the mouth gaping and the stench from within worse than anything he could imagine. He thrust his sword at it, felt the point crack some ribs, slowed its advance. He pulled back and chopped again, down onto the shoulder, a killing blow, and with no armour to impede it, the blade sank down into the chest. But still the thing didn't stop, and its fingers gripped his hair, pulling him close. Miltiades shouted and pulled backwards, tripping, and they went down together and he screamed as he fell at the horror of this dead thing coming down on top of him. The stink of it. The feel of it. The insult to all he knew of the natural and ordered world. He instinctively clamped his mouth and eyes shut as they hit the ground, and he felt its forehead clash against his own and a spattering of something liquid striking his face. He had one forearm trapped between their bodies, and he wormed it upwards, placing it under the thing's chin and thrust it away. He felt its bony fingers digging into his shoulder and the strength of it as it struggled against him to bend its face closer. He didn't need to look at it to know its mouth was gaping – the guttural, gurgling sound coming from its black gullet sickened him. He strained, tears leaking from the corners of his eyes, and managed to force its head aside, its sparse hairs sticking across his cheeks. He felt its teeth catching at the shoulder of his tunic, catching the cloth, its movements becoming more excited as it sensed the meat that lay so close beneath. All his wrestling knowledge, the time he spent in the gym, had left him. No moves, no tricks to unseat this horror. All he had left was a desperate, animal struggle to push this death as far from him as possible, for as long as his muscles could hold out.

He sucked in a breath, and screamed "Help me!", his voice shockingly raw and desperate to his own ears.

There were stumping steps, and a boot swung, grazing his face painfully, but connecting full force with the dead thing's head. It was thrown sideways. He scrambled the other way, on hands and knees, and heard crunches and curses behind him. He spun onto his back, still kicking away, and watched Olorus stand over the creature as it reached weakly for him, and the Thracian stamped upon its face, again, and again, until it was smashed in and the skull cracked, and still the king stomped until all movement was over, and it was truly, truly dead.

The king turned and stared at him, breathing hard. "It bite you?"

Miltiades shook his head. "Yes. I mean, no. It tried. I think it tore my tunic..."

The king limped over, and took hold of Miltiades' head, roughly shoving it to the side and tearing his chiton open. He stared, and grunted, releasing his hold. "You two?"

Miltiades glanced at the others. Zander sat on his heels, face a mask of horror. Teron was wiping his leg down with some leaves, his hands shaking. A high keening came to them. The scout lay nearby, hands over his bleeding face. The king grunted again, and limped over to him. He pulled one of the injured man's hands aside, causing him to cry out sharply. Olorus stared, then turned and stamped over to his horse, which stood nearby, trembling. He held his hands out, spoke soothingly, and the animal let him catch it by the bridle. He slid the rhomphaia clear.

"You think there are more of those?" croaked Miltiades. He pushed himself to his feet, and bent to retrieve his own sword. "Zander. Get up."

The king approached the scout, spat into his hand and lifted the blade.

Zander pointed. "What's he doing?"

"Olorus," said Miltiades, "wait-"

The king struck. The long blade cleaved through the scout's forearms and into his neck. Blood sprayed. The king wiped his eyes on the sleeve of his tunic, then swung again. This time the iron bit right through.

"Why?" shouted Miltiades. "Why?"

"He is a poor scout," said the king. "He told me three. But there were four."

"And so you killed him? You bloody killed him because he got the number wrong?"

Olorus frowned. "I kill him because I must." He bent, and grabbed the head by the hair, raising it up. He looked at the eyes, frozen open, then tossed the head into the waters of the river.

Riding back, Miltiades glanced back at Zander, who was riding a little behind him. Teron was further back still, sullen and avoiding eye contact. Miltiades had walked over to him after the action and clapped him on the arm.

"No shame in it. Many men shit themselves their first time in action. And this... this was unlike anything any of us have encountered before."

Teron had looked at him and blinked. "I'm a Eupatrid. I'm not like many men." And he had turned away.

Miltiades had felt a surge of anger at this rebuff of his attempt at kindness. They had been distracted then by the return of the other two Thracians, who the king called over and set about slapping around the head. Shame-faced, they had stood letting him strike them until he had had enough. They had then gathered up their weapons, chased down the other horses and set off for the Thracian bria.

Now, Miltiades slowed his horse and dropped back beside his slave.

"What's the matter?"

"What's the matter? Apart from encountering those living horrors back there?"

"Yes, apart from that. You can't fool me, Zander. Something else is bothering you. You keep looking at me."

They rode in silence for a full minute.

"I don't know who you are any more."

"What does that mean?"

"I mean, first back on Lemnos, then there on the riverbank... You're different. Changing. Suddenly you are leaping into action in a way I just cannot. This experience is changing you, and I... I feel just the same. I feel left behind."

"I feel just the same as always. It has just been about... about doing what needed to be done at the time. No more than that. That isn't courage."

"Yes, but you stepped forward when others – including me – did not. And what if you make a mistake? What if you are killed?"

"I have no intention of dying out here-"

"You think many men intend to die when they do? Did your father? Sorry, that was wrong... It's just...you are a good man, Miltiades, and a good master. Seeing the king execute that man back there just rattled me. I know; why should that rattle me after what we had just seen – but it reminded me of my place. I know I have it good with you. But if you were to die, and I did not, because I was too craven to be at your side as I should be... what would become of me? Sold or given away. Maybe to a master who doesn't care if I can read or what I think. Who sees me as just an automaton for getting things done. A disposable one at that..."

"I don't know what to say to you that isn't going to sound condescending..."

"Oh, just ignore me. I'm thinking too much. Something you seem to be doing less of. I'll try to copy your example."

"Zander, I'm sure if and when the time comes for you to act, you will not find yourself wanting. This is my expedition – I'm in charge, and so I have to act different to who I normally am."

Zander gave him a tight smile and nodded, but his eyes betrayed his worry.

Back at the bria, a crowd gathered to watch them ride in. A woman took note of the riderless horse and burst into tears. She was led away, wailing, by other women of the village. The king dismounted, and cursed as his injured leg threatened to give way beneath him. His warriors cried out and rushed forward to support him. Hegesipyle appeared in the doorway of the hall. Olorus saw her, and shrugged. She bit her lip, shaking her head. Miltiades saw the glint of tears in her eyes. Olorus waved her down, and she came to him, disappearing into his arms. He whispered to her, rocked her, and Miltiades felt a strange pang. What Athenian Eupatrid would allow themselves such a display of public affection? He had been taught to look down on those to the north as barbarians – yet here he was seeing something so much more human.

The Thracians headed into the hall, leaving the Athenians standing awkwardly together.

"Shouldn't we be heading back?" asked Zander.

"Yes," said Miltiades. "But we need someone to take us. Unless you want to steal the king's horses?"

Zander shuddered. "No thanks."

"Hey, Greek."

They turned. Hegesipyle had returned and was walking towards them.

"Uh...princess," said Miltiades, and inclined his head.

"You saved my father."

"Only partially. He saved me, too."

"I thank you for that, anyway."

"You're welcome. You speak Greek very well."

She raised an eyebrow. "It was my father's wish that I learn. He said it was necessary, because of how you Greeks spread."

"Ah."

"And what did you think, Greek? When you saw the Hades men?"

"Hades men? That is what you call them?"

"That is what the other Greek called them. It seems as good a name as any."

"The other Greek?"

"The other with your name. The other Miltiades."

Miltiades felt a jolt run through him.

"You know him?"

"A little. He was...a kind man."

"Do you know what happened to him?"

She looked at him with serious dark eyes, accentuated by the tattooed lines beneath each. "You have seen the Hades men. What do you think happened to him?"

Miltiades felt his gut lurch. "He had men. Warriors. They built a wall..."

Hegesipyle sadly shook her head. "That time, there were many of them. And they are very dangerous. They have no fear. They do not stop. They never stop... One bite is all it takes."

"What do you mean?"

"They are like the adder. Their bite is poison. If they tear the skin, you sicken and die. Then you become one, and so it continues. Unless someone puts a blade through your head or spills your brains."

"Ah, so that is why your father killed the scout..."

"Yes. What did you think, that it was just the cruel act of some barbarian?"

Miltiades didn't answer. "Where do they come from?"

"North. East. Over the mountains. Who can say? They just appear. Sometimes one. Sometimes more."

"But there has to be some origin. Some original cause. Logically..."

Hegesipyle surprised him by yawning broadly. She made no attempt to cover her mouth, and he was partly repelled, partly attracted, by the sight of her teeth and pink tongue.

"Um..."

"You Greeks. You talk so much. It is boring."

Again, Miltiades didn't know how to respond. To be so disrespected by a young woman was outside his experience. He wondered how to disengage from this discussion, even though he was desperate to learn more of the Hadesmen. Here must lie the answer to the riddle of what became of his uncle. He thought of the wall – Zeus, did that not protect them? Did that not keep them out? And why had his uncle not sent word, not asked for help? But the answer was already there – his uncle was a proud man, of a proud family. How many Eupatrids would willingly have conceded to the Pisistratids that they needed help? Until it was too late? Miltiades cursed the pride that seemed to be the downfall of his class all too frequently.

A sudden thought struck him like a slingshot. An image in his head of the men lifting a mad old woman over the wall...

Hegesipyle was walking away.

"Wait!"

She turned, frowning at the tone of his voice. He could feel his throat constricting.

"The Hadesmen. The ones we saw were very rotten. Obviously dead. Do they always look like that?"

"Yes."

He let out the breath he had been holding.

"Eventually," she added.

"What?"

"They all rot. Some faster, some slower. But the new ones do not look like that."

Miltiades suddenly felt weak. "What do they look like?"

"Those do not appear so different, if you cannot see the wound that changed them. That is when they are most dangerous. But you can tell - they cannot speak. There is nothing in their eyes... What are you doing?"

Miltiades was running to the horses. "Mount!" he shouted to the others. "Now! We must get back!"

"You better not take those horses, Greek. They belong to my father."

Miltiades hauled himself atop his mount, grateful to pull the move off smoothly. "I'm just being interesting, princess."

He kicked the horses' flanks, urging it into a canter, hearing the sound of hooves behind him as Zander and Teron followed. He felt absurdly pleased with himself for that exit, though a ball of worry sat in his gut.

"What is it?" asked Zander, pulling alongside.

"We may have let in the Trojan horse..."

SIX

....

PAN

They returned to chaos.

The first inkling was an oily cloud of black smoke rolling into the sky. Miltiades had already set a cracking pace that had exhausted all of them as they clung to their horses with weary battered knees. But when they saw the smoke, he urged them on faster still. Once they reached the wall they were momentarily stalled, until they remembered the tumbled section to the north. It was difficult going for the horses, to lead them over the ruins and through the debris, but Miltiades was already conscious of the insult he had done King Olorus' hospitality, and wanted to avoid making it worse if possible by simply releasing the horses into the wild. They had to push and pull the whinnying horses through, but finally remounted and rode on.

Back at the ruins of the encampment, they were confronted by the scene of shouting angry men, a tent burning down into nothing and at least four men lying injured on the ground. Miltiades spotted Photios tending to them, and swung off his mount, his legs buckling when he hit the ground.

"You!" An angry shout reached him, and Metramandes stormed towards him, followed by a dozen others. "Where have you been?"

Miltiades ignored the question. "What has happened to those men?" he asked instead. His voice shook a little – all the horror and exhaustion and tension of the day seemed to catch up with at once.

"Your bastard pirate's men, that's what! It's been a bloody shambles! Where in bloody Hades were you?"

But Miltiades was looking past the furious metic. "Shit! Where's the bloody boat?"

"Miltiades!" called Photios, limping towards them. The Athenian was aware of Zander beside him. Teron had disappeared.

"Who do you think you are?" roared Metramandes, and he shoved Miltiades in the chest. Miltiades' hand went instinctively to the hilt of his sword. The metic saw the move and bunched his hands into fists. Other men were gathering around them.

"Step back from me and calm down," said Miltiades.

The metic's eyes narrowed. He crossed his arms, but held his ground. "You lead us to this place and abandon us when there is danger? This is your idea of leadership?"

Photios arrived, his face strained. "Miltiades, terrible things have happened-"

"Quiet, old man. I am talking."

"No," said Miltiades. "You are shouting. I need to know what has happened. Is it the old lady?"

"How did you know?" asked Photios.

"You know about this?!"

"Where is she?"

"Dead," said the teacher.

"Wait!" shouted Metramandes. "This isn't good enough!" He turned to face the men gathered about them. "This cannot go on. This is supposed to be an economic undertaking, not a war - yet this man has continually led us into danger. First at Lemnos. Then he exposes us to...I don't know what. We need a change of leadership, I propose that I-"

"Shut up," said Miltiades. "I'm the leader of this expedition. I'm not an archon. You don't get to vote in a new leader, and you don't get to question my actions. If you don't like it, just leave."

"I have invested a lot of money in this trip. If the Pisistratids knew what you are up to..."

"Why? Going to go inform on me?"

"I am no informer." The metic drew himself up haughtily, and looked about him. "What do the rest of you say? Are you happy about this? Speak up!"

"They aren't going to speak up," said Miltiades. "Everybody knew what they were signing up to..."

"Not this," said someone in the crowd. "Not monsters."

"Look, I just want to hear what happened. Let me talk to Photios, and then..."

"No," said Metramandes. "We settle this. Now."

Miltiades was lost for words. He had the sudden sickening feeling that there wasn't going to be a way out of this without violence. The men there in the camp had no great loyalty to him, despite what he had said about their oaths. Enough of them – too many – were simply watching to see how things would unfold. Now, so far from Athens and everything that was familiar to them, before they had a chance to become established here on the Chersonnese and find success, they were too close to giving up. He sized up the metic – the man was much bigger and stronger than he. But if he drew his sword – Zeus, had he not faced enough horror this day without this?

And then, like a ghost, Tresantes was standing between them, a stalk of grass between his teeth.

"Get out of the way, Spartan," said Metramandes. "You think I am afraid of you?"

The Spartan shrugged, continuing to study the ground at his feet. But there was something coming off him – an intention towards violence - that gave the big man pause.

"Might I suggest," said Photios. "that you allow me to talk to Miltiades now, and then later we hold a full assembly to discuss the situation?"

Miltiades saw that he was offering the metic a way out, to back down while saving face. He prayed silently that the big man would take it.

There was a pause, then he nodded tersely. "So be it." He spun about and marched off, followed by a small knot of men. Others started to disperse, and Miltiades let out a long breath.

"Now," he said. "in the name of the gods, tell me what has occurred. And where is bloody Phillipus and the ship?"

....

They had been going about the business of setting up the camp, Photios explained. The ship was being unpacked, large tents erected for shelter until they could build huts. Firewood gathered. A couple of men tried some fishing from the shore.

Then Callias had arrived, with Crotus and Larmenes. The old lady was still attached to the end of Crotus' finger, until Photios had told him to stop. They tried to speak to her, to reason with her, but all she would do was stare with her rheumy eyes, clap her gums together and lunge weakly for them. Most grew tired of looking at her, and went back to their chores, complaining of the smell coming off her. A mixture of fish and rancid cheese.

They had discussed bathing her, or at least stripping her rags off her and washing them, but with no women at hand, felt too shy to do so. They offered her food, water, but she ignored their offerings. Eventually, they were forced to hobble her ankles and wrists together, as gently as they could, to keep her safe in one spot.

Crotus retired, complaining of a headache.

Larmenes stayed with her, watching while Photios drew sketches in the dirt with a stick, trying to get her to communicate that way. Then Phillipus appeared.

He had come to say the ship was unloaded. He glanced at the old lady, the looked swiftly at her again. His face went cold and hard, like a lamp abruptly snuffed out. He snatched up a thick stick from a pile of firewood, and strode forward, raising it-

"Don't!" cried Larmenes.

The stick smashed down, cracking onto the top of the old woman's shawl-covered head. Phillipus struck again, and Larmenes yelled, thrusting his arm between them, taking the blow, and then rolled backwards in pain, holding it across his body. Phillipus stood over the woman, beating with the club. She sagged backward, and the material of the shawl darkened and tore, and a spattering of dark blood sprayed the walls. Photios could only watch in shock, blinking as droplets struck his face.

Finally Phillipus stopped. His chest was heaving, legs trembling. He looked at the stick, dripping gore, and threw it from him in disgust, stumbling backwards. Larmenes turned over and crawled back to the lifeless body with the ruined head.

"What have you done? What have you done to old mother? Oh!" He patted at her shoulder, tried to pull a corner of the shawl over her ruined face, the horror of the deep dent in her forehead. "You bastard, Phillipus. You're lucky Crotus isn't here. He'd gut you, would Crotus. You're lucky. Lucky he is sick-"

"What?" asked Phillipus, his eyes dead. "What did you say? Sick? And he was with her?"

"You're just lucky, that's all. You better look out when his fever goes, he'll cut you-"

Phillipus bent and picked up another length of wood. "Where is he?"

"What?... No! You leave him be!"

"I'll find him myself."

And Phillipus had stormed from the ruins. Larmenes cried out, dragged himself to his feet, still holding his injured arm across his belly, and ran out after him. Photios followed.

"Stop him!" screamed Larmenes. "He's after Crotus!"

Men stopped, looking about in confusion. A small knot gathered uncertainly in the captain's path. Sailors and oarsmen from the trireme saw the confrontation, and jogged down to stand behind their trirarch.

"Get out of the way, you cocksucking idiots. You don't know what you are dealing with. I do."

"Don't let him, boys! Don't let him get Crotus!" Larmenes ducked down into a tent as the colonists swore at the seamen. The captain tried to shove one aside, and like a signal had been given, the fight was on. Men spilled in the dirt, wrestling and cursing. Fists flew, and more than one knife was pulled, cutting flesh.

It was Metramandes who put a stop to it, wading in to the midst of them, clouting colonist and sailor alike on the head, pushing them back, till enough sense prevailed for the two sides to separate.

"You fools!" he cried. "You haven't even heard him – look!"

And they turned to where he was pointing – Larmenes stood in the tent opening, tears running unashamedly down his cheeks.

"It doesn't fucking matter," said Larmenes thickly. "He's dead. He was my friend, and now he is dead."

And in the slow silence that fell, all watched him stand and sob.

"You see, you idiots?" shouted Metramandes. "He's already dead! You're fighting over a dead man! And now somebody better explain to me why..."

Those who were watching saw all the colour drain from Phillipus' face. "Back to the ship! Now! Leave these idiots to their death!"

He spun about, walking toward the dock.

"Now, hang on," said Photios. "Miltiades wanted you to wait..."

"Where are you going?" Metramandes yelled after the departing seamen.

"Where is he going?" asked Larmenes. "What did you do to Crotus?"

Photios noticed the tent flap shake. "Hey-"

The tent flap whipped aside, and Crotus staggered out of the tent. Larmenes spun and looked at him, jaw dropping in shock.

"You... You're alive?"

Crotus held his arms open and stepped forward. Larmenes half fell into his embrace, sobbing – and then shrieked as Crotus dipped his head and tore half the flesh from his cheek with his teeth.

One or two men had stepped forward at first, confused and smiling – for it was good news indeed if a man thought dead turned out to be alive, wasn't it? Others had stepped back, reasoning the opposite – those declared dead had no right to be moving about, and were best avoided. Most had just stood, confused.

Until now. Now men cried out as Larmenes thrust himself away from Crotus and fell backwards, rolling in pain, hands clasped to his bleeding face.

Crotus snarled and lunged at the nearest man, teeth gnashing so hard some must surely have cracked. He moved strangely, and it was this as well as the number of men gathered about that saved any more from being bitten. Crotus would focus on one man, then be distracted by the cries and movements of another, and so staggered back and forth, drool and blood dripping down his chin.

"What in Hades is wrong with him?" shouted one man.

"He's sick!"

"He's dead!"

"Kill him!"

"Kill him again!"

And finally someone picked up a stone and threw it, hard. It caught Crotus on the cheek, smashing his jaw bone and causing his mouth to hang to one side. The injury did not faze him in the least. Others took up rocks, and so a frenzy began. The increasingly battered body continued to lunge in pursuit, the face now a wreck, the ribs broken. Finally a braver soul ran up from behind and struck him on the back of the head with a large stone, wielded in both hands, and Crotus fell to his knees and keeled over onto his face. Others ran forward, and by the time Photios and Metramandes could get them to stop, there was nothing left of the head but a red paste and bones fragments smeared across the ground.

....

"What did you do with the rest of him?" asked Miltiades, feeling sick.

Photios pointed to the smouldering remains of the fire. "I thought to control the sickness."

"And Larmenes? What of him?"

"We put him in another tent. I have done what I can for his pain."

Miltiades nodded – then lifted his head. A ship had slid into view from behind the headland.

"Phillipus!"

Miltiades broke into a jog down towards the docks. When he got there, the trireme had been rowed in close, but still stood a good few boat lengths out into the water.

"Phillipus, you shit head! What are you doing?"

The captain stood grim-faced in the bow, several sailors standing about him armed with javelins.

"I can take you off. If you all come down to the dock, strip naked, and swim out one at a time."

"What in Hades are you talking about? We aren't going anywhere."

"Then you will die. And worse. All of you."

"You've seen this before, haven't you?" said Miltiades. "Egypt? Was this what you saw in Egypt?"

The captain blanched, but kept his mouth tightly shut.

"A Miltiades established this colony, Phillipus, and a Miltiades is going to make it grow and prosper."

"Then a Miltiades is going to become a walking nightmare."

"No. I understand this...this plague or whatever it is. I know how it is spread. How to contain it."

"So you have it contained now?"

Miltiades hesitated. "I will. Soon."

Phillipus shook his head. "Hubris."

"Go back to Athens, Phillipus. Get us our supplies and the families of these men. When you return, you will see."

"Risk more lives? Risk women and children? Is that what you are asking?"

"Life is risk, and the gods favour the bold."

"You're a fool, Miltiades." Phillipus gave a muffled order over his shoulder, and the oars dipped into the water, backing the trireme away. "But I will do as you ask. Though I fear when I return there will be nothing to return to."

Miltiades watched the ship slowly turn, and then proceed down the channel of the Hellespont and out of sight.

He turned to find Tresantes and Photios standing behind him. "And where were you while all this was going on?" he asked the Spartan.

"Building a shelter. For Rabbit."

"Right..." He shook his head. "I need you to come with me now. Photios, take me to Larmenes."

They headed back up into the ruins, which were slowly being put into some semblance of order. Miltiades was aware of eyes on him as Photios led him to a tent pitched some distance away from all the others. Photios bent to step inside, but Miltiades restrained him with a gentle hand on his arm.

"I need you to wait out here, master. Don't let anyone come in."

Photios looked at him, but nodded. Miltiades glanced at the Spartan, then pushed inside.

The smell made him gag. A hot reek of rancid sweat, vomit and something indefinable. He forced himself to move forward, to the simple cot where Larmenes lay twisted and writhing. A dressing was tied to his face, stained and black. His lips were dry and cracked. His eyes sunken and desperate, rolling around in their sockets. For a moment, they found Miltiades, latching on as if in some desperate hope that he brought salvation – and the fear in the sick man's eyes moved Miltiades, and caused him to lift his hand, as if soothe the man's brow... But the glint of sweat shining on the sickly skin gave him pause. Tresantes brushed past him, kneeling by the cot. He lifted Larmenes' head – the man groaned horribly as he did – and brought a ladle of water to his lips. Larmenes gulped greedily.

"Slow, slow."

The Spartan lowered his head – and in seconds Larmenes coiled onto his side and vomited those few mouthfuls onto the ground. When that was gone, still his body wracked him, drawing deep croaking sounds. Finally he rolled back, exhausted. The sharp stink of fresh vomit made Miltiades' own stomach lurch.

His fingers curled around the hilt of his sword. Tresantes noticed the movement, and one eyebrow lifted, but he said nothing. Miltiades moved closer. The man's eyes were closed now, thank Zeus. His chest pulsed with fast, shallow breaths. Miltiades realised he was holding his own breath, and forced himself to exhale slowly.

The sword came free. It had to be done.

Hadn't it?

"Is this a kindness?" asked Tresantes.

Miltiades shot a glance towards Larmenes, but he appeared past caring what was said.

"That. Or a necessity."

The Spartan nodded, and stepped aside, giving Miltiades space.

Miltiades considered, the blade still held by his side. It was the wrong weapon. It was made for hacking, for beating on an armoured opponent. But to bring it down on a man lying sick and helpless... It hardly seemed possible. Yet look at Olorus, so swiftly dispatching his man.

Trojan horse.

If he didn't act, he was risking others – possibly everyone, possibly the whole venture, with all the ramifications for Athens, desperate for a safeguarded food supply. But...it still seemed so bizarre, so unlikely, even when he had seen what he had seen...

But what had he seen?

He rubbed his eyes with his free hand.

And Crotus – was it truly as Photios had described, or was there another explanation? Was it some sickness that robbed the senses, dulled the feelings of pain? Was there definitely a connection between those incomprehensible dead things in the hill and this man before him?

He sheathed his sword. "We wait."

It took longer than he expected, in the end. Evening fell, with the cries of strange birds mourning the coming dark, and still Larmenes lingered. Photios coughed outside the tent, reporting that Callias was seeking him – the men were gathering for the meeting they had been promised. Tomorrow, Miltiades had hissed. Tell them we will gather and talk, like good Athenians must do, tomorrow.

"Very well," Photios had replied, though he sounded troubled.

Larmenes sank further into the fever, and now the veins running from the wound on his face showed as a web of raised dark lines beneath the pale skin. They pulsed with every beat of his heart.

Miltiades sat with his head in his hands, until he felt the Spartan shake his arm. He looked up to find Larmenes' lying with his eyes wide open, lips moving slightly. He appeared to be speaking. Miltiades knelt beside the cot.

"What is it, Larmenes?"

"...I see them..."

"Who?" asked Miltiades, then, before he could stop himself, added, "The gods?"

Larmenes stared into the air, eyes widening. Miltiades couldn't help glancing up at the roof of the tent himself, but there was nothing there. Nothing that he could see, anyway, in the flickering light of a small oil lamp.

"Don't let them..." whispered Larmenes. "Don't..."

And he started shaking, his muscles suddenly tightening. His jaw clamped tight, and then finally he slumped, released. There was a sudden new reek as his bowels voided.

"This was kindness?" asked the Spartan in the silence.

"This is learning," said Miltiades, and he leaned forward, watching. He tentatively raised a hand and brushed it down across the younger man's eyes, feeling the tickle of his eyelashes as he closed the lids.

At first, Larmenes appeared as he was, a dead man. His face – the unbandaged, unravaged side - relaxed, and took on that stillness that speaks of peace in whatever follows life. It was one thing that gave Miltiades hope; that no matter how badly life may end, there appeared to be something calm and quiet on the other side.

But then a ripple flickered across Larmenes' eyelids. Miltiades leaned back, breath catching. It was what he had been expecting, but that didn't make the reality any less confronting.

Larmenes' eyes cracked open. But it wasn't Larmenes anymore.

Now, he had to do it now. His hand went to his sword hilt, but the Spartan stopped him. He held a long slim knife in his other hand.

"This is better."

Miltiades nodded, tind held out his hand. Tresantes raised an eyebrow.

"I can do it."

"No. I let this happen. This is my responsibility."

"Then do it quickly. Do not hesitate."

Larmenes was already levering himself up off the bed, dead eyes fixed upon them. Miltiades forced him back and plunged the blade in one socket, deep until the width of the blade was impeded by bone. Larmenes fell slack, his weight pulling his head clear of the knife.

Miltiades looked at the smeared blood and other substances on the knife blade, and swallowed. Tresantes gently pulled it from his hand, then jabbed it into the dirt several times to clean it.

"We will need to build a bonfire. Burn him."

"Yes," said Tresantes. "But later. There isn't much night left – you should sleep."

Miltiades took stock, and realised how exhausted he felt. How spent. Gods, it was only their first day here. He had an overwhelming urge to just leave; just pack up and go. Why did he leave his home? Why was he not sitting in the seclusion of his courtyard, reading? He was not his uncle. If the other Miltiades had been overwhelmed and killed here, then he had no chance of making this work. It was laughable. The Pisistratids didn't have to kill him – they just had to give him an order to essentially go kill himself, and he jumped, he obeyed. And when news got back to his family – if news ever got back – the tyrants could shrug their shoulders and say "hey, we were just trying to guarantee the grain supply. If he couldn't hack it..."

Miltiades let Tresantes guide him out of the tent. The Spartan then bent and plucked at a handful of long grass.

"Aren't you going to sleep?"

"Yes. But after I feed Rabbit."

Miltiades looked up at the night sky. A familiar sight, yet here and now it felt so cold and distant. He was suddenly struck by such a feeling of loneliness.

"I'll come with you." He bent and pulled up some grass as well, feeling faintly ridiculous.

"Make sure you get some roots. She likes the roots."

They walked together to the edge of the encampment. The Spartan's small pack sat here, and, against the remains of a wall, was a small fenced in area. The rabbit was within, and sat up on her haunches as they approached, nose sniffing. Miltiades watched as the Spartan fed her the grass, gently stroking her long ears while she chewed. The rabbit did not seem to mind at all, and indeed settled under the touch after she had finished eating. There was a peacefulness to the scene, of watching something so much more innocent than a human enjoy some kindness.

"It wasn't just that I wanted to be sure..." The Spartan gave no sign of having heard. "I just couldn't bring myself to do it. In action, in battle, it is something else. Self preservation kicks in. But to just butcher a man lying there... I couldn't do it. Not until he had...turned..."

The Spartan kept stroking the rabbit, which had closed its eyes in pleasure.

"You would have done it, wouldn't you? If I had asked?"

"Yes."

"What's different between you and me? Am I a coward? Or do I just overthink things too much?"

"It isn't about courage or thinking. It is just about doing. I will tell you something, Athenian – this is the great secret of Spartan training, just this: to make a decision, then to act on that decision. Wholly."

Miltiades considered this.

"Can I ask you something else?"

The Spartan grunted.

"You say that you were labelled a coward by your own people... Do you mean that you actually fled in the face of the enemy? Something like that?"

"No. I was called coward because I disobeyed an order."

"Ah. No, I didn't have you pegged as a shield dropper. Can I hazard a guess, that the order had something to do with animals?"

The Spartan looked at him in surprise. "How did you know that?"

"It seemed to fit. Watching you."

The Spartan was silent for a long moment, stroking the rabbit, who twitched her nose at his touch.

"We were raiding our neighbours, the Argives. Not a full invasion, just a quick attack to remind them to fear us. We fought a small action, burned some farms. I was in one of the raiding parties. My officer ordered me to kill the oxen at one of the farms. Not for meat, nor for sacrifice, just to stop the Argives having them. There were calves, just born, with their mother. I could not see why they should suffer for an old argument over borders, which had nothing to do with them. So I refused."

"What happened?"

"I was arrested on the spot. Chained."

"And the oxen? The calves?"

"Were killed anyway."

"Did they make you watch?"

"I was unconscious by then." He smiled bitterly. "They didn't chain me easily, Athenian."

"No, I don't suppose they did... What is it, can you say? About animals. Why they mean so much to you."

The Spartan stared at the ground for some minutes before finally speaking. "In them I see the true hand of the gods, divorced of petty greed and malice, and I marvel."

"And in men? Do you see the work of the gods in men, as well?"

"In men I see nothing but disappointment."

"You should have been an Athenian, Tresantes. You are too deep a thinker to be a Spartan, I fear. Goodnight."

He walked to his tent, where he could hear someone snoring within. Zander was sitting in the tent mouth, his head nodding on his chest. Miltiades shook him gently.

"I wasn't sleeping..."

"Well, go and don't sleep in your bed, then. I'm just going to set a watch on the wall, and I'll join you.

"No need. Photios already took care of that."

"Ah. Good. Then goodnight. I don't suppose you packed away any of the good wine?"

Zander had, though its flavour was somewhat spoiled by the hide wineskin he had transported it in. Miltiades took a couple of gulps, and lay back on his blankets, his cloak spread over him. Zander was soon snoring gently beside him. He worried for a moment that his mind would not let him sleep, or worse, would hound him with nightmares. For now he knew that his uncle was indeed most likely dead - slain or eaten by unspeakable horrors - but before the grief he could feel hovering at the edges of his thoughts could take hold, the labours of the day caught up and his consciousness slid away smoothly into sleep.

SEVEN

························

PERSEPHONE

"**M**iltiades?"

He came awake, wondering for a moment where he was. Zander was gone, his bedding neatly folded.

"What is it?" he croaked.

"The watch reports movement."

He came fully awake, a snake of fearful nausea loosening his stomach. "Like what?"

"Riders."

Ah. Then at least all it could be was a mob of Thracians looking for payment of a debt...

He dressed quickly, pulling on his clean tunic and his cloak, and slipping his head and arm through his sword belt.

"Show me," he said to the man outside.

On the way to the wall, they passed Metramandes, supervising a dozen men collecting usable timber.

"Don't forget our assembly today," called the metic.

Miltiades lifted a hand in acknowledgement but didn't stop. At the wall, he found a man pacing nervously up and down. He looked greatly relieved to see Miltiades.

"Ah," he said, cocking his thumb back at the wall. "There's some barbarians here to see you."

"How many?" asked Miltiades, taking hold of the wall to hoist himself up.

"I'd say all of them."

Miltiades grunted. Half on top of the wall, he found himself staring at two score or more Thracians sitting on horseback, with another four score on foot behind them, all armed. At the fore sat King Olorus astride his horse.

Miltiades hauled himself upright on top of the wall, and nodded at the king.

"You," said Olorus, stabbing his finger at Miltiades. "You are a strange guest. You save my life, then leave very fast and rude. And you steal my horses."

"As you say, King Olorus. It doesn't look good. But I had my reasons."

"So today I gather some men, and come here. And all the way here I argue with myself – what do I do? Honour this man? Or destroy his little camp?"

Miltiades heard a noise from the sentry behind him. It sounded as if he was choking.

"And have you made a decision?"

"My daughter, Hegesipyle, says you rude and arrogant, and need lesson. But she said you asking about the dead men, and then leave my bria. So I am thinking... Either you suddenly very scared, or you think you got a problem back here at your camp... Is that your reason, Greek? You have a problem back here?"

"I did. But it is dealt with."

"All dealt with? Properly dealt with?"

"Yes." Miltiades felt the fingers on his hand curl at the memory. He forced them open. The Thracian watched, and nodded.

"So we have to trust each other. A problem like that – either at my bria, or here in your camp – is a problem for both of us. You see that?"

"I do."

"In that case..." The king threw a leg over his horse and dismounted, grimacing and rubbing his thigh. He looked up at

Miltiades and bowed his head. "I honour you, Greek. Miltiades of Athens. You save my life, and more than that – you save me from dishonouring my life by becoming one of them."

Miltiades noticed a sudden urge to urinate. He nodded stiffly in return.

"I thank you, King Olorus. And now, about those horses. I have a business proposition for you. And for something else you may provide, too..."

The king's eyes narrowed. "Now we talking. You and me, we going to be good friends."

....

"This is ridiculous," said Metramandes, surging to his feet.

"I'm sure he will be here soon," said Photios.

"Not good enough." Metramandes strode into the centre of the small bare space they had cleared in the ruins to act as the agora of their new town. "Comrades! Colleagues! I wish to speak."

The colonists were gathered in a loose semi-circle, some standing, some sitting. The hubbub of conversation gradually fell away and they looked at the metic with serious faces.

"We joined together in a venture. A business venture. A chance to gain land, money...and for some such as I, that most elusive prize of all, Athenian citizenship!"

There was some laughter at this, and Callias, standing beside Photios, could feel the positive regard they held for this outsider. For who wouldn't be chuffed to know that even while Metramandes was wealthier than they, they still possessed something he wanted?

"Leadership of this expedition has been sorely lacking. Now I know that Miltiades is a decent man, and comes from a respected Eupatrid family with a fine sporting tradition. But look at where he has led us... First, we are nearly involved in a very costly fight with the Lemnians."

"Which he got us out of with his courage!" hissed Callias under his breath. Photios patted him on the arm.

"And then we are brought here." Metramandes opened his arms wide and swept them about, inviting the assembled men to look at the ruined township they were camped in. "To this foul place. Now, none of us, I would say, could be called cowards...but that which we face here is beyond anything anyone could have imagined. Whatever foul plague this is, that can turn innocent men into ravenous creatures such as we have seen... Well, I say to you, this is no fit place for decent Greeks."

There was some applause at this, and many heads turned nodding to their neighbours.

"And where is Miltiades? Why did he seek to delay this assembly once already? Why does he not appear to answer these concerns now? I put it to you, gentlemen, that the time has come for new leadership. A new plan. A new beginning somewhere else. And I say-"

"There!" cried Callias, pointing.

Miltiades stood on a half-collapsed wall, hands on hips.

"Ah! Our missing leader," cried Metramandes. "At last! Just in time for the vote-"

"There isn't going to be any vote."

"Says you."

"Says me and my new friends."

More men clambered up onto the wall beside him. Men wearing pointed caps and patterned cloaks.

"This is Embades, that's Bolinthos. And these are a few of their friends. They work for me."

"Mercenaries. Barbarian mercenaries," snarled Metramandes.

"Let's call them keepers of the peace. Just like the Skythians employed by the Pisistratids."

"You think you can just silence debate?"

"No. I'm Greek, and an Athenian at that. I know that there always has to be debate. But the situation is too dangerous to allow any silly risky decisions made in a moment of panic. That puts us all in danger. I can't allow that. As duly appointed leader of this expedition, now of this polis, I won't."

Metramandes growled, looking about him at the men standing and watching silently, then back at the eight armed Thracians standing on the wall.

"You have led us awry. You exposed us to some plague."

"There is a sickness here, it is true. But I understand it better than you. We can survive here."

"Survive? Is that all? I came here to make money!"

"Money will be made. And grain will flow to Athens. And our Thracian neighbours will help teach us to defend ourselves against the Hadesmen. And we have the wall..."

"Didn't seem to do your uncle much good, did it? Can't see the previous owners here prospering!"

"We will finish it. Improve on it. And then we will be safe."

"Stuck on this little finger of dirt? With nothing but a...a vegetable patch to share between all of us? Listen, Miltiades, I came out here to get some decent land. If you can't keep your end of the bargain, then the whole thing is off."

Miltiades stared at the metic. "Understand this: we stay. Or rather, I stay. Those who wish to leave when Phillipus returns are free to do so."

There was muttering at the name of the captain.

"There is land enough on this side of the wall for all to have a decent holding. We will mount a watch on the wall itself to guard ourselves against any Hadesmen. We will build ships and safeguard the Hellespont. Your wives and children will be safe to join you. There will be a life here for you."

Miltiades looked around at the men's faces. They were hard to read – they were frowning, but that was probably because they were listening intently. He hoped.

"But hear me – while I said you are free to leave, I mean it. What you are not free to do is to try to convince others to leave with you or in any other way undermine me. I will suffer no betrayal-"

He hesitated. Thrice betrayed.

"Understood?"

"I'm sure we all understand you very well."

"No. I mean you, Metramandes. Do you understand?"

The metic's eyes blazed, but he nodded tightly.

"Then this assembly is over. Back to work."

Miltiades climbed down from the wall, finding Callias and Teron waiting.

"Cousin..." said Callias.

"Back to work, like I said."

"Well done," drawled Teron. "Handled like a true Eupatrid."

"Go and clean yourself again," said Miltiades. "I can still smell shit on you."

A watch on the wall meant fewer men to do the work of establishing a viable camp. In the end Miltiades designated three men to do sentry duty at a time, dividing the wall into thirds of about a mile each. And of course there were then six men missing at a time when it was time to relieve them, for the three going out and then the three coming back tended to dawdle. He found it hard to understand – there was something of the rebellious adolescent about the mood of the colonists when it came to this, yet it was for their own safety. It seemed that they somehow blamed him for the monstrous threat that apparently stalked the wild hills – but none came forward to say that they wished to leave when Phillipus returned. He hoped that didn't mean there would be a mass exodus, unannounced, on that day. It would be a terrible thing indeed if the expedition fell apart and he had to return to Athens and report that to the Pisistratids. What would they do?

The positive thing was that over the next couple of days, the ruins were cleaned up and put in some order, and a group of men under Photios went out onto the flat land to the south and drew up boundaries for plots of land. While they would be forced to plough by hand this time, they would soon be able to get some oxen in to help. To add to their stock of supplies, there were fish to be caught, and wild game too. Miltiades worried about how Tresantes would accept them hunting the latter, but the Spartan had shrugged when he first broached the subject.

After a couple of days, when it appeared that his command was being accepted, he relieved the colonists of sentry duty and instead told the Thracians to take over. Once he made himself understood, with gestures and drawings in the dirt, they were initially keen, happy to escape the boredom of the camp. But when Miltiades sent Callias to check on them, the young man returned to report that all but one warrior had disappeared to go hunting; and the remaining man was napping.

So it was back to using their own men, and instead sending the Thracians out to hunt, which they did with a gusto, and far more successfully than the Greeks.

Then Phillipus returned, the trireme cutting smoothly through the waters to the jetty. Any bad blood from the brawl seemed to have been forgotten in the excitement at seeing a link from home, and the pile of stores on the ship's deck. Even more welcome were the couple of dozen family members who had journeyed out to join their menfolk.

Phillipus would not dock the ship at first, standing grim-faced in the bow as he took in the burgeoning encampment. Miltiades spoke to him from the dock, assuring him that there had been no further outbreaks of the Hades plague, and finally the captain agreed to land.

"You should know something. Hipparchus is dead," was the first thing he said when he was sitting back in Miltiades' tent with a full wine cup in his hand. Miltiades had summoned Callias and Photios to join them, along with Zander.

"What? How?"

"Murdered. Or assassinated. Depends how you want to see it."

"What do you mean?"

Phillipus explained.

It was no secret in Athens that Hipparchus had an eye for beauty; especially if it came in the form of a well-shaped young man from a good family. At that time in Athens, it was generally agreed that one of the most beautiful of those was a young Eupatrid named Harmodius. The trouble for Hipparchus was that Harmodius was already attached to another man, Aristogeiton. Hipparchus, however, was never one to let a little thing like that stand between him and what he wanted. He began by making some overt moves on Harmodius anyway, sending messages and gifts. This left Aristogeiton seething – but what could he do? How do you tell one of the ruling tyrants of the city to back off? Then one day Hipparchus approached Harmodius publicly, in the agora. Aristogeiton was there, too, but Hipparchus totally ignored him and propositioned Harmodius. To Hipparchus' great surprise, he was rebuffed. The young Harmodius, dripping that arrogant contempt that comes so easily to those blessed by the gods with good looks, looked Hipparchus up and down and refused with a contemptuous laugh, before strolling off arm and arm with the triumphant Aristogeiton. Hipparchus was gobsmacked. He had got too used to getting what he wanted, and this insult was too much. He planned his revenge.

The time was drawing near for the Panathenaic Festival, the great religious holiday established by the old boy, Pisistratus himself, as a way of drawing the people together into a cohesive whole. All of Athens loved the Festival – there were sporting events to watch, and sacrifices to the goddess Athena that meant everyone got to feast on some meat. And it served as a rare chance for the girls of the Eupatrid class to put on their best robes, do their hair and makeup, and display themselves for future husbands while they took part in the procession taking a new robe for the statue of Athena up to her temple on the Acropolis. It just so happened that one of those eager young girls was the younger sister of Harmodius – and she breathlessly told her family how the Pisistratids had selected her to act as one of the basket bearers who walked at the front of the procession. Her!

But on the day of the practise run, when the girls and their families gathered at the base of the Acropolis, Hipparchus took his revenge. He loudly demanded to know what a strumpet like her was doing thinking she could lead such a holy procession... especially when it seemed obvious to everyone how close she was to her brother. How unnaturally close. Oh no, it wouldn't do at all – this procession was for virgins only.

While she ran home in tears, utterly humiliated, Hipparchus had sought out the stricken Harmodius in the crowd and grinned at him broadly. How do you like that, sunshine?

For this public insult, Harmodius and Aristogeiton made plans to kill Hipparchus. As an afterthought, they decided they had best kill Hippias, too – it seemed unlikely he would react well to the murder of his brother.

The day they chose was the Panathenaea itself. Nearly shitting themselves with nerves, they loitered in the early morning agora, knives concealed beneath their tunics. They had hoped to catch both brothers leaving their mansion – but Hippias was delayed at the last instant, and Hipparchus set out alone. Panicking that they would not get another chance, they leapt on him and stabbed him to death. The Skythians came running at the sound of this screams and turned the beautiful Harmodius into a pin cushion with their arrows. Aristogeiton they took alive.

Hippias was furious. His brother may have vexed him, but he was family. He had Aristogeiton tortured, certain that the attack must have been politically motivated, and that there were other accomplices. But Aristogeiton would not give over any other names – either because there weren't any, and he was a strong enough man not to just name innocents to possibly save himself, or because he was strong enough not to give up. Gossip around the agora said that Hippias had gone to see him, lying filthy in his cell. 'You just need to give me the others' names,' Hippias had said. Aristogeiton had looked at the tyrant from his puffed, blackened eyes, and said that if Hippias would take his hand, he would finally tell. Hippias stepped forward eagerly, taking the other man's outstretched hand. 'Well,' he asked, leaning in. 'Who were they?' Aristogeiton had brought his bloodied face up close, and said...'What kind of a piece of shit are you, to take the hand of the man who killed your brother?' And he laughed and laughed. He was still laughing, said the gossip, when Hippias cut his throat.

"Since then," said Phillipus, "things have become a little... tense in Athens. Hippias has changed. It isn't just grief. He suspects everyone. If I was you, Miltiades, I wouldn't give him any cause to remember that here you sit, in the right position to cut off Athens' grain."

Once the ship was unloaded, Phillipus put his oarsmen to work helping build more of the wall. It was a good call – the shared labour with those colonists doing the same that day helped to further wash away the bad blood of the recent violence.

"Besides," said Phillipus. "I'd rather know that I am sailing into a safe port, rather than having to spend time every visit trying to work out if it is safe to land."

"When will you be able to return?" asked Miltiades.

Phillipus scratched his beard. "As soon as I can. As long as I don't think it will give Hippias or his agents any reason to suspect me of any treachery."

"You mean, don't be so obviously attached to me, in case he decides I am an enemy?"

The captain grinned. "Something like that."

It was evening. Phillippus and Miltiades lay back on cots in the latter's tent, sharing a small amphora of wine. The captain turned silent, staring into the coals of the small brazier they had burning near the tent flap for heat.

"Tell me about Egypt," said Miltiades.

Phillipus opened his mouth, then shut it again, then glanced across at him. "No. I do not talk about that. Talking only serves to bring the horror back to life. I prefer it to lie dead and buried."

"Yes, but is it? If you cannot bear to speak of it, surely it is already there, haunting you. Maybe the opposite is true – your best path to be free of it is to stop trying to get rid of it."

The triarch frowned, swirling the dregs around in his wine cup. "Maybe... You are a strange man, for a Eupatrid. You think a lot. Maybe too much."

"Maybe."

"One day I will tell you. But not this day. I'm nowhere near drunk enough tonight. Just pray to the gods that you are right, and you can keep this place safe."

The next morning Miltiades watched the trireme pull out of sight down the coast, wondering how long until they would return. They had a good store of supplies now, and seed planted. They knew the best fishing spots, and the Thracians were doing an excellent job providing them with game. The ruins of the camp were looking more orderly, and wooden frames were going up for simple houses. There was a large pile of stones gathered to continue the work on the wall, under the supervision of the two stone masons, Hermolaos and Agathon. And no more Hadesmen had been spotted.

Later that day a Thracian rider arrived. When Miltiades appeared, having been summoned by the colonists on watch, the Thracian told him that King Olorus wished to see him. Miltiades bid him wait, and jogged back to saddle up the Thracian horses.

"You come, too," he told Callias.

"And Teron?"

Miltiades hesitated. He was going to take Zander or Photios, but the look in his cousin's eye moved him to agree. Callias grinned when he nodded, and called out to his friend. Miltiades watched them together. Their fondness for each other was obvious, but there was something in Teron's manner he did not like. He saw in him the same arrogance of some of the more beautiful Eupatrid girls – so assured of their place, so used to adoration. No one should be so sure of themselves, he felt. It just didn't seem fair to everyone else.

He told the young men to bring their swords, just in case.

The ride to the bria was more familiar. Miltiades felt that he would be able to pick his way unguided, soon. Once there, they were ushered into the hall of the king. Olorus was in discussion with an old man who stood by his throne – beside, not before. At least, he appeared old, but it was hard to tell as the man was wrapped in a long dark cloak, and hooded. Olorus raised a hand in greeting as they entered, and the man with him fell silent and turned to look. He appeared to be staring at Miltiades.

The man left the king's side and advanced down the hall – or rather, seemed to glide since they could not see his feet. Miltiades was conscious of adjusting his stance, balancing his weight on the balls of both feet, as if about to fight, and felt a similar shift in the other two. But the figure stopped, and threw back the hood. Underneath, he was a pale skinned man with a shaven head, tattooed on both cheeks.

"You," he said to Miltiades. "You have the look of someone who has been touched."

A rude retort rose up in Miltiades throat, but he stifled it as he looked past the man to the king, who was watching the exchange. This was obviously some kind of Thracian holy man or seer – it probably didn't do to mock them. It was bad enough back in Athens, where there were those who would stare amazed if you professed any doubt in the gods. Here? Who knew how they would react if you mocked their religious sensibilities.

The seer nodded. "Yessss. You have been marked. But for what? Show me your hand."

Miltiades awkwardly raised his hand. The seer hissed and caught it, pulling it to him, palm uppermost. He studied it, running one finger along the lines there. Then he spat, letting a fall of white spittle land. Miltiades jerked, but the seer held him firm, smiling as he rubbed the gluey mess over the skin.

"You shall live forever, Greek. It shall be written."

"Don't you fellows usually say 'it is written'?"

The seer stared at him for an uncomfortably long time. "This fate you write yourself, Greek. A black sea is rising, and you should run."

"You mean a flood?"

Miltiades looked over the seer's shoulder at Olorus, who was frowning in their direction. Shut up, damn it, he told himself. Don't get into an argument. This isn't the agora.

"An ocean." The seer suddenly dropped his hand – threw it down, more to the point, and turned away.

"Wait," said Miltiades before he could stop himself. "Did you...did you see anything there about betrayal?"

"I spoke all I saw."

The seer swept from the room without another word, and Miltiades wiped his hand on the side of his tunic. The encounter had unsettled him, but he tried to shake it off. "You wished to see me, King Olorus?"

"Yes," said the king. "We must speak of the future."

"King Olorus, I'm sorry, but I don't really go in for fortune telling..."

"I do not speak of the seer's words. Though you would do well to heed them. He has foretold many things, that one."

"And that's the thing," murmured Teron. "Predict the future often enough and you're bound to get it right once or twice."

Miltiades coughed pointedly, but couldn't help agreeing with the sentiment.

"I speak of you and us," said the king. "My men tell me your camp grows, and more of your people join you."

"That is so. Athens wishes Chersonnesus to be a successful polis."

"So. Your people will always seek to build here. As long as the grain flows from the cities of the Black Sea."

So the old fellow understood the strategic concerns. Miltiades nodded.

"Then we must be friends."

"That is what Athens wants. That is what I want, King Olorus."

The Thracian nodded, then sighed heavily, staring at Miltiades. "So you should marry my daughter."

"What?!" squawked Miltiades.

"Then we are bound, you and I. Your people and mine."

"But...but... Do you mean right now?"

"No! What a foolish idea. She does not even know you. You think I am some barbarian to just give you my only daughter? Here and now?"

That was pretty much how it worked in Athens amongst the Eupatrid class, Miltiades mused.

"I don't think she even likes me!"

"Then make her like you."

Miltiades conjured an image of her cold stare and fought to control a shudder. Make her like him? Then a thought struck him. "And have you told her?"

The king seemed to flinch. "Not yet. But soon."

Olorus clapped his hands and servants brought jugs of wine. Miltiades winced at the sight of the thick sediment swirling around the cup he was given. By the time they had drunk each other's health, his mouth felt full of it. He could see particles on Callias' teeth. Teron was nursing his still rather full cup – Miltiades suspected he had only been pretending to drink. That cheered him a little.

But...married? Him? It was not something he had pictured happening any time soon. He had never had any real interest in the insipid girls his mother shoved his way. Indeed, he had begun to become accustomed to the idea of remaining unmarried. He had certainly never entertained the idea of marrying a barbarian princess. Zeus, his mother would implode.

"Now I must show you something," said Olorus, his face turning grim.

They followed him out of the hall, accompanied by his warriors and the elders. They proceeded right through the bria and down a short path to a clearing, where a throng of Thracians waited. In the centre was a pit with a large wooden covering, such as you might find over a well, but this was square and easily four times larger than any wellhead. A man caught Miltiades' eye, as he was naked but for a breechcloth, and was held fast by several armed warriors. He looked ashen, but his eyes glared with defiance.

"What's happening?" asked Callias. Miltiades shrugged, but had a feeling whatever it was, it wasn't going to be nice.

There was movement on the trail behind them, and three women appeared. Hegesipyle and a companion – another tattooed noblewoman - were supporting a trembling young woman between them. The women formed up on the opposite side of the clearing. The prisoner did not look in their direction, nor did the girl glance once at him. She kept her gaze fixed firmly on the dirt at her feet.

Olorus stepped forward, and spoke. He turned to the woman, and his tone suggested a question. Hegesipyle put an arm around her thin shoulders, and hugged her. The girl nodded, and pointed a finger at the prisoner, without taking her eyes from the ground.

The king turned to the Greeks. "This man has done wrong. This man has forced this woman against her will, taken what he had no right to take. This day he dies."

The king shouted an order, and several men ran forward, taking up ropes attached to one side of the cover. They strained, heaved, and the lid slid away, revealing the pit below. Immediately there came a clacking, like the strains from a myriad of giant cicadas, and then the smell hit them, the smell of decay.

"Oh," groaned Callias.

"Father Zeus," said Teron.

Miltiades bit his lip and forced himself to take a step forward, conscious of the gaze of the Thracians. He swallowed carefully.

The pit was full of heads.

The heads were alive.

The clicking and clacking was the working of their jaws, as they gnashed the air. Those with one or two eyes still intact stared unblinking up at the people standing above them. Those without reacted to the excitement of the others. Some were mostly skulls, with the barest strips of skin and tendon holding them together. Few had ears or noses, lost amongst the biting, tearing mound of teeth.

Olorus met Miltiades eye, then pointed at the prisoner. The man had just enough time to finally look afraid, and raise his voice in protest, before the guards thrust him down into the pit. The crowed surged forward. The pit was at least ten feet deep. He landed feet first, and fell forwards onto his hands, dislodging heads, his arms plunging elbow deep into the rotting mass. He quickly thrust himself upright, standing and waving his arms, now streaked with corruption, to maintain his balance. Then he screamed, as one head latched onto the back of his heel. At the same time another got it's teeth into his toes, biting and chewing furiously. The man threw back his head and yelled, not daring to shake the head clear lest he fall.

Miltiades looked around the crowd. Most watched with avid delight. Some appeared a little nauseated, a feeling he could identify with. He felt eyes upon him, and looked across to find Hegesipyle staring at him as she rubbed the back of the young woman, whose face was buried in her shoulder.

Oh boy, he thought, just you wait till your father talks to you.

One of the guards reversed his spear and leaned down to shove the man with the butt. He fell sideways, and greedy waiting mouths took his fingers. Black tongues swirled to catch the blood that flowed from his wounds. He tried to rise, heads attached to him like foul ticks. He beat at them, knocking some away, but others were always beneath him, straining to catch hold. He was weakening, the horror and the blood loss robbing him of his strength to resist.

With a sudden desperate cry the man threw himself towards the side of the pit, landing right beneath the Greeks. He jumped, scrabbling at the edge. Miltiades was aware of Callias suddenly standing beside him, both of them staring down into the eyes of the man below. But his gaze was like a cornered animal, unseeing, and for that Miltiades was grateful. But then Callias was kneeling at the edge, reaching down and grabbing the injured man by the wrist. He hauled backward, the man's hand slick with mud and blood and putrid waste. Miltiades shot a look towards Olorus, who was watching him, a hand held out to check his warriors. The king's eyes narrowed, and his head tilted to the side.

"For the Gods' sake, help me," gasped Callias. Miltiades glanced back at Teron, but the other youth appeared rooted to the spot, face twisted in disgust. He looked again into the eyes of the condemned man – and somewhere, back in the darkest recess of his pupils, something was already burning.

He drew his sword from its sheath, and, kneeling, chopped down into the back of the man's neck. Callias lost his grip, and the man tumbled back into the pit like a stunned sacrificial ox.

Callias looked up at him.

"It was too late," said Miltiades wearily. "He was already infected, you understand?"

Callias stared, then nodded, then abruptly leaned forward and vomited weakly into the mud. A thin stream of bile ran forward, dripping down into the pit.

Olorus gave an order, and his warriors fished the man's body from the hole with hooks. He was dragged up, his head dangling back over the edge, and a warrior hacked it off with two blows of his rhomphaia. The head bounced among the others, and for a while its neighbours worked at it, biting at the ears and nose and lips. But after a few minutes, they appeared to lose interest, and fell silent. The man's grey, torn head lay quiet and bleeding amongst the corruption.

The dead eyes opened.

Miltiades almost expected to see some emotion in them, some rancour, or regret. But they were just the same as all the rest – empty.

He suddenly realised that Olorus stood beside him.

"You understand?" asked the king.

"Yes," said Miltiades. "I understand." He suddenly felt the urge to spit, a sensation of something poisonous in his mouth.

....

"You're very quiet," said Miltiades when they were more than half way back to Chersonnesus. His young cousin had ridden alongside him without having spoken a word since they mounted. Teron was riding behind. "What are you thinking about?"

"Did you see the girl with the king's daughter?" asked Callias. "Not the...victim. The other one."

Miltiades looked at his young cousin in surprise. That was not what he had expected. "Kind of. I confess I was a little distracted by the huge pit of heads. Why?" He noted a change in Callias's colour. Was he blushing? "Um... Attractive, would you say?"

"I would call her so," said Callias. "Even with those tattoos."

Teron snorted.

"Yes," said Miltiades. "I think one would grow used to them. They...set off the eyes."

"Bisanthe," said the younger man. "That's what her name is."

There was a pause. Miltiades wondered when he had found the time to dig up that piece of information.

"So what did that crazy old man mean?" asked Teron from where he rode behind them. "Something about you living forever?"

"Haven't the foggiest."

"Hey, I know," continued Teron brightly. "Maybe he meant you will end up being bitten by one of the Hadesmen. And then you'll never die. Not properly. Just keep on stumbling about the wilderness..."

"Fuck off, Teron," said Miltiades, and kicked his horse to move him further ahead. It was a relief when the land fell away, revealing the bustle that was his growing little polis below.

....

Phillipus returned, but this time with fewer supplies and no additional colonists. Those who had been expecting family members cursed him or slunk away dolefully.

"You owe me some money," said the trirarch. "I bought this lot of goods myself."

"Whatever for?" asked Miltiades. "This is a state-sanctioned colony. Why not go to Hippias? And why not bring more people?"

"Listen," said Phillipus. "Things are getting worse in Athens. Hippias has lost it. I didn't want to make it any worse for you. You know what he expects me to do on this trip? Map any defences you have built."

"Well, you can tell him about the wall. That's all we've got."

"He isn't interested in your wall. It's if you have any defences to stop a landing from the sea that concerns him. That's right. He's already planning on how to knock you off your stranglehold here."

"Shit. We haven't done anything that he should find alarming. Wait – has someone been saying otherwise in Athens?"

"Hades' ballsack, you know Athens. There is always talk, especially when it concerns a Eupatrid. All I'm saying is, you better do something to get in the good books soon."

"Like what?"

"Grain. Get some more wheat flowing. And you can't wait for whatever you're expecting to grow in your little fields here. You need to convince the cities in the Black Sea and Propontis to start trading with Athens again."

Miltiades tapped his teeth. "I need you for that."

"I know. I told my oarsmen this was going to be an extended trip." Phillipus grinned. "They make some nice wine in the Black Sea."

Miltiades ordered Callias to stay behind – and by extension, this included Teron.

"You need to be seen to be doing your share of the labour. Make sure you both do a stint or two rebuilding the wall."

"Oh," said Callias, a strangely distant look on his face. "If you say so."

Miltiades told Zander and Photios to come with him, and on an impulse extended an invitation to Metramandes.

"Me?" said the metic.

"You have a head for business," said Miltiades. "I could use your help bartering."

Metramandes tried to look indifferent, but Miltiades could see him puff up with pride. "Then I shall come."

They boarded the trireme, and at Phillipus' order the ship backed out into the waters of the Propontis, but instead of turning south to enter the Aegean, turned to the north-east and headed further up the straits. It took half the day, the men pulling against the current, until they slipped between the narrowing coast and out into the expanse of the Euxine, the Black Sea. The helmsman pulled on the great tiller,the port side oarsmen rested their oars, and the warship turned to follow the northern coast line.

Here the land was much less steep, the beach giving way to large expanses of meadow and forests. You could see what had lured Greek colonists here over the years – plenty of land for men to farm, timber for houses and ships. It was even here in colonies like these that the phalanx was born – replacing the older style of fighting where it was every man for himself in what could best be described as wild brawls, with the more collegiate idea of fellow citizen farmers standing together against outside hostile forces.

The first of the major Euxine poleis hove into view, a large city arcing around a small bay. Farms dotted the gentle slopes rising beyond the main township. Fishing boats were scattered about the bay. The city centre was a colourful mix of temples and public buildings. Most importantly, there were large warehouses down by the docks. This was a city with grain to spare for trade.

They docked, and Phillipus gave several hours' leave to the crew, who immediately headed for the nearest wine bars and brothels. Miltiades could see the captain look after them longingly, almost licking his lips, but he wanted the trirarch with them. He gazed about as they made their way to the agora and the government buildings. This was what Chersonnesus could become. This was what he could build.

They found the assembly room, and a slave ran to inform the leaders of the city that they wished to meet.

"I think," said Photios, "that I may take a short stroll."

"We'll be going in in a minute. I need you."

"You'll be fine," smiled Photios. "I shan't be long."

The old man walked off with surprising speed.

"Weak bladder?" asked Zander. Miltiades shrugged.

Shortly after, they were led into the chamber, which housed a row of benches, looking to accommodate maybe a hundred men. Today, three sat together in the centre.

"Welcome, guests, to Apollonia", said the man in the middle.

"Our thanks, and greetings from Chersonnesus. And Athens." That caused them to shift a bit and pay more attention. "We are deputised..."

"Wait, wait!" cried the man. The other two shook their heads and chanted "Quorum! Quorum!"

"Sorry?"

"If this is official state business, we must have twenty members of the oligarchy present to receive your deputation."

"Just to receive my deputation? Not even to vote on it, just to receive it?"

The trio nodded sagely.

"Well, can we get another seventeen members here?"

"Now?" asked the middle man, scratching his chin. "I suppose so. We will have to send the public slaves to track some down."

"Not Larmenes," said the man on the right. "He is on business in Bisanthe."

"And Cleotus has the gout," put in the one on the left.

"I don't care who I speak to," said Miltiades, "as long as I can put a proposition to you."

And so they waited, as the handful of public slaves were dispatched and oligarchs slowly trickled in. Finally they had the necessary twenty.

"Leaders of Apollonia," said Miltiades. "We come to ask why trade has fallen off between your city and ours. Athens has always been a good customer of the poleis of the Euxine. We would have it that the grain again flows from your fields to the markets of Athens."

"We have a new buyer," said the middle man. "He won't much like it if we cancel the contract we hold with him."

"You had a contract with us."

"Athens is far away. Darius is much closer."

"Darius? Who is Darius?"

The oligarch scoffed. "You Athenians. You act as if we are some country bumpkins, compared to you. But it is you who do not understand the world. Darius is King Darius, king of kings. The ruler of the Persian Empire. Our neighbour across the Euxine."

Miltiades frowned. "I thought the Carians and Lydians held sway on that coast."

"Then you are behind the times. All now give allegiance to the Persians."

"They seem to be spreading... But come, we are fellow Greeks. Why trade with the barbarians when you can trade with us?"

"Gold is gold. It knows no distinction."

Miltiades scratched his chin, thinking. "We can offer safeguards the Persians cannot."

"Oh?"

"The Athenian fleet is growing. We are best placed to protect your merchants from pirates, so your trade may indeed prosper. Why, we have even re-established our base on the Chersonnese. That is where we have come from. It is an interesting place. Very narrow. Very easy to blockade with just a few warships..."

That elicited a great muttering from the oligarchs. "Threats! Threats!" cried one.

"No threats," said Miltiades. "Just a promise. Trade with us, let the grain flow, and both our cities prosper. Deny us, and only one will gain."

The oligarchs bade them wait outside, and kept them there for nearly half an hour as they argued. Finally, they were ushered back inside by a sallow slave.

"Friends," smiled the middle man, though his eyes remained cold. "The full council will still need to sit and vote, but we are confident agreement will be reached. We are delighted to be in business with Athens again."

"You are wise," said Miltiades. He hesitated. "With business done, I wonder if I might ask you something. Have the people of Apollonia been much bothered by the Hadesmen?"

There was a beat of a second, and then the oligarchs cackled loudly.

"Are you saying," asked the middle man, a strange grin on his face, "that you have seen a Hadesman?"

"Yes." Miltiades frowned. "As have both these men." He pointed at Zander and Metramandes.

"Oh dear."

"Oh dear?"

"My friend, you have all been afflicted with the grassland fever. Or steppe fever, as it is also known."

"What do you mean? None of us are unwell."

"Oh, that is what makes the fever so pernicious. There are few symptoms – except for a certain excitability of the mind, and hallucinations."

"Hallucinations?" barked Metramandes. "What we have seen were no halllucinations!"

"Luckily," continued the middle man, "there is a treatment available, perfected by our doctors."

"The Hadesmen are real. I have destroyed one myself."

"You thought you destroyed one."

"We have lost men!"

"Who were probably killed by natives. The wild Thracians and steppe folk know all about grassland fever, and use it to their advantage. They sometimes dress in gruesome fashion when planning their thieving assaults on honest men."

"This is crazy."

"No, sir, you are crazy. Your wits are addled. Your humours are out of balance. You need treatment."

"I think we need to go..."

Miltiades signalled to the other two, and strode for the door.

"If you go now," called the middle man. "The deal is off. We want nothing to do with those who allow this sickness to spread. Such wild talk is dangerous. It impacts on production. Why, before you know it, you have a full scale panic on your hands, and no one will go out to work. No sir, that shall not do. You take the treatment, or go home empty handed."

Miltiades looked at Zander, who shrugged.

"And what is this treatment?"

"A simple herbal concoction, developed by our doctors. Drink a dose, and we are still in business."

The three huddled together.

"What do you think?" asked Miltiades.

"This is bullshit," said Zander. "They are batshit crazy if they think those things aren't real."

"Doesn't matter what they think," said Metramandes. "We need the deal, right?"

"Surely they wouldn't be trying to poison us," mused Miltiades. "What would they have to gain?"

"Exactly," said the metic. "Let's drink their crappy brew and go."

"Very well," said Miltiades, turning back to the oligarchs. "We will accept your medicine, but..."

"No, no buts. The Hadesmen are a figment of the fever. They do not exist. And as they do not exist, they are not to be spoken of. Understand? Now what about the crew of your ship – are they afflicted too?"

"No. No, it was just us." Miltiades saw Zander shoot him a look.

They were led from the council chamber to a nearby Temple of Apollo. In a small antechamber a small stooped priest stirred a large bowl. There were shelves lined with containers, and several large amphorae leaning against the walls. There was a smell in the air, almost fruit-like, and certainly not unpleasant.

"These three are for the treatment, priest," said their escort.

The priest nodded and set out three drinking bowls. He ladled a thin brown stream into each. The men stepped forward cautiously, each lifting a bowl, swirling the contents in the old habit of mixing wine to avoid a big mouthful of sediment towards the bottom.

"So... this isn't poisonous, right?" asked Miltiades. "No one has ever died from this? Or been struck blind?"

"Certainly not!" sniffed the priest.

"Have you ever taken this treatment yourself?"

"No. But I've never claimed anything so blasphemous as to have seen the dead return to life, either."

"Oh, let's just get this over with," said Metramandes. "Bottoms up." He threw the contents down his throat, and smacked his lips. "Actually, that isn't so bad."

Zander and Miltiades looked at each other, and then drained their own bowls. Their escort nodded and left the room.

"So how exactly is this supposed to work?" asked Miltiades. "How does this cure a man of seeing the Hadesmen?"

"I'm not sure about that," said the priest. "All I know is, those who take the treatment stop claiming they have seen them. Eventually..."

"Eventually?"

The priest nodded. "Some need more than one treatment. Though I've never seen anyone need more than three."

The three Athenians exchanged glances.

"So the medicine makes them recant their stories? That they have seen the dead rise?"

"I don't think I like the sound of this," Metramandes frowned, and put a hand to his stomach. "Oh."

"Priest, what exactly is in this slop?"

A deep gurgle was clearly audible from Zander's belly. He clapped a hand to it.

"Oh, this and that. Purgatives, mostly."

"Oh, shit," said Miltiades. Something was happening in his guts.

"Precisely," said the priest, looking up with a small smile. "There's a bucket in the alley behind the temple."

They ran. Or ran as well as they could, with clenched ass cheeks.

"Get out of the way!" roared Metramandes, shoving Zander aside and squatting over the wooden bucket set there. The slave went sprawling – and with that motion lost his battle of control. A jet of liquid shit instantly shot from between his legs. Miltiades stood, white-faced, grinding his teeth – then suddenly lurched forward and vomited copiously against the wall,

all the while fumbling with his breechcloth. This was too much, and he felt the sting of hot faeces blasting free behind him.

"Fuck!" croaked Metramandes, spinning around to vomit into the bucket.

Zander plucked at his stained tunic, peeling it away from his legs, then turned his head and threw up almost as an afterthought.

They stayed there in the alley for some time, before a slave appeared and beckoned to them. On shaking legs they staggered out of the stinking alleyway, to find Middleman and most of the other oligarchs waiting for them by the temple.

"So," said Middleman with a grin. "Cured, are we? Or do we need to hold you and give you another dose?"

"Oh no," said Zander, falling to his knees. "No dose. I didn't see anything. Not a thing."

"That's right," said Metramandes. "None of us saw anything."

Everyone looked to Miltiades. He was breathing hard, his stomach felt like he had been punched and he doubted he could sit happily for some time.

"Master..." croaked Zander.

"Fine. Have it your way. We didn't see them. We didn't see them tear men apart, or how they went on fighting when any other man would fall."

"That's all we wanted to hear. And so, we are in business."

They were shown to a public gymnasium where they were able to clean themselves, though the attacks continued every few minutes. All they wanted was to get away, and so they headed back to the docks, detouring several times into the back alleyways to find a quiet spot. The citizens of the polis seemed to recognise the situation, for none complained to suddenly find a stranger shitting behind their shop, and none asked them what the matter was or made any kind of eye contact.

Close to the ship, Photios caught up with them.

"Ah, there you are. I was talking to a... I say. You smell somewhat...unpleasant."

At the ship, the flute player blew a series of high pitched notes on his flute, and the oarsmen started returning from the taverns. Phillipus appeared drunk. As the ship backed away from the pier, and turned in place, the sea air seemed to do them some good. But as they hit the swells further out, the pitching of the trireme seemed to excite the last remnants of the emetic they had drunk.

"'Scuse me!" cried Zander, rushing to the side of the ship with one hand cupped to his buttocks.

"Again with the shitting?" said Phillipus. "Why does everyone shit on my ship?"

Later, when things had calmed, Photios gestured to Miltiades.

"I have a tale to tell you," said the schoolmaster. "While you dealt with the high and mighty of the land, I went for lowliest. I spoke to the beggars outside the Temple of Apollo. I have found that sometimes the truth is to be found in the meanest of places."

The teacher flushed a little as he said this, no doubt remembering with shame how Miltiades had found him. Miltiades wished he could think of something to say, but everything seemed wooden and awkward, so he merely gestured for Photios to continue.

"I found an old man from Cappadocia," he said. "Or rather, he was a young boy in Cappadocia, before he ended up in Apollonia. He told me of a day when he was very young, living in a coastal town. He told me he remembers how one day Persian riders appeared..."

••

The riders were weary, caked in dust, their horses blowing hard. The men riding at the rear kept an agitated watch back the way they had come, hands staying close to the bows carried in cases on their horses' flanks. The Persians rode into the coastal town, ordering everyone to stay inside their houses with the windows and doors barred and shuttered, and that none were to show their faces on pain of death. Some tried to protest, business owners mostly, and the reaction was swift. Several riders dismounted and beat the men ferociously, finally dragging them bloody into their homes, into the arms of their wailing wives, and slamming the doors on them. Everyone else chose to obey. It wasn't just the violence, or the fact that these were obviously household cavalry of the Persian king – it was the fact that the troopers were all quite obviously scared.

The streets were soon deserted, and the cavalry rode around, swearing and banging on any window shutters left slightly open for a peek. When the town looked empty and they were satisfied, they gathered again on the southern outskirts. Watching. Waiting. Unobserved except for one keen pair of eyes.

For one young boy was too curious to allow himself to be shut away, so had instead stolen up onto the roof of his family home. He was careful, always ducking down if he saw a Persian turn his way – but their attention was for the most part directed away.

A long time passed, and the boy was bored. He would have climbed down but he was fearful of being caught and beaten. Then one Persian rider gave a shout, and pointed, and as one they rose in their saddles, straining to see. The boy looked, too, wondering what it could be. The riders suddenly shouted to each other, and split into two groups, one galloping East, the other to the West.

And on the horizon, a black stain grew.

The boy screwed up his eyes, trying to make out what it was. And then the wind shifted, and he curled up on the rooftop, heaving himself dry of the bread he had for lunch and the porridge he had for breakfast. It felt as if he hurled up every meal he had ever eaten, and his very stomach besides, until his throat was raw from acid. Still, he was eventually able to pull himself up and peer over the low wall encircling the rooftop.

Before him stretched an army.

Though, as it came on, he saw that it was more mob than an army. It was one seething mass of people. In the front, before it, came a band of runners - like skirmishers before a line of heavy infantry. As they drew nearer the town, he saw they were about a score of young men, stripped down to breechclouts, their skin powdered in dust cut by rivulets of sweat. These youths were jogging ahead of the host, sometimes slowing, sometimes sprinting. They called back to those following them, waving their arms, and then running on. Now, as they neared the coast, and subsequently the town, they turned to the East, dashing along the flat plain.

Behind them, the great mass slowly bunched and turned after them. And now they were close enough for the boy to see them, and he never forgot them again till the end of his days. Nothing could have ever prepared him for the very wrongness of it. For here were the dead, walking. They were in differing states of decay – some mostly whole, some barely able to stagger forwards. Some wore armour, others rags or nothing at all. There were men and women, some children, but not many. They stumbled on broken feet or stumps, with splintered protruding bone and hanging intestines. And the clacking of their teeth was louder than the waves on the shore and the call of the sea birds.

As the boy watched, one of the youths tripped and went sprawling. One of his fellows swiftly ran over and pulled him upright, for the closest dead had been excited by this display and surged forward. But it was clear the man had badly injured his ankle and couldn't maintain the pace. His comrade kept glancing back, eyeing the distance between themselves and the hastening horde. Finally, he slipped the injured fellow's arm from around his neck and let him go, sprinting clear. The other man cried out, and fell, then jumped up, hopping forward as fast as he could go. But it wasn't fast enough. Clearly he was already tired. Bony fingers began to snatch at his back, and though he tried to force himself to ignore the pain and run, there is only so much the human body can endure. The living human body. The reanimated dead did not slacken, did not stop, and finally one hand, nearly stripped of all flesh, was able to wind itself in his hair and pull him down.

The boy had sometimes watched ants swarm over a grass-hopper or scorpion. More often than not it had been he who had fed the larger insect to them. And it was that image that came to his mind now as the dead clambered over each other to reach for the writhing fresh meat below them. The man's death caused a swirling whirlpool in the greater flood, but was not enough to halt it, for the others groaned, expelling dead air from their withered lungs, as they moved after the other run-ners who urged them onwards.

It took a long time for the sea to pass. The boy had long surrendered to his youth, collapsing down beside the wall and weeping.

Finally, when the nightmarish sound had passed, he dared to look again. Here there were still several dozen of the dead stalk-ing about, too far back to be driven mad by the running lures or the interest of their fellows. A few turned their dead eyes on the houses, and something deep in their brains urged them to turn aside and head for the town, some distant memories that here they would find the meat they craved.

The boy was unsure what to do – but then, with a drumming of hooves, the riders who had gone off to the west returned. They rode forwards now with their bows drawn, cantering past the dead who hissed and swiped at them, firing arrows into them as they passed by, turning in their saddles to deliver fi-nal shots straight behind them. Wheeling about and coming through again. And one by one, the dead fell, pin cushioned with arrows until one finally pierced an eye or nose or ear, and then whatever magic animated them was dispersed and they collapsed like piles of rag and bone.

When all were dealt with, the riders dismounted, and, cursing, dragged the bodies into one mound. Wood was quickly gathered, and pitch poured on from jugs. As the riders rode on to the east, after the main horde, a foul oily smoke curled into the sky behind them.

....

Miltiades stared into the water. "How many did he think there were?"

"He didn't know," shrugged Photios. "To his mind, there were more than the stars in the sky at night. Not a very accurate count."

"They were herding them. The Persians. Herding the Hadesmen."

"That was my impression as well. Or luring, rather. Seeking to draw them away from the inhabited parts of their empire."

Miltiades turned and looked back toward Apollonia, receding behind them. He drifted back towards the bow of the trireme, Photios following.

"What do we know of the Euxine? Does it end?"

"Yes, it ends. It is like a great bowl, they say."

"Then a man may walk around it."

"He might. If he did not need to find food or shelter."

"And how long would that take? How long would it take to walk all the way around this sea and end up...here?"

They looked back at the polis, its bright central buildings, its green fields receding into the distance. Its lack of decent walls.

"They are fools. Blind, stupid fools."

"They desire wealth. Like many men. And their wealth derives from their crops. How many, do you think, would go out to work the land if they feared being set upon by Hadesmen?"

Miltiades grunted. "And so instead they punish those who speak up. By calling them afflicted, and ensuring they recant. Still, this policy of theirs may well...come back to bite them."

"Indeed."

When they pulled in to the dock at Chersonessus, Miltiades was annoyed to find a large number of the men sitting around drinking and gaming with dice. Not all, he was pleased to see. The two stonemasons seemed to be missing, so hopefully they at least were still working on the wall. He spotted Teron.

"Where in Hades is Callias? Why are these men slacking off?"

"In answer to the second question, why shouldn't they? It has been nothing but work since we got here. And since you were all gallivanting off to civilisation – or the closest thing that passes for it around here - it didn't seem bloody fair to me that we all had to keep working while you had fun. I said it was up to them what they did."

"And Callias?"

"How am I supposed to know?"

"How are you supposed to know? Because normally he follows you around like a puppy, that's why."

Teron's eyes narrowed. "Well. I don't know where he is. But I can guess."

"Then don't keep me in suspense, guess away."

"Gone to visit that Thracian slut, I expect." Teron attempted to look unconcerned, but Miltiades could see that it was an act.

"I want to see him the minute he comes back."

"Good. I don't. By the way, you may wish to bathe. You smell a little...unsavoury."

Miltiades reddened and stalked off, glancing at the sun. It was too late in the day and he was too wrung out to chivvy the men into working. Instead he headed for the beach, stripping his tunic off as he went. The water was cold, and the salt stung his raw anus, but it was good to feel clean. Before long he was joined by Zander and Metramandes.

"A meeting of the minds," said the metic.

"Or the assholes," said Zander.

Metramandes laughed, and ducked under water. He came up, hair and beard dripping like Poseidon, and squirted a jet of water at the slave. Zander recoiled, tripped on some rock beneath the surface and fell backwards, struggling to keep his screwed-up face clear of the water but going under anyhow. Miltiades felt his own laughter rise from within him and with it, the loosening of muscles he hadn't even realised had been bunched so tight.

Later, he walked towards his tent, plucking at his tunic as it clung to him wetly. His feet were covered in sand, a sensation he didn't like, but he didn't want to get his boots wet since damp footwear felt even worse.

"You have a visitor," said Photios, coming down to meet him. "In your tent."

"Any sign of Callias yet?"

"Yes. He came with your guest."

"Ah." There was a strange sensation in Miltiades' stomach. "And where is he now?"

"Begging Teron for forgiveness and being ignored, I imagine."

"I'm going to have to do something about that."

Photios raised an eyebrow. "I can set you mathematic problems that would stump a genius, and that would still be easier than trying to sort out someone else's relationship problems."

There were oil lamps burning in his tent when he got there, and a silhouette thrown up onto the hide walls.

"Hello, Hegesipyle."

She turned and looked at him as he dropped the tent flap behind himself, her cool gaze raking his wrinkled damp clothing and bare feet.

"My father," she said, "is careful to always look the part of the king. Perceptions are important."

"Ah. How lucky not to be a king, then, and bound by such requirements. The joys of being a free citizen of Athens. Wine?"

She nodded.

"Usually," he said as poured – though first he had to surreptitiously wipe her cup clean with his finger tips, "couples would have a chaperone at such meetings. Especially in the evening."

She accepted the cup, rolling her eyes at him. "I hardly think my virtue is in any danger from your charms, Greek. Besides, there are four warriors lounging nearby. Were I to scream, I doubt you would live long enough to say two more words."

He felt absurdly pleased with how the meeting was going so far. Home town advantage, he supposed.

"Lucky for me you don't seem the screaming type, then. So... to what do I owe this visit? Do you... do you know about your father's plans? For us?"

She snorted. "Father is an idiot. Can I sit here?" She pointed at his camp bed.

He nodded, then lunged forward to scoop up his spare breechcloth and kick it under the bed. He tugged the blanket into place, smoothing it with his hand, then stepped back. She smirked, and made a point of lowering herself gently onto it. The sight of her on his bed, the lamplight glowing in her dark eyes, was arresting. He coughed, and made a show of making himself comfortable on a folding stool to cover. There was a pit in his stomach – he realised that her words had hurt. But what reaction was he honestly expecting? What was this now, vanity?

"I am sorry the idea holds no appeal for you. I will speak to him again and see if he will change his mind. If you like."

"Don't bother. He has a fixed idea about you Greeks. And if it wasn't you, I'd be marrying some other Thracian lordling."

"I am glad to hear I am preferable."

"Yes. I can't see you stopping me from doing what I want. Or beating me."

"Well...no... I wouldn't."

She leaned back, gazing at him over her cup, eyes glinting.

"So, Greek. Future husband. Tell me about yourself. What do you like to do? Hunt? Fight?"

"Reading," he muttered. "I like to read."

Her eyes widened, and she laughed open mouthed, not bothering to use her hand as cover. His cheeks were suddenly hot.

"Oh! Oh, my. Reading? And what is it that you read?"

"About adventure," he replied, truculently. "The old heroes. Theseus. Achilles."

"Ah. You wish to emulate such men?"

He shook his head. "The age of heroes is over."

"A sad thought." She fell silent staring down into her cup.

The silence grew, stretching out between them.

"You would have liked my father better," he said thickly. "Better than me."

"Why?"

"Oh, everybody liked him. No, correction, not everyone. The Pisistratids didn't like him. But he was exciting. He raced chariots, in the Olympics. Everyone knew his name."

"He liked horses?"

"No, not especially. He liked what they could do for him. But I think they were more of means to an end for him. He wasn't like Tresantes – you haven't met him yet."

"So, you think I would have liked him better," she shook her head. "You have offended me, Greek, to assume I would be taken in like that."

"I wasn't meaning just you. Like I said, tyrants excluded, everyone liked him."

"But not you."

"No. Not me."

Now he fell silent. An old pain stirred, like an ember suddenly hit by a fresh breeze.

"When my father ordered that I learn your language, Greek, and understand there was a world beyond the bria of the Dolonci, he woke something inside of me. A hunger. Do you understand?"

He shook himself, came back into the tent. "Yes. I think I do."

"Then you will understand why I will marry you. You are maybe not the most interesting of men. Your name may not be known by everyone. But you may help me see what is beyond the next hill, beyond the horizon. I want to see. I want to know. Do you understand me?"

He looked at her, noted the need in her eyes. "Yes," he said.

"And will you show me?"

"That much I can do."

She nodded. "But," she said, holding a hand up warningly. "Understand, that I will not love you."

Miltiades called Photios and Tresantes to him, and escorted the princess and her retinue of warriors back to the wall. Agathon and Hermolaos were there, with a couple of others, continuing to rebuild the fallen section despite the late hour. He was pleased with their work ethic – at least some could see the necessity of getting things done. There was now a shaped gap with blocks left as steps for horses to pick their way through, single file.

When the Thracians had passed through, and cantered off towards their bria, he turned to speak to the stonemasons.

"We should be able to get a gate hung in that gap," said Agathon, wiping sweat from his brow. "If you can spare a carpenter for a bit."

"I want more than that. I want you to have stones shaped and ready to fill that gap on my order."

The stone masons glanced at each other. "Faster to do a gate…"

"I do want a gate. But I also want it to be ready to turn into a solid wall."

He turned and strode off, Photios and Tresantes following. The stonemasons watched him go, then stood next to each other, staring at the gap. When he reached the central section, where the stone was properly mortared into place, he stopped, running his hand over the coarse side.

"Will it hold, do you think?"

"When it is all as well-built as this section? One would think so," said the teacher.

Tresantes hoisted himself up and sat, dangling his legs. "Depends on the size and inclination of the attacking force."

"I want a fighting step built. All the way along the inside, so we can properly defend anywhere we need to. And braces. I want strong beams all the way along, helping to brace it."

"This will all take time, and quite a lot of materials. It will delay the rebuilding of the polis."

"The polis will be a moot point if that horde shows up and we are not ready."

"So you think that they will come?"

"Where else would they go? Into the sea of grass in the interior? No, the only people there are the horse nomads, and they would be able to get away. The Hadesmen will work their way along the coast, destroying cities like Apollonia as they come."

"And thus swelling their numbers..."

Miltiades nodded. "We are going to need weapons, too. Javelins. Lots of them."

"We can do those things," said Photios. "But the men who are to stand at the wall and wield those weapons will need the courage to stand and fight."

"This wall will help them find it," said Tresantes, slapping the stone. "But you speak true – each man must find a wall within his heart, something worth defending."

And could that be this narrow finger of land, for any of them, mused Miltiades.

....

Later, Miltiades found Callias sitting alone on the beach, staring out at the sea.

"Where in Hades were you? What did you think you were doing?"

"I... I went to the Thracians."

"You had a duty to perform here, while I was away. Not to mention the risk to yourself, travelling alone... What if you had encountered a bunch of Hadesmen?"

"I didn't think about that..." Callias admitted.

"Evidently not. Imagine how it would look for me, taking your severed head back to present to your father with my apologies? What was just so bloody important about visiting those bloody barbarians?"

"You are marrying one of those bloody barbarians, aren't you?"

Miltiades paused. He sank down onto the gritty sand beside his cousin. "So it appears."

They sat in silence for a while, watching the small waves lap onto the shore. Miltiades was at a loss as to what to say, so he opted to say nothing.

"I just kept thinking about her," said Callias finally. "The look she gave me..."

"Who? Hegesipyle?"

"No! Not her. The other one – her companion. Bisanthe."

Miltiades frowned, thinking.

"But you didn't even speak to her, did you?"

"Not then. But I have now. Kind of. She doesn't really know much Greek. But I could teach her."

"Whoa, slow down. I'm to marry Hegesipyle to cement a deal between us and the Thracians. I don't think there is room for emotional entanglements in all this."

Callias didn't reply, but Miltiades felt him tense up. He cast about for another topic.

"And how did you get on with Teron?"

Callias' jaw tightened. "Fine."

"Fine," said Miltiades. "I heard he was quite upset with you. Which seems likely, given he seems to look on you as some kind of possession."

Callias shot him a look. "I told him it was none of his business."

"And how did he take that?"

"Not well. But it is the truth. I told him he couldn't assume that I wouldn't one day want to marry. That I would always want to be his... his friend."

There were tears in the corners of the younger man's eyes. Miltiades awkwardly reached over and patted him on the arm. Callias' head dropped at the contact, and he took a deep breath.

"I think you should end it with him. Thracian noblewoman or not."

"Like my father. You disapprove. You see something wrong with our relationship?" There was a challenge in the thrust of the youth's jaw.

"No," said Miltiades. "It is just that Teron is a massive dick. I think you would be happier without him."

Callias smiled bitterly. "You may be right. But it can be hard to escape emotional entanglements, can it not?"

Miltiades suddenly felt so out of his depth. This younger man seemed to have had much more experience in matters of the heart than he. Another pat on the arm was all he could think of, leaving his cousin uncomforted and himself feeling fairly useless.

EIGHT

....

SHADES

He walked along a beach, at night. The sea was flat, and the moon shone brightly upon the water and the wet sand, turning them both to silver, so that it was hard to see where the one ended and the other began. He may have been walking across a sheet of polished iron. The world was silent but for the slap of his feet on the firm sand. He became aware of a figure ahead of him, and something about the gait and stature made his heart leap. He hurried forward, but as he did so suddenly hit a softer, more water-logged section of beach, for his feet sank into sand like porridge and he had to pull each foot clear with a soft sucking gurgle. The figure still paced ahead, hands behind his back. It occurred to Miltiades that he might call out, but then he found he had no breath to do so, for now he was sinking knee deep and every step was taking everything he had. He looked up in desperation, for the figure was shrinking, and now he was up to his thighs, and hissing waves raced up the beach and surrounded him, pooling around him as they sucked back, causing him to sink deeper still in the slurry. But now he found his voice, and threw back his head and called...

"Miltiades!"

And then his uncle was there, looking down at him, and extending his hand. Miltiades clasped it, and his uncle drew him from the quicksand until they both stood again on firm silver sand. Miltiades, trembling, stepped forward, arms outstretched, but his uncle stepped back, pulling his black cloak about him and shaking his head.

"Uncle," he said. "I have been looking for you. Where have you been?"

"Do not seek me," replied his uncle. "For I cannot be found."

"But I have to find you," said Miltiades. "I must."

"Why?"

"Because..." But his uncle was sadly shaking his head, and Miltiades suddenly felt his heart may burst. "...Because... someone must love me."

His uncle covered his face with his hands. He looked at Miltiades between his fingers. "There is something you must know. There is no ferry here. There is an ocean rising."

"An ocean? But..." Miltiades turned to look at the sea beside them, but saw then that it was not the sea, as he had thought, but a wide river, for there were purple hills just visible on the other bank.

"A black ocean rising." His uncle suddenly retched, clapping his hands to his mouth. A stream of black liquid ran between his fingers, dripping down onto the sand. "You must-"

But he stopped and vomited up a great spray of black water, more than a normal stomach could possibly hold, and Miltiades could not help but jump backwards.

His uncle looked at him with wild eyes, and with a great effort said "Not just one. There will be-"

A second explosion of dark water sprayed from his mouth, and continued to come, pouring faster than the strongest fountain. With a last desperate look, his uncle seemed to be thrust away from him, disappearing behind a rising tide of black liquid, and now he was suddenly out of his depth, kicking with his feet to keep his head above the tide. He cast about, but there was nothing to see in any direction but rolling waves of darkness.

And then he felt hands pulling at him under the water.

Bony hands, with skeletal fingers. And he saw that he was not alone; the dark water was full of bodies, writhing and twisting, decomposing, parts of them sliding off into the noisome depths. And he cried, and fought to keep his head up, keep his lips sealed tight.

A single figure rose out of the depths before him, the head more skull than anything, a tight layer of decayed flesh clinging to it, eyes white and rheumy, and it clasped him to it, and when he tried to thrust it away, his hands passed right through it – he felt the ribs give way, and his arms were stuck inside of it, but still its hideous head bent towards him, the mouth opening, tongue black and swollen, gums rotted away revealing white, white teeth-

He screamed.

He sat up, flailing, wet with sweat. Someone was standing over him.

"Bad dream?" asked Zander.

"Fuck," said Miltiades, falling back onto his cot. "Holy fucking fuck."

"So that would be a yes. Lie easy and I will get you some wine."

Great Zeus, thought Miltiades. What is happening to me?

He gulped at the cup that Zander brought him, then pushed it back into his slave's hands and stumbled to the door of the hut. Outside, the sky was lightening with the approach of dawn. He strode forward, pleased to see the silhouette of a man on watch. He headed for the edge of the encampment – more a village, now, really – and gazed down at the water of the Hellespont. He shivered, part from the chill, part from the clinging hold of the dream.

As the daylight grew, he saw that the waters of the channel were still free of all shipping.

No ferry here...

And a terrible thought hit him between the eyes.

He ran for his hut.

"Get me a horse," he snapped at Zander. "And find Tresantes, I want him with me."

"What about me?"

"You stay here, and keep an eye on Callias."

In a short time he and the Spartan were cantering towards the bria of the Thracians. Tresantes glanced at him once or twice, but didn't ask any questions. Once at the village, they dismounted and strode to the hall of the king. It was still empty, the fire in the middle down to one or two small glowing embers.

Cursing, Miltiades wheeled about, and headed through the village, and along the path leading to the pit. When they got there, the cover was back in place. He took hold of one of the ropes.

"Help me."

Tresantes raised an eyebrow, but took up one of the other ropes, and together they hauled, but the wide wooden lid barely moved. At that moment, King Olorus came striding into the clearing, accompanied by Hegesipyle and a handful of warriors and advisors. He stared at the Greeks.

"My men tell me you come. I think, ah, good, he come to visit Hegesipyle, like a good suitor. But no, you are here. What you do?"

Miltiades looked at him, but continued to pull, then threw the rope down in exasperation. He strode to the king, causing the warriors to bristle.

"The Hadesmen. The ones who overran Chersonnesus. What happened to them?"

"We kill them." Olorus narrowed his eyes.

"And the Greeks?"

"All killed."

"By the Hadesmen? Or by you?"

Olorus frowned. "Why you ask this? You know what happens if you bit..."

"King Olorus," said Miltiades, his voice shaking. "Is my uncle... Is my uncle's head down in that bloody pit?"

"Ah," said the king. "Now I see. You think this of me? You think I take the heads of your kin, and put in my pit?"

"Did you? If he is there... If he is down there, in the name of all the Gods I must get him out. I must get him out of that foulness-"

"If he was there, he is not your uncle anymore," the king said grimly. "That man would be gone. But no, Greek, he is not there. That time, there were many, many Hadesmen. More than I had ever seen before. When we came to the wall, they had already overrun your town. The wall had not held. Most of your people were eaten whole, they did not rise again. Then the Hadesmen came for us, but we fought them in the mountains and valleys, and though many warriors fell, none reached our brias. All perished. All gone. And I swear to you by our gods, no Greek head went into my pit."

Miltiades nodded, but felt numb. He could not shake the feeling that the body of his uncle wandered, unburied, unclaimed, and that his spirit could never pass to the other side until it was allowed to rest. But what could he say? And even if the king was lying, and he gained access to the pit, how would he be able to recognise his beloved uncle in that mass of putrefaction? He realised in passing that Hegesipyle was watching him, but he couldn't read her face and was in no mood to try.

At a loss, he nodded tightly at Olorus, then spun about and marched from the clearing. If you don't know what to say, better to say nothing, he reasoned. His back prickled with tension all the way back to their horses, and the tight muscles didn't begin to relax till they were well on the way back to their encampment.

It was the midday meal when they returned, and Miltiades found Callias sitting with Photios while Teron tended a bubbling pot nearby. Tresantes went off by himself, as he usually did. Callias was a little cool at first, no doubt unhappy at having been left behind.

Miltiades spotted Tresantes running through the camp in great agitation. His stomach turned over. Had they been breached? But no, the Spartan was looking at the ground, peering behind stores, not running for a weapon.

"What is it?" he called, walking down to join him. "What's wrong?"

"Rabbit," said the Spartan. "She is gone."

Miltiades was taken aback by the stricken look on Tresantes' face. "Well, I'm sure she can't be too far... She escaped?"

"I do not know. I do not know. There is no burrow, no sign..."

"Well, she is a wild animal, so..."

Tresantes shot him a look that caused Miltiades to falter to a stop. Instead he said "Come and ask if anyone has seen her, then, rather than just running around. Come on."

The Spartan nodded, distracted, but followed him back towards the others.

"Listen," said Miltiades. "Tresantes' rabbit has gone missing. Have any of you seen it?"

Photios and Callias shook their heads. Teron lifted a spoonful of soup from his pot and sipped it noisily, smacking his lips.

"Teron? Have you seen the rabbit?"

"A rabbit? Let me think..." He stirred the pot, frowning. "Now you mention it, there may have been a rabbit around here somewhere."

"Where?" Tresantes began casting about.

"Colder," said Teron.

The Spartan turned. "What does that mean?"

Teron shrugged. Tresantes took a step towards him.

"Warmer. Much warmer. Deliciously warm, in fact." He took another sip of the soup, and smiled at the Spartan. They all looked at the bubbling pot.

There was no warning. There was hardly time to blink. Suddenly Teron was on the ground and the Spartan was on him, fingers around his throat. The young man starting turning red, eyes bugging.

"Tresantes!" shouted Miltiades. "Wait!"

The Spartan lifted the younger man's head off the ground, then smashed it back down. He was purple now, his eyes rolling backwards. And then Tresantes was flying sideways, tackled by Callias. Teron rolled away, gasping – but in a fluid movement the Spartan swept Callias off him and came up on his feet.

"Joking!" croaked Teron, one hand holding his throat, the other held up in supplication. "I was joking!"

Tresantes stood over him. "Then where is she?"

"In my tent, under my cloak. Don't worry, I pegged it down, it can't escape."

Tresantes sprinted away. Callias dusted himself off.

"You're an idiot, Teron. You know how much he cares for that thing."

"Gods, what a mad man. You should get rid of him, Miltiades."

"You're the one I should be getting rid of, Teron."

"Me? It was a joke, I was joking. Then next minute I'm choking, all because of his weird fetish. Honestly, have you ever met anyone who would put a stupid little beast above a human?"

"No," Miltiades admitted.

"You have to admit it is weird. He is just begging to get teased."

"But it isn't funny, Teron," said Callias.

"It is. Look, your cousin Miltiades is smiling."

"Oh, that isn't why I'm smiling," said Miltiades. "I'm just thinking about what's about to happen next."

"Why?...Oh, shit!"

Tresantes was sprinting back towards them, face implacable. Teron, laughing a wheezy, anxious laugh, ran behind Callias. "Help me! Call him off!"

"Just don't kill him, please, Tresantes."

Teron turned and tried to dash away, but the Spartan easily dodged across and tripped him up. Teron rolled onto his back and scooted backwards.

"You can't hit a man while he's down!" he shouted.

"Then get up."

"No!"

"Suit yourself." The Spartan dove onto him, managing to avoid the younger man's hands and feet and knock all the air from his lungs with an elbow. He ground his weight down onto Teron's chest. Teron groaned.

"Not nice when you can't breathe, is it? That is what it was like for Rabbit pinned under your stinking cloak. Is it nice? Do you like it?"

With each question, Tresantes lifted and dropped his weight again, forcing more air from the other man's lungs, and then not allowing him room to take a breath.

"Touch her again, and I will kill you."

Callias turned to Miltiades. "Cousin..."

"Come on, Tresantes. He has learned his lesson. Let him up."

The Spartan looked at him. "You are taking his part?"

"No. I just fear that we are going to need every man we have. Even a shit like him."

Tresantes nodded, and stood. He held his hand out. Teron looked at it, then accepted it, and the Spartan hauled him to his feet. As he came up, Teron suddenly lurched forward, butting with his head into the Spartan's face. Tresantes rolled his head backwards, the blow only partially catching him, and thrust Teron from him. Teron came straight back in, swinging wildly. Rather than retreat,

Tresantes moved into the attack, blocking Teron's arm and grabbing him around the waist. He thrust one foot between

Teron's legs, and hooked one out from under him. The younger man went down again. This time Tresantes dropped beside him, and took hold of one of his arms. He snaked his around it, bending the elbow joint until Teron cried out in pain.

"Are we done?"

"Ah! Yes!"

"Do you swear? Do you swear by all you hold dear?"

"I swear! I swear!"

Tresantes gave the joint one more squeeze, then released him. Teron lay moaning in the dirt. The Spartan nodded at Callias, Miltiades and Photios then stalked away.

"I'll kill him," muttered Teron. "One day, I'll bloody kill him."

"Oh, shut up," said Miltiades. "You will not. Take your medicine like a man and let it go. We can't afford stupid feuds. Now, we all have work to do, so let's get to it."

....

Miltiades spent the afternoon working in the encampment. It was looking good. Most of the rubble had been cleared away, and many men were now living in simple wooden huts, though most still used their tents for ceilings. A few fields were being tended, and a small flock of goats grazed on the hillsides. Vegetable gardens had been established, and some men who had worked as fishermen in Athens had procured a small boat and used it to add to their larder.

And gratifyingly, a couple of large grain carrying merchant ships had been seen sailing down the Hellespont. They had been too far out to hail, but hopefully they were bound for Athens. Nothing Miltiades could do at this point if they weren't, but he resolved to procure a galley or bireme from somewhere when he could, so that they would then be able to intercept such vessels and police this stretch of water. He was realistic enough to know that such actions placed them on the same level as the pirates they were ostensibly protecting the region from, but such was the way of the world. He harboured a secret wish to find ships bound for Lemnos and impound them, until such time as the Lemnians paid a fat ransom.

Later in the day he walked out to the wall, and saw that the stonemasons were hard at work dressing blocks ready to fill the gap. A few other men with carpentry skills had begun building a simple fighting step, but it was obvious that was going to be a big job unless he diverted more men to it. At least there was no shortage of good timber here, unlike the denuded slopes of Attica around Athens.

When he returned to their camp – really, it was fast becoming a polis: a tiny one, but a polis nonetheless –he went in search of the Spartan. He found him lying curled up, seemingly asleep, in the pen he had built for his rabbit. The rabbit itself was sleeping as well, nestled between the man's arm and torso. Miltiades stopped and looked at this scene. He was amazed that an animal could show such affection towards a human – and that a human should care so much for an animal he himself had seen as nothing more than something to hunt and eat. It gave him pause – it had always seemed to him that that was the natural order: man took what he could from the natural world for his own desires. He had always thought of himself as someone who questioned things – indeed, had he not often felt superior to some of his fellow citizens who just accepted things as they were? Yet now his eyes were opened and he found whole new areas that he too had just been accepting.

Such as, when someone was dead, that was the end of it.

"I'm not asleep," said Tresantes, though he kept his eyes closed.

"Good. How is she?"

"She is fine." The Spartan reached over and stroked the rabbit's ears. Her brown eyes opened momentarily then closed again in pleasure. She seemed to sink further into her spot. "They are more hardy than you would think."

"I don't think Teron meant to harm her."

"No. But he is unthinking, and that is just as dangerous as intent."

Miltiades nodded, but he wanted to change the subject. "I was wondering if we might do some training together. You and I. I'd like to learn to fight like you. I'm fine with a sword or spear, but I would like to be as good at pankration as you."

"If you wish. I am not very good."

"Your 'not very good' is a bloody long sight better than me! Tomorrow?"

The Spartan nodded, and rested his head back on his arm.

....

The next day, Miltiades stood before Tresantes down on the beach. He brought Zander, and Callias came as well. Of Teron there was no sign, but he doubted the youth would wish to willingly subject himself to any more punishment from Tresantes. Miltiades had made sure they scheduled this session for the midday break. As leader of the colony, he supposed he could have trained while the others all worked, but he was conscious of how that would have appeared.

"So, let us begin. Strip off," said the Spartan, pulling off his own tunic and breech cloth. When he turned to fold his clothes into a neat pile, angry ridge lines of scars were revealed across his back.

"What happened there?" asked Callias. Miltiades winced – he assumed it was from when Tresantes was stripped of his citizenship.

The Spartan stared at Callias questioningly, then reached around and touched his back. "Oh! These? They are my stripes from the Festival of Artemis Orthia."

"Festival? What kind of festival leaves you with scars?" Callias was thinking of the festivals they celebrated in Athens, which usually involved feasting and drinking. And some religious observance too, obviously. But mostly drinking.

"A Spartan kind of festival." Tresantes grinned. "It happens towards the end of the Agoge – our training. The young men compete to see how long they can stand at the altar of the temple, as the older men beat them with rods. Whoever stands it the longest wins great honour."

"So…you just stand there while they beat you?"

"Oh no. You are busy trying to steal as many cheeses as possible from the altar." Tresantes frowned. "It is very difficult to stack cheeses while you are being flogged."

"Did you win?"

"Alas, no. I could only stand and receive about two dozen blows before fleeing."

They all looked at him.

"You would have to really like cheese," said Zander after a pause.

Miltiades could not imagine how anyone could force themselves to receive such punishment, but then recalled the Spartan's trick with the lamp flame back on Lemnos. They were a strange people. He removed his own tunic and stood naked with the others. He glanced down at his body, and was more pleased than he had been for some time. The life here had agreed with him, at least physically. He had been eating more simply and more frugally, working more and sitting around reading far less. In response his muscles were more defined, and the thickening he had been noticing in his midsection reduced. Zander caught him looking at himself and rolled his eyes theatrically.

Tresantes began with some simple exercise – some sprints along the beach, squatting then leaping into the air - until their thighs burned. They next paired up for some basic wrestling drills. Miltiades worked with the Spartan. Though he outweighed the other man, he could feel the whipcord muscle under his skin, as they each took hold, one hand behind the other's head, the other grabbing an arm. He found it harder to unbalance the Spartan than he thought, while in turn Tresantes could easily send him staggering, and he only stayed on his feet because the Spartan held him up. It was a sobering lesson.

Miltiades was gratified that Zander was struggling with Callias, too. The younger man was fitter, with better balance, and the slave was soon cursing under his breath, especially when he was suddenly sent sprawling and Callias stood over him, chest puffed out.

"You're just showing off for the audience," grumbled Zander as he climbed to his feet.

Audience? Miltiades looked around. Hegesipyle was sitting on the grass watching, with her companion woman Bisanthe, and Photios. Photios waved. Miltiades was suddenly aware of standing naked before Hegesipyle, and fought the urge to cover himself. None of the others seemed to mind. Why should Callias? He was in peak condition. And slaves rarely had much room for modesty. Tresantes shrugged, reading his mind.

"In Sparta, it is customary for the men to train naked before the women. It encourages better performance."

Miltiades glanced back at the Thracian women. He could have sworn Hegesipyle was looking directly at his crotch. Appallingly, he suddenly felt his penis twitch. Oh no. No no no no no. He turned his back on her, but his member seemed to have a mind of its own, and continued its slow rise. Tresantes shook his head.

"This is not a phalanx drill. Spears are not required."

Miltiades turned bright red. "End of session!" he cried, and ran for the water. His erect penis bobbed painfully, and he was forced to hold it with one hand as he ran until he could mercifully plunge into the cold water. He dove under, wishing he could stay beneath the surface for hours, but was forced up. He came up spluttering, wiping salt water from his eyes. He looked back at the beach. Hegesipyle was lying on her back laughing, kicking her legs in the air, her lady wiping tears from her eyes. The other men were staring at him. Miltiades spat water in their direction and swam towards the pier.

..."I'd say you are off the hook," said Phillipus on his next visit shortly after. "The markets are full of grain, and no one is talking about you."

"Credit where credit is due!" cried Callias. "The people should be thanking us for safeguarding their food supply!"

"Trust me," said Phillipus. "With the way Hippias has been carrying on, it is far better to not be talked about."

"Still bad?" asked Miltiades.

Phillipus nodded. "Worse. The man is cracked. Sees sedition everywhere. Doesn't need much excuse...which reminds me, where is Teron?"

"Skulking about somewhere," said Miltiades, ignoring the frown that Callias gave him. "Why?"

"His lot have been exiled again."

Callias gasped. "Oh no!"

"Yep, the whole Alcmaeonid clan. All of them had to clear out of the city or face arrest and execution. For the public good, according to Hippias."

"More likely for Hippias' good."

"Of course. He suspected them of plotting to overthrow him. So out they go, and he has confiscated all their property."

"I'll find him," said Callias. "Let me be the one who breaks it to him."

They watched him go, then Phillipus turned to Miltiades.

"I'm not sure where that leaves you. Or him, rather. This colony legally being part of Athens, no member of the clan should be here, either."

Miltiades nodded slowly. "As much pleasure as it would give me to get rid of the little shit, I don't particularly want to be taking action like that without a direct instruction."

"Thinking the long race, eh?" Phillipus grinned. "True, tyrants don't generally last forever, even if the Pisistratids have enjoyed a particularly long spell. And the Alcmaeonids are fabulously wealthy... Not the best of enemies to make."

"No. And I prefer to have that little snake where I can see him. Gods above know what kind of trouble he could stir up if I booted him out and he hung around in a neighbouring polis... Or suggested to the clan they seize Chersonnesus for themselves and put the squeeze on Hippias that way."

"Well, you know best. I'd better go see to the unloading. This will be the last trip for a while, with winter coming on. You have a good stock of supplies, and I must say the place is looking good."

He held out his hand, and Miltiades clasped it. "Travel safe."

Hegesipyle returned to visit again, bodyguard in tow. This bothered Miltiades for a number of reasons. He was uncomfortable with how public this process was – he could imagine tongues wagging around the campfires at night, laughter bubbling about their leader and his wild, barbarian bride-to-be. It also pulled him away from his duties, and he did not want to be seen to be shirking. He understood leadership enough to know that the way to respect was to muck in with everyone else, not stand back or, even worse, be off wooing while everyone else worked. And finally, there was the matter of her last visit, when he had appeared like a randy satyr... Gods, he hoped she hadn't told Olorus.

"Hegesipyle," he greeted her, when she had dismounted.

He had no doubt that Callias was lurking somewhere nearby, disappointed at the absence of Bisanthe. Hegesipyle studied him solemnly.

"Miltiades," she returned – and then her face split in a wicked grin. "So... I guess you do like me, yes?"

He felt his cheeks burn red. He opened his mouth but nothing sensible seemed to be forthcoming.

She punched his arm, and turned to walk. He fell into step beside her.

"Don't be ashamed. It is natural."

"I just didn't want to offend you..."

She looked perplexed. "You Greeks are very...uptight."

"Not all Greeks," said Miltiades miserably. "Probably just me..."

She laughed. He realised he was making it more of an issue than it needed to be, and tried to relax. He sought to change the subject.

"No Bisanthe?"

"No. To tell the truth, she finds the attention from your young cousin a little wearying."

"Oh no. She doesn't like him?"

"She says he is kind, and pretty. But not like a real Thracian man."

Which of course made him wonder how he stacked up...

There was a cry from the direction of the docks. Miltiades heard someone calling his name. Men were hurrying in that direction.

"I think I had better..."

"I will come."

They ran down towards the shore, where a knot of men sur-rounded the small fishing boat they had acquired. Three men used this to fish the waters of the Hellespont. But there were only two standing by the vessel, white faced and trembling.

They saw Miltiades arrive. "They're coming..." said one, and promptly fainted away.

....

Miltiades summoned an assembly. There was no point in trying to keep whatever the news was quiet – he believed that fear was much more likely to grow in the spaces where there was no information. Better that everyone had the facts.

The two fishermen stumbled along behind Miltiades and stood with him on the rough stone dais serving as the speaker's platform. Once all the men in the immediate vicinity – a little over half the colonists – had gathered, the two fishermen looked at each other, and one stepped forward.

"Well," he began.

The sun was warm, and the Hellespont enticingly flat when Acheron, Dion and Charones pushed their small fishing boat away from the dock, and turned it up the channel, towards the Black Sea. They raised the small triangular sail, and the wind bit into it, filling it with a satisfying snap, and the prow lifted a little as they started to hiss through the wine dark water.

They passed a skin between them, revelling in the movement and the kiss of spray. They appeared to have the entire Hellespont to themselves, and life was good.

"Do you suppose anyone will ever catch on?" asked Dion.

Charones shrugged. "Not so long as we always bring back a full net."

But Acheron was frowning. "They would be less likely to catch on if only two of us were out."

Neither of the other two looked at him. It had been an ongoing argument. When Miltiades had asked for those with fishing experience to come forward, they had all three volunteered. The problem was that building was much harder, hotter and dirtier work compared to something they knew well. And with the size of the boat, they only really needed two men at a time to crew it and fish. They had originally discussed drawing up some kind of roster, so that each of them took a turn working in the camp or on the wall, while the other two went out, but somehow it had never taken off. Instead all three arrived at the boat each morning, engaged in a half-hearted argument about who should stay, then finally all boarded and sailed out of sight as quickly as possible before anyone could argue with them.

The camp was certainly grateful each time they brought back a load of fish shimmering like silver, and even Miltiades himself had congratulated them, but they still had the guilty manner of school boys skiving off from a lesson in the stoa.

By mutual agreement, they had decided this day to sail up to the mouth of the Black Sea, to investigate how manageable that larger body of water would be for a fishing boat such as theirs, or whether they would have to look towards something bigger. The only problem with that would be needing more crew.

"We have this sewn up," said Charones. "We are in the winning position here. As this polis grows, we will be able to be the biggest fish suppliers. We'll be able to run a fleet of boats, and our own market stall too. Zeus, maybe we can even sell to the Thracians. We stand to make a killing, boys. Best thing we all did was throw it in in Athens."

"Aye," said Dion. "I was sick of that overfished stretch at Salamis anyway. And more and more merchant ships coming in all the time..."

"Now what in Hades is that?" asked Acheron.

Dion and Charones looked at him, then in the direction he was staring. The distant shoreline was dark.

"What?"

"Don't you see it?"

Dion screwed up his eyes against the glare. "See what? The trees?"

"Trees?" scoffed Acheron. "Bloody funny trees. They're moving. That's a...I don't know, but its people."

"Shit! An army?"

"No armour. No banners. Let's take the boat in for a closer look..."

Dion and Charones exchanged a glance, but said nothing. Acheron turned the tiller, and the boat scudded in towards the shoreline. Acheron had the keener eyes, it was true, but as they sailed in, it became obvious that the dark mass was indeed a crowd moving along the coast. Like a cloud, it sometimes split apart, sometimes formed back together.

"Man in the water!" cried Charones, shooting out his arm to point.

They were all fishermen, and all shared the fisherman's horror of drowning. Or of being eaten alive by the creatures of the deep. They reacted instinctively. Acheron threw the tiller again, and the boat heeled over, running at an angle toward the shore.

Dion and Charones leaned over the port side, arms outstretched ready.

"I'm going to have to come off fast," grunted Acheron. "So we don't hit any shoals. Grab him and be ready for me to turn."

The boat hissed forward. They could see the man in the water, his arms thrashing weakly, like he was trying to swim, though in his confusion he was actually heading further out into the channel, if anything.

"Get ready!" cried Acheron.

"Nearly...nearly..." said Dion, leaning further out. "And... Got him!"

He hauled backwards, an arm in his hands. Charones lunged to get hold as well.

"Got you, matey! Got you!"

Acheron dug the tiller into the water, fighting to send the boat back away from the shore.

And Dion cried out in horror as the arm he held disintegrated in his hands. The white skin sloughed off and the man sagged. Charones stared, in the act of wrapping an arm around the man's back, under his other arm. And the stink hit him then, the foul, fishy reek of meat long spoilt. And the head came up, holes where the eyes should be, hole where the nose should be, and the worst hole of all, the gaping mouth, coming at him, fastening into his neck. He screamed, and blood spurted. His hands scrabbled at the thing's head, seeking to thrust it away, but like the arm, the skin kept parting beneath his grip, and all the time the mouth was biting, biting. Dion punched it, and Charones screeched louder as the blow drove the thing's teeth deeper. Charones tried to pull back, to stand, and the boat rocked wildly.

Acheron looked about for somewhere to put in, but now he could see the figures on the bank more clearly; the ruined flesh, the glint of bone. And already a score or more had noticed the boat and were plunging into the water. He directed the boat away, but the creature on the side was acting like a sea anchor, pulling at them, slowing them.

It had to go. Which meant...

"Dion!" he screamed. "Tip him over! Tip him over!"

Dion cast an agonised look at him, then hooked Charones's legs and with a cry threw him over the side. He closed his eyes. He did not want to risk making eye contact as Charones was pulled beneath the waves. Gods, he hoped it would be quick. To silence that awful screaming.

Lighter, the boat surged forward, out, deeper. Safe.

And when he could, Acheron turned it homeward, back down the channel towards Chersonnesus. And though his fingers ached, he couldn't bring himself to ask Dion to take over. To be honest, he could hardly look at his crewmate, though he had only done what he himself had asked.

···

And now he fell silent, standing before the assembly. Tears streaked his salt-bitten cheeks. He looked about, fearfully, wondering if he would see judgement in the solemn faces of the men looking at him.

Miltiades cleared his throat.

"We have to get the fuck out of here!" shouted one man, and then they were all on their feet, yelling, pointing, baying.

"I ain't going back! This is all I got!"

"Then stay and die, you ass!"

"Cowards!"

"Fuckwits!"

Miltiades held his hands up, but no one paid him much mind – or at least, not enough to still the noise. It looked like things could come to blows. He looked about, and spotted Metramandes watching him. Then he spotted Bolinthos and Embades standing off to the side with Hegesipyle. He beckoned them over.

The clanging gradually got the assembly's attention. That ringing sound they were all familiar with, of blade on blade. Those at the front quietened first, and that patch of silence gradually spread until the last voice was yelling "...and I told you, she was the one who..." before the speaker realised he was yelling into a vacuum and fell silent. They all turned to see the two Thracians standing with their drawn rhomphaia blades on the dais.

"The next man who speaks out of turn faces these two," snarled Miltiades. They didn't like it, he could see, but it worked, they held their sullen tongues. "Gentlemen, we will not become a rabble. We can defend this land. We can hold this polis. We will not let these...horrors drive us from what is ours. They are not an army, they have no general, no stratagems. We can and will drive them from our wall."

A man at the front raised his hand. Miltiades nodded.

"The wall didn't save your uncle, did it?"

A pain pierced his guts, but he didn't show it. "We have strengthened it. When we found it, more than half was just loose rock. Now most is properly set, thanks to Agathon and Hermolaos. And we can add more defences. I understand these creatures. We can do it. We can survive."

Another man put up his hand to speak.

"Miltiades, like many I have a lot to lose if we leave. I have put all I have into this place succeeding. How long will these things be here? How long must we hold out?"

"For as long as we must. But we can – we have food, we have supplies. They will move on when they find they cannot have us." He took a gamble: "Metramandes, you have been very quiet. What say you?"

The metic stood stroking his beard for some time before speaking. "Like any party, isn't it? The longer you stay, the harder it is to leave." That earned a few laughs, and the tension seemed to decrease a little, like a bow string given just a little flex. "I have never been accused of being the man who left while the lamps were still lit, the wine still flowing, and the flute girl feeling lonely. I'm for staying."

Miltiades laughed along with the rest. "There is another thing to consider – where would we go? We have one small boat. Phillipus is not due back for some time. The only way out is to march into the hills – right into their path."

And after that, there was little more to say. The assembly began to break apart. Miltiades stepped off the dais and headed for Metramandes.

"Thank you for that, you helped calm some nerves."

The metic looked at him coldly, all the warmth gone from his face. "You can pull that trick only so often, you know."

"What trick?"

"Threatening us, threatening fellow Greeks, with your tame barbarians."

Miltiades frowned, but the metic turned his back and stalked off, shouting out to his friends as if the exchange hadn't happened. He shook his head, and turned to find Hegesipyle behind him.

"I must go," she said. "Our people will be leaving."

"Leaving?"

"For now. We will abandon the bria and move deeper into the mountains, into the hidden valleys."

"Shit! I will come and see your father. Maybe your warriors can lead the Hadesmen away, into the gorges, like last time."

"No! You do not understand. There was much death and suffering last time we faced such a horde. The king will not wish to make his people suffer again. He will not help you."

"If you asked..."

She recoiled. "I am not asking! My people must die for you? For you stupid, greedy Greeks?"

Her sudden anger stung him, and he felt his own wrath rise in answer.

"Greedy? You make it sound like all we do is take. We do bring things, too, you know."

"Like what?"

He swept his arms about. "Like this! We bring this! Civilisation."

"And who says we want it?"

"Well, you should!"

"Why?"

"Because its better, that's why! Better than what you have."

Her eyes were like slits. "Oh yes, because we are just backward barbarians."

"That isn't what I meant..."

"You know what, Greek? You know why my father was so keen for me to learn your tongue? Because he knew you would come, and keep coming. If not you Athenians, then the Corinthians, or the Spartans, or Thebans... It doesn't matter. You all have the same hunger. Maybe you are not so different from the Hadesmen."

His jaw tightened. "Then go. But you can't always run, you know. Sometimes you must decide something is worth defending, and fight."

"This?" She looked about contemptuously. "This is worth dying for?"

"I have no intention of dying."

"No," She smiled then, sadly. "And neither did your uncle."

He couldn't speak any more. He watched her walk away, the two warriors falling in behind her, shooting curious looks at him over their shoulders.

"Miltiades."

He turned, sighing. The price of leadership was this, this constant demand for his time and energy. Zander hovered nearby, with Photios uncomfortable in his wake.

"Look, Miltiades, this is not an easy subject to raise..."

"Oh, good."

Zander squirmed, looking to Photios for support, but the teacher was gazing out towards the sea.

"You and I learned together, and learned to question together, right?"

"Zander, get to the point."

"We never put much stock in the gods. In fact, we laughed at those who saw their hand in everything..."

"I feel like there is a 'but' about to appear here."

"But...some strange things have been happening. That intruder in Athens. What the oracle said. That Thracian shaman... It feels like...like maybe the gods are trying to speak to you."

An image flashed into Miltiades' mind, of his uncle's ghost spewing black water. His guts turned to ice. With an effort, he kept his face neutral. "And say what?"

"Maybe we shouldn't be here. Maybe we should...run. Isn't that what the oracle said?"

"You heard me, Zander. Run where? There is nowhere to go. That seems to be a detail the oracle overlooked."

"We could make rafts, and cross the Hellespont. Or at least armour up and fight our way out. I am frightened that if we stay here we will be cornered and slaughtered."

"And what say you, Photios? Have you suddenly become religious too?"

The teacher looked at him, his brow furrowed. "I don't know if it is the gods. But... the very existence of these things is against all that is natural. That being so, it may be that in return nature seeks to guide us."

"Well, whoever it is could do a better job of it. Opaque warnings don't help. And anyway, why us? Or why me? And... Wait a moment. Tresantes!"

Miltiades left the two others behind him and jogged over to where the Spartan had stopped.

"A word," said Miltiades. "Let's talk strategy..."

The trembler frowned. "I am no strategos. I am a simple hoplite. I push and stab, that's about it."

"I thought all Spartans were trained to be resourceful... You know, the agoge and all that..."

The agoge, the Spartan training regime for their boys was well known throughout Greece. Sent out into the wilderness to survive by their wits, it was aimed at teaching the future war-riors to endure.

"The agoge? You mean shivering in a ditch until it is dark enough to sneak into some poor helot's hut and steal his bread? I'm not sure there was anything in that which applies to this situation. I don't know if anyone has faced this situation..."

And survived, thought Miltiades miserably. His shoulders slumped. What could he do, that his uncle could not?

"Look," said Tresantes after a while. "In battle, every phalanx pulls to the right, yes? It is unavoidable: every man cannot help but strive to get under the cover of his neighbour's shield on his right. And in so doing the whole formation crabs sideways as it moves forwards. Well, in Sparta we actually use that. We train the men who hold position on the right to go even further, until they are beyond the end of the enemy phalanx, then turn inwards. And the enemy help by moving across in the opposite direction. So once our right flankers are clear, they curve around the flank of the enemy, and roll them up. Simple. And very, very deadly."

Miltiades shivered, picturing what it would be like. Each man locked in place by his neighbours and those before and behind, and then to have this new threat slamming in from the side. It sounded near impossible to pull off, though. It was hard enough to get the city's farming class to line up and march for-ward all together, let alone carry out a manoeuvre like that.

"I don't understand."

"We use what the enemy naturally does against them. Maybe think on that." The Spartan clapped him on the shoulder and sauntered off.

Use what the enemy naturally does against them. Miltiades let his feet take him where they would, and found himself on high ground looking down on the coast. What do the Hadesmen do? Nothing but surge and destroy, like a plague of locusts... How did you disrupt and rout a foe who knew no fear, who just came on, like a wall... Like a wave...

Miltiades stood on the fighting step, looking into the distance. Nothing stirred.

"Close it," he said.

Hermolaos and Agathon jumped to obey, shouting instructions to the colonists serving as their labourers. The gates were lifted off their hinges, and the prepared stones slid into place, one by one, slowly shutting out the threatening view of beyond.

While that was happening, Miltiades ordered all the amphora to be collected from the township. The grain was to be poured onto canvas instead, and too bad if rats ate some of it. Wine was poured into skins until they were swollen, and the remainder tipped away into the dirt. Olive oil was poured into the sea, a thin film drifting away with the current.

"And now stakes," he said. "All you can make. And branches. And rope."

Saplings were cut, their branches stripped, both ends sharpened. Thick branches were lopped and dragged to the wall. Meanwhile the dressed square stones continued to slide into the gateway.

"And so here we remain," murmured Zander to himself.

The final planks were hammered and lashed into place on the fighting step. It was rough and none too steady in places, but now ran the entire length of the wall. Now Miltiades sent men over the top, and they laboured beyond it, shooting nervous glances at the ridges that hid what lay beyond.

The empty amphorae were buried in two staggered lines, their tops level with the ground. There were not enough to pack them in as closely as he would have liked. Sharpened stakes were set angled into the dirt, points at chest height. And shorter pegs were hammered into the ground, ropes tied tightly between them.

"Where did you learn your siegecraft?" asked Tresantes.

"Oh. From books."

The Spartan raised an eyebrow.

Next Miltiades ordered the men to look to their armour.

"Don't worry about your greaves," he told the hoplites. "You are going to be fighting on the step, so your legs will already be protected by the wall. And they will just add more weight." They couldn't afford for the fighting step to collapse beneath them...

"Shit!" said Callias. "I need cord! Something has snipped all the bloody cord on my curaiss! I can't tie it down!"

"Ah," said Tresantes. "That will be Rabbit. She does like to chew things."

Callias goggled at him. "You let her run around near my stuff? I'm going to be killed because of your pet? I hope you're the first bloody one I bite, in that case."

Those without proper arms were detailed off as javelineers. The store of missiles they had brought with them were unpacked, and he set some men to making more, though in the time they had these were nothing more than pointed sticks. A few men had hunting bows, but arrows were limited, and they did not have the resources to make more. Instead he set them to collecting stones, rounded to fit into a man's hand for easy throwing, and to pile them inside the wall.

All through the day they laboured, the women and children bringing watered wine and bread so they could keep at it. And none complained, or slackened, for all could feel the brooding weight of the distant mountains, could see the emptiness of the Hellespont running by.

In the late afternoon, a sentry cried a warning, and a jolt of fear shot through the workers. Some had already run and vaulted the wall before it was seen that it was not the nightmare they feared arriving, but three figures on horseback. Miltiades came running.

Hegesipyle, Bolinthos and Embades sat on their lathered horses. Miltiades jumped down, picking his way between the stakes and buried amphorae.

"It is too late," said Hegesipyle as soon as he reached them. He took hold of her horse's bridle. "We couldn't get through. They are behind us. Not far. Not far enough. Oh Miltiades..."

She looked at him, tears pricking at her eyes. "They are many." Her eyes widened. "More than when this wall failed your kinsmen."

"Get down," said Miltiades quietly. "And control yourself. A panic will feed on itself, and we will be undone."

She nodded, and swung from the back of the horse, her two warriors following suit.

"You will have to let the horses run free, to take their chances. They can't get through."

She bit her lip, and nodded, and spoke to the men. They frowned, staring at the spot where the gate had been, but dismounted, pulling the patterned blankets from their horses' backs. With a few slaps, the mounts were set free, and the three cantered off with tails held high, catching something of the nervousness of the men.

Miltiades led the trio of Thracians back to the wall.

"What is all this?" asked Hegesipyle.

Miltiades stopped and pointed. "We will use their numbers against them. Rather than let their full weight hit the wall, we will build a second wall before it. From the Hadesmen themselves."

"What do you mean?"

"You'll see. Unfortunately."

A watch was set all along the fortification, the rest of the men bidden to stack their arms nearby, but return to their huts and tents to sleep. Miltiades paused awkwardly outside his own hut.

"You can sleep in here," he said to Hegesipyle. "I can bunk in with Callias, or Photios."

The Thracian shook her head. "I don't think I am going to get much sleep. Do you have wine?"

"Um, yes."

"Then let's drink it. Since tomorrow we may be dead."

Zander raised an eyebrow, but left them to it. Miltiades himself mixed the wine, keeping it fairly strong. He supposed he ought not get drunk – what if the undead surge arrived tonight? – but the urge to add a little softness to the jagged spikes of worry in his mind and gut was strong. Besides, the presence of his intended wife was, as usual, unsettling. Especially after the way they had parted earlier.

And so they sat together, and drank. And when she held her cup out, he refilled it. And when she held her hand out for his, he took it, and sat beside her. And while talk did not come easily between them, something did become right, some merging of things, so that they came to rest closer and closer together.

And he suddenly felt her eyes dwelling intently on him, and he turned to her questioningly but she shook her head to silence him, and he felt it too. How life beat back in the face of death. In the most primal of ways. The hut suddenly felt boiling hot, and her arm was slick with sweat when he gripped it. She inhaled sharply, her eyes dark.

It had been a long time, but he was slow and considerate, and these qualities had always made him better at this than he knew. She cried out, and clung to him, sweating, muscles tightened, and then collapsed, her face pressed wetly into his chest.

"It doesn't mean anything," she said. "It doesn't mean I love you."

Yet when he touched her with his fingertips he felt her trembling.

Then she said "Put a light on", and he sat up and lit a lamp. She curled on her side, nestling back against him, watching the orange flame dance and the oily smoke spin toward the shadowed ceiling.

"I don't like the dark" she said. "There are monsters in the dark. I used to think so as a child, but then I grew up and laughed at my own foolishness. But now I see that the child was wiser."

"Yes. There are monsters. But they can be killed. You are safe with me." He regretted the words instantly: who was he to make such promises?

But she turned into his arms and held him tightly. After a while, he rolled onto his back and she lay gazing at his face. It was disconcerting, her being so close, so he gently closed his eyes.

"You have a grey hair growing out of your nose," she said, and he felt her long fingernails probing for it

"Hang on...ow!" He clapped a hand to his assaulted nose. She laughed.

"Oh, where is the mighty warrior? Why do all men carry on so? I sometimes think women should be the ones who do the fighting. We are made to withstand pain better."

"That's different," he said, and it came out more huffily than he meant, but she had surprised him, and he also felt a slither of jealousy thinking that her comment suggested she may have lain thus with another man before him.

"Do not sulk. Come, I will kiss it better." She dragged herself up onto him, leaning down and looking him in the eye, and he held her gaze. She lowered her face, and he felt her lips lightly peck him on the nose – but then they peeled back and she bit him instead. He felt her hot breath as she laughed, tugging at him. He laughed too, and strange tears leaked from the corners of his eyes, running down to join the sweat on his blanket.

Damn, but in this moment he tasted happiness.

NINE

························

ILIAD

Word came with the grey dawn. The host was upon them.

They didn't need scouts to tell them. A murder of crows filled the sky, and a great horrible moaning came on the wind. As did the stench – a sour reek like overripe cheese.

Many who had not already succumbed to their nerves sprayed their breakfast down the wall.

The first dead man came staggering out of the morning mist, almost like a scout coming on before the main force of an army.

A combination of factors had propelled him to the front of the horde. For a start, he was fresher than most – which made him something of a rarity. The bulk of the horde had been together for a long time, and their skin had become leathered beneath the elements, and their muscles and organs had shrunk away. They were not much more than walking skeletons, and they stalked along stiffly. And they were hungry, so very hungry, so that whoever they caught was generally devoured and left as nothing but a pile of pink steaming bones.

But this man, who had worked as a farmhand on the wheat fields of Apollonia, had been lucky – if you could call it that. He had seen them coming, this tide from the north, trampling the grain where it stood, and had time to hide himself inside a small shed amongst the farm equipment. He had knelt there, shivering, listening to the screams of the other workers, his knife gripped in sweaty fingers. And he might have been all right, might have survived, but for the very size of this river of dead. For although none of them had seen him hide, and they did not have the sense to come looking for him, force of numbers burst open the doorway as they flowed around the farm outbuildings, and propelled a couple to fall sprawling in through the opening.

As their dim brains perceived that they had fallen right on top of the very thing they craved, they had sought to bite him. He had fought them grimly, stabbing with his knife, feeling the blade scrape against their ribs as he punctured their dry flesh, but to no avail. He had cried out as their teeth found him, tearing chunks from his arms, his legs. His blade became wedged between bones and he couldn't pull it free. In desperation he had felt around, and come up with a hammer. And so he learned that they could be stopped, as he pounded their heads to a foul paste. But it was too late, the hammer at last fell from his blood-slicked fingers, and he had collapsed back, ill and feverish.

Then later when he came back - and became an 'it' rather than a 'he' - and shambled out to join the throng, its looser tendons meant that it easily overtook those who had passed by. And so as the flood poured on, finding its way across rivers choked with the floundering bodies of those who had gone before, as it ground through forests and crowded through valleys, it had come to be at the very fore.

And now it, too, was so very hungry.

It stumbled forward, no sense of urgency in its pace, despite the empty hollow gnawing that was all it knew. The wall stretching across before it made no sense to what was left of its brain. It did not see a barrier, and so came on. Likewise, the stakes and ropes before the wall meant absolutely nothing. Something hissed past it, and that did cause the ruined head to jerk and turn, following the movement, but the eyes saw nothing else, didn't focus on the arrow quivering in the ground.

It didn't hear Miltiades hiss at the archer to hold his fire, like he had fucking been told.

Behind it, others were emerging from the ridges and trees, limping, something horribly unnatural about their stiffened gait.

The fresh one was close to the wall now, and it looked to the top, where some objects were moving. It didn't recognise them as spear points and helmets, but movement heralded sweet succulent meat, and the scent of flesh and sweat reached some dulled sense, and so it quickened its pace.

And then with a crash, one of its feet went straight down into a buried amphora. The force of the drop shattered the knee, and the femur broke as all its weight fell forward. It lay still for a moment as if trying to make sense of why it was suddenly lying down, then slowly pushed itself up on its bite-pocked arms. But it couldn't fathom how to keep moving, how to get free, and pulled uselessly at the loose dirt. A moan escaped its lips, but not of pain, just of base frustration.

There was a rustling of excitement along the wall from the defenders who had witnessed this. These things were mindless idiots. Dangerous, yes, and disturbing... But if they didn't even notice basic traps like that, how hard could this be?

But then the farmhand's corpse managed to finally pull itself free, and though it could not stand on the ruined leg, it dragged itself relentlessly forward, right to the base of the wall, and began digging its fingers into the cracks between the stones, seeking to haul itself up. And meanwhile, more and more were emerging from beyond the ridge line, and from the trees, and down by the coastline.

And the momentary thrill of jubilation was replaced by a settling of cold fear, as the men realised what was before them.

They were thinly spread. But Miltiades reasoned that if the horde were following the coastline, then it was probable they would mostly fall upon the right. And so it was along that half that most men were stationed, with just a few clustered in small pockets of two or three hoplites, with another couple of poorer colonists with javelins, bows or even slings, further to the left.

The children and wives stood behind where Miltiades squatted on the fighting step, ready to serve as runners up and down the line. Hegesipyle and the two Thracian warriors also stood nearby.

"What about us?" she had asked.

"I'd prefer you stayed right out of it," replied Miltiades, holding up a hand to forestall her. "But I know you won't, and frankly this is a fight for everyone. I just can't help thinking of your father's face if he finds out I put you at risk."

"So I suppose that means I am to stand with the women, and act as a messenger."

Miltiades took her arm and drew her away, causing Embades and Bolinthos to frown.

"No, I need you and those two for a more important job. I need you to keep watch at the back of the wall, and if someone is injured...Bitten... I need them taken care of, do you understand?"

She nodded grimly. "Yes. Of course. We will do what needs to be done."

Miltiades caught her arm again as she turned away. "Just... Just don't cut anyone's head off. Keep it...as quick and neat as possible."

"You mean," she said, "don't act like barbarians?"

Before he could respond she had stalked over to the two warriors, and they leaned in, listening to what she said. They shot glances at Miltiades and nodded.

It was, he supposed as he peered over the wall, one less thing to worry about...

He heard Zander nervously clear his throat. "I can't spit," said the slave. "My mouth is too fucking dry."

Miltiades eyed the pair of javelins that he held gripped tightly. "You know how to use those things?"

Zander rewarded him with a tight grin – in their younger days, when prodded into gymnastic displays, Zander had always been better at throwing things than he: discus, javelins...

"The pointy end goes first, right?" Zander frowned. "Actually, one of these is just a pointy stick. We ran out of proper javelin heads..." He fell silent, staring dolefully at the sharpened stake.

Tresantes leaned back, squinting down the line in both directions.

"Your men are losing heart," he reported to Miltiades.

"Thanks," Miltiades replied tightly. He was clamping his teeth together, he realised. "What do you suggest I do about that?"

Tresantes stood up. "I suggest I go over the wall and kill some of those things."

Miltiades' eyebrows shot up. "Over the wall? What, me too?"

"No, just me." Tresantes smiled at him. "The men will be less fearful if they see me fight alone."

"By Apollo's left nut, you are mad," said Zander.

The Spartan winked, and pulled his tunic off over his head, and stretched, naked, in the growing light. Miltiades couldn't stop his eyes flicking to glance at the other man's penis – not out of desire, just interest, and the fact it was right there at eye height. The thing that struck him was the normality of the Spartan's cock and balls – his own felt like they were trying to retract up inside his body, they were so shrunken with nerves. Tresantes took up his spear, and cast it down over the wall, where it stuck quivering in the ground. He lightly swung himself over the edge, and lowered himself down – but then heaved himself back upwards again.

"What is it?" hissed Miltiades.

"You said stab them in the head, yes?"

"Yes! Gods, yes! Stab them in the head!"

Tresantes grunted, and dropped to the ground.

With a rasping groan, the dead farmhand pulled himself along the ground towards the Spartan, mouth working as if it was already chewing on a strip of flesh. The Spartan bent and touched his toes, whistling, then stood and swung his arms around in circles, frowning as he massaged one shoulder with his fingertips. The Hadesman was right beside him, reaching out for him with fingers stripped of flesh, the white bone points like claws. Still whistling, the Spartan yanked his spear from the ground, examined the point, then turned and drove it into the dead thing's face. The heavy iron point penetrated deeply, and the remaining life was instantly cut from the monster. It slumped, just like any corpse after any battle, instantly a more familiar kind of horror. Tresantes put one bare foot on its shoulder, and pulled the spear free. He put it over his shoulders, like a yoke, and picked his way forward through the tripwires and stakes.

Both sides had been watching. From the defenders came excited whispers, and then some cheers, as more and more men stood to watch the show. The dead had noticed him too, and many were drawn towards him.

Tresantes stopped, and stood with the spear now held loosely by his side. At least a score of Hadesmen were limping towards him, coming from an arc across his front. Even those too far away to clearly see him were attracted by the movement of their fellow dead – there was enough reason left to know that level of interest usually signalled food.

The closest one now staggered forward, speed increasing, its eyes wide and mad above the horror of its noseless and lipless face. It reached for him, and in one fluid movement he set his left foot forward, brought the spear up onto his shoulder in classic hoplite stance, and then thrust it forward into the dark hole where the thing's nose had been.

The hoplite's spearheads were made hard and heavy, built for punching into bronze-covered wooden shields and stiffened armour. The old dried flesh and bone of the dead was no match.

The point of Tresantes' spear bore right out the back of the Hadesman's head, and it dropped. As it fell, the Spartan braced and the thing's own weight dragged it free of the spear.

Another lurched toward him from the side, and this time he changed his grip to the underhand style, usually used for seeking a man's guts or groin in the thrust of phalanx battle. But Tresantes instead brought the point up beneath the thing's chin, and the force of the blow knocked it back off its feet.

There was scattered applause from the wall, and the Spartan cocked his head when he heard it, turned and waved at the defenders.

"Gods, pay attention!" hissed Miltiades, though the Spartan was too far away to hear him.

There were more upon him now. He spun as they closed the distance. Gone was the precise spear work now as he dispatched two, three with short savage jabs to the head. He retreated, jogging back a few paces, then set himself and drilled the closest dead man through the face. But there were more, pressing closer. The Spartan glanced back at the wall behind him.

"Come back," murmured Miltiades. "Come back, you idiot. That's enough."

"It is not going to help morale if they get him," said Zander.

The Spartan whirled, stabbing. The hoplite spear was a heavy thing, and he was not a big man, but he wielded it as if it were as light as a javelin. He jabbed quickly into three more – the first two collapsed, the last staggered. He kicked it to pull the spear free and turned his back upon it, and it threw itself upon him – the blow he had struck had not been deep enough, had cut too far beneath the brain, destroying the thing's teeth and jaw, but not killing it. Now as its dry dead hands clasped him, he dropped a shoulder and turned in, kicking its feet from under it. It fell, and he drove the spear down into its skull with both hands. But then as he turned, the spearhead would not come free – it was stuck, embedded too deep, the flanges caught inside the skull. And the others were on him, reaching. He angled the spear and dropped all his weight onto it, snapping the shaft with his knee. He spun it, came up stabbing, using the counter point on the end. The lizard sticker. So named for its brutal use, to stab downwards on the wounded enemy who lay thrashing in the dust as the phalanx ground forward. For nothing scared the hoplite more than the thought of an injured enemy suddenly stabbing upwards, blade tearing into balls and guts, and there's you, wedged in by your mates, unable to get away...No, better to grimly thrust downwards, driving the point into anyone at your feet, alive or dead, to get rid of the threat. And if it happened to be one of your own, one of your own boys from the front of the line, then they had better call out long and loud to avoid being slaughtered. If you could hear them over the din... In those moments of terror, it was hard to think...

Tresantes wasn't thinking, wasn't aiming, just drove the sticker into the chest of the monsters upon him, in this moment his long training overcoming what he needed to do. The square based point didn't have the same penetration power as the slimmer head, but the force punched them back a pace or two.

"Shit!" spat Miltiades. He looked along the line. "Archers! You, and you! Can you help him? Don't hit him! But get them in the head!"

The two men nodded and stood, drawing their bows. "Don't hit him," murmured one. "Apollo bloody save us."

They loosed, and the two shafts arced down into the growing crowd of dead, and were lost.

"The heads! I said the fucking heads!"

"It's not that fucking easy," snapped one to the other. "Let him fucking try..."

They fired again. One arrow flew into a gap, burying itself into the dirt. The other struck a Hadesman square in the eye, and the creature shook briefly, and dropped.

"Shit!" said the archer.

Tresantes had dropped to his knees at the sound of the arrows, somehow hearing the whir in the air above the groans of the dead. He struck out with the heavy shaft now, swinging it like a club, aiming at their knees. Brittle joints cracked, and the creatures fell. He stared into the face of one that crawled toward him – it had been female, not far past marriageable age, as far as he could tell. Somehow the sight of her grey dead tits swinging free beneath her unnerved him more than anything else he had seen. Both nipples were missing, and he wondered...

"Tresantes!" bellowed Miltiades. "Run!"

He jerked back into action, spinning and kicking back into the dead girl's face. He dropped his broken spear and ran for the wall, vaulting over the traps at its base. He leapt, and caught hold of the top, but found now that his arm strength was spent, and he hung there for an awful moment, and the sound of the dead groaning and coming after him was horrible in his ears – it was the not being able to see behind, the feeling of safety, relative safety, being just there, within reach. Then Zander and Miltiades had him, grabbing him by the sweat-streaked arms and hauled him over to collapse onto the fighting step with them.

"Did that help?" he gasped. "I don't know if that that helped..."

"Just get another bloody spear," said Miltiades grimly. "They are on us."

The dead had surged after Tresantes as he fled, and straight into the traps set by the Greeks. They came on as a thick wedge of corruption, and seven or eight of those in the front went down, legs shattering in the buried amphora, just as the first Hadesman had done. But unlike that one, these had no time to pull themselves free before the next undead tripped over them and fell, pinning them beneath a mass of writhing limbs. Others staggered past, or barely over, and hit the trip wires: they caught their feet, and pitched forward, straight onto the angled stakes set behind the ropes. Only one or two were caught through the head, the rest were pierced straight through chest and stomach and throat, and so they sank there, pinned, grunting, as still more dead clambered over them, tripping and sprawling.

But meanwhile more and more kept coming, not just at this point, but further along the line, attracted by the men standing shouting and swearing at the top. And the tangled mess spread on both sides, forming a knee deep then waist deep mass of confused movement. Some managed to make their way over the tangle, and now righted themselves and came to the wall, staring up with dead eyes, reaching with their scrappy hands. And now the hoplites reared up, stabbing downward with their broad-headed spears, the blades biting into skulls. Some were misaimed, and sheared alongside the skulls, sending flaps of dead skin curling, or punched down into shoulders or throats. Some spears were lost, caught deep within a falling body, let go of by men fearful of being pulled over. Most struck true, and the men held firm, drawing their spearheads free, their cuirasses scraping against the wall top as they drew their quivering arms back to strike again.

"Fire!" cried Miltiades. "Fire!"

And the call was taken up along the wall, and behind it as the boys ran along, calling in their high voices. Now the poorer colonists rose, with bows and javelins, and fired down into the writhing mass caught on the traps. It didn't matter where they aimed – the missiles helped pin those on top to those underneath, and added a further barrier. Javelins punched through leathery skin and desiccated muscle, skewering the dead. Arrows thrummed, every one hitting a target, becoming another piece in the confused mess.

The tangled mass of Hadesmen now stood chest high, and was such an awkward obstacle that half those trying to clamber over simply became stuck themselves, as one of their legs slipped down into a gap, or other trapped horde members grabbed hold of them in the effort to drag themselves free. Others simply overbalanced as soon as they started, their leathery limbs and tight sinews not allowing much balance, and they fell backwards, unblinking eyes staring up at the sky for a moment before whatever logic still lingered in their crumbling brains drove them to slowly roll over, push themselves upright, and try again.

The few that did fight their way across joined the thin line at the wall, reaching up, scraping more dead skin from their toes and feet as they tried to climb. They made no moves to defend themselves as the heavy iron heads of the Greek's spears bit into them from above. Some grabbed hold of the shafts, reacting to the movement, and pulled them from the grasp of the defenders. Those who found themselves weaponless took up stones from the piles at their feet, and dropped or threw them down, smashing in the Hadesmen's skulls.

Miltiades' arm ached. He had not wielded a spear so long for many years, and his occasional visit to the gym did not compensate. He had slain at least three of the horrors himself, but kept stepping back to squint along the line. They were holding. Clearly, they were fast becoming exhausted, but they were holding. Maybe he could rest some of the men, have them fight in shifts... but the terror of allowing one of those things to manage to scale the wall was too great. If the face of the wall was smoother, if they had had time to properly shape and fit the blocks, then maybe they could risk it. But he feared there were too many finger and toe holds still... And the height was slowly shrinking as the dead stood on more and more of their own fallen.

It was sickening. No human force could have kept up that kind of assault, in the face of such death. Men's hearts could stand only so much. It was the reason for the creation of the Greek style of warfare – one brutal, horrible combat that lasted as long as it took one phalanx to break the will of the other, and then it was done and the peace deal struck. This endless butchery was something new, something no man should have to face. Even the Spartans would surely quail at this. He glanced across at Tresantes, who was breathing hard but striking smoothly. Callias was on his other side, grim faced, his lips moving either in silent prayer or cursing. Teron was with him, his beautiful armour now grimed and scraped, but his well-balanced spear had brought down his own trio of dead as they climbed the wall like some monstrous grey lizards.

Miltiades felt a tap on his ankle, and he flinched, but it was only Bolinthos, with Embades behind him. The Thracian gestured towards himself and his mate with his thumb, and then raised a quizzical eyebrow. He pointed over the wall, then at the rhomphaia in his hand. Miltiades stood upright, checking on his forces, then gazed over the wall, forcing himself to look beyond the writhing mass of bodies – Zeus, like a disgusting mass of maggots, they were – to the field behind...and saw something wonderous. The numbers were thinning. They were definitely thinning. There were maybe a score or more still coming down the slopes and through the trees, but in small dribs and drabs.

"Be my guests," he said to the Thracians, gesturing at the wall.

They grinned, not understanding his words, but seeing his gesture, and scrambled up beside him. He was pleased to see they both recoiled momentarily at the sight from the top, but then they picked a gap and jumped lightly down on the other side.

"Cease fire!" yelled Miltiades, his voice cracking. He needed water. "Watch out for the Thracians!"

He need not have worried. The javelins were all spent, and all but a handful of arrows. The stones, too, were greatly depleted. Hardly anyone was still firing into the mass. Some men had even started using their swords, leaning dangerously out to hack down into the faces of the dead with their curved chopping swords. Tresantes was one of these now, spear gone, practically lying atop the wall, holding on with his left hand and feet while stabbing downward with his short straight xithus blade.

The two Thracians hefted their two-handed swords as the nearest Hadesmen turned hissing towards them, and cleaved their heads from their bodies with easy sweeps. Most of the others had not noticed them arrive, and continued to claw at the wall.

Before they could take action, there was a scream from further along the defences – a man was lying over the top, his legs held by his desperate mates as a trio of Hadesmen hauled on his arms. Embades sprinted toward the writhing knot, but even as he reached them, the dead were biting down into the man's neck and shoulders. The long rhomphaia blade sang through the air, splitting open the dead creature's skulls. The defenders started to drag the now silent man back up, but suddenly there was Metramandes, shoving them aside.

"Drop him! Drop him!" he cried.

They stared at him – but he yanked their grips free, and the man tumbled down over the wall. Metramandes looked down at the Thracian, who saluted with his blade and drove it down into the man's head.

Miltiades felt sick; so close to victory, to lose a man now...

Bolinthos meanwhile was jogging along, striking down and splitting rotten skulls. He then turned to the reaching hands of the dead caught in the logjam on the traps. He spat at them, then with a fierce cry swung his blade backwards and forwards, shearing their hands and forearms away, then lifted the blade and stabbed it down, repeatedly, into one clouded eye after another, snuffing out the little life that remained in each.

There was another tap at Miltiades' ankle, this time Hegesipyle, holding aloft a water skin with a tight smile. He squatted and took it gratefully, gulping it down.

"Cousin!" croaked Callias. "Can we join them?"

Miltiades hesitated. There was an urge there to stop, to leave it, let them go – but that wasn't a sensible thought. These weren't men. If they didn't take care of them now, the dead would continue to struggle, some no doubt eventually freeing themselves and going for the wall again. They had to be destroyed.

"Over the wall!" he cried, pitching his voice high to carry along the defences.

He turned and threw his spear down, and draped a leg over. He paused, looking to see that none of the bodies below were moving, and dropped. He staggered, and fell, landing in the rotten pile of meat and bones, running with foul liquid. Around him others dropped too, some keeping their footing, others like him losing balance on the uneven ground and cursing. He groaned. His cuirass had bitten painfully into his side. He thrust himself upright, a mouthful of hot vomit gushing free as he was forced to place his hands on the dead. He took hold of his spear and stepped towards the seething wall. One small corpse pulled itself free and upright as he approached – Athena! It looked like a boy barely in his teens, one arm totally missing, as were his ears and nose. Miltiades stopped and held his spear level and firm, and the dead boy ran straight into it, the point biting into his forehead. He continued to shove forward, head pushed back, mouth gaping. Miltiades cursed and ground his teeth, thrusting forward, but instead of penetrating, the boy's head suddenly turned, and the spearhead merely slid across his brow, slicing open the skin. The dead boy stumbled forward, clawing for his face with its one hand. He swung the spear like a staff, but the thing was in too close, and the counterweight missed. The shaft smacked into the side of its head, but not hard enough to drop it. Miltiades held the spear out crossways, holding the thing off as it reached for him – but his arm muscles were shivering, and it was pressing with some unholy might...

"Stand still!" a voice shouted behind him, and he froze. A spear head appeared over his left shoulder, its point blackened with undead gore. The shaft rested on his shoulder, and then shot forward, neatly puncturing the dead boy right between the eyes. The arm dropped, and it sagged, the spear head still embedded in its brain. Miltiades shoved, and the body fell free.

Tresantes stood beside him. Still naked, Miltiades noted. But he was glad that the Spartan's first priority had been to find another spear, not put his tunic back on. He looked both ways to take stock of the action. The colonists were hacking and stabbing at the dead they could reach in the tangled pile. Now that the main burst of adrenaline had left them, none were keen on risking themselves by getting too close to those grasping fingers, those champing jaws. This was different to the usual kind of victory, where you chased down the opposing side in a mad wave of joy to still be living, till you dropped from exhaustion and tore your helmet off to drink in great breaths of incredibly sweet air – provided you were far enough from the main field of battle, with its stench of blood and shit. But here there was no great joy, for the horror before them robbed them of that.

"My thanks," gasped Miltiades.

The Spartan nodded, and approached the pile. There were three or four Hadesmen within his reach that still moved – though all were safely pinned beneath other properly dead ones on top. Tresantes let his spear point track between them, as they growled and stared, then struck, skewering the largest looking one through the eye.

Callias limped over, and waved away Miltiades' look of concern.

"I tripped, jumping off that stupid wall. My foot went right through... Well, never mind. I really want to go down to the sea and wash it. Can I? I mean, we've won, haven't we?"

"Yes," said Miltiades, and a smile cracked his lips. "Yes, I believe we have. We bloody well have."

A horn blast tore through the air. They spun. Hegesipyle stood atop the wall, the other women and children clustered with her. They were staring into the distance, some pointing, crying out.

Hegesipyle looked into Miltiades' eyes, her hair flying behind her like a torn banner.

"What is it?" he asked, but he knew.

"Come back," she called. "Now."

The horde was big. Very big. It had been together for a long time, its numbers swelling whenever it encountered a settlement, slowly dwindling as its weaker, more dismembered members gradually fell apart, and were reduced to spindly husks pulling themselves along inch by inch. They had been Egyptians, and Phoenicians, and Cappadocians, Persians, Medes, Lydians. Bactrians. Sogdians. And yes, Greeks. But now they were united, past differences long forgotton, past love, hate, rational discourse, blazing jealousy. All that was left was the hunger...and maybe something more, for why else stay together, tramping along in solemn groaning procession. Yet they took no comfort from each other. Provided no help to each other. If one fell, it was left where it lay. And so the horde had marched on, with no plan, no destination. They moved as mindlessly as a plague of locusts, simply seeking to devour whatever lay in their path. And in their journey, passing along the coast line – for there was sense enough to stick to dry land– the horde bunched and stretched. Sometimes packed tightly, sometimes spreading wide. And so it was that a pack had pulled ahead of the rest. And it was this group that lay dead in depth before Miltiades' wall.

But now the rest had arrived.

"Back to the wall! Back to the wall!"

They grabbed what they could. They picked up the dropped spears – those that weren't broken. They plucked javelins from the bodies they could reach. Some arrows could be salvaged – mostly those stuck in the ground, for the others were held firm in the tight dead meat by their barbs, and needed time to be cut out. They were tired. Some jumped and pulled themselves up, others needed to be hoisted and pulled – especially the hoplites. Most had left their big round hoplons on the wall, but cuirasses and helmets were heavy. So with scraped skin, the defenders hauled themselves over, back onto the fighting step, and their movement was duly noted by the dead pouring out onto the plain, and a terrible groan filled the air as they came on.

"Oh fuck," said Miltiades, and Tresantes spat over the side and said nothing.

They came forward, so many more than before, much tighter packed than before. Drawn to the area where they had seen the most movement, where the traps had created the mound of dead. Hundreds of them. More. Thousands.

"We're going to die," said Callias.

"Worse," grunted Zander.

"Ready yourselves!" bellowed Miltiades, and his voice surprised him. It didn't sound like him at all. He jumped up onto the wall. "Let none pass! We are men of Athens, and we do not yield!"

A ragged cheer swept the battlement, and the men pounded their weapons on the rock.

"Hegesipyle! Get the women. Get all the lamp oil you can from the camp. Hurry!"

She nodded and ran, calling to the other women and boys as she sprinted for the stores. He turned back and watched the black tide of dead pouring forward.

Black sea of the dead. Black ocean rising.

His uncle had warned him – tried to, couldn't. Why? Was this somehow meant to be?

The legion of dead reached the tangled mass of bodies at a shambling run, and the leading corpses went down in a sprawl on top. Some were impaled on protruding stakes, adding another layer like a corrupt offering of meat on a skewer. But most were unharmed. They started dragging themselves upward, and some more were grabbed by those in the pile, still seeking to drag themselves free, and were held fast, their teeth gnashing in frustration. Others were crushed and held by the Hadesmen following, who also sought to clamber over.

And for a moment, watching the tangled mess, Miltiades felt a surge of hope – it might still work. The wall of dead would become even more tangled, maybe, and collapse backwards on itself.

But as he watched, the first of this new wave rolled down the front, into the space between the dead barricade and the wall. And before they could do more than crawl forward, more undead fell on top of them, adding a complete layer of death.

The height of the barricade was growing, and the front side of it was becoming more compacted, giving those behind it easier access to the top. And as they crested it, and tumbled forward, they added still another layer in the gap – and it didn't matter that all of these were unable to rise, because their layers themselves were creating a siege ramp.

Wrong. He'd been wrong. The undead barricade wasn't going to save them – it was going to be their doom.

Almost as if the dead sensed their victory, they seemed to concentrate in the space before him. The mound was growing so high now, that the Hadesmen in the back of the horde could see and were attracted by the movement and excitement of those staggering to the top.

The mound was now as high as the wall. And the gap in between was half way full.

"Knock them down!" he screamed. "Everything you have!"

Arrows and javelins sang, and the top rank of Hadesmen fell backwards, knocking down those behind. The range was short, and the dead were not fast as they waded forward, so the archers were able to put their shafts right into the horrible gaping faces. Likewise for the javelin throwers – for did not all Greek men value exercise and education, and so at some point in their lives, practise the sport? So their cast's, so close to their targets, were true, and a well-thrown javelin could pierce right through a Hadesman's rotten skull, the tip cracking through grey bone, dragging whatever hideous consciousness was left with it.

But the ammunition was soon spent, and the dead began to rise again.

"Here!"

Miltiades spun – Hegesipyle, with the fastest of the other women and boys, puffing as they carried heavy dark amphorae between them. He dropped to his knees, holding out his hand, and Tresantes was there beside him. Together they took up the first and tipped it over the wall, the lamp oil within splashing down over the grinding dead below.

"Pour it on! Pour it on!" he cried, and other men copied him, taking up the oil flagons and upending them.

Miltiades knelt and struck at a flint, his hands shaking, the spark not taking in the torch beside him. Hegesipyle prised the stone from his grip, and struck it, a bright glow burying into the torch head, she cupped in, blew upon it, and light burst forth. He squeezed her hand, and took up the flaring torch, feeling the heat scorch his face as he stood. With a savage cry he flung it down, and the oil ignited.

No great explosion as he had wished, just a rushing blue flame that ran across the surface of the dead. The shredded dry rags that wrapped their leathery limbs caught, and so too did the matted hair atop their heads. And now the flame changed colour, and the fast running blue was taken over by the crackle and surge of yellow flame. The dead did not feel the flames, and still sought to crawl and climb to them, but as the heat bit into them, their tight tendons and husks of muscle froze, and snapped, and they dropped, charred and barely moving.

But more dead fell, for they were not afraid of the heat or the flame. The weight of their numbers slowly smothered the fires, and all that had been gained was another layer of corpses. The mound was higher. At this point of the wall, they were looking up at the dead who fell forward. And they were getting closer. They would soon be raining down upon them.

"Callias!" bellowed Miltiades. "Run the wall. Get all the spare hoplites down below."

"But there is fighting all along the wall."

"This is the crucial moment. If we are breached here, the rest doesn't matter anyway. Run! Tresantes – get down there. Get them into a square, you understand?"

"Yes," said the Spartan. "We are about to lose the wall."

Miltiades stopped. "I hope not. But yes, we probably are."

The Spartan nodded, and dropped off the step. Miltiades turned to the men about him. "Hoplites to me! Light troops, make way, to the sides."

The men exchanged places – the archers and javelin men now armed with nothing but swords and daggers, while the helmeted spearmen formed up beside Miltiades.

"Get your shields," he told them, and they turned and shouted at the boys and women, who ran forward, lifting the heavy hoplons from where they sat against the base of the wall. None cared whose shield they took. They slid them onto their left arms, and faced the dead, spear or sword in hand, a wall atop a wall.

"Now steady," cried Miltiades, and he stared upward into the hollow eyes of a Hadesman balanced atop the great mound of dead, and the gap between was near full, and this foul thing now came staggering forward, part falling, right at him, right at this part of the wall. He gritted his teeth, and braced, and the thing came crunching into his shield, and he felt the weight of it – not the full weight of a living man, but this thing had the weight of horror, of nightmares, upon it. He thrust back, sensing more than hearing its clawed fingers and teeth scrabbling at the layer of bronze on the other side. And around him he heard men cry as more corpses fell against them, and they shoved, the grinding pushing match of the phalanx, but here there was no additional line behind them to add weight, to steady them. There wasn't even room to take a step back.

"Knock them back!" someone bellowed – it might have been Metramandes. "Knock them back to Hades!"

"Knock them back!" screamed Miltiades, and he shoved with all his might. The cry went up along the wall, a desperate paean.

Suddenly he stumbled forward, the weight gone from his shield as the corpse lost its footing and fell backward over the wall. Exhausted, he turned and smashed his hoplon into the nearest Hadesman to his left, sending it sprawling. It rolled over the edge, but landed only a short distance below thanks to the pile of bodies already there. The man beside him had barely time to grunt out "Thanks" before the next corpse came barrelling into him. He grunted again, bending beneath the strain. Miltiades drew back to strike again, but movement caught his eye and he spotted his own dead man coming at him. He just had time to turn and brace as it fell against him – and then another piled in behind.

The number of dead swarming up the slope did not appear to be slacking. They could not hold.

Miltiades could not risk turning to look behind. "Tresantes! Tresantes, are you ready?"

"We are ready," came the Spartan's voice, and its steady calm gave him heart.

"Get ready to break!" he yelled. "Do you hear me? Wait for the word-"

But with a cry the man beside him turned and jumped, the Hadesman toppling after him. Instantly two or three more appeared, fighting into the gap.

"Break! Break!" Miltiades gave a last shove, losing his shield as the dead clutched it, then spun and jumped. He landed heavily, twisting sideways as a Hadesman lying nearby reached for him. He was dimly aware of men yelling and landing around him, staggering upright and running as best they could. Thankfully, exhausted as they were, they were still able to react faster than the dead who fell after them. Ringing the spot where they had given way stood the hoplites gathered from the rest of the wall, shields held high, spears cocked over their shoulders. The defenders ran for the line, pushing through. Miltiades ran for Tresantes, conspicuous in his nakedness. The Spartan turned to let him slip through, then squared up again as Miltiades bent over, coughing.

"Miltiades," said the Spartain quietly, and the Athenian made himself stand upright and turn – in time to see a moving clot of a score or more dead breasting the top of the wall, flooding over.

"Dead! We're dead!" cried a man nearby, and he turned to run. Others stood, uncertain whether to join the arc of hoplites or flee.

"Stop that man!" croaked Miltiades.

"With pleasure," someone answered, and a hunting spear sailed through the air and caught the man in the small of the back. He collapsed writhing.

"Teron, fuck you," said Miltiades, but it worked, he could see it worked, men were coming back to the line, reinforcing it.

And the dead rose and came at them.

These men were fresher, had not been as hard pressed, and their iron spear heads jabbed forward viciously, crunching into the unprotected faces of the dead, dropping them at their feet. Behind them, beside them, the weary defenders thrust with sticks and slashed with their swords, or caught up stones and hurled them. Stick and stone and steel smashed and bit deep into the already ruined faces of the snarling dead, the horror lending them strength.

On the fighting step, the defenders were peeling back as the breach widened. But further along, all along the wall, scrabbling figures could be seen pulling themselves up and over. It was the end.

"Form a square! Women and children in the middle! To me! All to me!"

They were going to lose lives. It was inevitable. He hadn't let himself think it before, some primitive fear that giving it thought would somehow make it fact. But he had been fooling himself. Men were going to die, because of him. Because of his hubris.

Why were they here?

He was his father's fucking son after all. Glory chaser.

Some never made it to the safety of their fellows. They fell awkwardly, twisting an ankle under the weight of their armour, and collapsed. Or else landed fine, but were instantly knocked flat and helpless by a Hadesman or two falling straight down onto them. And once a man was down, and grabbed in the bony grasp of the dead, it was next to impossible for him to rise. For others would swarm him, like ants battling an armoured beetle, biting at the soft exposed parts, dismembering, carrying the pieces away.

It was a foul way to die. Death in battle was always horrible – the spearhead ripping into bowels, the heavy sword chopping down into neck and shoulder. The collapse into the mass of the phalanx, screaming as the counter weights beat down. But this was worse again. One had only to listen to the screams of the victims to hear how much worse this was – the horror of it. For it struck a man deep inside him, to find himself being eaten alive, especially by something that was not a part of nature, such as a lion or bear, which, horrible as it was for the victim, was only doing what was natural – these things, these things that existed outside of nature, and had no real need for the meat they were consuming so greedily.

But most, most, managed to get clear. They formed up, the best armoured taking the rear position, closest to the dead, and the light troops forming the front rank and the sides. The women and children and injured clumped in the middle. And they began a retreat – back to where? Where was there to go? Men held the cuirasses of the rear rank, guiding them, as they struck back at the following mob of the dead, with their yellowed teeth and yellowed bones, blackened holes in their bellies. And all tried not to look at the wall and the surging tide pouring over and after them.

They couldn't move fast. The more mobile of the dead caught them, some falling punctured by spear or with a head smashed open by a blunted sword. Others surged along the sides, grabbing at the shields, reaching for the flesh they craved. From above, mused Miltiades, they must look like some great injured beast dragging itself along, with a swarm of flies following to suck it dry. They laboured on. The two Thracians darted back and forth along the rear line, leaning over the shoulders of the hoplites to sweep down with their rhomphaia and cleave skulls in two. How they could have used a score of such warriors. They ground their way up the rise, and now the buildings of their little settlement were in sight – but what was the point? The huts were not fortified, they would not hold the dead out for long, even providing they could break contact and run for them.

Miltiades looked towards the jetty, hoping against hope to see Phillipus' trireme docked there – but it was empty. There was no escape that way. With much bellowing, Miltiades had the square wheel to the left, and head down to the beach. If they must die, they may as well die as Greeks, with the sea to their backs. Besides, they would not need a fourth side, and those men could reinforce the others.

As they began bypassing the huts, Tresantes drew back from the line and angled into the front corner formed by the light troops.

"Hey!" shouted Miltiades. He could see the Spartan looking at the numbers of Hadesmen on this side.

"I will be back soon," said the Spartan.

"Do not do it. Do not go after that fucking rabbit- Tresantes!"

But the Spartan had already shouldered through the line, and was sprinting up the slope. A number of the dead snatched at him as he sped by, and some went to follow, but he disappeared from sight too quickly, and the slowly crawling square was such a more obvious source of meat, and so they turned and resumed their assault. Miltiades ground his teeth. He dare not slow their march or stop, or they would be completely surrounded, and they simply did not have enough armoured men to adequately defend all sides. But he need not have worried, for they seemed to have moved hardly at all when the Spartan came jogging back down the slope, a club of firewood in one hand, and a cloak-wrapped object clutched to him in the other. He ran an arc around to the front of the square, beating two or three Hadesmen to the ground, and met them as they hit the beach.

"Open the line!" he yelled, and, startled, a few men at the front shifted enough for him to dart back in, chest heaving. Miltiades shook his head.

And so the square crunched over the sand, men swearing or crying aloud to the gods, the younger children wailing as their mothers hugged them grimly to their sides, urging them not to trip, not to fall. As they hit the water, the front rank plunged forward until they were waist deep, then splashed their way back to the sides and rear.

And so the dead followed them, stumbling down the slope, spreading around the formation, reaching for the living. When their hands and forearms were hacked away, still they groped with the stumps, strips of dried flesh waving like little war banners. They leaned in, teeth clacking, and fell back with their skulls caved in, and either stayed down if the damage was sufficient, or slowly drew themselves back to their feet if not.

Miltiades grabbed Hegesipyle and pulled her to him. He pressed his lips to her ear.

"When we fall, you must kill the children. Do you understand? Wait as long as you can...but don't let them be eaten alive. Do not allow them to die that way."

She nodded bleakly, then darted her head forward and kissed him, their lips barely touching through the narrow gap in the front of his helmet. Miltiades turned back to the line, and took his place. His right shoulder ached, and he had no shield, but he had picked up a broken piece of wood, and used that now to hold the Hadesmen at bay long enough to raise his chopping sword to his shoulder – Apollo's balls, how the thing seemed to weigh four times more – and swing it down, hacking into their heads. If he was lucky, they dropped, and the blade pulled free. Otherwise, they fought on, biting at the wood he held in their faces, as he wrenched to pull the blade out and strike again.

He risked a glance up the slope, and the sight killed what hope remained, for he could see, silhouetted on the top, a dense new rank, pausing as they took in the scene below. So this was it, he thought, nothing to do but die now. So why fight on? Why not just let it happen? A part of his mind was interested to find this spark, this will to live, that wouldn't let him drop his weapons and surrender. And there was a small surge of something like pride. Maybe, when he met his uncle in the afterlife – if such a thing really did exist, and Zeus Above, did he not hope with all his heart in this moment that it did – he would be able to clasp hands as an equal.

Dimly came a strange hissing.

He hacked and shoved. Rain? Was that rain? It didn't matter. He could die just as well wet as dry – but there were no clouds…
The hissing came closer.
"Arrows!" someone croaked behind him.
"They're shooting at us too?" he whispered, brain reeling. He squinted: there was nothing – wait, there, the next volley, a mass of shafts lifting into the air like a flight of deadly birds. He could see them, see them reach the zenith of their flight, and they pitched down – down into the rear rank of the dead. Pitched down and punctured heads. The figures on the rise – they were men, living men.
He choked, tears stinging his eyes.
The arrows kept falling, gradually falling closer and closer to the knot of defenders. Few of the dead were aware of the newcomers. They made no move to defend themselves, even when peppered with shafts. Some sported five or more stuck in their backs and shoulders, until a fatal shot hit them hard enough in the head to penetrate into the grey matter inside and end their horrific second existence.
"Hold on," murmured Miltiades. "Just hold on. We can make it." Then bellowing: "Hold them! Hold them! Don't fall now!"
He heard a child wail behind him and he looked back in horror - "Hegesipyle! No!" – but she met his gaze calmly as she

bounced a child in her arms, the mother sunken in exhaustion at her feet.

Back on the ridge line, the archers ceased fire and parted ranks, and scores of spearmen jogged down the slope in long lines. Their spears were shorter than those of the Greeks, and they carried light rectangular or oval shields of wicker. They seemed to wear little armour, and strangest of all – they were wearing long trousers.

These spearmen descended on the rear ranks of the dead, and began to despatch them. They seldom fought one-to-one, but instead crowded each Hadesman, so that two could hem it in while a third lined up a killing thrust. Their light shields worked well in this regard. Miltiades could see how easily they could be whipped into position, and while the cane did not seem sturdy enough to fend one of the corpses off for very long – he doubted he would ever forget the sound of their exposed bone finger tips scraping on his bronze shield-front – by working together they were able to jostle the dead into the right position.

All the weary Greeks had to do was stand firm and maintain their shield wall, gladly letting these newcomers finish the slaying. They were dark skinned, with piercing eyes, and called to each other in a strange tongue. Their clothing was exotically patterned, their heads covered by scarves. They grinned at the Greek defenders with white teeth, and called encouragement to them.

When the last Hadesman lay still, they reformed into a rectangular formation, and the archers jogged down to do the same, their remaining shafts clattering in the quivers attached to their belts.

"What now?" asked Callias.

"We hold our position," Miltiades answered.

"Our position is fucking tenuous," he heard Teron rasp.

He snorted. If the youngster was complaining, then he must be unhurt.

A small knot of men in armour strode down the hill, accompanied by banners and soldiers bearing horns and trumpets. One came forward.

"The wounded men will please to step forward. Step forward to that side." He pointed over in front of the archers. His Greek was heavily accented, but understandable.

Miltiades stepped forward. "Who are you?"

The man held up a hand. "First, please, the wounded will step forward. Then questions."

"They mean to shoot them down," growled Metramandes.

"We will take care of any wounded we have," said Miltiades. He turned back to his men. Looking at their weary, stunned faces. Apollo above, let there be none...

And they were lucky. There were wounds - cuts and grazes - but none from bites. It appeared that all of those who had been bitten had fallen and been consumed during the fighting. They were fortunate. Miltiades couldn't begin to imagine the horror of having to execute anyone now – especially if they were unwilling and fought against it. Once the newcomers had ascertained for themselves that no one was suffering from any bites, the tension reduced slightly.

"Now," he said, returning to face the officer. "We thank you for your relief. But we must ask who you are, and ask that you stand down. This is the polis of Chersonnesus, and I am Miltiades. We are a lawful colony of Athens. Who are you?"

The man pointed. A small fleet was rounding into the bay, huge Phoenician ships with striped sails and a double row of oarsmen. Horns blared.

"Kneel, oh Greeks," said the officer. "Kneel before Darius, King of the Persians. King of Kings."

TEN

MIDAS

They were herded off the beach, back into their settlement. But gently.

"I am Datis," said the officer. "Come, rest. Talk later. We have refreshments for you. We have cordials and sweetmeats."

So Miltiades led his weary force back into their little polis, where the Persians set up a small feast. They sat and ate, saying little, while they watched dark-skinned levies drag the bodies of the Hadesmen away, and later pointed as dark smoke from a huge funeral pyre boiled into the sky from beyond the wall. Down on the beach, ships docked side by side, and large bright pavilions were set up on the sand. Hegesipyle sat at his side, their knees lightly touching, and if any Greek was offended that a woman sat amongst them, none spoke, for surely such social rules seemed silly in the face of what they had just seen.

"Come," said Datis. "The king wishes to speak to your ruling men."

Miltiades pushed himself to his feet, his joints and muscles protesting painfully. He signalled to Photios, Metramandes and Callias to come with him. Teron seemed too exhausted to even protest his exclusion. The Greeks trooped down to where a large pavilion of gold silk sat in the centre of a ring of slightly smaller tents. Armed guards with short spears, the butts decorated with golden pomegranates, stood at the entrance. Inside, a throne was set at the far end on a raised wooden dais. Courtiers and officers stood about. A man sat on the throne, clad in shining silver scale mail, his hand on the hilt of a golden sword.

"Behold!" cried Datis. "The King of kings! Champion of Ahuramazda, Lord of Light! Prostrate yourselves before him!"

"Do what?" asked Callias.

"I think they want us to kneel," said Miltiades.

"To a barbarian?" growled Metramandes.

"Not kneel," said Datis. "Lie down. On your belly."

The Greeks looked at each other. Up on the dais, King Darius tapped his finger on the pommel of his sword. The soldiers standing around the tent shifted.

"Well," said Miltiades. "I suppose they did just save us from being eaten alive."

"That's right," said Photios. "Besides, it doesn't have to mean anything."

Miltiades faced the king, knelt, and slowly lay himself flat. After a pause, he heard the rustle of the others copying him.

"As it should be," growled a new voice, another speaking accented Greek.

"Stand, stand," said Datis.

They levered themselves up. Another officer had come to stand at Darius' side. A scowling teenage boy was also with him, seemingly dragged in reluctantly from another opening hidden behind the dais. The young man looked them over, sniffed, and looked away in boredom.

"We thank you for your timely intervention against the Hadesmen, oh king," said Miltiades carefully. "I am Miltiades, ruler of Chersonessus, colony of Athens. These are my officers. You are welcome as our guests, so long as your forces are encamped here."

Darius stared at him. The new officer cocked his head and frowned.

"It is you, Greek, who is the visitor…"

"Come, General Mardonius," said Datis. "Let us first talk of these daemons. What did you call them? Hadesmen? After your Underworld, yes?"

"Yes. You know of them? You have seen them in Persia, too?"

"Alas, yes," Datis spread his hands. "It has been the great task of the King to rid his lands of these loathsome creatures. Now all his subjects may sleep at ease, all across the great empire. In his kindness, the King has turned his burning eye upon those lands of his neighbours still beset by this peril."

"Your arrival was certainly most welcome and most timely… Tell me, had you been tracking the movement of the horde?"

"Indeed. Of course, once we saw they were upon you, we needed a certain amount of time to land our troops safely to engage."

Photios cleared his throat. "And what of the city-states around the Euxine? Were you in time to save them as well?"

"Alas, no," said Datis, shaking his head. "We were too late. The daemons had already destroyed those cities…"

"The people, anyway," said the other officer, Mardonius. "The Greeks. They're all dead. Or joined the horde. But the cities still stand."

Datis inclined his head in agreement. "Just so. And so that those who fell are remembered, and their efforts to tame the land not be in vain, the Great King has decreed that we shall resettle those empty cities with subjects from the empire."

"How bloody thoughtful of you," growled Metramandes. "Just expanded your economic hold by what, a dozen cities? Got here too soon, did you? Hoped we were all dead too?"

The Persians bristled.

"Curb your tongue, ignorant pirate!" spat Mardonius.

Miltiades held up his hand to forestall the metic. "As I said," he raised his voice. "As I said, we are very grateful to you. And are happy for you to be our guests. For as you see, Chersonnesus still stands. And so once you have rested, and resupplied, you may leave. With our thanks."

The officers exchanged a glance.

"Ah," said King Darius. "But there is the cost to consider." His accent was heavier than Datis and Mardonius, but his Greek was clear. "And restitution."

"Restitution," Miltiades repeated. "By whom?"

"By you."

"We didn't need you!" Callias burst out. "We could have beaten them!"

There was a pause, then the Persians laughed. The teenage boy stared sullenly at Callias from below his fringe. The king turned to him.

"You see, Xerxes? This one has some fire. This is what I want from you."

The young Persian burned red at being so addressed but remained silent. He sniffed and looked away. The king shook his head.

"You say you had been tracking the horde," said Miltiades slowly. "I, too, have intelligence on its past movement. And given that it originated in Persia, and was allowed to-"

"Encouraged," said Photios.

Miltiades frowned at him. "Allowed to move around the Euxine, then as far as I can see, it is you who owe a debt to me."

There was silence. The king spun the curved sword, the golden pommel beneath his fingers, the point spinning on the wooden dais, digging a shallow hole. Finally he clamped his hand down, stopping the blade, and looked up.

"You have pluck, Greek. And for that, you shall live. What is more, I grant you your colony. I leave you in its control. All I will take in return is some taxation on your income, and expectation of military service should I have need of you. In return, you will swear never to strike against me on land or on water."

Miltiades chewed his lip. But there was nothing for it. They were in no condition to fight, and would be quickly slaughtered by the numerically superior Persians. He needed time. Time to send to Athens for help... Or should he? Would Hippias send any aide? And what, exactly, did he owe to that crazed tyrant anyway? What did it matter who they were under, king or tyrant, so long as Chersonnesus grew?

....

Walking back up to the settlement, Miltiades could feel Metramandes seething.

"What?"

"I can't believe you did that!" the metic exploded. "Sold us out like that!"

"What else in Zeus' name did you expect me to do? Declare war?"

"It just sits badly with me. To be under a barbarian."

"It isn't that bad," said Photios. "They really aren't interfering much at all. In fact, they are being far more generous than we Greeks have been to people we have conquered."

"But they didn't conquer us! They...they cheated! And I tell you, it will sit badly with the men of my party."

"Wait a minute." Miltiades stopped and stepped in front of Metramandes. "What party? As in, a political party? Because there is no such thing out here, chum. I'm in charge. And that is it."

Metramandes stared at him, then stalked off muttering. Miltiades turned to Callias and Photios in exasperation.

"Can you believe this idiot? Not two hours ago we were fighting for our very lives, and now he wants to tell me his fucking party will be unhappy with me? What the fuck?"

"Well," said Photios, patting his arm. "He is a Greek. What do you expect? Politics is in our blood."

"Is a little gratitude too much to ask, though?"

"Ah, but that is the worst of all. Every time he feels he must be grateful to you just makes him resent you more."

"You want to know the worse thing about that prophecy? About being betrayed three times? It is knowing you are looking at one of the people who is going to do it, and not being able to do a thing about it."

"Hmmm," said Photios. "You never know. He may be one of the people fated to be betrayed by you."

....

"You are an exceptional man."

Miltiades shrugged. "I only did what any leader would do in my position."

"No," said the King of Kings mildly. "No, I have many Greeks under me. More than a score of Greek cities on the Ionian coast pay me tribute. I have watched them. Watched them bicker and jockey for position. No, you are not like them. You are more like...me." His white teeth gleamed in his tanned face.

They strolled along the beach, a ring of armed guards keeping a discrete distance away. The summons had come earlier that day. Datis himself had come knocking at Miltiades' door, to tell him that King Darius wished to speak to him. It was awkwardly timed. Alone, finally, with Hegesipyle, he had asked: "So...tonight?"

She had smiled. "You mean, will I still sleep with you now that we no longer seem at risk of being devoured?"

"Well," he said, face flushing red. "Yes, but I mean, only if you want..."

"Sometimes," she said, "Sometimes it is very nice to be devoured."

And then had come the blasted knock at the door. He had to hold his cloak in front of him to disguise the sudden appearance of his lust. As he followed the Persian officer he had spotted Tresantes sitting in the shade, gently tugging on the ears of the rabbit which lay alongside his leg. One of its brown eyes had blinked open and looked at Miltiades in such a smug way that he felt his irritation spill over.

"That rabbit is going to be the death of you one day."

The Spartan had simply shrugged in reply.

"I don't get it. You risked your life to go after it, but it is just an animal."

"Maybe so." Tresantes scratched its head, and it nestled down lower. "But I care for her more than any other."

Miltiades shook his head. "It is hard for me to understand."

"Then I feel pity for you." The Spartan turned his calm eyes onto Miltiades, and the Athenian was surprised to find how the words stung him.

The Persian general had called him on. But instead of heading to the great silk tent, they had continued further down the beach, where the figure of the Persian King had been standing staring out across the waters of the Hellespont.

"Go," said Datis, a little bitterly. "The Great King made it quite clear he wishes to speak with you alone."

And now they strolled along the shore, the small waves hissing across the sand near their feet.

"We had a wall to help us," Miltiades offered.

"A wall does not defend a city by itself. It needs men. And before you protest again, I would say men do not defend a wall unless they are led. Not against other men, and certainly not against the likes of these daemons."

"Forgive me for this, uh, King Darius – I appreciate the flattery, I really do – but I gathered our survival is more a source of irritation to your plans for expansion."

The Persian laughed. "You see, that is what I am talking about. A big problem that one encounters as King of Kings is a certain unwillingness by one's subjects to speak plainly. They are all too busy fighting for position. Persians, Medes, Greeks... All the same. Thus, I find you a little refreshing. So, let me be plain in return. Yes, I had not expected anyone to survive the daemon onslaught, let alone a piddling little place like this. You had a wall, you say. Well, so too did some of the far larger cities to the north. But they are now stripped bare like a cornfield after a locust swarm. This does make your survival somewhat exceptional."

"We only survived in the end because of your arrival. You could have let them finish us. Or shot us to pieces with your archers."

"Yes. But we watched your withdrawal, your choice of where to make your stand. By then I had determined that I wanted to meet you. Under my rule I have many subject peoples. Many seek to revolt at any moment, given any sign of weakness. The Empire is vast. I must rely on my generals and satraps to govern and keep the peace. I do have a satrap for Ionia, and he is a good man, Artaphernes. But he is not skilled with the Greeks under his control. You are a difficult people. This is where you come in."

Miltiades waited. He wasn't sure what to feel, let alone what to say. Not so long ago, you would have found him sipping wine and reading in his study, avoiding his mother. To be here, now...

"You must be well-regarded in your city, to be given this post. No doubt your family were well pleased with the honour."

He couldn't stop a bark of laughter escaping. "Hardly."

The Persian raised an eyebrow. "What of your father? Is he not proud?"

"My father is dead. But he and I never... saw eye to eye."

"Ah," The King stopped, hands behind his back. He was gazing further down the beach. A lone figure stood there, staring morosely out to sea. Miltiades saw that it was the Persian adolescent. "It is difficult between fathers and sons, some times. As father, you see how things should be, to your eye, but... The son will see things how he will."

They resumed walking.

"There will be another operation. Soon. I am taking my forces north, into the lands of the Skythians."

"Hunting the Hadesmen? The daemons, as you call them?"

"Of course," smiled the King. "Though of course, to then safeguard the area I will be compelled to bring it into the Empire. I need ships, to transport troops, and equipment, and for communication. Many of these ships will be provided by the Ionian Greeks. I want you there. I want you to be a leader amongst the Greeks, help keep them in line. But to accept you as equal, you are going to need warships. You don't seem to have any..."

"One. I can get one."

Darius nodded. "It is a start. In return for this, I will appoint you as sole ruler of your little city. And I will send you builders and carpenters to help you grow. Will you do this?"

Would he?

"Well, I suppose since we have already medized..."

"Why do you call it that?" frowned Darius. "We are Persian, not Medes. You should say 'Persianized', if anything."

"Ah. It is the nature of we Greeks to think we understand something, and refuse to change our mind if proven wrong. The kingdom to the East was always known as that of the Medes, before the Persians came. Anyway, I will do it. I will serve with you."

The king stopped and turned, holding his eye. The silence stretched out between them.

"Don't let me down, Miltiades."

And strangely, Miltiades couldn't help but take a liking to him. When you compared him to Hippias... But then a thought hit him:

Thrice betrayed.

....

The Thracians returned.

King Olorus did not even wait to send out scouts, but came himself, riding down from the mountains on a sweat-soaked horse. He rode with his cloak thrown over his head, his reins in the hands of two of his bodyguard who rode either side of him.

And when the party of riders with him saw the wall standing, and called to him, and he himself heard Bolinthos and Embades shouting from the battlement, he tore the cloak from his head. And when he saw his daughter Hegesipyle standing proud atop the wall, he slipped from his horse's back and ran as fast as his thick legs could carry him.

The Persians had stayed another week, before the tents were brought down, and one by one they had marched down and embarked on the ships standing out in the bay. King Darius, good as his word, left behind a party of engineers, who joined the Greeks in turning their tents into huts, their huts into houses. The blocks sealing the gate were withdrawn, and stacked for future use, and a strong wooden gate built and hung in place.

Miltiades had ordered a constant watch be kept on the wall. It appeared the Persian light troops had been thorough, scouring the land and shooting down any straggling Hadesmen, but he did not wish to take any chances. Who knew how many may even now still be stumbling slowly around the great Euxine sea? Or how many lurked in the Skythian grasslands?

Then a runner came from the wall, reporting horsemen on the horizon, coming from the northwest, and Hegesipyle had smiled and run for the wall, Miltiades struggling to keep up.

She turned towards him now, as she knelt and prepared to slip over the wall. Her lips brushed his cheek.

"Now we shall marry. But... best you do not tell my father of our recent sleeping arrangements."

And with that she dropped to the ground, and was swept up in the enormous hug of her father. Miltiades looked at the muscles that still bunched in the older man's arms, the long dagger in his belt, the score of bodyguards riding up behind him, and swallowed. He had absolutely no intention of raising that subject at all.

Somewhat sheepishly, Embades and Bolinthos followed their princess over the wall. Miltiades was tempted to shout and point out the perfectly good gate a little further along. Olorus spotted them coming over his daughter's shoulder. He moved her to the side, and waved them over. First he kissed each of them on the cheek. Then he hauled off and gave each a mighty slap across the face. Then he kissed them again. He looked up at Miltiades and raised an arm. The Athenian waved in reply.

The wedding was held a week later. Olorus demanded it be done in their bria, rather than Chersonnesus. It seemed the Thracian ceremony was similar to the Greek, involving a feast then procession to the groom's home. Except nobody wanted to trudge all the way from the bria, where the feast would take place, to the Chersonnese. So instead Olorus proposed granting Miltiades a temporary home in the village.

The food and wine were good, and put Miltiades at ease somewhat. It felt a little uncomfortable to be so far from what he now saw as his home, amongst these barbarians. They were a mixture of the familiar and the strange. He brought Photios, Callias, Tresantes and Zander with him.

Zander helped dress him in the privacy of his small hut, draping a clean cloak over his best chiton.

"Will I be expected to serve her?" asked the slave.

"A little, I suppose. But maybe she'll want to bring someone with her. You'll be all right with that, won't you?"

"It's just a bit strange. I've never worked for a woman. Apart from the gorgon, of course."

"Well, she doesn't count as human, does she?" Miltiades felt a rush of gratitude for this moment of normalcy between them. He had been conscious of the changes in their relationship since he had assumed this command. He had had less time to just chat. He was acting more like a master, he supposed, and in answer Zander had become somewhat quieter, more like a slave.

Once the feasting and the speeches were done, the libations poured for the blessing of the gods, a torchlit procession led them to their hut. They were accompanied right inside, amid much laughter and cheering, until Miltiades was able to thrust the last well-wisher out, and close the door. Even then, the crowd stood outside, singing wedding songs. Being in the Thracian tongue, Miltiades couldn't understand them, but could guess they were fairly bawdy by the pink tinge to Hegesipyle's cheeks. Worst of all, he could clearly hear King Olorus shouting the words. A strange people.

They sat together on the bed, side by side, strangely shy, until Miltiades reached over and took her hand. He squeezed it, and she turned to him with a small smile. He leaned over and kissed her, lightly, then more hungrily, and she wrapped her arms about him.

When they lay sweaty and spent, Hegesipyle suddenly sat up, and fished about their clothes on the floor. She came up with his knife, and crawled back into the middle of the bed.

"Um, what are you doing?" he asked, as she tested the edge on her thumb. "Hey!" She drew the blade across the pad of her thumb, then carefully squeezed droplets of blood into the centre of the bedding.

"It is best. There are many gossips in this bria." She sucked on her thumb.

"Oh," he said. "I hope I didn't... Back in Chersonnesus, you wanted to, too, didn't you? I didn't mean to make this...awkward for you."

"No," she said, looking aside. "That moment already happened. Before you."

"Oh. I see... Might I... Who was he?"

She shook her head. "It does not matter. He was a kind man, that is all. But he is gone now."

"Where?"

"Away for ever."

"Did you... love him?"

She placed a hand in the middle of his chest. "Let us not talk of what was. The past is like another country we cannot come to again. We are here, now, you and I. Let us just be here."

She pulled him towards her, and he allowed himself to relax, willed himself to just let go, but as he held her she murmured in his ear.

"But remember, nothing is changed. I will still never love you."

....

Phillipus returned. After a fashion.

A lookout positioned in a new wooden tower constructed on a hilltop shouted the arrival of the Athenian warship, and a small crowd gathered at the dock. At first the trireme overshot the pier, and had to backwater, with the cursing of Phillipus carrying clearly across the water. Then it came in too fast, crunching against the dock and causing it to sway dangerously. A couple of oars were even sheered off, the rowers acting too slowly to draw them inside. Finally the ship was tied up alongside, and men jumped across to start unloading the mass of stores lashed down the middle.

Phillipus jumped across and took Miltiades' hand. "You and I must talk. At once."

Miltiades was looking at the strange range of men hauling themselves stiffly from the rowing benches. They didn't look like oarsmen.

"What's going on?"

"Revolution," said the trirarch.

There was now a decent stone council chamber in the middle of Chersonnesus, with a wooden ceiling and benches for meetings. Miltiades sat on one of these, with a handful of colonists about him, including Photios, Callias and Metramandes. Phillipus paced up and down in the middle of the room. There were windows in the walls, but it was still gloomy.

"Now tell us," said Miltiades. "What are you talking about?"

"It was his lot." Phillipus nodded at Teron. Miltiades hadn't invited him, and hadn't seen him come in. He had an impeccable ability to lurk. "The Alcmaeonid clan. They've only gone and kicked old Hippias out of the city."

Teron whooped. "Ha! At last! The rightful order restored. The Eupatrids back on top, with us on the top of all of them!"

"Don't get too excited, sonny. It isn't what you think. It isn't what anyone was expecting. It isn't rule by the Eupatrid class anymore."

"Then what is it?"

"Demos kratia."

"Demos kratia? People rule? What does that mean?"

"Just as it says. The people are in charge now."

"But the Alcmaeonids threw out Hippias?"

"Yep. It was Cleisthenes."

Miltiades cast his mind back, to that day he encountered Cleisthenes by the temple. What had he said? That maybe things hadn't gone far enough? Was this what he meant?

"Tell us the whole story, for the gods' sake."

"Well," said Phillipus, smacking his lips. "It is a long and thirsty tale. So if someone could just..."

"Here." Photios limped forward with a wineskin. "Now explain yourself. The people have always been able to vote..."

The trirarch shook his head. "Not all the time. Not for everything. And not all the people, either."

After a decent pull on the wineskin, Phillipus launched the tale...

The temple complex at Delphi had suffered a terrible blow: a fire had broken out, whether from some campers' fire or an offering that got out of control, who could say, but the conflagration did extensive damage. The head priests were picking despondently through the rubble when a party from the Alcmaeonid clan, who were kicking about mainland Greece in their recently expelled state, arrived. The Alcmaeonids expressed themselves to be horrified at the damage done to the preeminent oracle in all of Greece, and offered to foot the bill for the repairs. All of them.

The priests were stunned and grateful. What could they do in return?

Oh dear, said the Alcmaeonids. What could be done? Here they were, banished from their beloved Athens, without the military might to force their way back in...

It was shortly after this meeting that something strange started happening. Every time an envoy arrived from Sparta, no matter what the question, no matter if it was state or personal, the answer came back from the Oracle herself: First free Athens.

This message was duly reported back to the Spartan kings, the senior of whom, Cleomenes, had no objection to interfering in the affairs of other states. He got the message, assembled a force, and marched into Attica. Hippias tried to resist with his small army of mercenaries, but the sight of all those flapping red cloaks and the steady silent advance of the Spartan phalanx broke them after the briefest of contacts. Hippias fled.

Cleomenes, like all Spartans, believed in the old ways. So he put the Eupatrids back in control, and expected that to be the end of the matter. He hadn't reckoned on Cleisthenes, the leading Alcmaeonid. Cleisthenes was not content for things to return to the old system of competition among the wealthy for position. He could see the ranks of the other families closing against the Alcmaeonids. Setting himself up as a new tyrant wasn't an option, so he cast about for another source of power, and found it. The people. All of them, right down to the poorest citizens. He launched his crazy idea – that the government of Athens should be done by the people, for the people. It was death to the old oligarchic rule by the rich.

The Eupatrids howled, and appealed to Cleomenes. The old Spartan king huffed and puffed at the scandalous nature of the idea, and seized control of the Acropolis. For you couldn't let an idea like this spread. Not when you sat on top of a huge slave class of helots yourself – Gods, imagine if they started believing they should have some rights... What would become of Sparta then? No, the whole mess had to be closed down.

But the people had tasted power, and they found it addictive. There was a revolt. The ordinary people seized control of their destiny. They stormed the Acropolis and kicked the Spartans out. Rule of the people was here to stay.

"And what of Hippias?" growled Metramandes.

"With the Persians, by all accounts. Working on King Darius to invade and put him back on the throne." Phillipus turned to Miltiades. "So, oh Miltiades, tyrant of the Chersonnese. I bring for you a hundred and fifty men and their families who felt they could not remain in Athens. Merchants, masons, bankers...all manner of men who were tied to the old regime and feared retribution. They approached me, as one of Hippias' old dogs, and asked for passage somewhere safe. I said I didn't know about safe, but I certainly knew somewhere where they would be useful. Of course, most of my actual oarsmen all preferred to stay in Athens and play at ruling the city. Ungrateful bastards."

"And what about you?" asked Miltiades.

"I'm staying too. I don't fancy working for a mob."

"That's good. Because I have a job for you coming soon. If you don't like working for a mob, I hope you have no objections to working for a king..."

With the influx of new colonists and the assistance of the Persian engineers, Chersonnesus grew more rapidly still. There was a proper market, a couple of potters, a blacksmith. One of the new merchants saw a chance and invested in an ox, renting it to the farmers to help in ploughing their plots. A small temple was built, and a second jetty run out next to the first. Miltiades finally had a proper little house of a couple of rooms, right next to the rebuilt council building. There were enough people now living in the little polis that Miltiades found himself obliged to spend a day a week taking petitions and solving disputes. One of the first brought to him was by one of the farmers, against Tresantes. The furious farmer accused the Spartan of assaulting him.

"Is it true?" asked Miltiades.

"He was beating the ox," said Tresantes. "So I beat him."

Miltiades rubbed his forehead with his hand. He felt quite tired.

"Well?" said the farmer. "Aren't you going to do something? He's a bloody maniac!"

"What happened to the ox, and the field?" asked Photios quietly, from his position standing behind Miltiades.

The Spartan shrugged. "I finished ploughing the field, and took the ox back to his pen."

Miltiades looked at the farmer. "He finished ploughing your field for you?"

"Yes!" shouted the man, glowing bright red. "But that isn't the point!"

"I ploughed it, and there was no need for any more beating," said Tresantes. "Of anybody."

"Well, there's your bloody restitution. You got your field ploughed for you. And you're in one piece. That's it, case over."

The farmer swore and stormed out. Tresantes turned to saunter after him.

"Tresantes. You can't go around fighting everyone who thinks differently to you."

The Spartan paused. "No," he said after a moment. "Just the ones who deserve it most."

"Did I make a mistake in bringing him?" Miltiades mused. Photios patted him on the shoulder.

And then came the summons.

A small galley pulled into the harbour, and a party of Persian officials brought word: Chersonnesus was to furnish a trireme for the King of Kings expedition into the land of the Skythians. Miltiades received the news sitting amongst his officers in the council chamber, and gave his assurances. They would come.

Oh, and one other thing, said the Persians. Here is your tax bill.

They handed over a scroll, and, bowing their oiled and scented heads, smiled their way from the small hall. Miltiades opened the scroll.

"Shit," he said.

Photios leaned over his shoulder, reading. His eyebrows shot upward. "So our survival and growth appears to come at some cost."

They were small, and vulnerable. They couldn't count on aid from Athens in the event of any trouble with the Persians. They were going to have to pay, and they were going to have to fight for their new masters.

"Can we even meet this?" asked Miltiades.

"We can. But it will stop anyone becoming rich overnight. The worst of it is that this money will be leaving the polis. Most money spent here stays here, and so we help each other – this will act as a drain. But we can cope. As you said, we must. We are in no position to argue."

The trireme was made ready, with one hundred hoplite class and seventy of the poorer colonists to serve as oarsmen. Armour, food and weapons were loaded on board.

Miltiades gave Photios power to act in his stead. Callias, Teron and Metramandes were to accompany the expedition, as was Zander.

"I do not wish to come," Tresantes had said when Miltiades approached him. "I do not wish to leave rabbit behind, nor do I wish to take her into battle."

Miltiades was annoyed. "You know," he said, "you are still a bloody Spartan at heart. You lot are always impossible to move beyond your homes. Them because of their fear of the helots, you because of your fear for that creature. Makes you wonder who are the masters, and who are the slaves."

But the Spartan had merely stared at him until he had felt discomfited, then returned to handing stalks of hay, one at a time, for his rabbit to devour like some small automaton.

Freaks and Greeks

They rowed north-east, up the Hellespont channel, and then out into the Euxine, hugging the coastline. Their initial progress was not as swift as it could have been, given that they had not rowed since their initial journey to Chersonnesus. But as the hours passed, they found their rhythm, and the beak of the ship cut cleanly through the cold water. It was still not until the next day that they found the army. They had been ordered to meet the Persian force at the mouth of the river Istros, that flowed into the Euxine from the west. There was no mistaking the place: a vast armada of ships had gathered there, high Phoenician galleys and dozens of Greek triremes. Tents lined the beach in a vast arc to the south, with Darius' gaudy pavilion unmistakeable in the centre. Phillipus had them aim for a stretch of empty sand, but then a small boat came out to meet them and guided them to a landing spot much closer to the wide mouth of the river.

"Nice to have friends in high places," grunted the captain as he personally steered the ship in to the beach through the shallow surf.

Miltiades and several of the others were led to the Great King's tent, and ushered inside. Darius sat on his dais-mounted throne, with his generals beside him. Other Persian courtiers and officers stood to the side, along with about a dozen men who appeared to be Greek.

"Ah!" said Darius. "Here he is! This is the man I was speaking of."

Miltiades felt all eyes turn towards him. He detected a certain coolness coming from his fellow Greeks.

"And now we are ready to commence operations. The last sparas of infantry will be arriving over the next days. This gives us time to discuss our entry into the Skythian interior. Our Phoenician detachment," The king nodded his head at a small knot of oiled and perfumed men with neatly coiffured beards. "tell me there is no suitable landing site north of the river, or at least not one to land such a large host. We would use up all of

our supplies in the time it took to get the whole force ashore."
The Phoenicians nodded their heads sadly. Miltiades wondered
if it had more to do with the fact they preferred to get back to
their own particular brand of piracy: trade. "So we must march
in from here, which means crossing the river. Ferries will take
too long. We need a bridge. The engineers tell me the river is
too deep. So it must be a pontoon. This is where you Greeks
come in. We will use your triremes to bridge the Istros."

There was a small hubbub amongst the Greeks, and Miltiades
heard Phillipus suck his teeth. Evidently the captains did not
much like the news.

"Miltiades!"

Miltiades jumped at the sound of his name. Darius was
pointing at him.

"You will be in charge of the bridge, defending it and keeping it secure until we return. For now, you are all dismissed."

The noise escalated as the various parties turned to make
their way from the pavilion. Miltiades stepped forward.

"Ah, King Darius?"

The king was looking at a map with his generals Datis and
Mardonius. All three frowned as they looked up at him.

"May I have a word? It's about the tax rate you have set for
Chersonnesus."

"Impertinent slave," growled Mardonius. Darius held up a
hand.

"What is the problem?"

"Well, it seems a little...steep."

Darius frowned. "I believe your little city exists because of
me. And is now all the better built because of me. But," He
smiled. "Surely, we can discuss it. But after the operation, yes?
Now, you will excuse me? Others await salvation from the depri-
vations of the daemons."

As Miltiades strode from the tent, another man who had
obviously been waiting outside fell in beside him.

"Don't hold your breath," said the man. "I've been waiting to talk to him about our tax rate for months." He held out his hand. "Aristagoras of Miletus. I'm kind of the leader amongst the Ionian Greeks. Or at least, I was..." He smiled, though he seemed intent on trying to break Miltiades' fingers in his grip. "You seem to be the new golden boy. Whatever did you do to earn Darius' respect so quickly?"

"Survive."

"Well, that is always the starting point, isn't it? Come by my tent and have a drink later. Meet the rest of the lads. Oh, and that man over there appears to be trying to attract your attention."

Miltiades turned – and there was Hippias standing off to one side, flanked by two Persian soldiers. The ex-tyrant of Athens gestured him over.

"Who is he?" asked Aristagoras.

"No one, now," said Miltiades. "But he used to be someone." He walked over.

"So," said Hippias. "I see you are here too, and doing very well. Regular King's pet, aren't you?"

Miltiades stood silent.

"Heard about my brother, I suppose? Knifed to death by two degenerates? You must be having trouble keeping the grin off your face, Philaid. You always held us responsible for your father's death, didn't you?"

"Good night, Hippias." Miltiades turned away.

"Wait, wait! Miltiades, listen! I have been trying to speak to the Great King, to urge him to take back Athens and establish me as satrap. But I can't get to him past his bloody generals and nobles. You can, though. You can get a word in his ear."

"Now why on earth would I want to do that?"

"Why?" Hippias stared at him. "Have you heard what they have done? They have given power to the masses! They have given my city to the riff raff – and I want it back!"

Miltiades stared at the other man – his glazed eyes, his open lips revealing his teeth, his sallow skin and the stink coming off him, and felt as if he was staring not at a man, but an ex-man. Another version of a Hadesman. His fingers curled, some part of him desiring to feel a sword hilt between them. The two Persians stirred, evidently reacting to some wave of violence coming off him, and Hippias, too, blanched and stepped back, blinking.

"At least hear me out," he said quickly. "Come to dinner. Come and speak to me. It is very lonely here, amongst these barbarians..."

"Sorry, Hippias," said Miltiades. "But I have another offer. I'm meeting up with the rest of the lads." And he walked away, flexing his fingers and wondering at fate, that they should meet here in this place, in these very different roles. He hoped it would be the last such meeting.

The rest of the lads, as Aristagoras termed them, were a curious bunch. A mix of tyrants and pirate chiefs who ruled the various small Greek poleis along the Ionian coast. They had all been under Persian control for some time, since the fall of the Lydian empire years before.

"It isn't so bad," said one, gulping his watered wine.

"Yes, it is," spat another. "Greeks under barbarians? Its unheard of!"

"Yes. Should always be the Greek on top of the barbarian, eh? Or behind." Aristagoras smiled lewdly. He looked at Miltiades. "Unless of course you prefer to be ridden by a bit of strange."

Miltiades smiled tightly amidst the laughter. Was he referring to Hegesipyle? He hadn't mentioned his Thracian wife, but he hadn't instructed his men to keep the fact secret either. He could imagine Teron spraying the news far and wide.

"So, the bridge..." he said, in the hopes of changing the subject. It worked.

"What a waste! What a waste of our bloody ships!"

"And it just wrecks them. Anchored next to each other, scrapes the shit out of the sides."

Ah, so that was it. No glory and it ruins the paint work. No wonder Phillipus was glum. The night wore on, and the wine flowed, and the company turned increasingly argumentative and surly. The main gripe remained the bridge, but other, older grievances between various cities readily bubbled to the surface. At last Miltiades could take no more, and quietly slipped out.

But the next morning, despite their protestations the night before, they did it. Who could argue with the King of Kings? The combined force of triremes were painstakingly rowed into the river, and brought alongside each other. Anchors were dropped fore and aft, and cables run out from both banks to bind them together.

"Not so bad..." said Miltiades. They had placed their own ship in the middle of the pontoon. The triremes shifted, and a deep groan emanated through the wood. Phillipus closed his eyes.

Boards were laid across the decks and lashed in place, and then the army of the Persians began their march across. The infantry passed first, with their patterned trousers and wicker shields, quivers at their waists and short spears in their hands. After them came the cavalry, leading their nervous mounts across as the boards became slick with liquid shit. All day the various contingents took their turn to pass across to the wilder lands on the northern bank.

And then finally, the Greeks were alone.

They set their camp on the southern bank, with a rotating squad of hoplites and light troops stationed on the northern shore, and sailors on duty non-stop to watch that no ship foundered.

Miltiades sat on the bow of their ship, watching the water swirl by, droplets falling from the taut anchor line. The river, it seemed, resented their attempts to conquer it, and sought to dislodge this impertinence from its throat like an old man trying to cough up a fish bone. Hubris, he mused, hubris. Mankind seemed determined to push against nature – was it not to be expected that nature would push back even harder? That brought to mind a discussion he had had with Photios the day before. He had found his old master standing on the northern end of the pontoon, staring into the distance.

"May I intrude on you and know your thoughts?" Miltiades had asked.

"I was just thinking about the Hadesmen," said the teacher. "And this war we fight against them. Is it just, do you think?"

"I'm not sure I would even call it a war, let alone just. Setting aside that this exercise is an excuse for Darius to add to his empire, I think the Hadesmen have to be destroyed. I don't know how they came to be, but they clearly don't belong on this earth."

"No? You think them unnatural? I am not so sure." The teacher frowned, and plucked at his lower lip. "Consider – why do they stay together, and walk in such large groups, if not for some feeling of fellowship, however base? And if they do seek the comfort of each other, then who are we to say whether they belong less than us."

"But they have less reasoning than beasts. You have seen them. There is nothing behind their eyes."

"Perhaps," Photios had said. "Or perhaps we just don't know what we are looking for."

Miltiades shook his head. "I don't see the value in developing any compassion for them. That doesn't help a man to kill them."

"Surely the truest mark of a man is that he may kill when he must, but still maintain compassion for those he slays."

There was nothing to be gained from developing any sympathy for the undead, as far as he could see. Though he had to concede that most they had encountered so far had been some kind of Other. How would he fair if their ranks included Photios, Callias and Tresantes? Or Zander? Could he despatch them with such impunity then? Could he sever what they had been from what they were?

His thoughts turned to his home in distant Athens. It was a very different place to the city he had left. Democracy. It was a hard idea to grasp. He understood that he was a victim of the bias that infected the ranks of the Eupatrid class – the view inculcated into all of them that their birth really did make them better than most of their fellow Athenians. So while it was one thing to allow the moderately well off to have the odd vote, like for who would act as archon for the year, allowing all the citizens to vote on everything was just so... extreme. What had Cleisthenes created down there? Was it a monster or something nobler? Would the mass of the people be nothing more than a seething, quarrelling destructive storm that would tear the city apart...or could something better rise from this experiment? Could men be more than they seemed, if given something bigger to be a part of?

And if they could – what did that leave him, the petty tyrant of a tiny far-flung outpost, at the beck and call of a foreign potentate? "Things may have to change more," Cleisthenes had said. And he did it, he changed the game totally. Apollo's balls, whether this worked out or not, they would be writing about him for generations to come...

What would his uncle do?

An image hit him right in the guts, a dark cloaked figure in the courtyard of his house. *Man of inaction, now must action take...* The pieces jostled together in his brain, like the shards of an amphora, but they could not form a neat whole. It was too deep and dark, like the cold fast flowing river water beneath him. He frowned. It was deep and fast, wasn't it?

He stood and stared downriver to where the flow emptied into the Euxine, then turned and studied the width of the waterway to where it disappeared into the West.

"You cocksucker," he murmured. "You didn't just watch, did you?" And with that he left the bridge.

That night, he called a meeting of the Ionian leaders. Once the wine was mixed and the libation poured, he stared at them each in turn. Aristagoras smiled and raised his cup, the rest maintained a sullen silence, still annoyed at the elevation of this Athenian upstart.

"Gentlemen, thank you for coming. I have a proposition for you... How would you like to cast a king adrift?"

···

The plan was simple. Pull the bridge apart and sail away, everyone back to their own polis. Let the Persian host wither and die, marooned in the great empty interior of the Skythian plains. And the Empire? Without a head, it would fall apart. Infighting and civil war would plague it for years. And the Greeks would be free.

There had been opposition, as expected.

"The Persians will destroy us!"

"The Persians will be busy. And weakened."

"If Darius survives..."

"He won't. Without us, he is doomed."

"What of the Phoenicians? What if they come and take him off? Not even the whole army, just him and his generals? They will put down any rising."

"The Phoenicians won't come to his aid," said Miltiades. "I'll stop them. I can close the Hellespont any time I want."

There had been some dark frowns at that claim.

Aristagoras cleared his throat. "If we do this... What of the empty poleis along the Euxine? The ones the Persians are seeking to annex?"

"I propose we divvy that land amongst ourselves. As restitution for the extortionate taxes the Persians have been demanding from us all. And to keep the land in Greek hands."

He had them at that. He could see their eyes glitter at the thought of those rich plains, those fields of golden grain.

"Tell me," said Aristagoras. "As one who was clearly Darius' favourite – why the sudden change of heart?"

"The Hadesmen," said Miltiades simply. "There is no way the horde that decimated this area could have crossed the Euxine themselves unless they were aided in some way. Why don't the Persians have their own ships for bridging? Unless they were already used – but somehow lost. I believe the Persians put bridges somewhere here to help the Hadesmen cross, but something went wrong, and they had to ultimately destroy their own ships. Maybe they were infested with the dead, and had to be burnt and sunk. Maybe there was a storm, and they all foundered. That is why they need us now. To their undoing."

They discussed it for many hours still, and there was shouting, too, as there was always when Greeks debated and the wine flowed. But in the end they agreed: they would dismantle the bridge, effectively destroying the Persian force, and the King of Kings with it.

"At night," Aristagoras stipulated. "It must be at night. We don't know who may be watching."

"It is going to be found out sooner or later," Miltiades answered. "But if it will keep you happy..."

"And not this night," Aristagoras continued. "Tomorrow. Or the night after."

Miltiades looked at him, and the rows of nodding heads, and shrugged. So be it.

But the next dawn brought some unwelcome news – they were no longer alone: a Persian cavalry squad was riding for the bridge from the North.

"What in Hades is this?" hissed Miltiades, as they stood gathered at the southern end.

"Looks like the banner of General Mardonius," said one sharp-eyed man.

"We can take them," urged Miltiades. "Strike when they are dismounting."

"No!" hissed Aristagoras. "We aren't ready! It will be...messy."

It was too late anyway. The squadron clattered across the pontoon. In the fore rode three riders abreast. As they reached the end of the bridge it was clear that the two outriders were helping support the man in the middle. It was Mardonius, looking white and drawn. As they reined to a halt other cavalrymen swiftly dismounted and ran forward, helping to lower the Persian general from his horse. And it was then the Greeks saw that his right arm ended abruptly a little way below his elbow in a mass of stained bandages.

"Oh my general!" cried Aristagoras. "What has happened?"

"Fucking Datis!" snarled Mardonius. "That is what happened..." His legs sagged below him, and his men cried out and carried him into a nearby tent. Aristagoras glanced at Miltiades and gestured for him to follow. Inside, the injured man was laid on a divan, his men fussing about and propping silk cushions beneath him till he snapped at them to leave him alone. He lay back, groaning and cradling his injured arm.

"I can still feel it," he hissed. "My fingers. All of it. As if it is still there."

A man brought him a cup of wine, and he took it and drained it in a single gulp. "More."

"Is that wise, general?"

"Fuck off, Greek. This hurts like the very devil. Ah, good." He took another cup. "Leave the wineskin."

"Did you find any of those undead creatures?" asked Miltiades quietly. He glanced about. There were still at least half a dozen Persian junior officers in the tent, all armed.

"Yes," said Mardonius after a pause, his voice muffled by the wine cup.

"General, were you bitten?"

Mardonius lowered the cup, his eyes blazing. "No. I. Was. Not. Bitten. That fool, that treacherous ass, he knew I was not bitten. It was a cut. A cut! But he yells out that I am doomed and strikes my arm with his sword. And now I am left like this! All curses upon his treacherous fucking head!"

"You are saying he deliberately-"

"Of course! Of course! For now he alone has the King's ear! While I am sent back here with you foul cretins... Enough. Get out. Fuck off. Leave me alone. And more wine!"

The Persians leapt to obey, and Miltiades followed Aristagoras as he bowed and left.

"That's the Persians for you. Or the nobles and royal family members anyway. They'd sell their maiden aunt to a brothel if they thought it would get them ahead."

"This doesn't change anything. We go ahead with the plan tonight."

"But... But the Persians..."

"We take them out. While they are sleeping. They won't know what hit them." Miltiades could sense the other man pause. He grabbed the sleeve of his chiton. "It won't be messy, Aristagoras. Quick and clean."

The other tyrant slowly nodded his head, but his eyes still looked troubled. "All right. But... Let me and the other Ionians take care of Mardonius and his men. We have been under their control longer than you. It will be more...fitting for us to be the ones to do this deed."

Miltiades nodded. "I'll take my men across and secure the northern bank this afternoon. When night has fallen we will fall back, releasing the ships on the far side first. You send men across to crew them as soon as you have..."

"Massacred the sleeping Persians?"

"Yes."

That afternoon, Miltiades and the small force of hoplites he had brought from Chersonessus squatted by the creaking end of the pontoon bridge. The sun was dipping behind the purple mountain range far to the west, and the endless plain before them was receding into the dusk.

"Riders!" called a sentry.

"What in Hades is it now?"

Miltiades hesitated. What to do? Form the men up? With their backs protected by the river, they could hold off any light cavalry coming upon them. They could still fall back, cutting the cables and anchors of the triremes as they went. Sure, a number of ships would be lost, and he couldn't see their owners being pleased with that, but it meant the plan would go ahead. But the noise would rouse the Persian troopers encamped on the southern shore. Would Aristagoras and the other Ionians have the sense to strike them down? If they didn't, Miltiades' small force could be caught in the middle and destroyed.

"Only patrol strength!" came the word.

He relaxed. A small force, probably sent to check that Mardonius had made it back. They could afford to let them pass, check on the general and then return to reassure Darius. He ordered his men to stand aside, and watched the riders approach. He frowned. They were carrying a banner, and the one at the front looked a little younger.

"It's the King's fucking son!"

His guts squirmed. He didn't know what to do, and then it was too late as the six cavalrymen swept by them. The young Persian prince, Xerxes, looked at Miltiades with a bored sneer as he passed by.

"My lord!" Miltiades called out, and the Persians slowed. "Is all well?"

Xerxes shrugged.

"Is your father... Is the king returning now as well?"

The sullen teen shrugged again, the hint of a smile tugging at the corners of his mouth. Before Miltiades could ask him anything else he urged his horse on, and clattered onto the pontoon.

"What does this mean?" asked Callias. "What do we do?"

"We stick to the plan. Their numbers are too few to change things."

"So we kill the king's son? I can't see him forgetting that in a hurry."

"It won't matter. He won't be surviving." But Miltiades felt restless, staring across to the far bank, where he could see a knot of men surrounding the newcomers. He hoped that all that had happened was the prince had become bored, and his sullen presence annoyed Darius until he sent him away. He turned and stared into the growing darkness. Surely the Persian host was not out there now, on the way back?

There was nothing for it but to wait. They lit a couple of fires, as to not do so would look suspicious. Several large bonfires blazed back in the main encampment, and the sound of drunken singing floated across the water. Finally, after several hours crawled by, the fires and the torches died away and the camp slept.

"Now," said Miltiades.

His men rose about him, the slight clatter from their weapons and armour causing him to wince. Squads moved to the massive cables, axes in their hands. Others boarded the first four triremes, moving to the anchor ropes fore and aft. They waited. Where were the crews?

Mitiades strained his eyes and ears, seeking any sign that events were underway. Impatient, he walked forward along the bridge, but all he could see were the dark lumps of the tents, and all he could hear was the creaking of the wooden ships and the rush of the river water below. Where were they? Were the Persians all dead?

He was now right in the middle of the bridge, and still no sign...wait, a figure, a man walking towards him. Miltiades crouched, his hand touching the hilt of his sword. The man stopped.

"Miltiades?"

"Aristagoras? Is it done? Where are the crewmen?"

"Ah," said the Tyrant of Miletus. "I'm afraid there has been a complication."

"Xerxes, yes I know. You've taken care of him?"

"Well... Look, I'm afraid there has been a bit of a rethink amongst the other commanders."

"A rethink? What in Hades does that mean?"

"Well, a couple of the others raised the very valid point that we all owe our positions to the Persian regime. And should we remove its influence over our poleis, well, there is some fear that many of us may not then hold onto power. You know what has been going on in Athens, don't you?"

"You fucking idiots. We can worry about that later. Right now we have a chance to cut the head off the snake. We cannot throw this chance away. Listen to me, Aristagoras. The bloody Persians let the Hadesmen kill everyone. They are using them like some kind of weapon..."

"But they aren't a threat any more in Ionia. We have very few Hadesmen, and the Persians are very good at taking care of any outbreaks. They have this whole communication network of riders to report them and stop them getting out of hand..."

"So you admire them? Apollo's balls, Aristagoras, I don't understand you. But it doesn't matter, we are going to act with or without you."

"Now, Miltiades..."

"What is going on?"

The voice was accented, and belonged to a new arrival. Miltiades grimaced. He hadn't noticed anyone approach as they argued. The dark figure slowly stepped forward.

"My lord," said Aristagoras, bowing.

"What are you Greeks doing?" asked Xerxes.

Miltiades' hand strayed towards his hilt again, but then stopped. There were other men further back - bodyguards? He looked at Aristagoras. The other man smiled, his teeth glowing white in the moonlight.

"We are just out for a walk, Highness, as you seem to be. Can't sleep?"

The Persian royal grunted.

"Well," said Miltiades thickly. "I will return to my men."

He nodded his head stiffly, turned, and walked away. What could they do? If the other Ionians wouldn't support them, there was little his small force could hope to accomplish. And just like that, the chance of freedom was gone.

Betrayed.

A day later, the main Persian host returned.

In the meantime Miltiades avoided the other Ionian tyrants as best he could. He could hardly bare to look at them, let alone speak to them. Aristagoras approached him a couple of times, smiling as usual, which seemed even more offensive to Miltiades as he struggled to remain civil. He just wanted to bellow at them that they were a pack of gutless bastards.

Then Darius rode back in, crossing the bridge and returning to the safety of the southern shore. Behind him his battalions of infantry came at the quick march, their scale armour jingling. Orders were then given to dismantle the bridge, and Miltiades ordered his men back across as they carried out the procedure they had planned, that would have set them free.

Phillipus inspected his trireme, drawn up upon the churned up mud of the southern river bank, sucking his teeth as he looked at the deep scores in the wood worn by the plank bridge and where other ships had butted against it.

And then came a summons from Darius.

"Don't go," whispered Zander. "What if he heard? What if he plans to kill you?"

"Well, I guess he can kill me here just as easily as in his marquee. And if hasn't heard anything, how would refusing to attend appear?"

But instead of being led into the great tent, Miltiades was put aboard a punt and rowed downriver to where a small Phoenician squadron had appeared. He was ushered aboard one of the high-sided ships, and then pointed towards the bow, where the familiar figure of the Great King stood. He made his way to the Persian, and bowed.

"It is a great and terrible place, the land of the Skythians," said Darius, without turning around. "A great sea of grass. It feels after a while that one is not moving forward at all, but merely shuffling ones' feet in one spot. I needed this." The king threw his head back and breathed in deeply. "The smell of the sea. It speaks to your people too, doesn't it? Perhaps even more than mine?"

"I believe it may be so."

"So be glad I did not take you into that interior, Miltiades. Be glad you did not suffer the storms that rage in a man's mind at the sight of such vastness."

"Then I am glad indeed, my lord."

"As am I. That I left such a man as you to remain here and guard our rear. You have done well." The king turned and looked him in the eye. "Haven't you?"

"If you say so, King Darius."

"If I say so," repeated the king. He turned his gaze back to the waters of the Euxine.

"Did you encounter many Hadesmen, King? Was the mission a success?"

"Yes. We found a large horde, which must have splintered off from those that assaulted you. We destroyed them, with some small loss. Including the hand of one of my key generals, unfortunately. But the people of this land can sleep safely, under the protection of the King of Kings."

Whether they want it or not, thought Miltiades, but did not say it aloud. And so the Persian Empire had grown larger still, slowly covering the known world.

"Yes," he said. "It would be a terrible thing for a large horde to return to Asia Minor undetected. I imagine the damage it could do would be extensive. Just as well there is no easy way back across the river."

He felt the king look at him, but avoided the eye contact. It would be dangerous indeed to raise what he suspected openly, that the Persians had deliberately facilitated the horde's depredations to ease their takeover of these lands.

"Do not worry, Miltiades. The Eyes and Ears of the King are everywhere. I will keep you safe."

A silence fell between them again, full of strain and discomfort to the Greek. Finally Darius spoke again.

"Tell me, how many of the various rulers in Greece speak the language of the Persians, do you suppose?"

"Not many."

"No. If we left it up to you, there would be no communication between us. Instead, to deal with you, we learn your awkward, ugly tongue. What does that mean, do you suppose?"

"I don't know, lord."

"Neither do I. But I wonder. Where does the Lie live, do you suppose? I fear it is within language. Maybe by learning to speak to one another, we have done nothing but open the door to the Lie."

And the king dismissed him with a wave, leaving him to walk back to the punt all the while with a feeling like a knife was poised to strike him in the middle of the back.

ELEVEN

SCYLLA AND CHARBDIS

Miltiades came upon Hegesipyle sitting with Photios outside the council building. There were scrolls scattered about them, and Hegesipyle was holding a wax tablet. She looked up and grinned at him.

"Miltiades! See? I am a student, just as you were!"

"Really?"

"Yes. Photios is teaching me to read and write. See, I am writing my name!"

She held up the wax board proudly, it's surface cut with childlike letters. Miltiades nodded, gazing past it to Photios, who appeared to have reddened.

"How interesting..."

"She has an enquiring mind," Photios offered.

"Yes, she does." He stalked inside the chamber.

As they lay together that night, she spoke more about the lessons they had been having.

"Photios told me that when you were a boy, what you liked best were the stories about the old heroes. Like Theseus – is that right? He is one you like?"

"He is one."

She nodded. "Yes. Photios said he must scold you to make you pay attention to numbers and other things. You only wanted tales of heroes. He said he guesses it made sense... You were a quiet little boy, so you dreamed of being great. Like Theseus."

"He said that, did he?"

"He said that maybe I am like the girl in the story – Ariadne? But that the labyrinth is inside you. What did he mean?"

"I have no idea." And he rolled over, but he didn't close his eyes.

The next day he summoned Photios to him.

"How do you suppose it looks," he asked, "for my wife to be taught by you, publicly, without my knowledge or permission? Can you imagine how that would go down if this was Athens?"

"I didn't think it was a matter of permission. And I didn't think we were striving to replicate the social mores of Athens. Forgive me, I thought you would be pleased."

"Pleased?"

"She seeks to know things. She wants to learn. Why, with a class full of students such as her, I..."

"Ah, and there we have it. It is all about you, and your failure to make it as a teacher."

"There were never any complaints..."

"Yet look where I found you."

The old man stiffened, and Miltiades felt a hot rush of shame. He clamped down on the feeling.

"Just...Just remember that I rule here. Please ask me before taking any action in future, especially when it concerns me and mine."

"Of course. I will tell your wife there are to be no more lessons..."

"No, those may continue. As you said, she wants to learn."

Photios frowned, and nodded his head. He turned to leave, then paused.

But before he could say anything, Miltiades jumped in. "Just stick to your job, Photios. And spare me the cheap analysis of my personal flaws."

Aristagoras arrived, unheralded.

It was months after the Skythian expedition. For the first week Miltiades had felt like he was holding his breath, expecting any moment the might of the Persians to fall upon them. He was scrupulous in making sure their taxes were paid on time and in full, hoping to reassure Darius of his loyalty.

Loyalty?

A bitter word. A word created by men as a form of heavy chain, to bind those with less power to those with more. He wondered if he ought to make some diplomatic moves to the new democracy in Athens, to see about a military alliance – but really, what could they do, so far away? So they were stuck. To slowly eke out their lives in this barbaric place, even less free than if they had remained in Athens.

At least the threat from the Hadesmen had dissipated. He maintained a watch on the wall, which was now stronger than ever, all the stones properly shaped and mortared. And occasionally one or two of the hideous things would stumble into view, either stragglers of the great diaspora or some local unfortunate who had encountered them. But these were easily dispatched. Miltiades ordered that every member of Chersonnesus should have experience in killing one, including the women and children. There were some rumblings at that, at how unseemly it was, but this was largely from the more recent arrivals. Those who had lived through the invasion just nodded grimly.

And then Aristagoras arrived, one evening as dusk was turning the sky purple and the waters of the Hellespont to black silk. Miltiades received him in the council room, alone. He noted the Ionian's eyes were a little...wild.

"Aristagoras."

"Miltiades! My thanks to you for receiving me!" He laughed then, and paced about the room, glancing into the corners and even twitching aside a tapestry hanging on one wall.

"We are quite alone."

"Ha! Yes, good, good! Hard to break old habits. His eyes and ears are everywhere. You'd be surprised – even here..."

"You mean Darius?"

Aristagoras bobbed his head. He stopped in front of Miltiades, who sat calmly on a wooden chair. One of the Ionian's legs was bouncing.

"You seemed quite chummy the last time we were all together."

"The last... Oh! Yes, well, things change. Should have listened to you, the man of the hour! If only you had been more persuasive!"

"Why? What is going on?"

The Ionian looked about one more time, then leaned in close. "Rebellion," he breathed.

Miltiades raised an eyebrow. "Really?"

"This time for sure. Why, it has already begun. By yours truly."

For a moment he couldn't speak. He let his breath hiss out between his teeth before finally responding. "We had the Persian king, his top generals and a good portion of his best troops at our mercy... And instead this is when you choose to revolt? Hades' balls, Aristagoras!"

The Ionian flashed him a sheepish grin. "Like I said, things change."

"What do you want with me?"

"You? Why, you, of course. The great commander who kept his head in the middle of some monstrous invasion. I need your name. Besides...you are already a part of it. Technically."

"What do you mean?"

"I believe word may have reached Darius about your little plan on the river. Word which is public knowledge, and thus cannot be ignored however much he may like you personally. He has to act. You are in danger."

"What about you? How did you go from calling it off last time – to protect your precious position, if I recall correctly - to leading this?"

"Ah. I had a spot of bother. See, I was hosting some wealthy individuals from Naxos. Good men. The finest. Anyway, this Athenian disease is spreading, so the commons on the island had risen up and taken control. Kicked the old oligarachs out and formed one of these demokratia things. The nobles came to me, and suggested that were I to help restore them to power, I could pretty much name my price. Now I won't lie to you and suggest I was uninterested. But I confess I was thinking bigger – to maybe gain control of Naxos and thus all the other little islands around it myself. Problem was, they have around eight thousand hoplites. So I went to see Artaphernes, the local Persian satrap, and pitched it to him. Give me the troops and ships, and I would give the Persians control of the central Aegean, with me as satrap. He jumped. Unfortunately, it didn't work out. Someone tipped off the Naxians that we were coming, and they got the jump on us. It was a complete debacle. Artaphernes was reportedly furious and demanding my head. So, it came down to either a messy and quite painful public execution...or start a revolt. And here I am, head intact."

"Zeus above." Miltiades shook his head. "The self-serving nature of the aristocrat never fails to amaze me... But tell me, how is that you still hold your position, if you are now in revolt?"

"Ah, now that is quite amusing. I presented myself to an assembly of all our citizens, and gave them my best oration on the evils of the Persian Empire. Even managed to get a little choked up and squeeze out a few tears as I talked of my dream for a free Miletus. They were eating it up. At the end, I declared our independence, quit as tyrant and sat down. You should have seen them. A couple of thousand jaws all falling open at once... They didn't know what to do. Then one fellow jumped up and moved that I be instantly voted in as archon with the power to deal with the current emergency, and that was it. They were all howling my name. I even sat shaking my head for a few minutes before finally standing and graciously accepting their request."

"I suppose the man who moved the motion was one of yours?" asked Miltiades drily.

Aristagoras grinned.

"And you think you are ready to take on the Persians?"

"Oh no, I know I'm not. But I could be. With you beside me. I tell you, the rest of the Ionian poleis are falling into line behind us. There will simply be too many spot fires for the Persians to put them all out. Besides, I intend to go and ask for a little help."

"Who from?"

"Why, the Spartans, of course. Have you ever tasted their famous black broth?"

···

"So," said Miltiades to his council. "It appears I am off to Sparta. Tresantes, I would like you to come with us."

"No," said the Trembler. "I will not return there."

"We could use your guidance in dealing with the Spartan kings and Ephors. You understand them. They are your people."

"They are not my people. I have no people."

"But still..."

"No! You do not understand the ways of the Spartans. My presence would hurt your chances, not help. There is nothing I can do - except say this: do not trust Cleomenes, the elder king."

Miltiades didn't have to ask what he meant by 'elder king'. It was well known that so great was the Spartan paranoia that they had developed a dual kingship, so they were never without leadership should one fall in battle. And of course, each could act as a check on the other's ambitions, and thus ensure the maintenance of the status quo.

"Why go at all?" asked Metramandes. "Why risk what we have by joining this revolt? You say Darius may know of the previous plot. So what? His nobles plot against each other all the time. It is the Persian way, they are used to it. Why not earn our way back into his good graces by seizing Aristagoras and handing him over in chains?"

"Hand a Greek over to a barbarian?" asked Teron icily. "Is that what we have sunk to?"

"It is too late for all of this," said Miltiades mildly. "The dice have been cast. There is no going back, only pressing forward."

"Why not consult the Oracle?" asked Metramandes. "See what the gods say?"

Miltiades shook his head. "Events are moving too fast for that. Besides, I tell you men may make their own fate. The gods told me...seemed to tell me...to run from here, but I stood and Chersonnesus survived. You all survived."

"Blasphemy," said Metramandes. "Blasphemy and hubris. See what comes of it."

Before they set sail in Aristagoras' trireme Miltiades formally laid down his position of ruler before an assembly of all the men of Chersonnesus. Callias immediately sprang up and moved that he be elected as archon with powers of a strategos and so loud was the acclaim that no one bothered to stand against him. It worked just as Aristagoras had said, and it left Miltiades with a queasy feeling in the guts as he stared out at the cheering throng. Was it that easy to manipulate the people?

His second act was visiting Tresantes in his simple dwelling. As expected, the Trembler was sitting in the small pen adjoining it, while the rabbit hopped about him, scratching at the earth. Miltiades watched it scoop pawfuls of soil and thrust them back between its two hind legs, then sprawl forward onto its belly into the divot, sides heaving with its fast small breaths.

"Here," he said to Tresantes. "I have brought you something." He held out the large round object, wrapped in linen.

The Spartan wiped his hands on his tunic and stood, taking it. He stripped the cloth from it, revealing a burnished hoplon shield.

"You are of the hoplite class. You really should have a full panoply."

Tresantes was staring at the design painted on the front. "What does this mean?" he asked flatly. "What are you trying to do?"

Miltiades frowned, then realised the other man was looking at the design upside down – from his angle, it looked like the 'Λ' shape that adorned the shields of the Spartans. The shape was that of the Greek letter L, for the Lacedamonians, which was the name the Spartans called themselves in their old Doric language.

"It's upside down! It's upside down!" he said quickly. He grabbed the edge and turned it in the Spartan's hands. "See? They are rabbit ears. Upright rabbit ears."

Tresantes stared at it in silence.

"Stylised rabbit ears, I grant you – but I wasn't sure an actual rabbit face would be very daunting for your enemies. This stands for listening, which is what you do. I see you listening all the time. I can't promise we will all adopt the design...but it means you belong here. You are of this polis. Do you...do you like it?"

Still the Spartan didn't speak, and Miltiades felt a little disappointed. Then he noticed the small wet star shapes dotting the shield's surface. The Trembler was crying.

"It is beautiful. I shall carry it with pride. I shall come home with it or on it."

The ancient pledge.

"Well," said Miltiades. "Let's settle for coming home with it for now."

The final act was saying goodbye to his wife.

His departure from Hegesipyle was more gut-wrenching than expected. They sat together in their little bedroom, holding hands. Tears brimmed in her eyes, but did not spill over. It frightened Miltiades a little to find how much he felt he needed the quiet nights with her. Not necessarily in a physical sense, just the peace that came from pressing your face into the nape of the neck of your woman.

"I'm sorry about this," he told her. "But I feel I have to go."

"Do not worry about me," she said. "After all, I..."

"Will never love me?"

She smiled, and they bowed their heads until their foreheads pressed together.

....

When they set sail, Miltiades could see straight away what a difference it made to have an experienced crew. The oarsman on Aristagoras' trireme knew their business well, and the warship cut sleekly through the waters of the Hellespont and down into the Aegean. To save time, rather than take the safer route hugging the coastline, they cut straight across the open water, heading towards the large archipelago of the Peloponnese.

Zander remained fairly quiet for the first stage of the journey, answering when Miltiades spoke to him but not volunteering much. As they rounded the cape of Attica, Miltiades sought him out, keen to try to bridge the distance that seemed to have developed between them.

"Strange to be so close to home."

Zander grunted in response.

"Could drop in on mother, if we wanted."

The other man laughed at that, and Miltiades smiled, feeling heartened.

"I would like to see the old dear's face when you tell her you are married."

"Oh, gods, yes. That may not go down so well."

"And then there are the facial tattoos..."

Miltiades rubbed his face. It didn't bear thinking about. "Look where we are. Compared to where we were not so long ago."

Zander nodded. "I know. One day we are scouring the agora for new books, the next we are in revolt against the largest empire in the world."

"We could be the subject of books."

"Yes. Yes, we could. I wish we were. I wish I could read ahead and see how this ends."

Miltiades opened his mouth to say something, but nothing comforting came to mind.

Callias stormed into the hut he shared with Teron and fell back upon his cot, throwing his arm over his face. Teron looked up from his own bed, where he sat burnishing his bronze greaves.

"You stink of horse sweat."

"Fuck off."

Teron paused his polishing and observed his friend. "It's that Thracian bitch, isn't it?"

Callias would normally have bitten at that, and there was a sharp intake of breath, but he didn't speak, just sat up and swung his legs over the side of the bed.

"I don't know why you bother with her," said Teron quietly. "She hardly seems to care if you exist. And I don't think your cousin would be pleased if he knew how often you sneak off to visit her."

"She...she intrigues me. She is different to the girls back home."

"I'll grant you that. Very different to the pale insipid ghosts your father was trying to force upon you." Teron carefully spread his polishing cloth on the bed, and lay the gleaming greaves upon it side by side. "But I'm sure that spoilt barbarian bitch will get hers sometime." He moved over behind Callias, resting his hands on the young man's shoulders.

"Whoa, you are tense." He started kneading the stiff muscles. Callias sat resistant for a minute, then slowly relaxed, leaning back against Teron.

"That feels good."

"I know." He dug his fingers deep. Callias groaned. "I always could make you feel good, couldn't I?"

"Yes," murmured Callias.

"Yes." He pressed his midsection forward, so Callias could feel the erection bulging beneath his tunic. "Yes?"

Callias exhaled deeply, then shifted around towards him. "Yes."

Teron bent, his lips brushing Callias' ear. "But go and bathe first. I meant it when I said you fucking stink."

They made landfall on the rocky coast of the Peloponnese at the village of Gytheum. Sparta boasted no great port like the Phaleron at Athens. The Spartans had no interest in making it easy for anyone to come to their lands, friend and foe alike. They were met by a small group of lean men with lined unsmiling faces, who provided horses and escorted them to Sparta itself. Or rather, the collection of interlocking small villages that constituted the city-state. The journey there took them through a series of fields worked by drab, downcast men and women – the helots, the resident slave population who provided all the labour that allowed the Spartans to spend their time in training for war. When other cities had sought to expand via colonisation, the Spartans had instead focussed their efforts on defeating their nearest neighbours, then creating an entire slave class to serve them. It was a strange situation, Miltiades reflected: the very thing that gave the Spartans their military lifestyle required it, for they lived in terror of a general uprising among the helot class. It was widely said – when there were no Spartans in earshot – that the helots would eat the Spartans raw to gain their freedom. It was like a man holding a wolf by the tail – while he kept his grip he was safe, but if he should stumble...

The capital was a dour place. Miltiades and Zander were used to the colour and spectacle of Athens. While this polis also boasted numerous temples, they were less colourful, more functional. And there was no teeming market place full of vendors and entertainment – instead trade was conducted at a series of small client villages in the surrounding lowlands. The men and women – even the children – had a hard look to them, and many stared with open suspicion. They were all clad simply, in a way meant to enforce the sense of equality among the Spartiate class.

But there was still wealth – when they were shown into the home of the king, Cleomenes, they found trappings of wealth in abundance.

"So much for equality," whispered Miltiades.

"All Spartiates are equal," Zander whispered back. "Only some are more equal than others."

"Oh very clever. Did you just make that up?"

"Shhhh," said Aristagoras with a frown.

Cleomenes came to meet them in the andron. He had no attendants, no guards. He was a big strong man, with grey at his temples. He had the same hard look as the other Spartans, but

seemed to have just a little softness compared to their sharp edges. A little more fat went into this man's diet.

"So what have you got?" he asked without preamble.

Aristagoras shook his head, sighing. "King Cleomenes, you must realise why we are here. The fact that the Ionians should have become the slaves of barbarians is a source of bitter shame and grief not only to us, but one that must extend to all Greeks. And especially to you."

The king's eyebrows raised, but he didn't speak. He flicked a finger to indicate Aristagoras should continue.

"You are the leaders of the Greek world. The best of the best. We beg you in the name of the gods to save us from our slavery. We are fighting – the Ionians have risen up as one and are fighting, but we need assistance."

"Against the Persians?"

"Yes – but they are easy! Easy! They don't have the stomach for a fight like real men do. Have you seen what they wear?

Trousers! And they fight with bows, like total pussies. Their spears are short. They weave their shields! I could go on...but I should probably tell you about their treasure."

Cleomenes' eyes glittered, and he leaned forward just a little.

"Obviously, we know it is glory that the Spartans seek – but it would only be fair that you received reparations. Here, look." Aristagoras pulled a map from his satchel and unfurled it. "These people are richer than the rest of the world put together. They have gold, silver, bronze, cloth, slaves. All of this is there for the taking. All of this is yours, if you wish it."

Cleomenes studied the map, his eyes sweeping across the Ionian coast, to Lydia and Phrygia, Cappadocia, moving east, until they came to rest on a marking far off to the right.

"What is that?"

"Which? Oh, Susa, the Persian capital."

"How long? How long to march there from the Ionian coast?"

"Um, hmmm, maybe...three months?"

Miltiades groaned. He could see the shutters close down in the king's face, see his eyes grow cold. He couldn't believe Aristagoras could be so stupid.

"You fucking moron," said the king. "You want the Spartan army to march three months inland from the sea?" He glanced out the window, obviously caught up in the horrific images of what would become of the Spartan homeland if left unguarded for so long. What the helots might do...

"It needn't be the whole force," said Miltiades. "And we needn't take their capital. Just force them to terms, force them to agree to the freedom of the Greek cities."

"Fucking amateurs." Cleomenes shook his head. "If you don't take their capital and kill their king, you really think they will stop? You think they could let you just sit there, independent? How do you suppose that will look to the rest of their subjects? They will have revolts from Egypt to Arabia. No, it can't be done. Amateurs. Get out of Sparta. Be gone by nightfall or I'll set the krypteia on you. They can practise their knife skills on your worthless carcasses."

He stood, and stomped from the room into the interior of the house. Aristagoras sat staring at the map, stroking his chin.

"Well-" Miltiades began.

"Come on!" cried Aristagoras, leaping to his feet and heading out the door in the direction the king took.

"This is not a good idea," said Zander. "We should not be doing this..."

They followed. They went down a hall, and turned right. They found Cleomenes sitting at a table alongside a young girl of eight or nine. Aristagoras stood before him, hands splayed out on the tabletop.

"All right, how much do you want? To make this happen? Ten talents?"

"Get out, Ionian. Before I show my daughter how to kill a man with your bare hands."

"Twenty, then. Twenty talents of gold."

"Ionian..."

"Thirty. Fifty!"

The king sat back, staring. His eyes darkened. "Fifty?" he asked.

Aristagoras grinned. But then the little girl, who had been glancing between them, shifted in her seat. "Father," she said in her high piping voice. "You had better go away before the stranger corrupts you."

And Miltiades saw it all, saw it happen. Cleomenes looked down, and his face fell as he suddenly caught a glimpse of himself from the outside. There was a flash of shame, and then his face twisted in anger. They had made the king feel bad about himself – something no king ever liked to experience. He pushed himself back and stood, face like thunder – and Aristagoras turned on his heel and fled from the room, leaving Miltiades and Zander to rush along in his wake.

"What now?" asked Miltiades once they were outside.

"We get out of Sparta by sundown, like he said. Before the secret police kill us."

"And then? We're stuffed, aren't we?"

"Oh no, not yet," said Aristagoras, beaming at them. "We'll go to Athens."

....

It was strange, Miltiades thought as he walked through the agora. Strange that while it was so hard to convince one man, it should be so much easier to convince thirty thousand.

Well, less than that. It wasn't like the whole citizen body gathered every time there was an assembly to discuss an issue. The farmers could hardly travel in from their fields just like that – even if they got the message that a meeting was on in the first place. It seemed to Miltiades that it meant that those with something important and meaningful to do were therefore the least likely to be available to vote. And what did that say about those who were?

In this case, nothing flattering. While Aristagoras spoke, standing on the speaker's rock at the top of the Pnyx, Miltiades had simply stood behind him, watching the crowd. He watched their eyes light up, and their jaws drop, as Aristagoras laid out for them the untold riches that could be theirs, if they joined the Ionians, their brothers, in their righteous struggle to throw off barbarian rule. He watched them devour every word, every promise of cattle and grain and gold. Every insulting dismissal of the Persians as a fighting force. They swallowed it all. And when the motion was put that Athens should furnish ships and men, they bellowed their acclaim.

Smyrus, one of that year's archons, had hinted as such when they had presented themselves after the long walk up from the harbour.

"You'll find the place somewhat changed since you were last here, Miltiades," he had said. Miltiades knew him a little – he was from the Eupatrid class, after all, and they all tended to know each other to some degree. "Do you know what they are talking of? Changing the archon elections to a lottery. A lottery! The feeling is that the wealthy still have an unfair advantage, and are more likely to secure the archonships. Well, they're right, of course. Easy to sacrifice some oxen and put on a feast for the neighbourhood when you have the cash. So, soon, everyone who wants to stand will simply put their name in an urn, and that is how we will pick that year's officials!"

"You don't agree?" asked Aristagoras.

"Oh, I always agree with the will of the people," Smyrus replied, looking at Miltiades the whole time. "There is also talk of commissioning statues of the tyrannicides. Very nice, expensive statues. I support that, too, of course."

"The tryannicides?" asked Miltiades.

"Yes. Those upstanding boys who slew the tyrant Hipparchus."

"That was over a messy love triangle, wasn't it?"

"Oh no," Smyrus' eyes glittered. "They were true democrats to the core. Anyway, we shall have to hold an assembly to discuss your request..."

The whole time, since they had entered the city gates in fact, Miltiades had felt the pull and push of his family home. And once the vote was decided, there was nothing else for it but to make his way there to visit. He took Zander with him, and the two walked silently up through the agora. The frequent use of the word 'citizen' struck him – vendors greeted customers with it, who used it in return. "Sweet cakes, citizens!" shouted the bakers. "Wine! Citizen, try my vintage!" cried the vitners. "How much, citizen?" asked the customers in return. There was something a little forced about it to his ears, but he couldn't deny the buzz of energy in the city. Something was happening here.

Neither he nor Zander recognised the slave who opened the street door to them. Miltiades had to explain who he was, while the man stared suspiciously, until Zander lost patience and shoved him aside. While his slave disappeared into the interior of the house, swearing, Miltiades headed for the women's quarters.

"Can I help...Why, Miltiades!"

He turned. His cousin Nicomedes came out of the andron, wiping his chin. "We weren't expecting you! So good to see you! Have you been in to see your mother yet? You're not back for good are you? I mean..."

"No, Nicomedes, I am just here on business. Don't fret." He left his cousin standing red-faced and knocked on the door of his mother's room.

"Oh do come in," his mother crooned. "I am quite decent, I assure you..."

He opened the door, and she shrieked.

"Miltiades!"

"Mother. How are you?"

She was wearing makeup, he could see, and her dress seemed to be more stylish than usual. And a thinner material, too.

"I thought you were Nicomedes."

"Clearly."

Her eyes narrowed. "Kiss me, my boy."

He went over to her, and brushed his lips against her cheek. Her skin felt clammy, and he had to fight the urge to rub his mouth on his cloak.

"Let me look at you. You seem...larger. The air over there must be agreeing with you. You're not thinking of returning, are you?"

"And dislodge my dear cousin? He has moved in, hasn't he?"

Her cheeks flushed. "He is acting head of the family while you are gone. It is only right that he should live here."

"I agree. It is pleasing to find you have...company."

There was a pause.

"I'm married," he told her, and cursed himself. So hard to fight the boyish desire to share things with her, so hard to get rid of that historical binding.

"Oh? I didn't think you would find many Eupatrids over there. Although some may have been banished from their various cities here on the mainland, I suppose. I'm assuming she isn't Athenian. I mean, I couldn't be that lucky, could I?"

"She isn't even Greek."

She stared at him. "Then it isn't a marriage. You are talking about a concubine. That's different. I'm sure even your uncle was not above using the locals to satisfy his baser hunger. But he would never have considered making the mistake of calling one his wife."

Miltiades suddenly felt hot and sick. He thought of her, her eyes, so piercing, framed by her tattoos. And he felt so far away from her. So very much in the wrong place. And all he wanted was to go...home.

He left shortly after, waving off his cousin and calling for Zander.

"There are hardly any slaves here I know," fumed Zander. "They have been sold or sent to work on the farm. There is going to be a lot to set right when we come back..."

"If we come back," snapped Miltiades, pushing through the street door.

He strode down the street, barely aware of Zander calling for him to wait up.

A hand plucked at his cloak and he stopped. "You are known," whispered an old crone, searching his face with her rheumy eyes. Her voice was strongly accented. He couldn't quite pick it, though he had heard it somewhere before.

"Famous now, are we?" asked Zander, coming up and gently unpicking her grip.

"Not by men," she croaked. "Not yet. You are known by others."

"A fortune teller," said Miltiades. "No thanks. Go tell someone else what the gods have in store for them, there's a good granny."

She spat. "Not your little gods, Greek. Deeper. You are known by something deeper. Older. You must listen – there is something you must know..."

"That's enough. I don't want to hear it. If you knew who I am, then you'd know that I'm the defier of prophecies. The gods counselled me to flee, and I stood and fought. I turned back the tide. Me, Miltiades. My uncle couldn't do that, my father couldn't do that, I did it. Now piss off."

He left her staring at him and lunged away, colliding with a man and sending his tray of pastries falling to the ground.

"Oy! Watch out, citizen!"

"And stop using that bloody word!" roared Miltiades. "Like some smug school boy who has just learned a new curse. You sound like an idiot."

The man stopped retrieving his cakes and drew himself up. A few people had stopped to watch the exchange.

"What's your problem? Don't like being one of the people, that it?"

"Look at his clothes," chipped in a helpful bystander, his dirty hands marking him as a potter. "Bloody Eupatrid bastard."

"That right? Well, your bloody high-and-mightiness, your sort ain't in charge any more. And if you don't like it, you can do the pissing off, not that poor little old lady."

Miltiades could see a certain fear in the man's eyes, as if he couldn't quite believe he may get away with talking to someone of the highest class in this way. At that moment the little old lady in question fired off a barrage in a guttural language, staring at Miltiades.

"You must listen-" she croaked, switching to Greek.

"She doesn't sound like a citizen to me," offered the potter. "Must be just a metic."

"Well, he can mouth off to her all he wants then, can't he?" asked a woman with a fish in her hand. "If she's a metic and he's a citizen."

"Yes, but what about my bloody cakes? He can't ruin a fellow citizen's cakes then swear at him like that. I have rights."

The crowd nodded agreement with that, and turned to look at Miltiades. At that point Zander stepped forward, dropping coins into the confectioner's hand. The man did a quick count, eyes squinting.

"Well, that's all right then."

"Come on," said Zander. "I know your mother winds you up, but starting a riot seems a bit much, even for you."

Back down at Phaleron, they had to wait for an hour before Aristagoras finally reappeared, seemingly a little drunk. He held an armful of wineskins in his arms.

"Let's toast!" he cried. "To our new allies, and an end to barbarian... barbarities!"

As the crew slipped the moorings, and the oarsmen settled into their places, Miltiades poured a libation over the ship's side then sent a long jet of wine into his own mouth. It was good.

"Let's go home," he said, and followed those pleasing words with another long stream from the wineskin. And another.

....

A pounding headache and a dry mouth woke him. He pulled his cloak from where it covered his face and gasped as the full sunlight hit him. Above, the square sail was taut in a strong breeze. Men sat along the sides of the hull, talking. About a third of the oars were dipping in the water, helping speed the trireme along.

"Are we nearly there?" he asked no one in particular. His back ached from the hard deck. Obviously they hadn't beached the ship last night – a risky move.

"Yes," said Aristagoras behind him. The man looked disgustingly fresh. Had they not spent the remains of the afternoon drinking together? He was sure the Ionian had been matching him pull for pull. "But there has been a slight change of plans. I need to get to Miletus, so you have to come with me."

"Miletus?" He sat up, sending harsh stabs through his temples. "I don't want to go to Miletus. You were supposed to drop us back at Chersonnesus. What the hell is going on?"

"Things are moving swiftly. The Athenian warships will be close behind us. We have to strike now."

"Well, just drop us where you can, and I'll hire a ship to take us home."

Aristagoras chewed his lip, then shook his head. "I can't do that. I need you. You're the reason the Athenians are helping."

"Me? You're the one who did all the talking... I just bloody stood there."

"But it was you they were all looking to."

"Looking to me? Nobody is looking to me, I assure you. You should have seen them in the agora, they bloody hate me..."

Aristagoras was shaking his head. "Not them. Not the commoners. The better men, the Eupatrids. They voted to go along because you, one of their number, are involved."

"Weren't you paying attention? It was a vote. And it was the greed of the masses that you triggered, with all your tales of gold and...what?"

"Yes, yes, there was a vote. But didn't you notice how many of them looked to see which way the Eupatrids were voting first? Didn't you see how all their hands went up once they saw which way the real power, the old power, was voting? You can't change the order of things just like that. You can give an ox a vote, but at the end of the day, he is still just a beast of burden. Look at me – still in charge, from tyrant to duly elected archon just like that. The name changes, but not the form. It's the natural order."

Miltiades frowned.

"So that is why I need you, why the rebellion needs you. To reassure your fellow Eupatrids that there is money in this for them, and they in turn guarantee the support of the masses."

"So I'm a prisoner?"

"No! For the gods' sake! Not a prisoner." Aristagoras grinned. "Some kind of figurehead, yes, but not a prisoner."

"Then at least let me send a message north, to let my people know what is going on."

"Sure," said Aristagoras, nodding. "No problem."

But it was a problem. When they reached Miletus, Miltiades couldn't find a ship heading north. All of the biremes and triremes were busy keeping the Phoenicians in check, and the merchant ships were pressed into service to ferry hoplites from up and down the Ionian coast, especially from Ephesus, the most powerful Ionian Greek polis after Miletus.

"It will be all right," said Zander, though the crease between his eyes belied his confidence. "They will be fine until we return."

Twenty Athenian warships sailed into the harbour, disgorging armoured men, and the elected polemarch, Melanthios. All together, the rebellion had mustered some six thousand hoplites, with another thousand men acting as light troops. Confidence was running high. *But that's because they can't picture how many bloody Persians there truly are,* Miltiades thought bitterly.

His confidence was not increased when at the first joint strategy meeting the Ionians voted to march north west and attack the seat of the local governor, at Sardis.

"But the Persians will be gathering to attack," he said to Aristagoras, when he caught him alone after the meeting. "Why not pick the ground to fight on, and wait for them here?"

"Because Sardis is a soft target," Aristagoras smiled. "We'll singe the king's beard, and he will be more interested in suing for peace than allowing this war to drag on. You'll see. We will get some very reasonable tax rates when this is over."

"Is that what this about?" Miltiades asked his retreating back. "Tax rates?"

Melanthios wouldn't listen to him either.

"Yes, I realise you have had some exposure to the Persian ways, Miltiades, but that doesn't make you an expert," the

Athenian commander said. "Aristagoras seems like a top-notch sort of chap, and this is his backyard after all. I'm content to let he and the other Ionians lead the way." He leaned in close. "So long as they are the best sort of men, you understand." He winked, and patted Miltiades on the shoulder.

So Miltiades and Zander found themselves marching inland, further from the sea, further from a ship home. Sardis, the headquarters of the local satrapy, was as poorly defended as Aristagoras had said, and not extensively fortified. They reached it after two day's march, with the light troops scouting ahead and stopping word of their advance reaching the city. It fell quickly. The gates were breached, and the hoplites poured down the streets, kicking in the doors of the local businesses, grabbing anything of value. Miltiades did not enter the city, but fretted outside. This was not going to stop the Persians. This was only going to spur them on.

....

Inside, two grizzled hoplites slouched down an alley. They weren't happy. Pickings had not been good, and their line boss, one of the sons of one of the gentry, with barely a whisker to his name, seemed determined to lead them where the shops were already trashed and all the best of the locals who hadn't fled already enslaved. So they had separated from their unit in the hopes of finding something better. At the end of the twisting little alley they came out onto a wider street, and right in front of them was what could only be a temple for one of them weird Eastern gods. They exchanged a look, and kicked in the door. A bald priest came at them, yammering in his barbaric tongue, and the taller hoplite head butted him in the face, his helmet smashing the man's nose.

"Bloody dark in here," muttered his smaller friend.

"Then light a torch. And hurry up – I want to see what's in here to nick before some other bastard stumbles on the place."

There was a flash of sparks, and then a taper bloomed in the dark, the yellow light bobbing deeper inside.

"Dunno if there is much here. All wood. Some nice tapestries, though....Ah, shit."

"What?"

"Got too close, this one is alight. Its fine, I'll just rip it down before it... Shit!"

"What are you doing?"

"I think we better..."

"Run!"

Outside, Zander pointed to the column of black smoke boiling into the sky.

"Now what in Hades do you suppose that is? Was destroying the city part of the plan?"

"No," said Miltiades. "I don't think it was... Aristagoras!"

The Milesian came jogging out of the gate, ahead of a babbling torrent of Greeks. His face was smeared with soot.

"What in Zeus' ballsack is going on?"

"Slight change of plans," Aristagoras replied grimly. "We're retreating."

"What happened?"

"Someone has torched their temple to Cybele. Lovely temple complex, all carved wood. At least, it was. Shit. The Persians are not going to like this."

"You are scared of them, aren't you? For all your big talk, you're scared of the Persians."

Aristagoras just looked at him, and jogged off, throwing his helmet to a slave to carry for him.

"Fuck," said Miltiades. "Fuck, fuck, fuck."

The Greek force marched back for the coast, and the perceived safety of their walled cities. Now all their talk of their superiority over the Persians left them, as they glanced worriedly over their shoulders for signs of pursuit, for signs of the dreaded Persian cavalry catching up with them.

And sure enough, word came that a large Persian host was moving to intercept them, and was likely to overtake them just short of Ephesus. There was nothing for it but to stand and fight. With no cavalry of their own to hold the Persian hazarabas at bay, marching on was inviting disaster. The enemy cavalry could raid and pick them off at their leisure. They needed to bloody the Persians soundly if they were to get away.

Aristagoras and the other Ionian commanders ordered a stop, and the host turned and formed up alongside the River Cayster. Its' broad expanse formed a natural barrier on their left flank. Unfortunately, there was nothing but open rolling ground to the right. Cavalry country.

The Athenian contingent formed up on the left, alongside the water. The land was boggy, but they were the most experienced hoplites in the army, so best placed to deal with difficult terrain. Next came the hodgepodge of troops from the smaller cities, then the Milesians, with the Ephesians taking the place of honour on the right flank, as it was their city the fight was taking place closest to. To counter the threat of being flanked by the Persian riders, all the light troops were spread out on the far right, their arrows, rocks and javelins hopefully being enough to keep the riders at bay.

Miltiades approached Aristagoras, standing on a small rise behind the line.

"If I can borrow some panoply, I will fight down amongst the Athenians."

"No, stay here with me."

"Here?" Miltiades glanced about. There was shimmer of dust as the Persians formed up beyond the Greek lines. "But a commander's place is in the front rank."

"Oh, Miltiades, you are so old fashioned. The new ways of generalship are about keeping back so you can watch what is going on."

"What about leading by example?"

"What kind of example does it set if the commander goes down in the first few minutes? No, no. We are staying right here. But if you really want to make a contribution, I'm sure we can scare up a javelin or two and you can send your slave to join the psiloi guarding the flank."

Miltiades looked at Zander, whose eyes had grown wide.

"No. He is staying with me."

"Suit yourself." Aristagoras shrugged, and turned back to watch the field.

Beyond the Greek line, the Persians were formed up. Local troops from Lydia with round shields, and rows of Persian sparabara: the front ranks armed with their wicker shields and short spears, while the rear ranks strung their bows and nocked their arrows. There had to be nearly twice as many men as in the Greek ranks. They had sent all their cavalry, over a thousand, out onto their left, ready to circle behind the Greek lines. At least, reflected Miltiades, Aristagoras had been right about the disparity in equipment and fighting styles. Once the phalanx was close enough, their armoured hoplites could chew through the more lightly protected Persians – and hopefully rout them before the cavalry could push through on the right flank.

But then he noticed a disturbance in the middle of the Persian lines. A gap was opening, the men suddenly shifting and sidestepping, and into this space ran more men carrying old fashioned tower shields not seen for a hundred years. They were nearly as tall as a man, ungainly to wield – but these seemed light, made of the same wicker as the sparabara shields. The men carrying them formed up and turned, making a solid wall on both sides of the gap, like a corridor.

"What on earth are they playing at?" murmured Aristagoras. "Are they going to send some more cavalry through there? Fools. We'll pin them in between us."

"I have a very bad feeling about this," said Zander.

A dozen young men came sprinting through the gap, blowing horns.

And then, staggering after them, came the dead.

They spilled out in a steady stream, turning their dull eyes from the blank walls on either side of them to the delicious running men to their front. They groaned in longing, stumbling through the dust, hands reaching out. The runners kept ahead of them, calling and blowing their horns, heading toward the Greek phalanx. And behind them, rolling them up, pressing them forward, came another wall of tower shields, their blank features giving the Hadesmen nothing to grip or desire to rend.

"Holy fuck!" cried Aristagoras.

"It's all right," said Miltiades. "There aren't so many. Maybe two hundred... We dealt with far more."

"They're...they're disgusting..."

And then Miltiades noticed it – the shimmer in the lines of the phalanx.

"Oh gods," he said. "Hold firm. They must hold firm."

For disorder was death to the phalanx. Every man was locked in place, his shield providing shelter for the man to his left, while he himself was protected by the man to his right. He pressed forward into the man ahead, and felt the reassuring pressure from the rest of the line behind him. Hemmed in, his hearing dampened by his helmet, his vision cut to slits, each man truly relied upon the nerve of his fellows. The phalanx was a powerful formation – so long as everyone held together. No one wanted to be abandoned and trampled if the lines gave way. So every man's senses were on screaming high alert, feeling for any change in the lines, any sense that others were giving way.

The horn men were now in easy javelin range, but all the light troops were out on the flank, where the cavalry were pressing forward. And now they dropped to the ground, throwing cloaks over themselves as the dead surged forward. Several were unlucky, the closest dead not fooled, and were set upon, suddenly blooming red as bony fingers and broken teeth tore at them. The front rank of the phalanx shook with revulsion. And the dead came on, rushing for the hot dense pack of meat before them. Closer. Closer.

The phalanx broke.

Men thrust backwards, screaming, dropping their shields and spears, turning their backs, seeking to burrow between the ranks behind them. And the Hadesmen grabbed at them, dragged them down, teeth pulling hunks of flesh from their calves and thighs, men screaming as their toes were bitten off in crunching mouthfuls. And the rows gave way, the rear ranks turning to run, the damage then spreading left and right. And out on the flank, the psiloi had exhausted their missiles, and fallen back, and now the hazaraba came sweeping in.

Down along the river bank, the Athenians were falling back, but holding their formation, pushing back any panicking Ionian seeking to burst into their midst, and spitting the few dead that came close on their long spears. But they aimed at the chest or throat or groin, as was the custom, and merely overbalanced the Hadesmen, who writhed in the dirt, unable to keep pace with three or four heavy thrusting spears left embedded within them.

"Come on!" cried Miltiades, and he grabbed Zander by the arm and ran for the Athenian troops. He thought he heard Aristagoras calling after them, but he didn't stop, just clenched his teeth and pumped his legs, both glad not to have the encumbrance of armour but terrified he would feel the bite of a Persian cavalry lance or arrow in his back any second. Or the bite from something even worse.

"Oh, hullo Miltiades," Melanthios greeted them gloomily. "What a complete fuckup. I should never have put my name up for polemarch."

When they reached the Athenian square, the hoplites at the front had snarled and shoved them aside, until a line officer recognized Miltiades and ordered the ranks to open and let them in.

"At least you have kept the men together. The Ionians have scattered."

Melanthios winced. "I've lost about a quarter of my men. They bolted with the rest before I could get the square formed. Rear rankers, not the best men. Silly bastards. We may rally a few on the way back to the shore. If we make it."

He was watching the squadrons of cavalry cantering to and fro across the battlefield.

"If we keep the square tight, they can't do much. I think they'll prefer to slaughter easier pickings."

"All they need to do is pin us down long enough for the infantry to catch up."

Miltiades shook his head. "I don't know that they will. I think they will be using the infantry to fan out and control the Hadesmen. The Persians can't afford to leave them running riot throughout the empire."

Melanthios shuddered. "I didn't get too close a look at them... but they are truly foul. To be honest, I didn't really believe the stories... Men that will not die..."

"Not men," said Miltiades. "That part of them is gone. The part that remains is just some ravenous beast." He paused. "No, not a beast. Nothing so natural as that. These are the opposites of beasts and men. Oh, and tell your men – if we encounter any more, stab them in the head."

The advice was spread to all the hoplites – tapped on the shoulder, they yanked up their helmets long enough to take in the message, before nodding grimly and settling their bronze back into place and turning their attention back to the plain before them. And it was as well – the Ionian hoplites quickly threw away their shields and helmets, some even pausing long enough to tear off their cuirasses, all the better to be able to run. Of course, this made them more vulnerable to the Persian cavalry, but faced between the two horrors, why, being spitted on a barbarian pig-sticker seemed eminently preferable to being gnawed on by one of those maggot-dripping horrors. This made the Athenian square the most obvious source of meat as it slowly ground westward. And in response, the Hadesmen ceased the pointless pursuit of the screaming men outpacing them and turned their attention to it. A kind of slow moving chase began, as across the battlefield the shambling dead headed for the square, while it continued to march onward, the rear rank guided by their comrades, who held the back of their cuirasses and led them over the broken ground.

And they were slowly overtaken – but at least not in any headlong rush: the dead broke into awkward stiff cantering runs for the last few yards, when their lust overcame their mobility difficulties, but it meant they came upon the square, either from the back or the sides, not as one foul block but as dispersed individuals and small groups. The hoplites cocked their arms, and rammed their heavy iron-headed spears into the eye sockets and nasal cavities, and if the point penetrated deep enough, the Hadesman dropped like a stone. If not, they were forced to thrust and grind, though the dead helped by pushing forward, burying the blades deeper into their own rotting brain matter.

"Spears! Spears!" was the cry, as many men had to relinquish control of their weapons as there wasn't time to wrest them free. So those in the second ranks around the square passed theirs along, glad not to be the ones facing the dead. And slowly, leaving a trail of corruption in their wake, the square pulled free until only a few barely ambulatory corpses tottered in their wake, soon to be felled by Persian arrows from the sparabara following up well behind.

The journey back to the coast was a nightmare. The men were forced to walk in their armour the entire way, while the injured and wounded were helped along inside the square by the Athenian psiloi – those who had been able to escape the slaughter and regain the relative safety of their comrades. Whenever Persian riders approached, the hoplites were forced to turn and present their shields, to limit the chances of being taken down by a dart. Whenever they were pressed too close, Melanthios would send some of the younger men out to charge them at the run, but the riders would deftly turn their mounts and canter away, leaving the Greeks heaving in their dusty wake.

When night fell, the march continued. There was no way any man wished to sit in the dark and make camp, not with those horrors potentially stumbling after them. The only thing that saved them was how many easier targets ran hollering and screaming in the darkness. With such a victory in their grasp, no cavalryman was especially keen to risk his life against the prickling Athenian hedgehog as it crawled across the plain. They were certainly easy to follow: a trail of gear lay abandoned in their path – a helmet here, pairs of greaves there, a sword. Melanthios yelled at them to maintain their discipline, but the journey was long and frightening and hoplite gear heavy – it was made for a definitive clash of arms, not the sort of mobile warfare the Persians practised.

"The sea! The sea!" came the cry the next day, past noon. Lips were cracked and dry, food bags empty... but at least the Greek ships rode the swell at anchor out in the bay.

"Yes," said Melanthios to Miltiades, as the Athenians boarded for the voyage home, watched by the glum citizens of Ephesus who were now largely defenceless before the oncoming vengeance of the Persians. "I can spare a ship to take you back to the Chersonnese – especially if you let it load up with grain for when it returns. In fact, I'll send three. But then you had better get ready: the Persians are going to want to retake that which they believe to be theirs."

"Will Athens send more help? If I need it? If I ask?"

"Maybe. It is hard to guess the will of the people, sometimes. They are apt to change their mind very suddenly. I wish you well."

So a trio of warships shipped anchor and turned to the north, as the remaining seventeen triremes beat a retreat back across the Aegean for Athens. Leaving behind the Ionian coast, and the rebellion.

TWELVE

MINOS

H omecoming.

It was not something Miltiades had much experience of. Not as a boy, slouching back home after lessons with Photios in the stoa, while Zander fussed alongside him, nervous of being punished if they returned too late. Not as a young man, when he returned after his year of duty as an ephebe, manning one of Athen's border forts. Not any time, until with the death of his father the family home became his, but then he didn't really go anywhere anymore, and besides, as he found now, it wasn't the building that made it a homecoming.

It was the pull in the guts, the iron in the chest, the inability for the eyes to settle anywhere, certainly not on the furrowed brow of Photios as he signalled from the dock, not until they had settled on her, and he had jumped the gap as the trireme settled in alongside the pier, and he had pushed past his advisor to take her into his arms.

"You have been gone a long time," she murmured in his ear.

"Um, I need to talk to you," said Photios behind him. "And welcome back, by the way."

"Later," said Miltiades, marvelling at how sweet human skin and hair could smell. "Later."

Miltiades kicked the door to the council chamber open with his foot, causing it to bang loudly. The men inside jumped, and at least four of the five gathered there had the grace to look sheepish when they saw who had disturbed them. Miltiades strode up to where the fifth man sat on his chair.

"Been having a fucking good time, have we?"

Metramandes regarded him coolly. "Miltiades. You've returned."

"Well observed. Now would you mind telling me what you are doing, sitting in my fucking chair, giving orders in my fucking city?"

The other men, all merchants or artisans, shuffled for the exit, but Miltiades held out an arm. "No, no, please do stay. You seem to have made yourselves right at home, so you might as well stay now." He turned back to Metramandes. "And you, lever your arse out of that chair. You are not the leader here."

"Well, technically that isn't true..."

"I left Photios in charge."

"Yes, but this is a democracy, isn't it? That is what you told the people. And since I didn't like the inaction here, I moved a motion to put a more democratic form of government in place, and we were duly elected."

"I am archon here."

"Yes, but you weren't here, were you? And nobody knew when – or if - you were coming back. And meanwhile, business was stagnating. Somebody had to take some action."

"How jolly. Where is Phillipus? Where's my ship?"

"On a mission. I sent him to Corinth to look into a trade agreement."

"Corinth? Fucking Corinth?" Miltiades laughed mirthlessly. "You'll be lucky if you ever see him again. He'll have just disappeared into their wineshops and brothels. Need I remind you that we are in the middle of a revolt, here? We need all our assets, including that ship."

"All the more reason to seek alliances with strong city-states." Metramandes thrust his jaw out.

"Corinth couldn't give a shit what happens to an Athenian colony. Anyway, I'm back, so your little council or whatever you want to call it is dissolved."

Metramandes' eyes narrowed. "Is it?" he asked softly.

One of the other men cleared his throat. "Now come on, Metramandes. The agreement was for the subcouncil to act up until the return of the duly elected archon, Miltiades. Or we received confirmation of his death... Ah, anyway, he's back now, so surely...?"

Metramandes didn't take his eyes from Miltiades. "Just seems to smack more of tyranny that democracy, this giving of orders. Maybe we should put the matter to the people."

"Maybe I should have you turfed over the wall. How would you like that?"

Metramandes slowly raised himself up out of the chair. As he straightened up, Miltiades remembered just how big he was. He forced his face to remain impassive, and to avoid stepping backwards.

"You will push things too far one day." Metramandes shook his head.

"We are at war, Metramandes. We don't have time for this. We need to prepare."

Later, he found Tresantes.

"You could have done something."

The Spartan raised an eyebrow. "I did do something. I chose not to kill him. I didn't think you would like that."

"I meant you could have tried to talk him out of it."

"I did tell him not to. But he went ahead anyway. That left only kill him or wait for you to come back. Do you wish I had killed him? I can kill him now, if you like."

"No! No, I do not want you to kill him. Thank you anyway. I suppose." He turned then to Callias. "What about you? Did you speak up?"

"I wasn't there." Callias flushed red. "I've been patrolling the wall a lot. In case any of those things come back. I have a good system running there – we won't be surprised. Ever."

Miltiades grunted. At least his young cousin had taken responsibility for something. Gods, ruling was one pain after another – why did men lust after it so?

....

The next day, word came that Miltiades was needed at the wall. Urgently.

He jogged the entire way, surprised to find Tresantes standing grimly alongside it. The men on guard duty were fidgeting and anxious.

Miltiades approached the gate, but Tresantes caught him by the arm.

"Do not open the gate."

Miltiades frowned at him. The Spartan slowly shook his head. The Athenian took hold of the ladder beside the entry and climbed up onto the battlestep instead. He gasped. Beyond the wall was Olorus, with his entire war band, all fully armed. The old King was in the front, mounted on his horse, his helmet pushed back on his head. His eyes narrowed when he saw Miltiades standing behind the wall.

"Greetings, King Olorus," called Miltiades. "To what do I owe the pleasure?"

The king pointed with his sword. "You have something of mine. I want it back."

Miltiades blinked, confused. "What do I have?"

"My honour."

"I don't understand... Wait, I'm coming over."

"No!" Tresantes hissed from below him, but it was too late, he already had his legs over the edge. With a shrug at the Spartan, he shoved himself off and dropped to the other side. Turning, he surveyed the host spread before him. The view was worse from here. He forced himself to approach the king, and stand before his horse, which stamped and snorted.

"King Olorus, what is it? How have I angered you? Do you wish to see Hegesipyle?"

The Thracian king winced. "I want the boy," he growled. "Callias."

"Whatever for?"

"He has dishonoured us. Justice must be done, and so he is mine now. Give him to me. Or pay."

"Threats, king?" asked Miltiades softly. "I don't understand. How has he dishonoured you?"

The king looked around, then leaned over, the lines around his eyes deepening like black fissures in granite.

"He took one of our noblewomen against her will. Bisanthe."

"I can't believe it. Callias isn't like that."

"You are calling me liar?"

"No. I just don't see how it is possible... She...she definitely said it was Callias?"

"Yes. That boy has been pestering her for months. She tell him no, but still he comes to see her." The king struck his chest with one mighty fist. "I am fool, for I know this but I do nothing. I found it funny. Funny! And then this boy shows he is not such a boy afterall. He attack her in the dark. He beat her. He steal her honour."

Miltiades looked at his feet, thinking hard.

"You know what this means, Miltiades. You must give him to me. He goes in the pit."

Sharp intake of breath. He was shaking his head without even meaning to, and the king sat back like he was stung.

"You do not want the other, Miltiades. I swear it. We are not Hadesmen. We are worse."

"Let me talk to him, find out what he says. Give me time."

"Hour. You have an hour. We be right here."

Miltiades walked stiffly back to the wall, where the gate cracked open and he slipped through, into a circle of worried colonists.

"Gather the men. Quietly. They are to bring their panoply, but muffled. I don't want the Thracians to know we are getting ready to resist. Tresantes, come with me. We have to talk to Callias."

Miltiades explained as they walked.

"Do you think he could be capable of something like that?" Miltiades asked him.

"You know him better than me."

"Yes, but maybe my perception is skewed. I see him as harmless...but maybe he isn't."

The Spartan frowned. "Sex and desire can make a man do strange things."

"That is what I am afraid of."

They found Callias with Teron.

"Get out," said Miltiades to the Alcmaeonid.

"Cousin, what's going on?"

"Sit down. We are in deep shit. And all because of you."

"Me?! What did I do?"

"I'm staying," Teron announced.

"I told you to get out. Tresantes, throw him outside, would you?"

Teron stood behind Callias, gripping his shoulders. "I am staying, because I love him. You can have your pet Spartan throw me out, but I will crawl straight back in."

Miltiades glared at him. "Suit yourself. Now, Callias, tell me about Bisanthe."

The young man looked down, and went red. Miltiades felt his stomach drop away.

"I'm sorry..." he mumbled.

"Zeus on high, do you realise bowhat you have done?"

"I didn't think it was that bad..."

"Not that bad? Not that bad to rape her?"

Callias looked up, blinking. "Wait...what?"

"They are saying you raped her."

"I never touched her! Well, I did try to kiss her, but she told me to piss off... I think. She doesn't speak much Greek. I mean, I'd never force... Wait, gods, she was raped?" He burst into tears.

"King Olorus says the girl is naming you as her attacker. What did you think I meant?"

"I used to sneak off to visit her, that's all. But I stopped. I haven't been there in a couple of weeks. Why would she say that?"

"I can vouch for him," said Teron. "He has been with me the whole time these past two weeks. We have not been apart. It is not possible for him to have done it, no matter what the barbarian says."

Callias looked up at Teron sharply.

"You can swear to this? Swear to the gods?" asked Miltiades.

"Yes."

"By all you hold sacred? Do you swear on Callias' life?"

There was the faintest of pauses, almost unnoticeable. "I swear," said Teron.

"Then get your armour on. But not you, Callias. I need you to stay back here out of sight."

Back at the wall, a host of colonists stood ready, out of sight at ground level. Men were quietly lacing up their cuirasses, or taking cloth covers off their round shields.

"What in Hades is going on?" demanded Metramandes, stomping over. He had at least brought his panoply, Miltiades noted.

"A slight problem with the neighbours. When I signal – if I signal – I need the men to mount the fighting step and be ready to repel an attack."

"Someone said this is about Callias and some girl. Are we really going to war with the Thracians because of him? You reminded me yourself – we are in the middle of a revolt, here."

"It won't come to that."

"But you are perfectly willing to risk us all, risk what we have built, for one boy? Tell me, Miltiades, would we all receive such care? Would I?"

"Just get ready."

Miltiades climbed up onto the step beside the gate, and looked down at the mass of Thracian warriors. He noticed a couple of clumps of men at the back hiding what looked to be notched tree trunks, obviously to serve as rough ladders. Shit.

"King Olorus!" he called.

The king sat upright on his horse, squinting. "Where is my property, Greek?"

"He says he didn't do it, and I believe him. And he has a witness who says he didn't leave the polis in the past two weeks. How long ago was the girl attacked?"

"Don't trifle with me, Greek. Give him to me, or face what you get."

"No."

"So be it." Olorus turned and shouted to his men. They bellowed in reply, clashing their weapons together and rising to their feet. Javelins were brought back, ready to throw, lances readied, rhomphaia swung and cut the air. The men at the back hefted their makeshift ladders.

"What would you do, old man? Make war on your own child?"

Hegesipyle appeared on the fighting step on the other side of the gate. Below her, the hoplites and light troops stood looking up at him, ready to pour up the fighting step to defend the wall. Miltiades stopped himself mid signal, and looked back to the Thracians: they had stopped dead. Olorus was holding up one hand, his face stricken with pain.

"Hegesipyle," he said unevenly. "Come down here."

"What? You gave me to this man in marriage before the gods, and now you seek to take me back? Is this the Thracian way?"

"It is the way of kings. And of fathers."

"And foolish old men."

"Come down here. Or else be seized when we raze this pit of thieves."

"I stand with my husband – as law and custom dictates."

"I am king. I decide the law."

"As my heart dictates, then."

"Do not stand with my enemy."

"Even worse – would you make war on your own grandchild?"

Both Miltiades and the king stared at her, at the hands she held gently to her stomach. Time slowed, thick as honey.

"Well, Greek," said Olorus finally, his voice hoarse. "You saved my life once, only to kill me today. So be it. I am done with you."

He kicked his horse, turning it around, and slowly it picked its way between his men. They fell in behind him, trudging back for the hills. He never looked back.

Miltiades slowly climbed down the ladder on shaking legs, and waited for Hegesipyle to do the same.

"Stand down," he told the men.

They walked back side by side, and after a little while her hand stole across into his.

"Are you going to say anything?" she asked him quietly.

"I...," he said. "I don't really know what to say..."

She squeezed his hand. "Are you displeased?"

"No, no. It just isn't a position I ever really saw myself in. My relationship with my own father was...difficult. So the thought of a child... I just fear, that's all."

"What is it you fear?"

"That he...she...won't like me..."

She laughed, and he felt a little of the knot in his guts untangle.

"When?" he asked.

"Oh, many months. You cannot even see anything, yet. But we should be ready. You must think of names."

He walked in silence for a while. "Cimon," he said. "If it is a boy, I like Cimon."

They had not taken more than a dozen steps when Hegesipyle burst into tears.

"What is?" asked Miltiades in surprise. "You don't like the name?"

"My father!" she sobbed, covering her face with one hand. Her other clutched for Miltiades'.

"I'm sorry," he said at last. "I forget. I was never close to my own father, and I forget it is different for other people. I'm sorry he did that. Sorry you were forced to choose..."

"He is a stupid, selfish man," she said, turned her head to blow her nose clear onto the ground, one nostril at a time. "But I love him."

"Of course." They walked on. "And...and me?"

She glanced at him, at his furrowed brow, and smiled through her tears. "I told you. I will never love you."

"Oh."

She laughed a little, in exasperation, and drew him close to her so that they walked with arms about each other. "I forget. You, too, are a stupid man."

"I'm afraid so. Very much so."

....

A ship arrived – a battered bireme, pulled wearily into the dock and made fast. As the oarsmen dragged themselves wincing from the lower levels, Aristagoras stepped lightly ashore and demanded to be taken to Miltiades.

"What news?" asked Miltiades, once the Milesian had a cup of wine in his hand.

Aristagoras winced. "Not good. The rebellion is basically done."

"Who still stands?"

Aristagoras took a deep pull. He pointed at Miltiades, then, after a pause, at himself.

"Ephesus is taken. Miletus, too. My crew and I are the only ones to make it clear. All the smaller states will be folding or being mopped up. We're screwed."

"What is the fate of those who have been retaken?" asked Miltiades, though the answer seemed obvious to him. Mass executions and enslavement – what else could a king do, or else risk appearing weak and allowing further rebellion to foment and spread?

"Ah! There's the genius. Mind if I pour some more? Do you want...No? Darius is being exceedingly magnanimous. He is reinstalling pro-Persian tyrants, but that is about it. He is even having his administrators recalculate fairer taxation." Aristagoras let loose a short bark of anger. "Amazing what you can achieve with a little rebellion."

"I can't believe he is being so generous. After the burning of the temple..."

"Ah, well, that. That he is blaming on the Athenians. And you."

"Me?? I had nothing to do with it."

"Not what he heard. Got any nuts or anything? I'm famished."

"Aristagoras, tell me what in Hades is going on."

"Let's just say the king's mercy only goes so far. I'm not on that list, and neither are you. We are being held mutually responsible for taking a small internal disagreement and making it more international. Involving outsiders – that is, the Athenians. He is taking a dim view of that. The revolt of a subject state is one thing – Zeus' balls, the Persians are used to that – no, it is the interference by outside states that really vexes them. He figures now he has to do something about the Athenians or look weak. And somebody in Sparta or Athens must have let slip about our little expedition."

"So what do I do? Should I write to him? Go and see him?"

"Not if you want to stay attached to your ball sack."

"Shit! What about you? Do you...want to stay here?"

"Nope. We are just stopping to take on water, grain, whatever you'll give us. Then I'm taking a leaf out of your book and setting up shop in Thrace. Going to live amongst the barbarians. Oh, don't make that face. We won't be anywhere near you. I'll sail on as far as the Strymon River and set up a polis there. Should be far enough from the Persians, with thousands of hairy Thracians in between, to live like a lord."

"Do you think..."

"We'll be fine. I managed to talk around the Athenian assembly, didn't I? I'm sure I can make a good deal with some halfwit hill dwellers."

"Aristagoras, the Thracians aren't idiots. They are a very proud people..."

"Yeah, yeah. I'm sure they're...Oh, that's right. You're bedding one of them, aren't you? Sorry."

"I'm married to one."

Aristagoras waved a hand. "That's great. Whatever does it for you. Well, we'll be on our way as soon as we can." He grinned. "Don't want old Darius catching me here with you."

"Maybe we are too small to worry about," said Miltiades. "Maybe things will just calm down."

"Maybe," said Aristagoras. He swallowed the dregs of the wine, and winced.

....

What was there to do but wait and see?

As he walked about his growing polis, watched the bustle in its little market place, the distant figures out working in the vegetable plots and grain fields, heard the tap and chip of the mason's hammers as they shaped more stone, caught the warm smell of bread baking...as he took all that in, it was easy to forget, to let down one's guard. It all seemed so permanent. So right. Photios sat amongst half a dozen young students at one end of the simple wooden stoa they had built – one end was already nearly completed in stone. Tresantes lay on his back while his rabbit played about him, jumping up onto this chest and racing about his recumbent form. Down on the beach, Phillipus oversaw work on the trireme, and one of their two biremes, drawn up onto the shore for a fresh coat of pitch while the other bobbed alongside the new dock. Permanent. And as much as the thought lurked in the back of his head that so it may have seemed to his uncle, still...

There was something else, something he wasn't used to. A feeling of...superiority. Had he not stared down the gods themselves, if he allowed himself to believe that the messages to cut and run had truly come from them? This little polis was smaller, to be sure, but he felt larger than he ever had in his life. No more standing with head down in the shadow of his father, or reading of other men's exploits by the wavering yellow light of a smoking lamp. Now he stood forward on his own terms, with men under his command, and a woman by his side, a child on the way.

No, he would not simply abandon this, turn tail and flee. There was room enough in this wide world for Chersonnesus and the Persian Empire. Darius could be brought around – he was reasonable. He had built something here. Something good.

And so the gods reasserted their dominace, by taking it all away.

THIRTEEN

···

THE WOODEN HORSE

The boy tried to tiptoe past the andron, but his feet were heavy and clumsy, and he must have made a sound, for he heard stirring within – the hollow tinkle of an empty amphora rolling across the tiled floor. Movement, then a rough hand grasped him tightly by his narrow bicep and yanked him inside – he stumbled, slipped, held upright by the strength of the man clutching his arm.

"What are you doing, sneaking about like that?" The voice was slurred and gravelly. "I called for you. When I call for you, you come running. Understand?"

He nodded, lips pressed tight, trying not to breathe in too much of the sour stink of the man's breath. Did not want to be contaminated. Did not want to be like him.

The man let go. His hands were fumbling at the thick leather belt about his tunic. "You know what you need? A bloody good lesson is what you need... Here!"

And the belt sang through the air, catching him across the arm, curling around to lick hot fire along his narrow back. The air shot out of his lungs, so all he could do was hug himself and make a high keening sound.

The sound enraged the man.

322

"What in Hades is that? Are you crying? I'll make you cry!" The belt came searing down again, and he found his strength now, and turned, ducking beneath the man's other hand as it flailed at him, darted across the room, cornered, turned, eyes darting about as the man stood in the middle of the room.

"Oh ho. That's my boy. That's better sport. Now – you better run all right! Go on, run." The man stepped aside, leaving a gap and the open door. The boy tensed. The man came at him, came at him, bloodshot eyes, stinking hot breath, teeth like a snarl. "Run!"

"NO!" roared Miltiades, sitting bolt upright in bed. The gentle hands of Hegesipyle were on him, her voice in his ear, shushing him, whispering to him.

There was the hissing sound of the surf down on the pebble-strewn beach, a voice somewhere raised in drunken song. The room was dark, no moonlight entering through the narrow high windows.

"A dream," he said thickly, rubbing his face. "A fucking nightmare, actually."

"I tried to wake you. You sounded very...afraid."

Miltiades stared into the darkness. "Yes," he said, allowing himself to sink back into the welcome of her arms. "I was."

He felt her breathing deepen, her body twitch, as she easily fell back asleep. He lay still, so as not to disturb her again, though his thoughts were disturbing, turning to dark cloaked figures, an oracle with gaping mouth, a seer with piercing eyes. He shook his head, and spoke into the black night. To whatever forces were listening. Maybe to the shade of his dead father, too.

"You can all say what you like, you fuckers. But I am not running anymore."

....

The day dawned overcast and dreary. At first a sea mist hung in the leaden sky over the waters of the Hellespont, a claustrophobic cloak of haze. But by mid-morning, a stiff breeze came up from the south, swirling it into clots and shreds, and the surface of the strait was chopped rough. There was something about that wind that seemed unwholesome – at least that was how it seemed to Gelon, the man on watch on the beach. It made his eyes water, so that he had to squint. Not that there was much point, he couldn't see far. Though at least the damned fog was likely to be blown away sooner or later.

Gelon was a farmer. He had come here after larger Eupatrid landowners had encroached on his land back in Attica, and threatened him with violence if he tried taking the matter to court. Here, he had secured a nice little plot on the southern tip of the peninsula, beyond the polis. The soil was good, back from the rocky gullies that lined the shoreline. He sighed. He should have been there now, working it, but no, everyone had to do their time as sentry down on the wall or here on the beach.

A dark shadow caught his attention, out on the water. He strained, rubbing his stinging eyes. A ship? What idiot would risk his vessel sailing in these conditions? Unless...

He fumbled at his belt, untying the horn he had slung there with suddenly shaky fingers. Not like him to be so clumsy. He licked his dry lips, tried to summon some moisture from back in his throat as he watched. Yes, it was definitely a ship, tacking along the shoreline. He hesitated – a single vessel did not seem to constitute an invasion, but he had his instructions. He blew one long note, then counted to five and blew again.

"Where?" asked Miltiades, arriving at the beach with Zander, Callias and a dozen others. All were armed, though not in armour. This was Miltiades' quick reaction force, made up of men whose livelihood was earned right there in the polis itself, and so most quickly able to assemble.

Gelon pointed. The ship appeared smaller – it had turned towards them, and now it's sail flapped taut in the stiff breeze, and a white crest of water appeared at its bow. It was coming in fast.

"What the blazes are they doing?" said Callias. "They'll run aground if they don't tack!"

The ship burst from the last tendrils of fog, and they saw it clearly. A medium sized galley, with one square sail. No oarsmen, no crew – just one lone figure at the tiller. They could see him, bearded, dark skinned. He saw them watching and raised one hand high in greeting.

Miltiades put his hands to his mouth. "Turn about!"

Instead the man grinned, and reached behind his back. Less than twenty feet from shore, he pulled forth a small curved knife. He saluted them, and calmly drew the blade through his neck. With a bright spurt of blood, he fell.

The ship smashed up onto the shore.

As it beached, something happened. The front splintered and folded and burst open, and a score of figures were tossed out amongst the debris and surf.

"Shit!" cried Callias. He took a step forward, but Miltiades caught his arm.

"Wait! Something's not right!"

The men in the wreckage were staggering upright, their clothes tattered, while others came stumbling from the dark hold. The wrecked ship turned sideways, and rolled, but still more figures came crawling out into the shallows.

"Hadesmen! Hadesmen! Quick, don't let any get by us! You, blow again. General call to arms!"

Gelon nodded, white faced, lips already puckering as he raised the horn. Miltiades turned to Zander.

"It's all hands on deck, I'm afraid. Do you want my spear or my sword?"

"I'll take the spear," Zander answered glumly. "I want to keep as far from the fucking things as possible."

"Come on," said Miltiades, drawing his curved short sword from its sheath. He smacked Zander on the shoulder as the slave lifted the heavy spear into the thrusting position, while behind him the horn blasted out its brassy flat note of warning.

He splashed through the ankle deep water towards the wreck, wincing at the cold bite of it. Alongside him the other men shook out in a loose line, calling encouragement to each other, the last moment of pause before such contact was lost in the action. Miltiades felt the weight of his blade, the shimmer of nervous energy in his muscles. His first target splashed towards him – and he saw he was wrong, they weren't wearing tattered clothes at all. It was their whitened skin hanging in strands, loosened by the seawater, torn by the collision, exposing the mottled grey tissue beneath. A sharp fishy stench rolled out of the bowels of the ruined ship as it lay like some dying sea creature vomiting up its last meal.

Miltiades groaned. The dead thing coming at him was a woman – had been a woman. She looked to have been roughly around Hegesipyle's age when she died. When she was killed. She was naked. Most of her breasts had been cruelly bitten away – providing suckling for the hideous dead spawn in mockery of nature. Strange how the female ones seemed so much worse. As if he could more easily accept men as monsters...though it made sense, considering the monstrous acts he had seen men do...

Then another part of his mind marvelled at how he could have time to think such things, how time seemed to shift in speed like the wind, now faster, now slower. But then a low groan caught his attention and he saw his error – while fixated on the female, another creature was coming at him from the side, was almost on him. He saw what had saved him – the thing was eyeless, blind. There were two empty sockets where its' eyes should be. He thought he saw the flicker of movement within one, the curling segmented legs of some sea creature lodged deep in the socket. The thing was seeking him by other senses, cocking its head for sound, the noseless nasal cavity searching for his warm scent. He vomited then – a short sharp spray of sour wine and bread, but he kept his head up, his eyes on the creature, let it jet down his front. He stepped back, judged the distance, and whipped his blade sideways in a backhand cut.

The tip slashed through the front of the eyeless thing's face, splintering bone and leaving it a tattered mess. The force staggered the creature, but to his horror he saw he hadn't cut deep enough, hadn't destroyed the necessary part of its brain, as it regained its balance and reached for him, grasping for him though it could not possibly feed with the ruination that was its face. He drew his arm back past his head, to deliver a downward hack between its outstretched arms, when he felt cold fingers scrabbling at his back – the girl-thing was on him. It caught hold of his right wrist, straining forward to bite him, but the blade of the machaira sword somehow lodged in its throat. Miltiades felt the rasp as it penetrated through to her spine, the tip catching between two vertebrae. Meanwhile the thing to his front came at him, and he was forced to try to hold it off with is left hand. It, too, was naked, providing him no handhold. He was forced to make his hand a claw and dig his fingertips into its swollen rotten skin, thrusting with all his might to keep the awful mess at bay. He could not stand it, would go insane, if it was able to press the sodden mass of leaking tissue and bone fragments against his face. They lurched a few steps sideways, then a small wave washed in, the impact enough to cause the faceless Hadesman to lose its balance. Miltiades cried out and shoved, and it went down sprawling. He brought his left hand up to clutch the sword hilt double handed, and with all his might swept it upward – the tip tore free, cleaving through the dead girl's jaw, snapping her head up. He used the momentum to spin, and cut down, the heavy blade chopping halfway through her skull. He pulled it free, and sloshed to where the other was pushing itself up onto its feet. He smashed its head in with another heavy blow, his arms numbed from the impact.

Breathing raggedly, he spun about, panicking that he was about to be taken from behind. He saw that his men were giving good account of themselves – he saw Zander pinning one monster beneath the water with his spear, while another man waded over and dispensed the killing blow to its head with his own spear. There were shouts higher up the beach – more men were running down to join them, pulling on what armour they could, stringing bows or untying bundles of javelins as they came.

Bodies littered the shoreline. In the shallows, the Hadesmen were clumsy. And as they all were coming from the same point, the defenders were able to ring them in, stabbing and slicing as they came.

Somewhere, someone was calling his name.

He looked about, trying to keep an eye on the battle and look for the source at the same time. It was the man with the horn – Gelon. He was waving wildly, then pointing out to sea. Miltiades followed his pointing arm.

Another ship was racing in from the mist.

He tracked it with his eyes – it was going to hit the shoreline not too far to the right. He had to handle this, had to get his people organised. They could not afford to leave any unaccounted for. He staggered up the beach, calling men to him. Some he sent on to join the fight behind him, the rest he called together and led to his estimated point of impact. He could see the lone helmsman on this ship – he appeared to be fighting at ropes or chains that held him to his position – he wasn't interested in steering the ship the whole way in. But it didn't much matter – it did slew sideways a little at the last moment, but it still struck with enough force for the same strange bursting of the bow to happen, the same tumbling of more foul Hadesmen. Three or four archers started firing, and a couple of men jogged in to lob javelins. This ship remained more intact, the hole in the front smaller, and they were able to almost plug it with the fallen.

But where there was a second ship, he supposed there would be... There! Out on the Hellespont, another two – no, three – sailing along in line abreast. In ragged formation their helmsmen put them over, and they turned bow on to the beach, gathering speed as the wind snapped their sails full. These were going to hit further south, down near the dock – Zeus, if they could launch their trireme, they could sink these vessels with their foul cargo. The biremes could land boarding parties, to turn them back about, send them back to the Persian coastline. But there was no time for that, already he could see more sails out on the water.

It was an invasion force. An invasion of the dead, being delivered up and down the entire coastline. Darius had not forgotten, had not forgiven. He was giving them back the ending he had saved them from. He was injecting the infection right into the heart of their polis, inside the safety zone afforded them by the wall.

The wall...

"Fall back!" he roared. "Fall back!"

Those closest who heard him, busy hacking and stabbing at the Hadesmen in the shallows, looked back at him questioningly – they were unaware yet of the doom being carried towards them. Already, the next three ships were running aground, disgorging their poisonous cargo.

"To the wall!" he shouted, running back towards the settlement. "Everyone to the wall!"

The wall was their hope. Just as it had served to keep the dead out, it could now keep them in. They would be safe beyond it, could maybe kill most of the dead from the top of it, if they could lure them there. Then send in teams of hunters to root out the rest. They could do it, they could survive. If they could make it.

There was a wild hubbub in the streets. People were running in from the direction of the fields, their farming implements still in their hands, responding to the sound of the horn from the beach, still blaring its alarm. Miltiades resolved to reward Gelon for his efforts – if he survived. Men were pulling on their linen corslets, tugging the shoulder flaps into position, while women and children held helmets and shields.

"To the wall! Head for the wall! Now! We can't hold the beach!"

They stared at him stupidly for some minutes – they had not planned for a move like this, stupid of him not to have thought of the potential for this... But to use Hadesmen so, to risk trying to control them – Apollo, how did they get them into the ships? This was beyond anything he had imagined. Human troops attempting an opposed beach landing would be full of fear. Not these things.

Now people started to heed him, started to stream out of the polis in the direction of the wall. He looked about for his officers.

"Photios! Find Hegesipyle, make sure she is all right. Tresantes, down to the beach, have the men withdraw towards the wall. Metramandes, gather some of the best armoured men and establish a rear guard – try to draw the Hadesmen after you, but slowly, right?"

"What about us?" asked Callias.

"Help get everyone moving for the wall. I'm going ahead – I'll have a defensive line set up to cover everyone else. Now go, go!"

Miltiades jogged through the people hurrying for the wall. He was conscious of the need to get there quickly, to stop anyone keeping on heading into the hills once they were clear – there was no safety wandering dispersed in the wilds – but equally aware that he didn't want to appear to be fleeing by running faster than the others. So he felt compelled to pound along at a medium pace, in the middle of the pack. He glanced about as he ran, noting those nearby with bows or a javelin or two. He'd have them standing along the top of the wall to give covering fire for Metramandes, Tresantes and the others.

"Of all the days to be pitching my fucking ship!" gasped Phillipus, falling in beside him.

"I'm glad you're here, I'll need your help organising this lot."

Phillipus glanced sideways at him. "I don't know. I wouldn't be here if my ship was in the water. I'd be clear of this shit. I can't face them, Miltiades. Not again."

"Phillipus, keep it together. I need you."
The trirarch grunted.

....

Photios hurried to Miltiades' house. He rapped on the door, glancing nervously about. The streets were mostly deserted. He had a knife in one hand, his knuckles white as he squeezed its hilt. He heard a groan from inside, flung the door open and stepped through, blade ready to strike. Hegesipyle was kneeling on the floor, bent double over a bucket.

"My lady! Are you injured? Is there a...?"

She waved one wet hand at him. "I'm not injured. Just-" She bent forward again, croaking, a thin stream of bile dripping into the bucket. "Very sick."

"We must go. We must get to the wall."

"Having trouble walking without vomiting..."

"It doesn't matter. The Hadesmen are here. We must-"

Hegesipyle screamed. Photios felt two hands like claws grab him from behind, and a burning sensation as teeth sank into the flesh of his shoulder. He turned, stabbing wildly, conscious of his skin tearing like old parchment. One of the dead things was there, dripping in the doorway. He stabbed at its head, but his blade was neither heavy enough nor his muscles strong enough to penetrate its skull. The point made thin punctures, nicking the bone beneath, then sliced down the thing's cheek, laying open the white flesh, revealing the yellow teeth. The thing shoved him backwards, mouth working as it swallowed the strip of his flesh it had stolen. He backed up until he crashed into the wall, struggling to stay upright, trying to manoeuvre the tip of the knife up beneath the thing's jaw. But it was so strong, pressing forward. Then a bucket slammed down over its head, spraying vomit over both of them. It bent forward, but instead of biting, simply slammed the bucket into his head, the wood rubbing his face raw. The knife fell clattering from his fingers.

It fell backwards, hauled off him by Hegesipyle with all her strength. It went clattering into the corner, kicking at stools, falling across a table. The Thracian woman grabbed up a pottery lamp, threw it, smashing into pieces against the bucket, which now served to armour the creature's head.

"Leave it, let's go!" he cried. He staggered, waving off her arm. Zeus above, the wound on his shoulder burned like fire. The grim fact sat there – bitten, he was bitten – but he forced it away. He glanced out the door – no one and nothing in sight. They slipped out, Hegesipyle with her hands crossed over her stomach, whether in a need for protection or because she felt sick he did not know. They turned the corner, and stopped. The Hadesmen were all about, stumbling up the streets from the direction of the docks. There was no way that an old man and pregnant woman were going to make it through that...

"My lady," he said, clasping her hands. "Wait until you see a gap, and then make your way as quickly as possible for the wall. Metramandes and some others will be just beyond the buildings."

"What do you mean? What about you? You can't stay here."

"Tell Miltiades...Tell him... Well, it doesn't really matter, does it?"

And he turned, and went hobbling into the street, calling as loudly as he could. The dead saw him, heard him, came shambling after him. He felt a quiver of fear rattle up his spine – he was faster than them. Just. He glanced back and was relieved to see Hegesipyle slip around the corner. So, at least it had worked. Rather too well, he felt, looking at the mob in his wake. He could hear the distant bark of Metramandes. Big blowhard. He felt a pang – could he not maybe lose his followers somehow, and go after Hegesipyle? Catch up with the rear guard?

But no, he couldn't. He was bitten, wasn't he? He had already lost his seat at the table of men. His fate was cast. All that was left to him was the choice of what to do with his remaining time.

"That's right, this way. You are all late for class!" he shouted. It helped, talking to them. And not looking at them, as they engaged in this slow speed chase. His wound burned, and he realised he was saturated. Blood? Yes, on the one side, but his tunic clung to his thin frame with sweat, too. "You are all very naughty boys. Come on, come for your lesson!"

What did he have to teach them? One last lesson – how an Athenian died. He stumbled, tripping forward but catching himself on his hands, pushed himself upright, lost precious ground to them. Another thrill of fear lanced him. What a horrible way to die. His nerve was failing him. Panic was sitting just below the surface. He imagined giving yourself in battle was one thing – the swift strike of sword or spear – but this, giving oneself to be eaten alive... He couldn't see it ever making an epic poem.

He turned a corner – there were more up ahead, come from further down the coastline. Well, that was that, then. He looked about for a weapon – better to go down fighting, surely? Or maybe end his own life, now, swiftly, on his own terms, but there was nothing, nothing. He backed up against a wall, felt fresh wetness down his leg – was he pissing himself? Oh the frailty of it. They were coming, reaching for him, their dead eyes, so wrong, fixed on him, mouths working in anticipation.

It was too much. Too much. He threw his cloak over his head. One final gift to himself. He didn't need to see this. He just had to endure it for as long as it took.

....

The wall was up ahead. Miltiades could see a row of figures standing along it – gods, how had they got there so quickly? The front of the pack was getting close now. But now there was a ripple of movement along the wall, and the first four or five runners, the closest, went down sprawling. He frowned. They couldn't all have tripped, but they weren't getting up. The next couple of men ran right past their prone shapes, calling and waving, but they too went down, and he saw – arrows. Archers. Archers on the wall.

The Persians had seized it.

"Stop!" he cried, sliding to a halt and holding his arms wide, straining to stop the headlong flight of those coming behind.

Others were still making for its shelter, yelling, thinking the shots were due to confusion, or that they could bargain their way to safety. The bows bent, and they were shot through with shafts. Finally the mob understood, and pulled away, crying out in fear.

"Fuck!" cried Miltiades. "Fucking Persians!"

Phillipus grabbed his arm. "The ship. We must fight our way to the ship."

"It's beached..."

"We'll launch it. It's on rollers. Come on."

"We can take the wall!" cried Callias. "We can push them off!"

"Fuck, boy, there are too many! And you don't know how many more are behind it. We don't have enough armour here!"

"Then we can wait for Metramandes!"

"No good," Miltiades interjected. "Then the Hadesmen will be on top of us. We can't fight on two fronts like that."

Miltiades desperately tried to think. The sparabara would most likely stay put on the wall. As long as they stayed out of bow range, they were no threat. It had to be the ship.

"Form a square! Form a square!"

Others took up the cry. Callias and Teron were there, trying to push men into position, but too few were properly armed and armoured. People were turning and fleeing in all directions. Order was fast breaking down.

"To the docks! To the docks!"

Miltiades saw he needed to lead the way. Holding his arms aloft, he strode back towards the polis. He could see a block of men ahead, slowing withdrawing towards him. Metramandes and the rear guard – they could rally around them, smash their way down to the beach and get out on the ships, the trireme and the two biremes.

It was working, they followed him, back towards the settlement. Screams – a straggling line of Hadesmen were coming up at them from the coastline, where the shattered remains of half a dozen ships foundered on the shore. Miltiades called to Callias and pointed. The young man nodded, settled his helmet on his head and ran towards them, shouting Athena's name. Others followed, running to meet them, smashing at their heads with swords, spear butts, rocks. Teron swore, ran to join them. Miltiades felt shame, but his lungs were heaving as it was – he couldn't be everywhere, do everything. Here was the true bitter draught of leadership – having to risk the lives of others, ask them to do your bidding.

Still there was death and chaos. Stray Hadesmen got through, grabbing at the fleeing people. Miltiades saw one man clap another on the back – his friend? – and the man spun in terror, lashing out with his sword, the blade taking half the other man's face away. He fell without a sound, and while the swordsman stood staring in horror, a Hadesman crawling along the ground sank its teeth into his ankle. The wounded man shrieked, stamping down on the thing's head, but then Miltiades had run too far past to see what else transpired.

Then up ahead he found the rearguard.

Metramandes looked back in surprise as Miltiades called to him. He had a thin double line of men in most of their panoply, the back line guiding the front, as they stabbed with their spears at a thick mob of the dead staggering after them. On the edges, men in no armour and some women protected the flanks, hacking down the Hadesmen threatening to overtake them and spill around the edge of the formation.

"Where are you going?" cried Metramandes.

"Persians on the wall. We need to get down to the ships instead."

"Shit! Halt! Hold them, boys!"

The line stopped, the front rank set themselves, bracing their spears as the dead came for them. The second line, most shield-less, leaned their weight into the front line. The Hadesmen plunged on, some skewering themselves on the spear points by their own momentum, their collapse either pulling the weapon free or tugging it from the hoplite's hand. The line bowed, the men called out, digging their toes into the dust, shoving back. Others were running up, exhausted, throwing themselves into the back, bracing the line.

"We'll push down to the left. You'll need to pivot the line and follow us."

Metramandes stared at him. "There is no way these boys can pull that off. I don't know how to do that."

"Then where's Tresantes? If anyone can... Wait, where's Hegesipyle?" He looked at the knot of women and children standing tearful and ashen faced in the centre of the loose crowd of men behind him – she wasn't there.

Zander was at his side, holding a shield and helmet. "Here. They aren't yours, but their owner isn't going to complain. And I'm afraid I broke your spear." He held up a three foot long piece of the shaft. "The butt spike came off, too, in one of their heads. Now, you get everyone down to the ship. I'll find her. I promise."

Miltiades looked at the grim face of his slave. "You aren't wearing any armour. You'd never survive. Besides, she is my wife. I'll get everyone heading for the ships, then cut up into the town. Then you find Tresantes, tell him to take charge."

He pointed down towards the beach, and the survivors ran that way, cutting through the dead who blocked their path, or else becoming entangled with them and going down sprawling and screaming for help. Back at the fighting line, those on the right tried to slowly move back, and turn, but a gap appeared, and within seconds one or two Hadesmen had managed to push through. With the men packed in so tight, once the integrity of the line was lost, they were at a disadvantage. It was hard to use swords, while all the undead needed to do was bite and tear. The men on either side of the gap yelled and pulled away, opening it wider, and a mass of Hadesmen fell through. The line was broken.

"To the ships!" yelled Metramandes. There was no holding them now.

Down on the beach, Phillipus and a dozen or so of his oarsmen ran for the trireme, cutting at the lines securing it steady. Others joined them, taking hold of the wooden warship.

"Heave!" yelled Phillipus, and they strained, the rollers slowly, slowly revolving beneath the hull, the ship so slowly creaking towards the sea.

On the dock, a crowd of panic-stricken colonists surged along and leapt down into the small bireme. Ropes were cut. Some tried manning oars, swearing as newcomers jumped and landed on them, pinning the oars with their weight. Then there was greater panic still – someone screamed "One's on the boat!" and the entire crowd surged to the far side, tipping it. The few sailors on board shouted to get back, get back, but there was no reasoning, and the edge of the boat dipped below the waterline. Water sluiced aboard, pouring down into the hold, the weight only helping to pull it down further. The ship slowly settled, the people splashing and blowing in the shallows.

Miltiades felt sick – but it was now or never. He ran to the trirarch, went to grab him, stopped, shouted instead until Phillipus turned toward him.

"Take it to the end of the dock. Get everyone on board you can. I'll meet you there!"

"Miltiades, stay here. Don't go back up there!"

"Keep control, Phillipus. And don't just fucking leave!"

He didn't say anything else, just turned his back and faced inland. He could see the shattered remnants of the rearguard fighting down the slope. The dead seemed to be everywhere, drawing inwards towards the beach. He became aware that he was gritting his teeth. The helmet he was wearing was a good fit, but missing any kind of cloth or leather lining, and sat painfully on his head. He had the shield. He had his sword. Somewhere up there was his wife and unborn child. He expected to feel fear – and it was there – but the need to find Hegesipyle was so great. He jogged forward, making the most of a small gap in the numbers of the dead to head back up into the town.

Zander stood watching him go. Behind him, the trireme was afloat, and men were clambering down inside to take position at the oars. People stood screaming on the shore, thinking they were being left, or else plunged into the water, swimming for the ship. Callias was organising a ring of defenders, while Teron was pushing and kicking people towards the dock. No one else seemed to notice the one man running back into danger. Zander glanced about. He supposed one advantage of not wearing any armour was that you were faster. Was he fast enough? He still held the broken shaft of the spear. He considered it. No one had asked him to go. Who would blame him if he didn't? Zeus' bollocks, it wasn't him that chose all the stories about heroes to read.

....

Hegesipyle had been watching from behind a flapping sheet of awning half torn from a food stand when she was grabbed from behind. She had arrived there at the edge of the township, determined to swiftly explain to Metramandes and lead a party back to rescue Photios. But when she got there, she found the rearguard had already retreated further than she'd hoped, and the crowd of undead massed between her and it denser than expected. She could have chanced it. She was armed - she had fashioned a club from a strut. She could have run around the edge of the throng, trusted they were distracted enough. She felt her legs tense ready – but something held her back. She found herself instead lurking there, with her hands pressed to her belly. Too risky. Amazing how this change in her had happened, that a good enough risk to her own life was so complicated as it now related to two. And it wasn't as if she could stay here... Every minute passing left her more alone and exposed. And then the hand grabbed her from behind, and it was time to fight for both those lives, for the man who loved them. She spun, striking with the strut, and connected with her attacker's head – but unlike the undead, he did not simply stand and take it, he instead rolled with the swing, so that it only caught him a glancing blow to the forehead. She was so surprised she didn't react as he stepped in close and held her arms down.

"Please do not hit me again," said Tresantes.

"What are you doing here?" She felt tears of relief pricking at the corners of her eyes. Gods, what a poor excuse for a Thracian princess she was becoming! Her legs suddenly felt weak and wobbly as he released his grip.

"I am going to get Rabbit," said the Spartan. He hesitated. "I must get Rabbit, you understand?"

She nodded. "It is all right, Tresantes. You must do what you must. I'll wait here..."

He fidgeted, glanced at the hand she had again placed across her stomach. "No," he said, shaking his head. "I cannot leave you."

"Well, then, let's go look for her together."

He smiled sadly. "It is too risky. You are with child. I must get you to Miltiades. I must see you safe. Then I will come for her."

"I'm sorry," she said, tears overflowing despite her desperate attempt to hold them in. "I don't want... Photios already... I just feel so...suddenly useless."

"It is all right," he said gently. "Come. We will make our way to the ship."

"The ship?"

"Yes. See? The hoplites have stopped, and everyone is returning from the wall. Something is wrong. The only other way to escape is by sea. And you are not useless – I need you. You must watch behind us as we go, and bring your painful club with you. We will have need of it yet."

He took her hand, and drew her from her hiding spot. He had his Spartan short sword in his other hand, the straight stabbing blade. As soon as they broke cover a Hadesman came lurching at them, hands outstretched, mouth wide. Tresantes stepped forward and thrust cleanly through its nose deep into its brain. It fell, and he stamped and pulled to draw the blade free. It was smeared with dark brown fluid. He looked at his hand, frowning: it was also coated in the viscous slime. He really wished he had a longer sword.

··

Miltiades tried to stay as low as possible, but it was difficult with the weight of the armour he was wearing and the shield. It was made to fight in a particular way, as part of the phalanx, not for these kind of manoeuvres. But he dared not shed any of it. He made his way to their little house, hacking down two or three Hadesmen that came at him – luckily for him, one at a time. He called her name as he kicked open the door, and instantly had a monster barge into him, his head ringing as its head slammed into his helmet. He shoved it further back into the room and swiftly spun around – she wasn't here. The thing came at him again –was it wearing a bucket on its head? It couldn't see, it was clawing for him. He stepped aside and cut, taking off one of its arms at the elbow. It staggered and flailed, and he chopped at its neck, missed, hit the bottom of the bucket and smashed it to pieces. He kept his grip on his sword, recovered, and struck again, dropping the thing to the ground.

He called her name again, dropped down and peered under the bed. No, she was gone. He groaned as he laboured to his feet. Where would she have gone? Or was she making her way here now, and if he left he would miss her? Indecision gnawed at him. Athena above, it was easier to order squads of men than make a simple decision like this. He stepped out of the door.

And around the corner came a group of at least a dozen. They looked terrible. They had obviously caught someone recently, for their white and grey bodies were splashed with bright red blood. But unlike a natural beast of prey, who may be sated after a successful hunt, these things continually craved more. Nothing could ever fill the emptiness that was the only thing left for them to experience. Maybe it was the lack of life they feel, he mused as they came for him, and it was this lack they sought to bury with the meat of the living.

Was it her? He set his grip, squeezing the sword hilt. Was it her? He took the weight of the hoplon onto his left shoulder, angled his feet to brace for their assault. Did they kill her?

He fought. The first went down quickly, head split from crown to jaw line. The blade came free clean, and he chopped diagonally at the next – a mistake, a blow meant for a living opponent – the blade hacked deep, through the clavicle, shattering ribs, tangled in bone fragment and sinew. He stepped left, pulling, drawing the dead thing after him. He kicked at it, felt its pelvis crack. Two others coming from the left, hands scrabbling at the shield to get at him. He slipped his arm clear, shoved, and they went down. He tore his helmet from his head with his left hand and swung it overarm down onto the Hadesman stuck around his sword. The heavy bronze felled it like a priest's sacrificial mallet, but the next was on him. He let go of the blade, threw the helmet like a shot straight into its face, snapping its head back and felling it. More. He lunged for the shield, pulled it free, just had time to get his arm through the strap when they were on him, he couldn't keep his footing, he went down. His head cracked against something. Three of them on top of him, on top of the shield. The bronze rim of it bit into his cheek but he didn't notice. His vision was narrow, black haze at the edges. He tried to writhe further under the hoplon, pull his legs up, afraid he would feel teeth tearing at his shins. Their suffocating weight, the dead fish stink of them. Their blank eyes right there, right next to him, and their teeth rasping on the bronze. He tried to push, tried to smash their ugly faces in, smash their terrible teeth, but their weight was too much. One dragged closer, a thin river of sea water and corruption pouring from the holes in its head. It joined the blood and sweat on his face. And tears. Oh fuck, it was too much, too much.

"Athena!" came a cry, and a sound like an axe hitting a tree, deep resounding 'thunk'. "Get off him you fucking freaks!"

There were grunts, and groans, and more heavy sounds, and then the weight was lifting off him – wonderful, wonderful. He took a deep ragged breath.

"Miltiades!"

He looked up, blinking. "Zander?"

"Get up! We have to get out of here! We have to get to the ship!"

"Hegesipyle..."

"Come on!"

The slave grabbed his arms, hauled at him. As soon as he came upright, a wave of dizziness and nausea washed over him. He retched, nothing coming up. Stumbled.

"Oh Zeus! What is wrong? Can you walk? Shit, here come more! Pick up your sword! Pick up your fucking sword!"

Everything was moving so slowly. Like wading through deep water. No, thicker – like honey. But foul, dark honey. Athena, how thirsty he was. He looked about and reached for the sword hilt, the blade still embedded in a Hadesman. The thing's head was bashed in. Zander stood in front of him, a club held two handed, swearing. Down the street came another mob of the dead things, more from the sides. Hardly seemed worth fighting on...but if his slave was going down fighting, then so must he. A good Eupatrid served as an exemplar to his community.

But then came a ripple through the ranks of the dead, and he caught a flash of bronze, and – what, rabbit ears?

"Tresantes!" screamed Zander, his voice high and shrill. "Tresantes!"

He squinted. It was the Spartan, barrelling through the dead from behind, running with his hoplon on his shoulder, the V of the rabbit ear motif resplendent. His momentum battered them aside, clearing a path. He reached them, panting, spun around.

"What is wrong with him?"

"I don't know. He is pretty out of it, though. I don't think he can walk."

"Fuck it!" cried the Spartan. "I do not have time for this! I have to find Rabbit!"

"Hegesipyle..." groaned Miltiades.

"Gods!" The word tore from Tresantes' throat, raw. He looked down at Miltiades. "Hegesipyle is safe. I took her to the ship. She is with Phillipus. Come, Zander, lift him. We have to be fast! I have to come back! I must find Rabbit! Follow me!"

Zander yanked Miltiades up, ignoring his groans, and got his arm over his shoulder. Tresantes eyed the gathering Hadesmen and pointed with his sword. "This way!"

He launched into a run, seeming not to notice the weight of his shield. He ducked his head and crashed into the ranks of the dead, and Zander staggered along with Miltiades into the gap. The Spartan's short sword flashed left and right, then he shoved forward again, setting his legs, thigh muscles bunching.

"Othismos!" he shouted with a laugh. "The push! This is how we train, dead men! I have pushed for hours against a tree! Think you can stop me?" He shoved on, and they burst through and into the clear. Tresantes immediately spun around, covering them, as they limped on down to the sea.

The trireme was positioned at the end of the dock, crowded with people. The other bireme was dragged halfway to the water, but now surrounded by bunches of Hadesmen squatting over mounds of meat and entrail. Others staggered down the jetty – down the end, the last living colonists were jumping across to the ship.

"Can you manage him?" asked Tresantes.

"What? No! Look at all of them! Come on, help me get him to the ship first. Please!"

The Spartan looked back at the town, face stricken, swore, and lifted Miltiades' other arm over his shoulder. Together they ran for the dock, Miltiades' feet dragging and stumbling. The Hadesmen on the jetty itself were focussed on the living on the ship, and so didn't see them coming until it was too late. They barged them aside, knocking them off and into the water where they splashed and hissed. At the end, Tresantes kicked the last off the edge. The ship sat a few feet away.

"Here!" cried Callias, appearing at the side and reaching for them.

"You must try to jump," Tresantes said.

"Hurry, more are following!" cried Zander, looking back.

Miltiades nodded, got his balance, and tried to jump with legs of lead. He missed, fell short, his foot skimming down the hull, his chest banging into the side. Hands caught at him – both from above and below: Hadesmen in the water had hold of one boot, were trying to drag him down, or lift themselves up out of the chin deep water.

Zander and Tresantes leapt across. They all took hold of him and hauled him clear, the things' grip slipping free.

"Get us out of here! Phillipus!" cried Callias.

The captain barked an order, and the oars strained. The ship moved forward.

"Wait!" cried Tresantes. "I am going back! I must find Rabbit!"

"Stop him!" croaked Miltiades, sitting up. "Grab him – he'll be killed."

Tresantes stood poised on the edge of the ship, but Callias grabbed him from behind, pulling him back down. Zander jumped on top.

"Get the fuck off me!" roared the Spartan.

The ship angled out further into deeper water. Tresantes groaned. Then: "Shit! There she is!" cried Callias.

Impossibly, a small brown shape was there hopping along on the shoreline.

"Rabbit!" cried Tresantes. "Turn in! Turn us in!"

"We will not," said Phillipus grimly. "The dead are everywhere."

Tresantes turned back to shore with a strangled moan, held fast by half a dozen men. Ropes were produced to bind his hands and feet. On the shore, the rabbit had stopped and was sniffing the air, ears turning left and right. She stood up on her hind legs, head questing from side to side. It was like she was staring out to sea. The movement caught the attention of the closest Hadesmen, and one bent and reached for her. She skittered sideways, stamped a foot and rose again.

"Rabbit!" cried Tresantes. "Oh Rabbit, run! You must run!"

The dead converged on her. A hand brushed her ears, grabbing for her, and she dropped, spinning about. She flicked her back feet and bounded between them, around them, as they lunged at her. She paused and looked out to sea one more time, nose twitching, mouth frowning, before dropping her head and disappearing up the beach and into the empty town. She did not stop again.

The fight left the Spartan all at once. He collapsed like a rag doll, drawing his knees up into his chest and weeping. The men let him go, some patting him like a child.

"He's been bitten! Miltiades has been bitten!" shouted Teron.

There were cries of alarm. Teron bounded forward, pointing at Miltiades' face. "Look at him! He's infected! Throw him overboard!"

Phillipus strode forward, face like death. Colonists watched in fear.

"No!" cried Hegesipyle, kneeling by his side. "You will not touch him!"

"Get away. Or you go over, too."

"And me, too, then," said Zander, stepping in between them, hands bunched into white knuckle fists.

"That isn't a problem," said the trirarch.

Miltiades frowned, trying to make sense of it. Bitten? When was he bitten? He touched his face, flinched as his fingers found the deep arc cut by the edge of his hoplon. "My shield..," he muttered.

"His shield!" cried Callias. "He said it was his shield! And look at it – there is no bottom cut."

"Then the fucking thing probably didn't have a jaw!" cried Teron.

"Someone pass me a shield! Here, look – the shape is the same. He's cut, not bitten."

Phillipus stared long and hard. Finally he nodded. "Very well. But we keep a watch on him."

Hegesipyle put Miltiades' head in her lap, and Zander sat beside them with a sigh.

"That's twice," said Miltiades, looking at him.

"Twice what?"

"Twice you saved my life in less than an hour."

Zander waved a weary hand. "Not bad for a slave, eh?"

"No," said Miltiades. "Not bad for a free man."

Zander looked at him "What do you mean?"

"I'm setting you free, Zander. You are now a free man. As soon as I can sit up straight, I will set it down in writing."

"And I'll act as witness," Callias laughed. "In case he later claims it was the blow to the head and he can't remember!"

"Free? I'm free?" Zander stared out across the water, at the hill sides slipping by. "Free."

It was hard to get any words out of him after that. He withdrew to the bow of the ship and sat huddled in a cloak, chewing on his finger nails.

....

There weren't many words from any on the ship. The horror and loss were too great. Some sat like Zander, stunned and non-responsive. Others slipped from group to group, asking if anyone had seen this person or that. The few children who had made it were silent. There were few who had not lost a friend or loved one, and all had witnessed the foul feasts that had sprung up around any who had fallen. The shrieks of the dying still rang in their ears, or the low monotonous moan of the dead, or – worst of all – their own names, screamed from the torn and blood-flecked lips of loved ones brought down, as they cried out for help, or maybe just a quicker death.

There had been moments of heroism: the man who tackled a Hadesman barehanded, allowing a woman and her child a chance to make it to the trireme. The teenager who turned back for his father, dragging him free of the dead grasping hands with fierce strength, before teeth could find the bare flesh unprotected by armour. The woman who stood back to back with her husband, choosing to die fighting with him rather than leave. Moments that the poets could sing about, if they had been noted. But they had been lost in the chaos and fear, and those who had survived were unwilling to speak of them. There had been cowardice, too. Pan had danced his weaving dance amongst them, blown on his infernal pipes, and many had lost their reason. Some now sat on the boat who had stolen their own lives back by the abandonment of another. Some had pretended not to see, not to hear. And now as they watched the coastline slip past, were slowly coming to realise that they must spend the rest of their days burdened with that knowledge. Know thyself.

The ship made slow progress. Only about half the oars were manned, and in a lopsided manner at that. Phillipus eventually restored some semblance of order, moving them about until the two sides were equally powered, and moving the refugees – physically, when necessary – until the weight was balanced.

"Where to?" he asked Miltiades.

"Athens."

They did it in stages, stopping well before dark to draw the ship up onto a beach by rope and rollers. They lit large fires and set sentries. Some went hunting, or bartered with locals, to eke out the small amount of supplies they had aboard. And the nights were a disturbed chorus of moans and muffled screams, as their nightmares played out in their troubled minds.

"What of you?" Miltiades asked Tresantes. "Do you wish to kill me?"

The Spartan barely look at him, shook his head wearily. "I have drunk my fill of death."

Miltiades tried to engage him some more, but the Spartan had withdrawn again. Miltiades left him to his brooding. He didn't have the heart to try too hard himself – he, too, had drunk his fill from that bitter cup. The loss of Photios tugged at his guts. Apollo, if he had lost Hegesipyle and his unborn child...

Finally, the ship slipped into the Euboean channel, on the last leg back to Athens, and here Phillipus swung the tiller and turned them in towards the shore.

"What are you doing?" asked Miltiades. "There is plenty of daylight left. We don't need to stop."

"Prior arrangement," replied the trirarch, nodding his head at Zander, who stood in the bow with a sack in one hand. Miltiades frowned and made his way forward.

"What is going on?"

Zander did not meet his eyes, but continued to gaze towards the approaching shoreline. "I'm going home, Miltiades."

"Your home is Athens."

"No." He shook his head. "Or perhaps. I have to find out." He looked at his old master then, eyes bright with unshed tears. "I must go and stand in the land of my people. I must find out where I belong."

"I...I just assumed you would stay with me."

"Am I not free to go?"

"Of course you are. I told you, you are free. It is just that I thought we were...I thought we were friends."

Zander laughed. "Oh, Miltiades. I have known you for a very long time. I knew the boy who used to hide from his father in the slaves' quarters. The boy I walked to lessons with. The young man with his scrolls and books. I have been many things to you...but was I a friend?"

"I thought so."

"Yet you never gave me my freedom. Not even after your father was killed, and it was yours to give. Not till now."

"To be fair," said Miltiades, forcing his tone to sound light, "you hadn't saved me from any man-eating monsters till the other day. Though you did save me from the Medusa many a time..."

He stopped talking – his voice was suddenly cracking.

"Brace!" cried Phillipus, and the trireme thrust up onto the pebbly beach.

Zander prepared to jump down.

"Zander," said Miltiades. "Might we part with an embrace, at least?"

The other man hesitated, then nodded. He turned to Miltiades, avoiding his eyes, but his grip was strong as they clasped each other. Miltiades tried to speak again, to say something, but his tongue was thick in his mouth, and he could think of nothing to say. After all, it was not like it was right for him to beg his ex-slave to stay, was it?

Then Zander pressed a scrap of parchment into his hand, and slid over the side, splashing up onto the beach without a backward glance. Miltiades waited, poised to wave, but the other man disappeared into the interior, and the ship lurched as the crew started shoving it back out into deeper water. He felt hands slip around his waist, Hegesipyle's sharp chin on his shoulder. She exhaled, her breath warm in his ear. He hoped she didn't speak, for he had the terrible feeling that he may cry. He patted her hands, gently pulled away from her and stalked to the stern, away from as many eyes as possible. He unfolded the tiny scrap.

It read: 'They promised me the same thing to spy on you.'

Betrayed.

···

FOURTEEN

SIREN'S SONG

They limped into Phaleron.

Miltiades thought about assembling them on the docks, speaking to them all. Thanking them for their bravery in the face of the unbearable. Apologising for how very different things had turned out to what they had expected. But once they had tied up, and he spoke to Phillipus about the hire of a boat shed, many had already started to disperse, wandering away into the noisy bustle of the port. A few lingered, those who did not know anyone here, who had joined them in Chersonnesus from other places. These Miltiades did speak to, promising to try to gain them Athenian citizenship for their pains. Meanwhile Metramandes gathered them up like a mother hen, promising to find them lodgings within the metic community. Callias took Tresantes by the arm and led the unresisting Spartan away to his father's house, Teron trailing along behind. And then there was nothing for it but to head towards the city, with his wife beside him.

He felt so sick at heart. The apparent betrayal by Zander had cut him to the quick. He told Hegesipyle what had happened. She asked if that meant that the slave had actually betrayed him, or simply been propositioned.

"After all," she said. "He cannot help it if they approached him. And if he did not act on it, then where is the harm?"

"Because he should have told me," he answered. Was she right? Was that all there was to it? He tried to think back – what chance had Zander had to actually report on his doings anyway? Unless he was sending letters back on the ship somehow... But Phillipus was no friend of the Pisistratids, despite working for them... The thought that, despite whatever the temptation may have been, there was no actual act of betrayal at least cheered him a little. Besides, the man had saved his life. Twice.

The road between Phaleron and Athens was busy as usual, with merchant's carts and travellers heading in both directions. Some recognised Miltiades and waved and called out to him. Others he was aware of looking and pointing him out to their friends. One man even came up and clapped him on the back, declaring him as the man who had helped lead them to safety after the retreat from Ephesus.

Then they entered the city itself – the noisy, crowded, self-important polis of his birth. In the agora, the old Pisistratid house had been knocked down, and new council rooms built in their stead. All signs of the old rule of tyranny were disappearing. There was even a new set of ten statues in a row nearby, each named for an Athenian hero. These, apparently, were the names of the new ten tribes of Athens – another of Cleisthenes' reforms: he had mixed up the people, making sure that all the Eupatrids were not clustered in one tribe. This way, each tribe had a fairly even mix of old money, farmers, merchants and urban poor.

Soon they were walking up the lane to his family home. He was recognised by the slave attending the door, and ushered inside. He found Nicomedes in the andron, busy with paperwork.

"Cousin Miltiades! Back again?"

"Hullo, Nicomedes. That's right."

"Um...Visiting or staying?"

"Staying."

"Oh, what a relief." He pushed the papers away from him. "Then I can leave all this to you. I cannot get my head around it all. Managing the estate, I mean."

"You get used to it."

"Well, I daresay you may. I recall you like to read."

Miltiades went to point out the difference between farm accounts and the tales of Theseus or Achilles, but didn't have the strength. "Well, anyway. I'm back. I need my room back."

"Oh." Nicomedes had a fine house, but it was further out away from the city centre. "And what of Callias? Is he well?"

"Yes. You will find him at your home. Oh, he has one of my men with him. Tresantes. I would appreciate it if you could put him up."

"You do not wish him to stay here?"

"I don't think he would wish it. There was...some trouble."

"Trouble? Did...did Callias acquit himself well?"

"He was exceptional."

Nicomedes nodded, relieved – then frowned. "I am happy to say I haven't seen hide nor hair of that young decadent, Teron, since Callias has been away. Let's hope it stays that way."

"Ah. Yes, well..." He suddenly remembered Hegesipyle, standing quietly behind him the whole time. "Oh! Cousin Nicomedes, this is my wife, Hegesipyle."

The other man goggled at them both. "You have brought your wife to the andron? I thought she was a servant or something."

"She is a Thracian princess," Miltiades bristled. "And in my home she goes where she likes."

"Of course, of course. I merely meant that I never clap eyes on my wife outside the women's quarters. And even then, I often have both eyes closed, if you know what I mean."

He laughed, and Miltiades smiled tightly. He took Hegesipyle by the hand and led her further into the house. Nicomedes was right – in little Chersonessus, in their little house, they had lived a life unfettered by the usual social conventions expected of his class. "Come on. We may as well get all the unpleasantness out of the way in one go."

He sent a slave ahead into his mother's rooms, but was still kept waiting some minutes before he was beckoned inside. His mother sat regally on a lounge. She held her arms out.

"My boy!"

Miltiades walked forward stiffly, and gave her a brief awkward embrace. Some kind of scented powder stuck to him everywhere he made contact with her.

"And what is this?"

"Mother, my wife, Hegesipyle. Daughter of King Olorus of the Dolonci."

His mother stared at her.

"What's the matter with her face?"

"Mother!"

"What are all those lines?"

"They're tattoos."

"Tattoos? Tattoos?"

"These are the designs of my people," said Hegesipyle quietly. "They mark me as a noblewoman of my tribe."

"They mark you as a barbarian, you mean. Honestly, Miltiades. How is she supposed to go into society looking like that? And she is so brown – like a field hand!"

"For Athena's sake, mother! She is my wife! I love her!"

"For now. Well, when you tire of her, you can divorce her and we'll find a nice Athenian Eupatrid for you. One that isn't too put off by the idea of where you have been thrusting your spear."

Miltiades' jaw dropped.

"You know," said Hegesipyle, eyes narrowing. "You are one fat, evil old lady, aren't you?"

Then it was his mother's turn to gape open-mouthed. "What?..."

"In my country, if you dare talk to me like that I would drag you out of that chair and stick a-"

"Out!" cried Miltiades. "We are leaving."

"You aren't giving my room to that creature!" cried his mother after them.

Outside, he sagged against a wall, reaching for Hegesipyle. "I'm sorry..."

To his surprise, she laughed. "Do not worry. She is a jealous old woman used to getting her way. I have dealt with a stubborn king all my life. I can handle her."

"I can't."

"Of course not." She kissed him. "It is different for you, because she is your mother."

He grabbed hold of her. "Listen. We are going to live our way, not theirs. Things are changing here – truthfully, in some ways that frighten me. But surely we can let go of the stultifying ways of the past and be free."

She hugged him back, but if he could have seen her eyes, he would have seen that they were troubled.

....

Far across the Aegean, across the lands of Ionia and Lydia, deep in the heart of Persia, in the glittering royal city of Persepolis, deep within the Apadana palace, Darius, King of Kings, dined with his family and nobles. His son Xerxes sat to his right, poking at his food and slouching in his chair. Further down sat his general Mardonius, eating with his left hand, his right lying on the table. Darius had ordered the casting of a solid gold hand to compensate for his loss, and Mardonius never wasted an opportunity to bring his disfigurement to everyone's attention, scratching at his beard with the curled golden fingers, or leaving it, as now, lying on the table in plain view. His brow was beaded with sweat – though he professed otherwise, his health since the injury had remained poor. His cheeks were sunken and eyes fever bright. If Darius wasn't so sure Datis had struck him maliciously, he would be beginning to wonder if the man might indeed have some slow burning version of the daemon sickness.

If Mardonius was hoping for some reaction from Datis, who sat across from him, he wasn't getting it. Datis made a point of never looking at or noting the golden hand. Darius knew he had doubled his personal bodyguard, and, except when dining at the king's table, had a slave taste his food. Darius sighed. If only they could all just get along. Still, the constant jockeying for position kept them busy, kept them from planning a more drastic redistribution of power.

He clicked his fingers, and a servant stepped forward bearing a pitcher of wine. He poured, and as he did so leant in close to the king's head.

"Sire," he breathed. "Remember the Athenians."

Darius dropped his spoon and slowly turned in his seat to face the man. "What did you just say? What the fuck did you just say?"

The man went white and stood with his mouth opening and closing like a hooked fish. His eyes darted beseechingly down the table.

"Oh, you are a dead man," said Darius. "But first you are going to tell me who..."

A chair scraped sharply back from the table, and someone leapt forward.

"Allow me, sire!" cried Datis, sinking his carving knife into the man's neck. Blood spurted. The servant looked at Datis wide-eyed, tried to speak. The general sawed with the knife, severing the windpipe. The servant sagged, lifeless. Datis bent and cleaned his blade on the man's tunic, then clicked his fingers at the nearby guards.

"Thanks," said Darius, fingers drumming on his chair. "Thanks so much. Now we don't get to find out who put him up to that."

"How convenient," muttered Mardonius.

"Forgive my hot head, oh King," said Datis, bowing. "It is a heavy burden I bear, that I must care so deeply for your honour and reputation that I cannot stand the utterance of such a public insult."

"Oh please," said Mardonius.

"Still," continued Datis as he resumed his seat. "The man had a point. Embarrassing as it was to have it aired like that."

And here it comes, thought Darius.

"We have regained control over the Ionians, thus asserting our dominance. But our honour is stained and position weakened by the fact that the Athenian terrorists have so far got away with an attack on our people and destruction of the Temple of Cybele."

"And what would you have me do?"

Datis held up his hand. "There is more, sire. The Naxians fought off the failed attempt by that idiot Aristagoras – an attempt made in our name. Thus, again, we are seen as powerless to adequately punish a small island. There are those in Egypt and other valuable parts of the Empire with rebellion in their hearts. If we do not act..."

"Yes," said Darius. "Quite. But consider what happens if we fail in such an endeavour? We can spin the other things. We re-conquered Ionia. Naxos is all the fault of the Ionian leadership. The stakes are high. I do not wish to be the first Achaemenid king who actually hands over less land to his successor."

That made Xerxes look up.

"Then let me lead an expedition to punish the Greeks. Let it be in my name. Any failure with be mine alone, but the victory goes to you."

Darius sucked his teeth.

"My king, we have seen how effective our weapons are. Why not test them on a greater prize?"

"Attacking a piddling little place in the middle of nowhere is one thing," interjected Mardonius. "Assaulting a well-fortified, well-defended city-state like Athens is something else again.

Any commander worth his salt understands that. Our men would be slaughtered landing in their harbour. Our weapon... contained. The rest of the coastline is too rocky. It won't work."

Datis looked pained, but did not glance in Mardonius' direction. "My King, it just so happens that there is one seeking refuge in your court who can act as our guide. We will not have to assault the Athenian defences head on. There is a back door, and he is the key."

"Summon him," said Darius.

"Why, as it happens, he is outside right now."

Mardonius groaned and rolled his eyes. "This is ridiculous..."

Darius silenced him with a look. "Call him in."

Datis clapped his hands, and the doors at the end of the room opened. A cranky, grizzled looking man entered the hall and stood at the end of the table.

"So," said Darius, switching to the Greek language. "My general here says you can guide us to a suitable landing spot in Attica. Is that so?"

"Yes," said the man.

Darius ignored the lack of honorific in the man's response. "You used to live there?"

"I am Athenian."

"Yet you are willing to help us? You know what we intend to do?"

"They have it coming," said Hippias. "I hate those cunts."

....

Miltiades sat frowning at the papers lying scattered about him. What in smoking Hades had Nicomedes been doing? The accounts were in a mess, and no planning had been done for the coming year and the needs of the estate.

Just then he became aware of the sound of raised voices out on the street, then clearly cutting through it he heard Hegesipyle yell "Go away!" She was answered by raucous laughter. A slave suddenly stuck his head in the andron.

"Master! The mistress!"

Miltiades shot up from his chair and ran to the outside door. Two more slaves were there, peering out into the street. He heard Hegesipyle shout again, voice high with outrage.

"Stand aside!"

He threw the door open, and Hegesipyle stumbled backwards into his arms. He was aware of a group of men grinning in the street, then she was spinning in his grip, going for his eyes.

"Whoa! Hegesipyle! It's me!"

He pulled her past him as she relaxed slightly, breath panting. He looked at the men outside. One balding fellow stepped forward.

"Fancy digs for a brothel, chief."

"What did you just say?"

"She yours, is she? What's the rate? Feisty, ain't she?"

"What? Get the fuck out of here!"

"Hey, easy, champ. Settle down. If she ain't available, she ain't available. Don't have to get all sniffy."

"She's my wife, you stupid prick!"

"Wife? Really? And you let her go walking around on her own, looking like that? What were we supposed to think? If she looks like a whore..."

"Get the fuck away from me before I kill you. Zander!" He caught himself. "Someone bring me my sword!"

The man stepped back, hands up. "No need for that, captain. Honest mistake."

Miltiades watched them saunter down the alley. They went slowly, turning back and grinning at him. Just before they turned the corner, Baldy made a rude gesture then ran to join his mates, cackling loudly. Shaking, Miltiades went back into the house.

"These countrymen of yours!" hissed Hegesipyle. "They are pigs!"

"What happened?"

"You were working. I grew bored in here. I wanted to see more of the city, so I went walking. I was looking around the marketplace when those men started following me. Saying terrible things to me. What kind of place have you brought me to?"

"A woman walking about by herself," said Miltiades gently, "well-dressed, and obviously foreign... I guess they thought you were a hetaerae."

"What is that?"

"A...a companion."

"A whore?"

"Yes... An expensive one, but yes."

"I am no whore! I am a princess of the Dolonci! My father commands hundreds of warriors! My father..."

She burst into angry tears. Wiped at them furiously.

"I know, I know. I am sorry. In here, you are safe..."

"I do not want to live in a cage!"

"Not a cage, a sanctuary. And it will get better, I promise. You will become used to the city, and the city will become used to you."

"Why should the city care?"

"Because although I may not be a princess of the Dolonci, I am the head of the Philaids, one of the oldest families of the Eupatrid class in Athens. That's why."

She smiled a little – and then there came a thumping at the door, which chased the smile away in a heartbeat. Miltiades waved the slaves away and threw the door open. "You can fuck off, too," Miltiades told the man on the other side.

"Sorry?"

He was well-dressed, and looked familiar. "My apologies," said Miltiades. "There has been some trouble this morning. You are?"

"Aristides. We met once, some time ago. But I'm afraid I am here on some official business, Miltiades. May I?"

Miltiades let him in, and led him in to the andron. Hegesipyle followed, and although Aristides looked mildly surprised, he didn't comment.

"What is this official business?"

"I regret to inform you that charges have been laid against you."

"Charges? What charges? For what?"

"Treason."

"What the fuck?!"

"You are being charged with acting as a tyrant over Athenian citizens."

"That is crazy! Who is charging me?"

"Well," Aristides hesitated, looking uncomfortable. "Let's say that I suspect those behind the charges have deep purses and a certain reputation for enjoying power themselves..."

"The Alcmaeonids! I bet it is the fucking Alcmaeonids! But why come after me?"

"You honestly don't know? Why, you are quite famous, Miltiades. And in this new day of democracy, that is a new kind of currency. And you aren't famous in the old ways, because you built a pretty temple or theatre, or won at the Olympics. You are famous for something new, something hard to replicate. I warrant they are fearful of just how powerful you could become. Hence the move to strike you down now."

"But the charges are rubbish. I was a tyrant, true, but that was because that was how the Pisistratids wanted it. I didn't have any choice."

"Well, that is what you must say to the jury."

"Jury? You mean to the Areopagus, don't you? The Eupatrid court?"

"No. There is a new court, a people's court, established by Cleisthenes. It is them you must convince. I have been voted in as Hegemon for this case, and will be overseeing the selection of five hundred and one jurors in the morning, selected from all the people by lot."

"I don't know what's worse – facing a bunch of jealous, bickering Eupatrids, or a bunch of everyday citizens..." Miltiades shook his head.

"Yes, well. I'd spend the day preparing your defence, if I was you. Good luck." Aristides nodded to Hegesipyle and left them.

"What will happen?" asked Hegespyle. "If they convict you?"

"A fine, I suppose. Or banishment. Or..."

"Or?"

"Death. But hang on! That is only in very rare cases. There hasn't been a death sentence in years."

"But why risk it? Let's get out of here. Let's find Phillipus and just sail away."

"Where would we go? All that I have is here."

"Back to my homeland. Back to my people."

"Would your father even allow that? Besides, if I go now, they will see that as proof of guilt. I will be convicted in my absence, and the family property seized. I can't allow that."

She eyed him coldly. "You could allow that. You just choose not to."

"Look, I'm not going to be convicted. I'll just explain what happened, and everything will be all right."

The next day Miltiades put on his best chiton and cloak, kissed Hegesipyle, and made his way to the Pnyx, where the court was to be held. He had not done much in the way of preparation, since it seemed to him impossible that he could be blamed in any way for what had happened. A crowd had gathered to watch the proceedings, and an assortment of pie sellers and other peddlers were doing good trade. The jurors had all been picked and were seated on rough benches set before the speaker's platform. A hubbub arose when they spotted Miltiades coming. The crowd parted for him, and he was gratified to receive a number of pats on the back from people as he passed through. Maybe it would indeed be all right after all.

He stood at the base of the stone platform, and Aristides nodded to him then mounted it and held his arms out for silence. A priest took the auspices and declared all correct.

"This Heliaea is formed to hear charges of treason brought against Miltiades of the Philaid clan," said Aristides. "Let the litigant come forward."

Miltiades scanned the crowd – a large man in rich robes stepped forward.

"Metramandes!" he gasped. "Wait! This man can't bring charges against me – he's a bloody metic, not a citizen!"

"I can assure you," said Metramandes with a smug smile. "That I am indeed a full Athenian citizen. Now."

"Who sponsored you? Wait, don't tell me – it was the fucking Alcmaeonids, wasn't it?" It was a smooth move by the rival clan, he was forced to acknowledge. This way they kept themselves out of direct involvement. "Was that all it cost for you to betray me? Citizenship? Are you that cheap?"

There were mutterings and frowns from the jury at that, and he realised he had stumbled. Metramandes smiled but otherwise ignored him.

"Hegemon of the court," said the big man. "I am ready to make my speech."

Aristides nodded. Metramandes mounted the platform, and in his rich, rolling voice addressed the assembled jurymen. He began by thanking the Athenian people for their great gift of citizenship, remarking that no other polis in all of Greece could live up to what their city had achieved. He spoke of his admiration for their daring and innovation in taking government from the entitled few and bestowing it upon the collective wisdom of the many.

Miltiades sought to control his facial expressions. He felt like groaning aloud and rolling his eyes at the obvious flattery, but did not want to antagonise the jury any further. Instead he looked about, suddenly spotting Hegesipyle standing on the boundary of the assembly space with other women, slaves and metics, all of whom were forbidden to set foot in that hallowed space. Though, he thought to himself, it was not so hallowed when it was being so liberally coated in bullshit, as now.

Metramandes continued, praising the economic strength of Athens, foretelling that her prosperity was sure to continue to grow, taking the city into a golden age. Why, he said, that was what had first lured him to the city. Never in his wildest dreams had he thought that he would one day be seen as worthy enough to be counted among Athena's blessed, as one of the citizens of her own city. He bowed his head, and the jury smiled and some applauded.

Fuck, thought Miltiades. He wished Photios was here, to offer some advice.

Which was why, Metramandes continued, he took it as such a great insult, that one of Athen's own should turn against her in such a way. Here he turned and stared coldly down at Miltiades, and the crowd looked at him, too.

That this man, this Eupatrid, should go against the will of the people and rule some of her citizens as a tyrant... well, it beggared belief. That this man, whom Metramandes had once thought a friend, should prove so false... Well, something had to be done. Somebody had to stand up for what was right. And so Metramandes himself – however reluctantly - had decided to bring charges against Miltiades, that he might answer for what he had done to the very people he had wronged.

Specifically, he charged Miltiades with acting as an unelected, unselected tyrant. Of refusing to allow Athenian citizens to assemble and vote on matters pertaining to them. Of enforcing this with the aid of foreign, barbarian mercenaries-

"They weren't foreign!" cried Miltiades. "They were bloody Thracians! They live there!"

-just as the Pisistratids had done before him. He had threatened the lives of citizens if they disobeyed him. He had held them captive in a dangerous location. Worse still, he had offered up tokens of submission to the Persians and become their vassal. He had aided them militarily in their expansionist agenda. He was on first name basis with the Persian king!

His actions showed his values. He consorted with barbarians. He sold grain for profit to the Persians, when the whole point of the exercise had been to secure the grain supply for the demos of Athens. He was impious. He hadn't even taken a decent Athenian woman for his wife, instead parading his painted consort through the streets with no thought for the feelings of decent folk.

Miltiades stared at Metramandes. His fingers curled into fists, and it was all he could do to hold himself back from mounting the platform and throwing the bigger man off. His eyes sought out Hegesipyle again in the crowd, but he could no longer see her. He suddenly felt quite alone. Why could he not return to how things had been before, to the quiet of his study and the gentle joy of a new book purchased from the marketplace?

Metramandes wound up, again thanking the people for allowing him to do them this small service in return for their bountiful generosity. He paused for a moment or two when he had finished, eyes gazing upward, and actually seemed to be blinking away tears.

"Do you have any witnesses who can support these assertions?" asked Aristides coolly.

"Why, apart from myself, I can call upon a scion of that well-respected family, the Alcmaeonids." He threw out one hand, and Teron stepped forward, looking noble and wise. Miltiades snorted. Teron flashed him a look and mounted the dais.

"Identify yourself," said Aristides.

"Teron, son of Timon, of the Alcmaeonid clan."

"And you can support the assertions made by Metramandes?"

"I can. I was there."

Aristides frowned. "How did you come to be there?"

"I accompanied my friend, Callias of the Philaids."

"And do you swear by the gods that all that has been spoken is true?"

"I do. Miltiades is guilty of treason. He acted as a tyrant and sold us out to the Persians. I swear by all I hold sacred."

A thought hit Miltiades so hard he almost staggered. He had heard this young man swear before – to him, that Callias had not left his side while Miltiades had been absent, and so could not have possibly been responsible for raping that Thracian woman. He recalled the look Callias had flashed him... Not because Teron was lying about Callias leaving, but because he had left himself... Callias must have thought Teron was lying to protect him, but he was really lying to protect himself. Miltiades had been too busy to give it much thought, but now it was obvious: it was this jealous little bastard who was responsible for the assault on Bisanthe, and thus the beginning of all their problems.

And then Aristides was calling him to the platform to mount his defence. He walked up slowly, mind reeling. His shoulder collided with Teron as the young man passed him. He turned and faced the five hundred and one faces watching him.

"Members of the jury," he began, then frowned and shook himself. "Rather, fellow citizens..." He watched Teron walking away, and his voice trailed off. He felt sick. "Hey, Teron!" he called, his voice sounding raw to his own ears. The young man stopped and turned around.

"You were there because you stowed away, right? Against your family's wishes? And remember – you speak before the gods."

The younger man stared up at him, then nodded with a smirk.

"And the first time we faced the Hadesmen, what did you do? Think hard, now."

Teron frowned, and then his face flushed red. All eyes were on him.

"You shat yourself, didn't you? You shat yourself right down your leg." There was laughter at this. It wasn't fair, he knew.

Those laughing had obviously never faced one of the undead themselves – had probably only heard stories. Cold fury burned in Miltiades guts. He hated himself for what he was about to do, but the urge to destroy Teron was too great to hold back. "I guess when the exit is so well-used, it is hard to hold things in at times of stress." He blew the younger man a kiss.

Now there was a storm of laughter, and Teron mouthed a foul word at him. It was part of the curious Athenian attitude to sex that certain sexual activity between men was seen as completely normal – but a man regularly allowing himself to be penetrated was somehow less of a man, indeed there was something decidedly womanly about him. Miltiades did not share that view, but knew the comment played well to the prejudices of the masses, especially when it was aimed at one of the old ruling class. As he said it, he knew he was condemning Callias as well to gossip and knowing, mocking smiles – Teron himself had announced their friendship, but now it would be seen through a different lense. Callias, who had stood by him through so much. Gods, but Teron had it coming.

"I'm surprised," Miltiades continued over the noise. "That you even knew what to do with your cock, when you raped that poor girl."

There was uproar. Rape was a capital offence, and such an accusation not made lightly. Teron turned and stormed from the area, shoving people out of his way. Such behaviour would only raise further questions. He knew the ordinary people were generally only too ready to believe incriminating rumours about the wealthy.

"There's your prize witness, metic. Oh, I'm sorry, citizen," Miltiades called across to Metramandes, who frowned at him with dark, thunderous looks.

Miltiades felt sick in his stomach. He had no doubt upset the momentum of the attack against him, but at what cost? He had betrayed Callias...

...that damned prophecy. Was this the end of it? Had he betrayed enough – been betrayed enough - to satisfy it?

Aristides called for order, but it was several minutes before Miltiades was able to speak again.

"While few of you actually knew my father, most of you knew of him. Three times he was the winner of the four horse chariot race at the Olympics. You know he is long dead...but what many of you probably don't know is who killed him. I can tell you: it was the Pisistratids. Hippias and Hipparchus, jealous and paranoid, murdered him one night. Or had him murdered. Either way they were responsible. I see some of you nodding – you can well believe it, right? You remember what their reign was like, what it turned into. So, you must keep in mind that is the context in which I agreed to this expedition, and its structure. Tyrants wanted a tyrant to rule the colony. If I had gone against their wishes, then I would probably have been killed, too. All that I did, I did to keep the colony going. Sometimes that meant being flexible – but that is the Athenian way, isn't it? We aren't like the Spartans, so bound by the old ways that they are scared of change. Athenians embrace change – just look at how the city was grown over the years."

"Do you have any witnesses you would like to call up?" asked Aristides.

Miltiades hesitated. Who could back him up? Photios was dead. Zander gone. Callias he had sacrificed himself. Tresantes? But he was Spartan, and so depressed he was probably unwilling to appear. Phillipus? If he was even ashore, would he be sober?

"Actually, there is a man I would like to send for. He can attest that I planned to start the revolt against the Persians before it actually began. It may take some days to track him down, but I wish to send for Aristagoras of Miletus."

"Can't be done," said Metramandes.

"I can call who I like. The case will have to adjourn until he can be found and brought here."

"You can't call this one, unless you can travel to the afterlife like Orpheus. Aristagoras is dead. Killed by the wild Thracians near the Strymon River."

"What?? How do you know that?"

"We already sent for him, so he could testify to your relationship with the Persian king."

"Then..." Who? His mind was reeling. Aristagoras dead? He could just imagine the smug idiot inciting the local tribes... He tried to think of the name of one of the colonists who could back up what he asserted –someone who would not be afraid to stand up against the Alcmaeonid clan.

"I would like to speak, if Miltiades agrees."

He looked up. He recognised Melanthios, the leader of the Athenian contingent from the Ionian campaign. He readily assented, and the other man mounted the platform.

"I cannot speak to all that has been asserted. But I can say this: in the retreat at Ephesus, Miltiades' help ensured most of our men returned to Athens. His knowledge of the ways of the Persians and the weaknesses of the Hadesmen was vital. I do not believe he is false."

He nodded at Aristides and Miltiades, and left the platform.

Miltiades pondered, chewing his bottom lip. It helped, but was not a ringing endorsement. He was afraid to surrender the platform and wrap up his defence. It felt like too near a thing.

But then someone was calling out "Make way! Make way! Let us through!", and three men came striding through the crowd towards the platform.

"Hmmm," said Aristides. "Something is up."

"Who are they?"

Aristides cocked an eyebrow at him. "Ah, but of course. You have not been here. The shorter man is Phaenippus, who is the Eponymous Archon for the year. The taller, older man is the Polemarch, Callimachus. The young fellow is a bit of an up-and-comer. Name of Themistocles."

The trio mounted the platform, and Phaenippus stepped forward, holding out his hands for silence.

"Citizens! I apologise for interrupting these legal proceedings, but I bring grave news. We have received word that a large Persian fleet has put to sea, and even now is making its way across the Aegean. Captain Themistocles here can attest that it numbers around six hundred vessels. There can be no doubt that their intention is the annexation or destruction of Athens." He nodded at Callimachus, who stepped forward.

"At the conclusion of this trial, all ten tribes must gather at their allotted meeting places and elect a general. Messengers are speeding through the city right now. I am mustering all ten lochoi, and expect each tribe to furnish one thousand men with hoplite panoply. There will follow a meeting tomorrow with all ten strategoi, myself, the archons and council to discuss our defence."

Both the jury and the watching crowd erupted. Phaenippus grabbed hold of Aristides. "Get this wrapped up straight away, will you? We need to move."

Most of the crowd started to disperse, heading for the designated meeting places for their tribes. Even some of the jury were already standing, ready to go.

"Members of the jury!" cried Aristides. "We will proceed immediately to the vote. There is no time for a secret ballot, and so instead I will ask for a simple show of hands." He looked sideways at Miltiades, then spoke again. "You heard the words of Melanthios. Miltiades here has experience in fighting the Persians and their infernal weapons. In this, our hour of need, shall we banish such a man?"

Metramandes sputtered, but Aristides waved him to silence. "For us to worry about such things as trials like these, we have to have a city. The city must come first. So now we vote – is Miltiades guilty or not guilty?"

There was no need to count. A very clear majority raised their hands for innocence, and just like that it was over. The jury immediately broke up, the men heading to their meetings. Aristides clapped him on the back and left. Metramandes stormed off. Miltiades walked slowly off the rock, his legs feeling like they may give way. He felt dazed by the speed of events. He wanted to rush back home and tell Hegesipyle, but dutifully headed first to the lower end of the Pnyx field, where his tribe was gathering. He could see that someone was already talking, gesticulating, and there came shouts of agreement from the several hundred already gathered. When he was close enough to hear, the man speaking spotted him, and pointed.

"Here he comes!"

He stopped dead as they all turned towards him – and burst into applause. Hands grabbed his. Others pushed him forward, and he found himself propelled towards the front of the crowd.

"Here he is! What about it? Who wants Miltiades as our strategos?"

The crowd roared and stamped their feet. The man grabbed one of Miltiades' hands and raised it above his head. Men from other tribes meeting nearby turned to look, such was the noise.

"Miltiades! Do you accept? Will you lead us?"

So far. He had come so far in so little time. It was overwhelming. He nodded. They roared again, and chanted his name. They picked him up and bore him through the streets on their shoulders.

...the crowd bit him. Bit him deep

....

FIFTEEN

MILTIADES

atis was grinning, and had come to the bow of the warship expressly for that purpose. He had been keeping his face stern and commanding all day, but was now allowing himself the chance to gloat, here where no one could observe him. At least, not from the front. He hoped that from behind he looked every part the leader. Here at the front of his command.

His command.

Oh, the power - headier than any wine, sweeter than the most expensive candied sweetmeat. It was definitely better than sex. The look on Mardonius' face as he watched them march from Persepolis...priceless. He would have winked, but Darius had been making some final speech about the honour of the Empire, all praise to Ahuramazda...blah blah blah. And since then, he had been so busy – too busy to really enjoy it.

The force he was collecting was the equivalent in size to a city, so it was no wonder... Stores, weapons, water, ships, horses, certain other requirements... The logistics of an invasion like this were staggering.

But now, finally, they had put to sea. Behind his flagship there followed a force of some 600 ships. When he looked back at them, why, he practically felt his cock harden. So he had come here, to the bow, to just take a moment to enjoy it, savour it, and dream of what lay ahead. Why, after this, who knew where he may end up?

"Datis?"

He winced. That voice. That damned nasal voice. He should have forced the traitor to travel on a different ship – what had he been thinking?

"Yes?" He turned around and faced the Greek. His naval commander, Artaphernes – some distant relative of Darius, of course, since there was no escaping taking some of the royal family along – was following behind, shrugging apologetically.

"This man," said Hippias, jerking his thumb back at Artaphernes, "tells me we aren't heading straight for Athens. Why?"

Datis chose to ignore the insult of being questioned by this minion – for now. "Because we have other business to attend to first. Don't worry, Greek. We will come to Athens in good time."

"Word will reach them. The longer we take, the longer they have to prepare."

Datis shrugged. "So? What can they do?"

"Don't underestimate the Greeks, Persian."

Datis thought for a moment whether he shouldn't just have the man thrown overboard. It would be humorous watching to see how long he stayed afloat. But no, they were counting on him to lead them to the landing zone. "Quite," he said instead.

"I have been writing a list. Of all those I intend to execute once I'm back in power."

"Oh? A good idea. Show them who is the boss, yes?"

"That's right. It is a long list, which will keep me busy for some time. I am impatient to start!" The ex-tyrant stared at him, then turned and stalked off.

"Sorry about that," said Artaphernes. "I tried to keep him away from you..."

"Doesn't matter. The price we must pay for his information." He shook his head. "Executions? He doesn't seem to have understood what our plans are. How are the ships looking? How are the transports?"

"They look fine at this point. But they are riding much higher in the water at the moment. Once they are full, they will probably start to take on some water."

Datis nodded. "Well, they just have to hold out long enough."

The fleet sailed past Samos and across the Icarian Sea, aiming south west for the cluster of islands known as the Cyclades. Here, in the middle of the Aegean, lay Naxos. They were expected. Ever since the failed assault organised by Aristagoras, which had triggered the Ionian revolt, the Naxians had lived in fear of reprisal. Anyone even suspected of Persian sympathies was exiled from the island, to avoid the risk of betrayal from within. When the Persians landed, the people retreated within the walls of the city, where a large stock of food was already in place.

But there are always those who are looking to exploit a situation, Datis knew. Especially amongst the Greeks. He had enough troops come ashore to ring the city as a show of might, then settled down to wait. It didn't take long for overtures to be made: what, exactly, some leading citizens wanted to know, would they have to do to avoid destruction? And if that could also involve certain men being put in charge, then they felt they could deliver on whatever Datis wanted. Fine, replied Datis. But you must understand that by defying Persia, you set a dangerous precedent. You can't escape unpunished, or it would look bad for the empire. But Darius was nothing if not magnanimous. All he required was for the entire population to be relocated into the empire, where they could pay taxes and have an eye kept on them.

That's it? asked the conspirators. No fine? No executions?

Just open the gates, replied Datis. Board our transports, and continue your lives in the fertile valleys of Lydia, instead of scratching a living on the thin-soiled rock that is Naxos. And sure, you guys can be in charge.

The gates opened. The Persians entered the city, quickly putting down those few who tried to fight, and loaded the entire population onto the waiting transport vessels. From there, they sailed westward, arriving at the holy island of Delos, where they stopped to take on fresh water. The local inhabitants fled for the hills at the sight of the fleet crowding into their harbour, and word spread about a terrible smell wafting ashore from the transport vessels. Datis ordered a huge pile of incense be lit on the shore, and the reprovisioning continued. Other smaller islands like Paros were commanded to donate supplies.

They sailed on to the town of Eretria on the southern end of Euboea, which had also supplied troops to the Ionian revolt. This time, there were none from inside who wished or were able to betray the city, and in the end it took an assault by the sparabara to take it. When the fighting was over, the people were told that they were to be relocated to the empire as punishment, and were led out of the burning city and down to the ships. Troops prodded them with spears as they climbed down into the dark holds. They were packed in, and the hatches closed.

"What about food? Water?" someone, an elder, would cry up through the slats.

"There are crates down there. Open them," would come the reply.

Hands would grope in the dark, and the long boxes found.

"Smells off," someone might say, before others in their eagerness and hunger wrenched the lids off anyway.

And unleashed their death.

An ugly, panic-stricken death, down there in the stuffy darkness, with the pink-tinged sea water sloshing around their feet.

And so the fleet, its invasion force ready, came ultimately to Attica.

To Marathon.

....

Miltiades arrived at the meeting in the council house to find most of the others already there. He was not surprised to find Aristides and Melanthios had been elected as strategoi for their respective tribes. He did not recognise the others, but when he counted he came up one short – someone was missing. Phaenippus called the meeting to order anyway.

"So, we must look to the defence of our polis. As he has had recent experience with the Persians, I would like Miltiades to address the meeting."

Miltiades nodded. It was quite nice, being deferred to in this way.

"We must commence barricading Phaleron and the nearby beaches at once. The Persians will be at their most vulnerable when they are trying to land – either way."

"What do you mean, either way?" asked Aristides.

"Whether they are seeking to invade us with normal troops, or destroy us with Hadesmen."

One of the other generals laughed. "I've heard enough gossip about these monsters. Surely, they are nothing but a bogeyman that parents use to scare their children into behaving?"

"I can assure you, they are real. They are the dead returned to the world of the living, but without any faculty other than sight, hearing, smell and a very disturbing appetite for flesh."

"I can second that," said Melanthios. "I know full well that there are some in Athens who have ridiculed the stories of the men who were with me in Ionia. But Miltiades speaks true. I would not have believed it myself if I didn't see it with my own eyes. Fear them, for an entire phalanx disintegrated at the sight of a few hundred. If they come here in greater numbers, we will have a hard time convincing any of our men to hold the line."

"Even in defence of their homes? Their families?" asked Phaenippus.

"They are truly awful to behold. They are an insult to nature. We have all seen death, including violent death in battle, but these things are far more disturbing. And that isn't even taking into account the sound of them... The smell... Gods, I can still smell them," Melanthios shuddered, and fell silent.

"But hold we must," said Miltiades. "Men may hold, if led effectively. And if they have faith in each other and their leaders. And they have proven that faith, by electing us. If we don't hold, and those things make their way into the countryside, then Attica is lost to us. We will be besieged in our city for years, as the numbers of the Hadesmen swell. We will lose all our farmland, our orchards, our olive groves. The city will ultimately starve and fall. They must be stopped at the coast, and destroyed. So we must fortify all the possible landing sites, to hold them up and help give courage to the men defending them."

"That won't be necessary," said a voice from the doorway. It was the young man he had seen at the trial – Themistocles. "The Persians are not headed for Phaleron."

"Themistocles!" said Phaenippus. "Where have you been?"

"Gentlemen, excuse my lateness. As soon as I was elected strategos I took my ship and went scouting for the enemy fleet. They have turned north and are heading up the Euboean channel as we speak."

"Where on earth are they headed?"

"Maybe they have given up?" asked one of the others. "They are sailing home?"

"That is the long way," said Miltiades. "Something else is up."

"I found out something else, too," said Themistocles. "Hippias is with them."

There were oaths, and wishes that they had killed the old tyrant rather than exile him when they had the chance.

"Wait," said Miltiades. "The Pisistratids. Where was their family from again?"

"You have it, Miltiades," said Themistocles. "They hail from the north east of Attica."

"Shit! He's guiding them! There is a landing site up there! What was it called?"

"There is," said another general. "There is a bay there, where ships may beach. The Bay of Marathon."

"Zeus' ballsack, this is an emergency! We must march at once to that bay!"

"Hold on," said Callimachus. "We cannot leave the city undefended..."

"Listen! If we don't defeat them utterly there, there won't be any city. We will need every man."

"Assuming your claims about them intending to use these creatures against us are correct."

"Oh, he is correct," said Themistocles. "Eretria is emptied. They have taken the entire population. That can't be good."

"Did you get a count of ships?"

Themistocles shook his head. "Not completely. We were chased off by a couple of warships. But there are hundreds. At least five hundred, I should say. A pity we don't have more triremes – we could have attacked and sunk them there, rather than letting them gain landfall before we can thrash them."

"At Chersonnesus," said Miltiades, his voice shaking slightly, "they put maybe ten shiploads of Hadesmen ashore, and we were overwhelmed. If they have some hundreds of transports... we are talking about thousands of the dead. Maybe twenty thousand or so..."

There was silence.

"We must send for aid," said Callimachus. "We must send runners at once."

"Who will come?" asked Aristides.

"Plataea will help."

"Plataea can send maybe a thousand men. We need more."

"Who else can we turn to?" Phaenippus asked. "The Thebans? The Corinthians? They will laugh at us. They will either not believe the danger, or prefer to leave us to our fate."

"It is their fate, too," said Miltiades.

"But they haven't experienced it themselves. They won't believe it. There are none here who could convince them – not even you. No, in their jealousy of our wealth and power they would choose to see us fall. But for little Plataea, we are alone."

"The Spartans may come," said a quiet voice.

"Who in Hades are you?" asked Phaenippus sharply.

"This is Tresantes," Miltiades told them, relief flooding through him at seeing the other man in the doorway. "He is a valiant man, and was a citizen of Sparta."

"You think it possible?" asked Callimachus eagerly. "The Spartans will come?"

"Wait – was a citizen?" asked Phaenippus at the same time.

Miltiades gestured for Tresantes to come in. "Do you think they will listen? Will they understand?"

"Perhaps," said Tresantes. He smiled mirthlessly. "The Spartans eschew riches, but what they value most of all is their reputation. It will appeal to their vanity...if you beg them."

"Beg them?" Phaenippus reared up in outrage.

"We can beg them if we have to," said one of the strategoi. Some nodded, while others shook their heads.

"Or..." said Tresantes.

"Or what?" prompted Miltiades.

"Tell them if they do not march, the disease will find its way to the Peloponnese. And then the Helots really will eat them alive."

"Well," huffed Phaenippus. "That sounds more like it. We can certainly tell them that."

"But if you do," continued Tresantes. "They will hate you for it. For instead of appealing to their vanity, you will be shaming them into action with their greatest fear. It will work, but they will never forget it. Or forgive it."

"If it gets them here, so be it."

"Just...understand. That once you have released that hatred, even though they come to your aid, there will be a reckoning. Someday."

"If it means we survive, so be it," said Miltiades roughly. "Who should go? Will you go?"

"No. I have told you before. I cannot go back."

"We have a man," said Aristides. "A champion cross country runner. He can take shortcuts across the mountains where no horse can go. He can get a message there very quickly. Pheidippides is his name."

"Good. Send him. And we must march to Marathon. And hold the Hadesmen there until the Spartans come to our aid."

"How long do you suppose we have?"

"Not so long as we would like."

The meeting broke up. Phaenippus and Callimachus bent their heads together, composing a letter to the Spartans, while Aristides and several others ran to find the champion, Pheidippides. Miltiades decided to head back home. As he left, Tresantes caught him by the arm.

"I will come with you. I will fight with you."

"I am glad – but I thought you had had your fill of death."

Tresantes looked away.

"Wait," said Miltiades. "You aren't planning on dying, are you? We didn't save you just so you could throw your life away."

"I am not planning on dying, no. But if the Fates decree it should be so, then I am ready."

"Look, I'm sorry to sound uncaring, but...all this over a rabbit?"

"You do not understand."

"Then help me."

The Spartan looked at him. "When I left Sparta, I left everything I had been behind. My home. My family. Even my name. I wandered, lost and alone. I felt there was nothing left inside of me, and nothing in the world outside for me. I was a void. But then one day, in the wilderness, starving, I came across rabbit. She was very young, just a kit. Abandoned, and hemmed in by crows that pecked at her. But she fought them. So small, and fragile, yet still she fought. I chased the crows away, saved her. And in so doing, saved myself. For in caring for her, I found something again. Something worthwhile. But now... I am empty once more."

It was a long speech for a Spartan, and left Miltiades with more questions than answers. But now was not the time to delve any further. "Well..." he finally said. "I have to tell you that I will feel far better to have you fighting with us once more. And I know that will make Hegesipyle happier, too. But come – we must prepare."

The call went out, and was answered. It had been many years since a general call up had been ordered. They came in their thousands: farmers, potters, bakers, builders, merchants: for the army of Athens was made up of its ordinary citizens. Each was required to bring their full panoply and food for several days. There were grey beards and smooth chins. Men who carried their own battered gear, and others who strolled along with a slave or two puffing under the load of their heavy armour be-hind. Many women and children lined the road for some miles, farewelling the men of the city. Miltiades made his goodbyes to Hegesipyle in private. Her drawn, worried face as he left was like a stab in his guts. He had to wipe tears from his own eyes as he left the house, which was why he did not wish her to farewell him on the road. He did not wish to be seen in such a state: not that he was ashamed of his love for her, just that it was a private thing, not for display.

He slung his hoplon over his back, already wincing at the weight of it, and picked up the heavy bundle made up of his cuirass, greaves and sword belt. His spear was leaning against the wall, and he was grateful for its support as a walking staff

"Well, well," said a familiar voice. "Fancy one of the top commanders carrying his own gear. Must be trying to impress the ranks."

He turned. Zander, leaning against the wall. Trying to look casual, but tense.

"Well, I did have a slave who used to do it for me."

"Still have slaves, don't you? He must have been good, if you haven't replaced him."

"To tell the truth," said Miltiades, and damn if he was not misting over again, "to tell the truth, he was indeed irreplaceable."

Zander nodded, and drew circles in the dirt with one toe. "My timing is excellent, I see. Looks like quite a fight coming."

"Yes. It is looking quite definitive. Our very own Trojan War."

There was a pause. Miltiades felt the pressure of time, that he had to get moving. Zander gazed down the alley.

"You know, I never reported anything..."

"I know. I understand."

"I'm sorry I left you like that. I should have talked to you, but I was...confused."

"Understandable. Uh...how was your home?"

"Home. Hmmm. Good...but not really my home. To be honest, it is a fairly backward little place. Not like here. I found some relatives, but..." He shrugged.

"So... what will you do now?"

"I don't know."

"You know, you're an educated man. You could find work as a teacher."

Zander looked up. "Me? A teacher?"

"My child will need a tutor one day. And in the meantime, I could use a foreman to help run the estate. It's a mess."

"You're offering me a job?"

"And to be honest, I could use your help more than ever to manage mother."

"So...you are offering me the chance to do what I was already doing...but for money?"

"Yes. How does that sound?"

"Strangely appealing."

"You should have just come in. Or knocked."

"Either felt strange."

A moment of silence fell between them. Comfortable. Companionable.

"Zander, you have stood with me twice before as my slave, and twice saved my life. I don't have the right to ask, but will you come and fight with me one more time? As a free man?"

"Yes," said Zander, looking him in the eye. "Yes, that I will do. But you can carry your own gear still. It will make a good impression on the men."

The column struck out north-east, following the road that wound across the Cephisus Plain and around the base of Mount Pentelicus. They marched as far as they could on that first day, then camped amid the olive groves of the plains estates. At first light they resumed their trek, and by midday had come to the coast. They drew up on the lower slopes of the mountain. Below them stretched the plain of Marathon, down to the bay. Another road looped around along the coast to the south, also leading to Athens. The northern section of the bay was protected by a thin finger of land that ran out into the sea, the Cynosura Promontory. The land at that end of the bay, back from the promontory, was wet and marshy, but the southern end was dry and flat.

"This is a good position," declared Callimachus. "We can guard both roads to Athens, and have the advantage of the high ground. There is a spring nearby for water, and even a shrine to Heracles. That will give the men heart."

Miltiades agreed, and dared to let hope flourish in his heart. "We must build a barricade, too. It will help slow the Hadesmen down, and give the men more confidence."

Trees were felled, their branches sharpened into points, and dragged to the front of the Greek lines. The tribes came in one by one, taking their positions along the line, the men finding their positions and dumping their heavy loads. The smell of shit soon filled the air – a gathering of that many men was a messy affair. Squabbles broke out as some man squatting behind a tree was disturbed by others sent to fell it.

And then word came from watchers further down the coast – there were sails approaching. The Persian fleet was here.

Callimachus looked up at the sun. "They will not have enough light to come ashore today. They will have to keep at their oars all night and then land in the morning. Good. We will be rested, and ready for them. Gentlemen, a council in my tent, if you please."

....

Out on the water, Datis studied the dark line on the mountainside, Artaphernes beside him.

"Signal the fleet. Transports to the front, to be ready on the signal. Warships to the rear. And go and get that Greek for me."

Artaphernes grinned and bowed. Datis watched the ships manoeuvring behind him until the cranky old Greek arrived, followed by four guards. Datis signalled to his captain, who barked a series of orders. The flagship raised more sail, and the water hissed at the prow as they cut through the water into the bay.

Hippias stared at the Attic coastline with clenched fists. "At last," he growled. "At long last." He frowned. "What are we doing?"

The ship turned, now sailing almost parallel to the shoreline some hundred yards out. The sun had disappeared behind Mount Pentelicus, cloaking the slopes and plain in darkness. Only the white foam of the small waves showed where the land met the sea. Datis trusted his captain to know his trade, and keep them deep enough.

"Well, Greek," he said. "You have kept your word. You have guided us to this most excellent landing site, and so the Athenians will be punished and King Darius avenged. For that you have his thanks."

Hippias nodded. "In the morning, we'll show those ignorant bastards who they are dealing with..."

"We are actually commencing landing now. And I thought it might be rather nice for you to lead the way. After all," he grinned. "It is your land, isn't it?"

Datis nodded to the soldiers, and they sprang forward and lifted Hippias before he could move.

"What are you doing, you Persian dog?!"

"Nice. Over the side, if you please."

While Hippias flung himself about as hard as he could, the four muscular guardsmen easily carried him to the side of the ship. They swung him, and launched him far over the side. Immediately, the captain signalled the helmsman, and the flagship swung about and began to tack back out of the bay. Datis pointed to a pair of men amidships, and they brought brass horns to their lips. A deep blatting note carried across the water. Out to sea, a series of sails went up on the transport vessels, and their tillers pointed towards the beach. The flax snapped taut, and the ships surged forward. There were splashes on either side as crewmen jumped clear and swam for the nearest warships.

"And so it begins," said Datis. "The fall of Greece."

....

"They're coming," said Miltiades. "They are landing tonight! Shit! We should be down there to meet them!"

"In the dark?" asked Themistocles.

The two stood on a small hillock that rose near the base of the mountain. It was just possible at this distance to make out the dark shapes of ships heading for the shore.

"I don't know," said Miltiades, gripping his head with both hands. "Now I don't know. I thought they would land during the morning, and be coming up at us in bunches... But now..."

"Will they come tonight?"

"I don't think so. They rely on sight, mostly. And for some reason, they tend to stay in large groups. Some wander, but most seem to prefer to stick together."

Themistocles raised an eyebrow. "So there is some human feeling left?"

"I don't know what it is."

"Well, we should go and report to the others. But listen," he gripped Miltiades by the arm. "Don't say too much about your uncertainties. As our resident expert, it is a little disconcerting when you start espousing how much you don't know."

....

Hippias surfaced, spitting seawater and obscenities. He took a couple of half-hearted strokes towards the hull of the ship, but it was already too far away. He turned, and struck out clumsily for the shore. He was not a strong swimmer, and he had swallowed quite a bit of water. He soon felt his strength desert him, but when he stopped kicking and let his feet sink beneath him, he found that he was already touching the bottom. He bobbed forward with renewed energy, despite the water seeming to pull at him. He staggered ashore, and flopped onto the pebble-strewn beach, chest heaving. He was home.

....

Miltiades followed Themistocles to Callimachus' tent. He was dismayed to find his cousin, Nicomedes, hovering outside. He had been wishing to escape any such confrontation since the trial, but now it seemed unavoidable.

"Miltiades!" said Nicomedes, hurrying over. "A word!"

"Now is not the best time, Nicomedes." Themistocles clapped him on the shoulder, and slipped into the tent.

"Have you seen Callias?"

"No, I haven't. Not since..." The trial.

Nicomedes wrung his hands. "I can't find him anywhere. I don't think he has answered the call to arms. Oh, the shame. As if things weren't bad enough..."

"Look, Nicomedes, I'm sorry about..."

"There's nothing to be done," said the other man, waving him away. "I suppose I shall have to disown him."

"Look, let's wait and see. Maybe he is with one of the other tribes." Miltiades didn't say that he thought Callias had probably chosen to fight alongside Teron, in his tribe. It was too awkward to talk about.

"Miltiades?" said Aristides, holding open the tent flap. "We are ready."

All Miltiades could do was lamely pat the other man on the arm and then leave him outside.

....

Hippias sat up. He could hear a ship moving in the darkness, and soon the white foam glowing at its prow showed where it came. It was coming in fast. They were going to wreck ships and lose men, but Hippias couldn't care less. The Persians had plenty of both. He scrambled aside as the prow of the ship crunched up onto the beach. Despite it hitting no rocks, it seemed to crumple inwards, timber cracking, the hull rupturing. Typical shoddy Persian craftsmanship. It was a wonder they even had a bloody empire. The troops inside were thrown about – he could see their dim shapes moving.

"Who is in charge? Where is your officer?" he demanded, walking forward. "Don't any of you ignorant bastards speak Greek?"

The smell hit him at the same time as the closest figures noticed him and came lurching at him through the shallows. The closest lunged at him, mouth gaping, going for his throat. The top of its head smashed into his jaw, and the thing bore him down to the ground. As it scrabbled at him, he felt something in his mouth: a tooth. It had knocked out one of his teeth. He spat, and it landed in the sand beside him. And he laughed bitterly then, as other creatures came and squatted beside him, for he saw then his folly, his blindness, and that all he would ever possess of Attica was that small patch of sand where his tooth would lie forgotten.

After that, he was too busy screaming to laugh.

....

Dawn was not far off breaking when the quiet word went around to arm and assemble. Some men rubbed the sleep from their eyes, but most had been awake through the long hours, listening to the sounds of splintering wood down on the beach as ship after ship piled onto the shoreline. There was another sound, too, a terrible growing chorus of groans. It turned men's bowels to water and had them reaching for their wine skins, for one last pull. No fires were permitted, so those few who could eat ate their porridge cold and raw. They pulled on their armour: the rich buckled on their polished bronze that would glow golden when the sunlight hit it. Others strapped down the stiff material of their linen armour. The poorest tied on their simple leather jerkins. Helmets were pulled on – the impersonal full helmets for the wealthier hoplites, simple bronze caps for the poorer. Then all took up their shields, the broad round hoplon, each bearing the device of Athena's owl. All men, rich and poor alike, bore these shields, for it was with them that the phalanx was formed. Swords and daggers were set in their sheaths and baldrics, and finally the spears were taken up, each one eight feet of heavy cornel wood, the triangular iron heads dull in the dim light. A forest sprang up, as ten thousand shafts were lifted into the air and the men shuffled into their positions. Eight ranks deep they stood, the traditional depth, the one that worked best. The men knew their file-mates, knew the men in the files to either side. Richest at the front, with their fine armour, and the most to lose, poorest at the back, where they could provide the best help by providing the backbone of the phalanx when the pushing started.

They formed up behind the barricade of felled trees, thrust their spears into the ground by their butt spikes, and rested their shields against their legs. Waiting to see what full dawn would bring.

They had been told what they were facing. The stories had gone around, and those who had served in Ionia had been sought and questioned. But still, many shook their heads, finding it too hard to believe. Hades was a jealous god, not one to release the dead back to the world lightly. How could it be possible that he would let so many escape at once? Punishment, some said. Some impiety has brought this punishment upon us. But all could hear it now, the ongoing moaning, so different to the sounds of a crowd of the living, like a dark parody of it.

The sun crested the distant hills on Euboea, and light spilled across the scene.

The wreckage of hundreds of ships lay across three miles of beach. Miltiades, standing out beyond the barricade with the other generals, felt his heart sink. There were so many. So many. Hadesmen beyond counting milled about across that arc of land. Thousands of them. More than twenty thousand, surely. Forty? Sixty? Fear gripped his heart, and in the silence of his comrades, he recognised the same. Already, the rattle and glint of the phalanx was attracting the attention of those dead on the edge of the pack – a few were peeling off, stumbling slowly in their direction. Soon the whole herd would be on the move, coming at them. And he saw now that they were wrong. They would be overwhelmed. The barricade would not matter, as the dead were so many they would flow around the sides and the phalanx would fall. And the Hadesmen would stagger inland and along the coast road, and all of Attica bowuld be poisoned with their presence for generations to come.

Greece would fall.

He turned and looked at the faces of the men behind him – they had not pulled their helmets down into position yet, so he could see the look in their eyes. As he watched, a fat black fly alighted on the cheek of one man.

"Ow, fuck!" cried the man, and he swatted at the insect. Full and heavy, it was unable to escape in time and burst on his face, leaving a foul smear of black rotten fluid. Those who had seen pulled back in disgust, clapping hands to their noses. There was a buzzing in the air, and Miltiades saw that there were more flies hovering. He looked down the hill – the air above the dead appeared darker: it was alive with flies. At the same time, the rotten meat smell of the host rolled over them, and many leaned forward to bark up whatever they held in their stomachs. Of course, he thought: these were fresher, not like the dried out husks they had fought at the wall, with their sour cheese-stink. And he saw how it would be... The dead staggering inexorably up at them, the smell in their nostrils, the carrion flies crawling into their eyeslits, drinking the sweat from their eyes, buzzing into their gasping mouths... It would be unbearable. No man could hope to endure the horror of that.

"Here," said a voice, and he turned to see a wealthy man in beautiful armour take the corner of his own expensive cloak and wipe the foulness away from the other man's face. He held the man's chin and rubbed his cheek clean, frowning in concentration, like a mother with her child.

"Thanks," croaked the first man.

"No problem, citizen," said the wealthy man.

And there, in that moment, Miltiades saw it. That there was something about this silly, self-important city, with its silly argumentative people, that was worth saving. An idea had been born, an idea that was still an infant, but must be allowed the chance to grow and become all it could be.

The people must be given the chance to grow and become all they could be.

And then it seemed to him that he perceived a cloaked figure standing at the base of the hill.

"Who is that?" he asked, turning to Themistocles, who was standing closest to him.

"Hmmm?" said Themistocles, not able to take his eyes from the horde before them. "Who?"

There was something very familiar about the man, and as Miltiades watched, the figure threw back his hood, and his golden hair and beard caught the light. His heart leapt into his throat. "Uncle... What..."

The figure seemed to be looking straight up at him, then turned and pointed at the darkness spread across the beach. Flooding across the beach. A wave.

And the words came back to him, even as he realised that his uncle was no longer there.

He turned and looked at the phalanx squatting on the hill, like some slow-moving armoured beast. Like a... tortoise...

...tortoise must rise up and run...

...run...

...run, said the oracle, said the seer, said his uncle...

RUN...

...but not away.

And he knew what they had to do.

"Council!" he cried. "Council, now!"

The nine other generals and Callimachus clustered about him.

"We have to attack," he told them.

They stared at him.

"You have to be kidding," said one. Others were already shaking their heads. "Give up this position? Go down onto the plain? We have the high ground!"

"That doesn't matter, not against these things. We have to go down there. Pin them against the sea and the marsh, kill them all. Now."

"No way."

"If Miltiades thinks this is best," said Themistocles slowly, "then we must consider it."

"There isn't time. We can't debate, can't argue. We have to go. Now."

"We should vote, then. Those in favour of holding here?"

Five hands went up, including Aristides.

"In favour of attacking?"

Three hands: Miltiades, Themistocles and Melanthios. Then a fourth. Then fifth. They looked to Callimachus, who pulled at his lip.

"You have the casting vote," said Miltiades shakily. "You are going to either doom us or give us a chance."

Callimachus glanced back at the phalanx. "I think... I think... We should call an assembly. Put it to the vote. Let the people decide."

"There isn't time!"

"But the demos..."

"You are war archon! Make a decision!"

Callimachus blinked. "I am not some experienced general. I was selected by lot." He snapped his fingers. "That's it, that's democratic. We will draw for command... Take turns. Whoever is in charge today can decide how he wants to proceed."

"You must be kidding," said Miltiades. "You want to leave the most important decision in our history up to chance? Are you out of your mind?"

"Steady on," said one of the others.

"Yes, let's leave it in the hands of the gods," said another, and there was a lot of nodding.

"Well, if my name comes out, I am giving my turn to Miltiades," said Themistocles.

"As will I," said Melanthios.

They each wrote their name on a scrap of parchment and dropped it into an upturned helmet. Callimachus reached in and stirred them around with his fingers.

Hurry up! Miltiades screamed mentally.

At last the polemarch picked one out and read it.

"Aristides."

Those who had voted to stay put grinned. Aristides stared at the ground.

"General Aristides," said Callimachus. "What are your orders?"

"I think," said Aristides. "I think that Miltiades was there at the start of this, and so it is only just that he be here at the end. I am handing over my day of command to him."

Callimachus frowned. "You are sure? His opinion differed to yours. We will be bound to follow the orders of the commander."

"Quite sure," said Aristides, looking up and meeting Miltiades' gaze. "Just don't fuck this up."

"Thank you," said Miltiades. "Now, there are two things we need to do. You won't like them, but I am asking you to trust me. The first is, we need to extend the line. We must contain the Hadesmen so they don't lap around the ends of the phalanx. So we will pull the rear four ranks out of the centre and put those men out on the wings."

"The centre will be too weak!" exclaimed one strategos.

"Men will be fighting alongside strangers!" said another.

"Citizens will be fighting alongside citizens," said Miltiades calmly – more calmly than he felt. "That is all that matters. And if you didn't like that, you really won't like this..."

When he told them, they looked at him as if he had gone insane.

"You must be fucking joking!"

"Impossible! Completely impossible!"

"Control your faces!" barked Miltiades. "The men are looking to you. Now, pass those instructions along to your line leaders, and take your positions."

"I shall be on the right flank," declared Callimachus.

"I will fight in the centre," said Miltiades. "Now, call the phalanx out."

The lines rippled, and the solid block dissolved as the men of Athens streamed around the barrier and formed up again lower down the slope. More than a few glanced back at its perceived additional safety, asking each other "What the fuck are we doing??"

Miltiades' tribe would be in the centre. He spotted Tresantes easily – the only man with a shield bearing a different device. He called him over.

"I want you beside me. On my left." That meant his shield would be covering the Spartan: he would do his best to make sure he came through the battle alive.

"No," said Tresantes. "On your right."

Miltiades hesitated. This made the Spartan largely responsible for his safety – but wasn't that the same thing? To protect Miltiades, he would need to keep his head. He nodded. "On my right, then."

The other commanders paced through the middle of the phalanx, ordering a chunk of men from the rear, four ranks deep, to step back and reform on the sides. They did so, eyeing their new neighbours with suspicion. Callimachus strode to the last rank on the extreme right of the formation, and took the lead spot, his grim determination now that the die was cast helping shore up the resolve of those nearby.

In the middle of the formation, Miltiades turned and faced those behind him. Their faces were pale, tight.

"For Athena!" he cried.

"For Athena!" they thundered, and the deep resonance of it shook him.

"For Athens!"

"For Athens!"

"For the living!" He tugged his helmet down over his face and lifted his spear skyward. "Spears!"

Their helmets went down, and they took up their spears. The front two ranks held theirs over their right shoulders, the points of the second rank extending over the shoulders of the first line.

He turned, and stepped into place, feeling the clack of Zander's spear as it knocked against his helmet. Tresantes' shield locked over his right side.

"Now, forward!" And the cry went down the line, and as he took a pace forward the whole formation shuddered into movement. A great din went up as men lurched against each other, and the spear points wavered. But as they went forward, they found their rhythm, and the lines closed up once more. Miltiades could feel the comforting presence of Zander's shield pressing against his back as they went, the men on either side of him. Down the slope they marched, momentum building. Men began calling out to each other, urging each other on.

"Come on, boys! Come on!"

"Kill the fuckers!"

"Eat my fucking spear!"

"For the polis, lads! For your wives! Your children!"

"Athena!"

There were quieter voices, too, unheard in the metallic jangling and hoarse shouts, whispering an endless sentence that was perhaps a prayer: "Oh fuck oh fuck oh fuck oh fuck oh fuck oh fuck oh fuck oh fuck..."

Down they came, the density of the formation keeping upright those who staggered on a loose rock or shrub root. The line bowed a little here and there – impossible to keep the formation totally straight – and there were injuries as men accidentally jabbed each other, especially third and fourth rankers cutting themselves on the bobbing butt spikes of the spears of the two front ranks.

The noise and the glitter of the morning sun on that mass of bronze caught the attention of the Hadesmen, and slowly their ranks were turning, surging forward in response. These newly dead, with their stink of decay, with their halos of flies and midges, with their undreamed of hunger. As the outer layers turned, and growled their stinking breath at the sight of so much meat coming towards them, the inner thousands felt the stirring, sensed the excitement of their brethren, and worked their jaws, turning inland. Almost fifty thousand undead, driven by one single purpose.

Miltiades saw them ahead, saw them turning, saw the great mass of them, saw their density. Now, he thought, now now now now now now now

"RUN!" he bellowed.

"RUN!!!" came the answering cry all along the line – and the great beast jumped forward. With the weight of their armour, with the weight of their horror, with the weight of their city, they sang and spat and shouted and swore, and leaned forward into a run. Ten thousand men, in full armour, began to run at the enemy before them. Never before had it been done. Never again. Years later, men could stand at the bar of the wineshop and command hushed admiration from the youngsters gathered there by uttering those two words: "We ran."

With a great clanking roar they gathered speed. Full battle rattle. The distance to the dead shrank, and the Hadesmen stumbled towards them on clumsy feet. Muscles straining, they ran with weight meant for brief battle. Breath rasping, skin rubbed raw by bouncing bronze. The phalanx started to shiver, to shake apart. Impossible to keep it together, not like this.

But the run carried them, carried them forward:

Through the gut-churning stench that would have halted them...

Through the curtain of bloated carrion flies that would have broken them...

Through those moments when sight could finally register the horror of the torn, dismembered things before them, that would have ended them, would have been their death...

The formation held.

The men held.

And as they drew near, Miltiades felt Tresantes knock his helmet against his own. He fancied he dimly heard him shout "I'm sorry", and then the Spartan pulled clear, and sprinted ahead of the line. He had withstood the agoge. He could run in armour longer and faster than any of them. He charged the dead ahead of them, at the last moment taking a great running leap and disappearing into the horde, his spear flashing.

Behind him, the Athenians roared.

Ten thousand armoured men smashed into the sea of the dead. Crashed into them. Slashed into them. The spears of the first rank shivered and splintered, spear heads embedded deep in skulls, shafts spun about and butt spikes driven and stabbed. Hundreds down in moments, the bronze machine pressing forwards, and those behind driving down with their spear butts, pulverising the dead at their feet, that fear of attack from below, that retraction of testicles, driving their strikes.

They yelled their defiance into the dead faces. With savage joy they cut into them. So easy, against foes who did not seek to defend themselves. Stab and stab and stab. Cut them down. Butcher them.

The living return these dead things to the realm of Hades.

But now the forward motion was slowing... The weight of the phalanx not enough to keep it moving forward forever, not against this many, not against this grim counterweight. Their chests heaving with exertion. Gagging down the foul air. Straps cutting into shoulders. Right arm deadened from the impact. Left quivering under the weight of the shield, each man giving cover to the man on his left, grateful for the protection of the man on his right.

"Strike!" cried Callimachus on the far end. His spear was gone. He held his hand back and another was passed into it. He didn't have the balance quite right, wasn't holding it in the middle, but struck anyway, stabbing into the face of the ghoul before him.

Now the sword work, now the spear play. They set their feet, struck. The dead fell. Fingers grasped at shields, tried to pull them down. Hands thrust into gaps. And faces, faces full of biting teeth, pressing forward: men, women, young, old, even some children... The hoplites hacked, and stabbed. Some, weaponless, punched, their knuckles torn to pieces on the unfeeling faces even as they shattered them.

Miltiades had used his spear, and Zander's, and now held his gore-slick hand up and felt another slide into it. Felt Zander rap him on the helmet: 'I'm still here.' He cocked his arm, thrust forward, the iron head biting through the eye socket of a Hadesman before him. Another grabbed his shield, tugging it down, and he stumbled, but the man to his left was using his sword and swiftly sheared off the thing's arms with a flurry of desperate blows. Miltiades pulled his shield back up into position as the next one came at him – and he stared for a moment in wonder.

"Hippias?"

It was hard to fathom. Here, amongst all these dead, the Fates deliver him this...

The ex-tyrant came at him, hands outstretched. He had been disembowled, his ribs wrenched open. There was barely enough meat left on his limbs to allow him to stand and move. Yet he was here... His father's killer. Miltiades made a stab, but Hippias was knocked sideways by another of the undead, and the blow went wide, merely scoring a line along his already torn scalp. Now Hippias was reaching for him over the hoplon, had wrapped one thin arm around his neck and was pulling him forward. Miltiades butted with his helmet, leaving a dent in the dead man's forehead and sending him down. He couldn't stop – the line was advancing. He had to keep his position. So he stepped forward, stamping down with his boot with all his strength. He felt it sink into Hippias' torso, felt the sole grind on bone. Then he stepped forward again, bringing his other foot down hard on the old tyrant's head, felt the skull crack. He stamped again, and more bone shattered.

And thus my father is avenged, he thought, and felt empty, and wondered if he would feel anything later. Should he survive.

For he detected, then, a difference in the movement about him, the strange currents of battle. From his position he could not see, but the noise and movement had finally pulled the attention of every Hadesman on the beach, and all of these thousands were now striving to get at the living. Over forty thousand pairs of hands reaching, seeking to pull skin to teeth, to rend and tear. This force, this weight, now came to bear on the phalanx.

In the centre, the pressure in the front lines was almost unbearable. The men behind pushed forward, their shoulders set against their hoplons, placed square in the back of the man in front. The front ranks of the dead were equally forced forward – though not with the same combined force, as their dead brothers and sisters sought to pull themselves through the press to reach them, rather than push together. And in so doing they lost some of the power they might have commanded. But it was still enough.

Miltiades found himself crushed between the living and the dead. His spear was caught, he couldn't withdraw it, doubted he had the space to wield it anyway. Hadesmen were pressed close to him – teeth were rasping against the side of his helmet, and he was staring into the red eyes of a noseless woman, carrion air pouring from her greedy mouth. He let go of the spear – it didn't budge, so tight was the press – and worked his hand to his sword. There was just room to draw it, skin scraping off his knuckles on the back of his shield as he pulled it up and out. There was not enough room to strike, so he was forced to pull it down, and angle the tip up under the dead woman's chin. Then he thrust, and all the dark fire went out of her eyes. She slumped, falling to a sitting position, then was pinned forward, head crushed against the lower rim of his shield by the next Hadesman coming at him.

Then he felt it - the line was being forced back. Immediately there was a counter effort from the men behind him, but there were only three of them, like all along this middle part of the line. They couldn't match the mass before them. He took a shuffling step back – thankfully the woman's corpse flopped sideways in the temporary gap.

Miltiades couldn't see it, but all along the centre, the ranks were being pressed backward. And now men were falling, pulled out of position by the grasping hands, going down with a cry like a man being submerged under water. And the slight pause while all the nearby dead turned and groped for him, reaching for any exposed flesh, pushing their greedy faces down to rend the suddenly exposed backs of legs, buttocks – this pause gave the next hoplite in line just enough time to move up into the gap. Though more often than not, now, the line instead moved back, and all he had to do was pause for a moment to take the front position. In this way a score of men were taken, then double that. Their high screams cut through the moans, the shouts, the crack of iron on bone.

But out on the right flank, Callimachus could see. Glancing along the line from a slightly raised mound, he could see what was happening. And he saw, too, that the eight rank deep wings were holding, were still pressing forward, and before them was the sea. And he saw what they could do.

"Turn!" he shouted. "Turn!"

He pushed around to the left, and the men in his file followed. He plunged into the shallow surf, debris from the ships banging into his greaves. The entire right wing slowly bent, turning inwards towards the knot of dead in the centre.

Out on the left flank, the men on the edge found themselves sinking into the edge of the marsh land. It was an area none of them wanted to be in, stuck in thick mud while trying to fight. Aristides, stationed there, could see that if they stayed in line, they would be forced further into it. He made a snap decision.

"Double time!" he cried. "Come with me!"

The Hadesmen were at their fewest at this point, and the hoplites were able to crash through them. Now Aristides also turned them inwards, reset the line facing along the beach, into the masses before them.

And so the dead were caught in a tightening vice. As the middle slowly gave way backwards, the momentum pulled the Hadesmen after them. And meanwhile the two wings ground inward. The phalanx was ruptured by the move, and more men died. Men who hadn't understood what was happening and found themselves suddenly out of line, and overwhelmed, and went down screaming in fear and frustration. Some suddenly yelped as something beneath their feet latched on to their calf, and down they went sprawling while their file mates stabbed and jabbed. Make sure they're dead, boys! Just 'cause they're down, don't mean they're properly dead! Kill them! Smash them! Grind them!

A moment came when the tide turned again. The men in the middle – in some places there were but one or two men left of a file of four – felt the pressure lessen, and now ground their feet and pushed back. They pushed. A hoarse roar came ragged from their throats. They felt it. Here they were, together. The polis, the demos. They loved each other in that moment, could weep for the action of the man on the right, as he pulled his hoplon up, set it to make sure his neighbour was safe. Life or death. Life over death.

They killed. They beat the Hadesmen down. They knew that they once were fellow Greeks by and large, once were fellow men, and women, but now there was nothing to do but send them back to Hades, deliver them again to the kingdom of the dark god, let him take them again to his bosom.

The dead died again, fighting. They had no morale to crack. There was no moment when they would turn and run. They thought nothing of the dead thing before them going down with a sword stroke through the head – all they saw was an opportunity to finally have a turn to lunge at the walking hot meat before them.

So the killing went on. And even now, as victory approached, in their total weariness, more men died. Sword arm numb, too weak to strike properly. Blows going wide, thrusts misaimed and failing to penetrate. Arms grabbed, teeth sunk into forearm. Frantic screams and hammering blows, striving to pull away, despite the tearing of flesh.

There was no system for replacing the exhausted men at the front of each file. The phalanx was designed for a quick decisive battle in which one side would give way and victory be achieved. Men stayed in their spot unless they were stabbed or their formation collapsed. This ongoing meat grinder was something else again. Some men simply dropped from exhaustion, no longer able to suck in enough putrid air – if they were lucky, they were seized by their mates and dragged clear. Others were dragged away in the other direction, by less gentle hands, with skinned finger tips like bone talons. Some simply lay where they fell, unconscious or lying with their eyes closed, reduced to being small children again by the scale of the horror, hoping that the monsters would not notice them.

Alone, each hoplite would easily have been overwhelmed and brought down, like giant armoured beetles slowly dismembered by swarming ants. But together, by holding together enough, they presented a wall of bronze – shins covered by greaves, shields sheltering them from knee to chin, helmets on heads. The Hadesmen shattered their teeth trying to bite through all that bronze. They bent their grabbing fingers backward till they snapped. They rubbed the skin from their faces trying to push between the shields.

The two wings slowly drew inward, as the centre now stopped: they didn't have the force to push any further into the dense pack of the dead before them. There was not an unbroken spear in the entire force. The swords were slick and heavy with gore. Feet squished in boots soaked through with sweat and blood and fluids.

Slowly, the nightmare drew to an end. The Hadesmen horde grew thinner. Those in the middle were distracted and confused by the noise coming from the left, right and in front. Less weight was therefore brought to bear on each of the sections, providing some slight relief, like a puff of sea breeze on a hot summer's day. The men sensed it, and rather than pull back out of fear of falling now, so close to the end, redoubled their efforts.

"Athena!" they croaked.

They could see each other now, glimpses of shields slathered in brown blood, glint of sunlight on helmets. The rise and fall of blades.

Here Callimachus fell, striding forward along the beach, through thigh-deep water, eager to meet up with the men of the left wing. Hands seized him from under the surface, and he was borne down, his armour pinning him to the sand. He was already exhausted, so could not hold his breath for long, and although the men behind him cried out and searched for him, feeling about with their hands, and finally pulling him clear, it was too late – he had drowned.

By the end, they were climbing over piles of the dead.

And then that glorious moment, when in one place, then two, then three, shield clanked against shield, and they stared laughing into the eyes of their brothers. Some could not comprehend, and kept trying to strike at the warriors before them, till their file mates gently wrested the swords from their swollen knuckled hands.

The end.

....

SIXTEEN

⋯⋯⋯⋯⋯⋯⋯⋯⋯⋯⋯⋯⋯⋯⋯⋯

ICARUS DESCENDING

"Ah, shit," said Datis, watching from his flagship. He had positively hooted when the rising sun had first revealed the Greek formation slowly trundling down towards the black mass of the undead. If they wanted to get it over and done with and be eaten alive by lunchtime, then so be it. And when they had suddenly picked up speed over the last few hundred yards...well, the whole way the Greeks chose to fight was crazy. But then as he watched, the roiling black mass had bit by bit been whittled away and then crushed between those glittering bronze blocks.

"Looks like we switch to Plan B."

"Which is?" asked Artaphernes.

"Sail around and seize Athens."

"Shame we threw out the tyrant," said Artaphernes. "That was just what he wanted us to do, wasn't it?"

"I imagine the other one has his eyes on rule, too. We'll see – he is pretty young." Datis grinned. "He may need some guidance. Signal the rest of the fleet."

⋯⋯⋯⋯⋯⋯⋯⋯⋯⋯⋯⋯⋯⋯⋯⋯

Miltiades dropped to his knees, dragged his helmet from his head with shaking hands. His hair was glued to his scalp with sweat. He was aware of someone – Zander – bending and embracing him from behind, an awkward armoured hug. Men were crying, dragging free the bodies of their fallen comrades. Others were walking amongst the Hadesmen, looking for any signs of life and swiftly skewering any that still moved.

Miltiades staggered to his feet, kicked at the piles of dead about him.

"What are you doing?" asked Zander.

"Tresantes," gasped Miltiades. "I must find him."

Zander caught his arm. "He is there." He pointed towards the shore.

Miltiades could hardly believe it, but there he stood. Or he guessed it was the Spartan. He was standing in amongst the wreckage, in the shallow water, completely coated in red and black gore. Shieldless. Empty handed. Staring out to sea. The very personification of Ares. Miltiades hefted his sword, approached cautiously from behind.

"Tresantes?"

The Spartan turned, the whites of his eyes the only counter to the red crust that covered his face and head. He stared at Miltiades, as if trying to place him. Finally his lips cracked open.

"I live," he said.

"Are you bitten?" asked Miltiades, tightening his grip on his sword.

The Spartan looked down at his arms, flexed his fingers. "No... It is strange." He looked aside. "There was someone here... There was someone here, and he said they would let me... That I could... If I wanted to, I could..." He shook his head, as if trying to clear it.

"What do you mean? Who was here?"

"He was there," said Tresantes, pointing at the field of dead. "He spoke to me, while I was fighting... How did he...?" He looked around in confusion.

"It is all right, Tresantes," Miltiades said softly. He assumed it was some kind of post-combat reaction that the Spartan was suffering, having somehow come through alive.

"He said... No, it can't be... It isn't possible..."

"What is it?"

The Spartan looked at him then, his eyes closer to normal. "It is nothing. I am fine. You do not need that sword. At least, not for me. But we must look to the other men."

Miltiades wanted to ask him more, but it was clear that Tresantes did not wish to speak further about whatever it was that he thought had happened to him.

They lay their dead in a line. There were 192 of them. Miltiades had feared this moment, when they would have to execute anyone who had been bitten – but, thankfully, those who had fallen had all died. Due to their armour, and the nature of the battle, they had either had their throats torn out, or the major arteries in the backs of their thighs severed, and so had bled to death if they hadn't been killed outright. There were plenty of other wounds: cuts, sprains, gouges, but these were the usual injuries that occurred within a phalanx. Slaves were detailed to collect wood: the Athenians would be cremated on a funeral pyre, thus removing any need for desecration of the dead by now destroying their dead brains before they could return from Hades' grasp.

Then: "Sails!" somebody shouted, and pointed. Out to sea, a column of ships was forming: warships and fat galleys. Miltiades stepped up onto a rock and called the hoplites to him. Zander passed him a skin of watered wine and he drank deep.

"Oh men of Athens!" he called. They sank down and listened. "We have won here a victory that will go down in history as one of the greatest! But...there is one thing more I must ask of you, or it will all have been for naught. Even now, as you can see, the Persians are setting sail. I do not believe they have given up. There are troopships and warships out there: they have more than enough men to seize Athens. They have about 70 miles to sail, and it is unlikely the wind will be with them all the way. There are 26 miles between us and home. We must get there first. We must march – now."

They nodded wearily. There was nothing else for it. The city was lying largely defenceless.

"We're with you, Miltiades!" cried a ragged voice, and they roared hoarsely. Miltiades dipped his head in acknowledgement, tears stinging his eyes, and felt a new energy course through his veins.

They dumped what they could – many abandoned their breast-plates. They took up their shields, and fresh spears from the baggage train, and then formed up in their tribes. Some boys piped the beat, and they set off, back along the same mountain path they had used yesterday.

Tresantes shouldered his pack – and started walking north.

"Tresantes!" called Miltiades. "Where are you going? We are going this way."

"Not me. My way lies north."

Miltiades felt his stomach heave.

"But why? Where are you going?"

The Spartan stared into the distance, then turned and smiled.

"To find someone." He turned and walked away.

....

The next morning, the Persian fleet sailed into the bay of Phalerum and there, lining the shoreline, awaiting them, was the Athenian army.

From the ships, the Persians couldn't see how thin the formation was. Couldn't know how many men had dropped out during the march from exhaustion, or how many were now barely standing, their muscles quivering under the weight of their shields and spears.

From the Persian perspective, attempting a landing now would be suicide. And yet the fleet lingered, cutting across the harbour. Waiting for something.

"What are they doing?" asked Zander. "Are they going to attack, so we can get this over with, or are they going to just fuck off?"

"It's strange," answered Miltiades. He glanced back across the plains towards the city behind them. "It's as if they are waiting for something... Wait, look there!"

"Where?"

"The Acropolis!"

Zander squinted. "I don't see anything..."

"There was a flash. Like some kind of signal! Come on!"

Miltiades grabbed Aristides and Themistocles, and told them to maintain their position. He leaned his shield against a wall and set his helmet beside it. Now in just his filthy chiton, with his sword belt over his shoulder, he led Zander in a slow jog back towards the city.

"What do you suppose it means?" gasped Zander. The three miles back to Athens had never felt as far as they did now.

"That someone is prepared to sell out the city," Miltiades answered grimly.

"Who would do such a thing?"

"You mean, who would put their own profit ahead of the wishes of the people? Why, somebody from my own bloody class, that's who."

Zander saved his breath. They still had to get through the city and up the steep ramp leading to the Acropolis itself. Once they were through the gate, the streets were strangely deserted. The women and elderly were nervously awaiting the outcome in their homes. A few hundred people were on the walls themselves, pointing out the Persian ships to each other and the block of men waiting by the harbour. Miltiades and Zander hit the Panathenaic Way and hurried along it to the base of the Acropolis. Zander grabbed Miltiades by the arm.

"Wait! We should get some help. We don't know how many conspirators there may be up there."

"There isn't time. Come on."

"Miltiades, stop! Listen to me: you don't need to do this alone. You don't need to do this at all. You're already a hero."

Miltiades turned and looked at him. "What are you trying to say?"

"Just let me go for some help. Please."

Miltiades nodded tightly, and watched while Zander jogged back down the Way. The ex-slave glanced back at him twice, then turned a corner. Miltiades turned and strode up the hill.

Like the city streets, the temple precinct was strangely empty. He loosened his sword in its sheath and walked quietly as possible across the flagstones towards the low wall on the western side. There was no one there. He jogged lightly up the steps to the Temple of Athena, and made his way along the colonnade. There was a room at the rear north western end of the Temple with large open windows looking out over the city towards the harbour. As he neared the door, he was sure he heard voices. He slid his sword free, and stepped inside.

"Hello, Callias. Teron."

The two had been standing close together – embracing? – and now leapt apart in shock. Miltiades saw a burnished shield leaning by the window and a bulging sack on the ground. Both of the young men were also armed with swords.

"What are you doing?"

"Nothing!" said Callias quickly.

Teron laughed. "Oh no, we are doing something all right."

"You mean like trying to betray the city to the Persians?"

Callias flushed red. Teron frowned.

"I'm restoring the proper order."

Miltiades slowly moved a little further into the room, to give himself more space. As neither of the other two had drawn their swords, he kept his down by his side.

"What is that supposed to mean?"

Teron rolled his eyes. "I'm giving Athens back the government she should have. Proper government."

"Which is?"

"Rule by the best men, of course."

"Like you?"

Teron sneered. "Well, certainly not like you. You might have the blood, Miltiades, but you don't really have the stomach for it. I thought you did, but I was wrong."

"Whereas you...?"

"Me? Why, I'm born to rule."

Miltiades shook his head. "No one should rule just because of who they are. It should be because of what they have done, for the people."

"Oh, that is just beautiful!" laughed Teron. "Please, hold on a moment while I carve that somewhere."

"Cleisthenes built this system. He was a Eupatrid, and an Alcmaeonid, just like you."

"He was a class traitor! A naïve fool!"

"Does the rest of your clan believe that?"

"You want to know if I am acting alone or at the behest of the family, right?" Teron grimaced. "Some have fallen under Grandpa Cleisthenes' spell. But there are still plenty of right thinking men in the family."

Miltiades made a show of looking around. "There doesn't seem to be anyone else up here, though."

"Yes, well, talk is cheap, as they say. Actions speak louder. What did you just say? A man should be able to rule because of what he has done? Well, I shall earn that right today."

"You would be a lonely ruler. Do you not understand what they were intending to do? They were going to kill everyone."

Teron looked at him coldly. "It doesn't matter who you rule, so long as you rule. The city would be repopulated with settlers. Later..."

Miltiades turned to Callias, who had been standing looking wretched the whole time. "What about you? Is this what you want?"

Callias opened his mouth, but Teron grabbed him and pulled him backwards. In the same movement he drew his sword. "Oh no. You aren't going to divide us. Callias is mine."

"Yours? Callias, do you hear that? Anyway, listen, this is over. You can see the army down at the harbour. The Persians are defeated: they can't land now. Give it up. You failed."

"Oh?" said Teron. He bent and thrust a hand into the sack, and pulled something out. He thrust it forward. It was a head. And not just any head – Miltiades saw the eyes flick open and the jaw start to move. The thing's lips pulled back and it snapped its teeth together. Teron stepped back toward the window. "What if I just tossed this over the wall? Who do you suppose would find it down below? Some small child, maybe? It would only take one bite to start it, to bring this place down."

This corner of the temple stood close by the wall ringing the top of the Acropolis. At the base of the steep slope was a poor neighbourhood of huts and narrow lanes. It would be all too easy for someone to unwittingly be bitten by the hideous thing before it could be found.

"Teron, don't do it."

"It is tempting to make you beg, but I think we both know I'm going to do it anyway." Teron grinned, keeping his sword pointed at Miltiades, his arm cocked to throw. He saw Miltiades' legs tense, and laughed. "Do you really think you could get to me fast enough?"

"Miltiades! Get down!"

Miltiades threw himself to the floor, and heard the thrum of bowstrings behind him. Teron cried out, as three arrows buried themselves in his torso. He looked down in disbelief.

"Gods, no!" Callias yelled, and ran to him. Teron sagged into his arms.

Miltiades twisted around – Zander was at the door, with three of the Skythian police force.

"You think...this is over?" said Teron, staring at Miltiades. He snarled and suddenly pressed the severed head against Callias, and it's teeth sank greedily into the young man's neck. Callias cried out, clapping a hand to the wound. Teron pushed him away. "Run, Callias! If you love me, run and hide!" Teron fell to his knees, and thrust the head against his own arm. It bit again. Three more arrows smacked into him. He laughed, blood bubbling on his lips. "Too...late..." He twisted towards the window, took a dragging step...

Miltiades pushed himself to his feet, strode across and whipped his sword sideways. Teron's head flew off, bouncing across the floor in a trail of blood. Callias had backed up against one of the other windows, staring at the scene in horror. He glanced out. Miltiades held a hand up to stop the Skythians shooting.

"Callias..."

Callias looked at him. He burst into tears. "What a mess..."

"Callias, listen to me. You are a good man. I know that."

"But you betrayed me! You made me a laughing stock! You unmanned me!"

"I know. And I am sorry. But you mustn't leave. You mustn't let the infection spread..."

Callias looked out the window again. If he jumped, the fall would kill him, but he was already infected. Would already come back as one of them.

"Callias," said Miltiades. "Please. You are a man. You are of the best of men."

Callias pushed himself upright. He turned and faced Miltiades. And walked towards him. Face calm, he dropped his hand from the angry red bite on his neck. He fell to his knees.

"For the city," he whispered. "For the demos."

He closed his eyes.

"For the demos," said Miltiades. And struck.

....

"Still nothing," Artaphernes reported. Datis couldn't be sure, but there seemed to be a touch of satisfaction in his tone.

"Stupid fucking Greeks," grunted Datis. "Cannot trust them to do anything right. Including betraying their own city. Tell the captain to set sail."

"Heading?"

"Back to Persia. No point staying here any longer. We're fucked."

"I don't know about 'we'," said Artaphernes, walking away from him. "I'm not the one in command of this expedition."

Datis closed his eyes wearily. When he thought about it, maybe execution wasn't so bad. At least it offered a relief from the endless jockeying for position in the court. He guessed he would soon see.

....

"Miltiades," said Zander gently. "Miltiades, there is something you should see down below."

Miltiades sat slumped next to Callias' body. He had covered it with his cloak, now soaked with blood. The Skythians had dragged Teron's body away, leaving a red smear in its wake. Miltiades dully supposed that some temple slave would be tasked with cleaning that up. They had taken Teron's head, too, impaled on several arrows after Zander warned them of the danger it would soon pose. He was holding Callias' hand, feeling how cold it was, how it was stiffening.

"Miltiades."

He shook himself, levered himself painfully up from the floor. He stood beside Zander, looking down across the city and out to the harbour.

"The Persians have gone," he said after a moment.

"Yes. But that's not all – look north."

He leaned out, not sure what he was supposed to be looking at – then he spotted it: a column of men marching toward the city. The sunlight glinted on armour and spearheads.

"Looks like a couple of thousand, at least," said Zander. "Who are they?"

"It's the Spartans," said Miltiades.

"Draw the men up. Reform the phalanx," he told Aristides, Themistocles and the other strategoi.

"You want us to fight the Spartans now, too?" asked one incredulously. "Besides, your day of command was over yesterday. Its somebody else's turn today."

"Don't be ridiculous," said Aristides. "Reform the phalanx, like the man said." He grabbed Miltiades by the arm. "We aren't going to fight them, are we? Aren't they here to help?"

"Yes. But it wouldn't be the first time that the Spartans came and changed the government in Athens, would it?"

The weary men were wheeled about, and faced the oncoming force. Now the red cloaks of the Spartans were clearly visible. There were many anxious glances: what were they doing? Then Miltiades ordered that all spears be downed, and shields rested. The men gratefully obeyed. He paced out to the front alone. The column of Spartans halted and three men walked forward.

"Well, Athenian," said one, who seemed to be the officer in charge. "We were quick marching here to assist you, as requested, when our scouts brought word that a battle had already taken place at Marathon and you were victorious. It seems you need not have called us to come all this way after all."

"We are grateful to you," said Miltiades. "At the time of the sending, things were looking fairly bleak. But by the grace of Athena we have been victorious, and the Persians have fled our shores."

The Spartan officer nodded. "That is good. Let us hope they have learned their lesson sufficiently and do not seek to return, less they feel the wrath of the Spartans. Now tell me – is it true? They have somehow managed to open the gates of Hades and use the very dead against their foes?"

"It is true."

"It is hard to believe." The officer gazed at the phalanx before him. "Your men look ready to collapse, and your lines are somewhat thin."

It was hard to tell if it was merely an observation, or some kind of veiled threat.

"There are many stragglers coming in. The fight was hard, and the marching fast. But we have the heart to defend our city."

The Spartan raised an eyebrow.

"We had hoped to see you sooner, actually," Miltiades added.

The officer gazed at him coolly. "We could come no sooner. We were observing the Festival of Carneia. It is forbidden for our men to march at that time."

Miltiades nodded. "They do say the Spartans are a pious people. Possibly to a fault."

A smile touched the corners of the officer's mouth. "Well," he said. "Possibly. We shall march to Marathon and inspect the bodies of these Hadesmen. We wish to acquaint ourselves with them... In case they should ever return to our lands."

He snapped an order, and the column wheeled, heading for the mountain road that would take them to Marathon.

Miltiades was finally able to dismiss the men.

....

That night, they ate in the andron; Miltiades, Hegesipyle and Zander. The mood was solemn and introspective. Zander mixed wine for them, and Miltiades led the libations.

"To Callias," he said, tipping his cup and splashing wine upon the ground. He frowned. The small puddle reminded him of blood, now.

"To Callias," said the others, and spilt more.

"And Photios," said Hegesipyle quietly.

Miltiades nodded. "Yes," he said, blinking back hot tears.

There was to be a public celebration of the great victory. The wealthy citizens donated oxen for slaughter in honour of the gods, the meat to be served at a public feast. But first the citizens gathered in the Pnyx, with the women, metics and slaves crowding around the boundary. Miltiades ascended the speaker's rock, and the crowd roared. He held his arms out for silence.

"People of Athens. Citizens. My fellow citizens. By the grace of Athena we have survived. I propose the construction of a new stoa in the agora, in honour of this great victory. Let the names of the dead be inscribed within it, so that future generations may know of the time when we stood together against the might of Persia. Of the time they opened the gates of Hades upon us, but we withstood it."

The noise billowed over him again. Every part of him sang with it. It raced through his veins, into his heart. It awoke something...the infection at his centre, slowly growing in power.

He was no longer the same. Something was new. But maybe something was missing, too.

"But this is not the end." He paused, one hand held aloft. He held them. They were his. "For I have seen, now, that this polis is blessed by the gods. We have begun something here that must not be allowed to wither and die. It must go on. It must grow. But, citizens, we have enemies. There are those who will be jealous of our favour, and seek to hold back the tide of change. We cannot allow that to happen. And so we must be strong. And willing to strike."

He stared down upon them, their rapt faces.

"I propose the formation of a fleet of seventy warships, with accompanying hoplites. With this force I will give Athens her security. I will strike down our enemies." He pointed out to sea. "The small islands of the Cyclades like Paros and Delos gave aid to our enemies. They must be punished. So too must those who have given us insult, such as the people of Lemnos who sought to stop me in my mission to the Hellespont, thus jeopardising your food supply. They must be punished, and in return you will be rewarded with the spoils of a just and noble war!"

They loved it. They loved him. They howled their support. He bit them with this picture of a glittering future, and they were infected.

There hardly had to be a vote. The motion was moved as a matter of course, and with a roar it was voted into law. The Athenians would take what they deserved.

That night, Hegesipyle lay beside him. Her mind was too full to sleep, and the child within her was restless. She felt hot, her hair sticking to her forehead. She slowly levered herself out of bed, careful not to wake Miltiades. Though given how much wine he had drunk, it seemed unlikely that he would stir. She walked out into the central courtyard, where the air was cool, and saw that the moon was casting soft white light. There was a man seated there, and at first she thought it might be Tresantes or Zander, but then she saw that this wasn't so. The man looked at her then, and beckoned. He had golden curled hair and a bushy beard. As she drew towards him, she saw the likeness of Miltiades in his face. He was wrapped in a black cloak. He smiled, but it seemed to her that his eyes were cold as the stars, distant and lonely.

"Hegesipyle," he said. His eyes drifted to her belly. He nodded. "He will be a great man."

She wrapped her hands around her stomach. "Hello, Miltiades," she said. For had she not known him, this sophisticated man who came first to the land of the Dolonci, before her husband of the same name? This man who had wooed her, bedded her, then been swept away like debris when the tide rises. She swallowed. "Are you a ghost? Or am I dreaming?"

He smiled. "Listen. There is something you must do. You must tell Miltiades to stop."

"Cannot you tell him?"

"His mind is closed to me. You must tell him to stop."

"I don't know if he will listen... He is...changed."

He bowed his head, then was suddenly standing before her. "There is something I must show you," he whispered, and placed a cold hand across her eyes...

...she saw a walled city, and fire. A night attack. Men were running, casting aside their heavy shields. She saw the device of Athens, Athena's owl, on the shields as they fell ringing... ships were burning... It was a rout... Men falling from the walls, from ladders...

...he was there, shouting...trying to turn the tide, trying to lead them back to the walls...a spear thrust to his thigh, the blood spurting... men running to the ships...fleeing, fleeing... he was dragged to his flagship and dropped in a corner...

...a fire within...fever...the stink of gangrene in the wound... his cheeks sunken...body devoured from within by the fire...

...anger...so much anger...the people screaming with rage at the loss, the waste...

...he was there, dragged from his home...lying on a cot before the people...a court...judging him, damning him...the pointing fingers...

...he was there, tears leaking from his eyes...sick, and lost...

...he was there...it was over... his last breaths...over...

She woke, with a cry in her throat. She was alone in their bed, the day just beginning to dawn beyond the shuttered window. Her heart ached. Her hands went automatically to the swelling of her stomach.

"Don't go," she said to him, holding a cloak tight about herself. He was in the courtyard with Zander, preparing his equipment. They both looked up at her.

"What are you talking about?" Miltiades asked. "You look feverish. Go back to bed."

"Don't go," she repeated. "Something bad is going to happen."

He frowned then, and walked over to her, taking hold of her arms. "Don't get yourself worked up into a state. Nothing is going to happen."

"I saw it. I saw you fail. I saw you...die." She choked.

"You mean you had a nightmare. That is all."

"No! I saw...your uncle. He said-"

"Enough!" His grip tightened. "I don't want to hear this. You had a bad dream. Do not dwell on it. I will be back soon."

"Even if it was just a dream, what then?" she asked. "Will it be over? How long before you go and fight again? What has happened to you?"

"I am only doing what I must. For the city. For you. For our child."

"No! Don't you dare say that. You are doing this for you." She closed her eyes and took a breath, then drew herself up taller. "I love you," she said simply. "Don't do this. Don't go."

"You once said that you would never love me. Now you try to use it as a shackle, to hold me back."

"Then what a fool I am," she said bitterly. "When I seek to keep you alive. My husband. The father of my child..." She clapped a hand to her mouth and ran into the house.

"Fuck!" yelled Miltiades. He swung around, his gaze falling on Zander. "That fucking Spartan chided me once for not understanding what it meant to love something. Well, now I understand all too well. I still see him, and his stupid sad moping face, and I feel the daggers that woman sinks into my heart... So now I see, all love does is give pain and make you vulnerable!"

He stormed off into the andron. Zander looked from one door to another.

"Please don't smash anything important," he muttered after Miltiades, then went in search of Hegesipyle.

She was easily located by the sound of her crying in a room to the side. He coughed to let her know he was coming, and walked in. She smiled at him tightly, knuckling tears from her eyes.

"I don't know what else to do. How do I stop him? Can you stop him?"

"I don't think I can."

"No. He won't listen. He is so caught up in this... What has happened to him?"

"He has changed. Men change."

"I liked him better before." She held her face in her hands, shoulders shaking with silent sobs. Zander stood waiting. Finally she stilled, and then looked up at him. Their eyes locked.

"But we have to hope, don't we? We must not give in to despair, though it is easy. We must do the hard thing, and keep trying. We must hope that those we love will find their way back to us."

He could only nod, and leave her there.

....

Down at the docks, the ships were putting to sea. Seventy Athenian triremes, loaded with hoplites and the materials of war. A crowd was there to see them off, chattering excitedly. The strain of imminent annihilation had lifted from them, leaving them in a celebratory mood - like when the sun reappears from behind storm clouds. Miltiades and Zander walked to the position where Phillipus had his ship tied up. The trirach waved as he saw them approach, and ordered some crewmen to take their armour and weapons and stow them away.

"A glorious day!" he shouted to them as they jumped across onto the deck.

"Are you drunk?" asked Miltiades. His mood had not been great, due to a last minute scene with Hegesipyle, who had physically tried to stop him from leaving. Grim-faced, fierce as any warrior, she had clung to him, and he had been forced to call some of the house slaves to help pull her off. Weirdly it had been his mother who appeared and drew her weeping away into the women's quarters. He had stormed from his house wiping at his own angry tears, swearing.

But now, here amid the bustle, he could feel his spirits lifting.

"Drunk? Me?" The trirarch grinned. "Only a little."

The sun was warm, and flashing on the waters of the bay. Ships were turning and sliding out to sea, their oars chopping at the green water, the high fluting of the pipe boys carrying in the air. Miltiades breathed deep. He felt a little drunk himself.

"Orders?" called Phillipus.

"Take us out, trirarch," he said, and fixed his gaze on the horizon, where the sky met the sea, and all the possibilities in the world seemed to await and nothing was yet written. "I'm hungry."

EPILOGUE

She lifted her head, for she had been sleeping, but a sound had caught at her attention.

A longed for sound, almost forgotten, like the patter of rain in the middle of blazing summer.

She hardly dared to breathe until it came again – but there it was: the low rumble of his voice, calling to her, and she rose up.

He saw her, and the hard lines in his face softened, and he knelt slowly on his weary battered knees.

He spoke her name.

"Rabbit."

And she ran to meet him with a sudden fierce joy filling her heart.

THANKS

Thanks first of all to Shane and Jo, of Tar and Feather Publishing, for their infectious enthusiasm and encouragement. Without them, this book would not exist.

Thanks also to my wife, Sandra, my very own warrior woman. Her ongoing support, with just the occasional bit of eye-rolling, is vital to me.

To Nick Hamilton, thanks for the gorgeous artwork.

And thanks also to Snuff, Pippin and Lucy, who taught me that small packages can contain the fiercest hearts.

SO HOW MUCH IS TRUE?

Quite a lot, really.

Our main written source for this period is Herodotus of Halicarnassus, a Greek writer born around 484 BC (about six years after the Battle of Marathon). His work, 'The Histories', has survived intact and explains the origins and course of the Greco-Persian Wars. While there is debate about the accuracy of some of what he wrote (and he himself presents versions of events that he says he was told about but found hard to believe), he is regarded today as a generally reliable source, backed up by other written fragments and archaeological evidence.

In seeking to explain the recent past, Herodotus went right back to describe the rise of the Persian Empire, which took him back to King Astyages of the Medes. Astyages comes across like a traditional villain, seeking to maintain his position through any means, including the killing of his grandson after he was warned by the Magi that the boy would one day unseat him. There followed that classic trope used in countless stories through the ages – the man given the job couldn't go through with it and hid the child with a poor herdsman. Of course there is no avoiding fate – the boy is Cyrus, who goes on to lead a revolt by the Persians against the Medes, and so the rise of the Persian empire begins.

Meanwhile, in Athens, an upper class man named Pisistratus decides that rather than share power with the other Eupatrids, he would rather rule outright. There follows three attempts to seize control by force, first after pretending to have been assaulted by enemies, then with the ruse of the tall woman impersonating Athena, and finally with his band of mercenaries. Once in power, he ruled for years, and did a lot to develop the city.

When he died, his two sons took over. Their rule continued much like their fathers, fairly benign, and included seeking to safeguard the grain supply by establishing a colony on the choke point of the Hellespont, led first by the brother of a famous Olympian named Miltiades, and then by his nephew of the same name (the hero of our story). But this calm began to unravel after Hipparchus was killed in a love triangle, and Hippias responded by becoming increasingly authoritarian.

Across the Aegean, the Persian Empire had continued to grow under Cyrus, then Cambyses, and then Darius (who did take the throne, according to what was told to Herodotus, when his was the first horse to neigh at dawn, thanks to his wily groom) and now included the Ionian Coast, which meant dozens of Greek colonies now found themselves chafing under 'barbarian' rule. Not that the Persians were particularly difficult masters – they gave their subject peoples a lot of latitude. It was just the Greek prejudice against the Other.

Miltiades, who had married Hegispyle, daughter of the local Thracian king, was one such ruler who found his little colony swallowed by the Persian Empire. He was compelled to join an expedition against the Skythians, and did reportedly come up with the plan to maroon the Persian king in the hinterland by destroying the bridge they had erected across the Danube. The other Ionian leaders would not go along with him, and the plan failed.

In Athens, a democratic revolution took place, led in part by a wealthy member of the Alcmeonid clan named Cleisthenes. He reorganised Attica to ensure the classes were more mixed, and extended the democratic power of the citizens (which meant that women, slaves and those not born to Athenian parents still missed out – this was a brave step forward for more equal rights, but certainly did not include everyone).

In Ionia, matters came to a head and the Greeks revolted. According to Herodotus, this was largely due to the intrigues of Aristagoras, the tyrant ruler of Miletus. Realising that they needed help, he travelled to Sparta where he was rebuffed by the king (due to the timely intervention of the king's daughter, according to Herodotus) but was more successful at Athens, where he was able to persuade the Assembly to send military aid. And here we see the downside of Athenian democracy – it was possible to whip the crowd up into a kind of frenzy which reduced critical thinking: the mob could easily become a mindless beast.

The revolt had some early successes, including the taking of Sardis (during which the Temple of Cybele was burned to the ground, presenting the Persians with a terrific casus belli). But one by one, the cities were brought back under control by Darius. And he had certainly noticed the actions of Athens (and Eretria, which had also sent a few ships). The story goes that he had a slave who every evening, at dinner, would whisper "Sire, remember the Athenians" in his ear. Or so the Athenians liked to believe, anyway. It was pretty cool to think that you mattered so much to the king of the biggest empire the world had ever seen...

Miltiades, meanwhile, had been driven from his stronghold and returned home – along with his new wife (we unfortunately do not have any information on how she found Athenian society). As soon as he set foot back in Athens he was sued in court for his tyrannical rule on the Hellespont. He was able to defend himself and escaped the charges – perhaps in part because he was known to be experienced in the ways of the Persians, having accompanied the king on an expedition into Skythia some years before.

In 490BC the Persians launched an invasion to punish Athens (and probably begin the takeover of Greece). They were led by General Datis, and guided by the ex-tyrant Hippias, intent on regaining control of his city, even if it meant at the point of Persian swords. They landed at Marathon.

The Athenians marched out to meet them, and camped in the foothills above the coast. And there the two armies sat for some time. The Athenians were worried about attacking, as the Persian archers would be able to bombard them as they approached, and they didn't really use cavalry, whereas the Persians did (they had built special horse transports to bring their mounts along). They were content to hold the Persians in place and wait for the Spartans to arrive (they had sent for help earlier, little knowing the Spartans were delayed by a religious festival). The Persians were not eager to attack uphill, into the barricades the Greeks had built. Their weapons and armour put them at a distinct disadvantage in close quarter battle – they were used to a more mobile style of warfare. And if they tried to march on the city, they would expose themselves to an attack in the flank.

At some point, something changed. There is some conjecture about this, but it seems that the Persians were making ready to send some of their forces around to seize Athens – and rumours quickly spread that fifth columnists would be ready to hand the city over to them (and this was an all too common risk at the time). Maybe they began by boarding their horses, since the cavalry didn't feature in Herodotus' account of the upcoming battle.

Whatever, the Greeks had to act. Herodutus describes an unlikely scenario where the ten generals of the ten tribes had decided to take it in turn to command, and on his appointed day, Miltiades, who had gone from defending himself in court be being voted in as a strategos, led the Athenians down onto the plain to attack. Knowing the risks they faced from being overlapped by the larger and more fluid Persian host, Miltiades extended the Athenian line by taking extra men from the centre. And to minimise the time they would be in the archers' 'beaten zone', he ordered the hoplites to attack at the run.

Now, Herodotus has the Greek hoplites charging over a seemingly impossible distance. Their gear was really heavy, and the formation itself was extremely difficult to keep together. But it is very likely that they did charge through the 'beaten zone', that patch of land where the Persian archers were most effective, to minimise their exposure to the missiles. And once they made contact, that was it. This was the kind of fight the phalanx was designed for: close quarters. We know 192 hoplites fell, as their names were inscribed after the battle, and the funeral mound looks about right for that number. Herodutus says some 6400 Persians died, which seems pretty steep, but once they gave way, certainly large numbers would have been lost.

The victorious Athenians then had to march straight for Athens to stop the surviving Persians from landing there. It was here that rumours began of a mysterious shield signal from the Acropolis, which was scandalously attributed to the Alcmeonid clan (though Herodotus says he finds this hard to believe).

The Spartans arrived, too late to help, but did go and look at the bodies. No doubt they had a professional interest in the arms and armour of the Persians and their allies, realising this probably wasn't an end to the conflict.

After his great victory, Miltiades died in disgrace. He convinced the assembly to allow him to lead an expedition against the island of Paros, for purely personal motives, and in this failed attack he was injured and developed gangrene. Furious, the people put him on trial – this time there was no escape: he was sentenced to death, though this was later changed to a massive fine of fifty talents. He died in jail, and the fine was paid by his son, Cimon, who would later go on to be an Athenian statesman and general in his own right.

So the great hero of the 490 invasion was brought down, tragically, by hubris.

How much longer Hegespyle lived and how she died, we do not know.

Of course, the troubles with the Persians did not end there. Darius was succeeded by his son Xerxes, who inherited a fractious empire. He set about putting down a number of revolts. But then in 480BC his imperial eye turned westward' once again...But that is the subject for another time...

Also by Timothy Bowden

Undead Kelly

"a ripping good yarn"
Iron outlaw

"best zombie novel I've read thus far..."
Scary Minds

Melbourne, 1880 Something evil has appeared in the Australian outback - the dead are rising, and stalking the lonely bush tracks. Officially, they do not exist, their attacks attributed to the work of natives or madmen. But one man knows they are real, and is determined to expose the truth. Ned Kelly. Because somebody has to stop the rot...